LIFE'S A STAGE

Merlo sat down at the board and started punching buttons. The shop lights dimmed, and a castle sprang up. I gasped. It wasn't from a fairy tale—it was real! The blocks were real stone, they had to be, and there was none of that translucency at the outside edges. The definition from this console was very high: the scene looked just as real as the live actors would—the drawbridge wasn't just wood, it was old, and it had a rotting board in the middle. The moat had scum.

Then the staging area darkened, the store lights brightened again, and Merlo gave a satisfied grunt.

By Christopher Stasheff
Published by Ballantine Books:

HER MAJESTY'S WIZARD

Starship Troupers
Book One: A COMPANY OF STARS

A COMPANY OF STARS

Book One of Starship Troupers

Christopher Stasheff

A Del Rey Book
BALLANTINE BOOKS • NEW YORK

A Del Rey Book
Published by Ballantine Books

Copyright © 1991 by Christopher Stasheff

All rights reserved under International and Pan-American Copyright Conventions. Published in the United States of America by Ballantine Books, a division of Random House, Inc., New York, and simultaneously in Canada by Random House of Canada Limited, Toronto.

Library of Congress Catalog Card Number: 91-91863

ISBN 0-345-36889-4

Manufactured in the United States of America

First Hardcover Edition: September 1991
First Mass Market Edition: September 1992

Cover Art by David Mattingly

*With thanks to
all the good people
with whom I have acted and run tech
over the years,
none of whom is in this book;*

*And
With most especial thanks to
Edward Stasheff,
my father and teacher,
who helped me develop the concept for this book,
actors, technical systems, plot lines,
and who helped me greatly with
the characterizations, especially
Horace.*

1

So she said, "Darling, I'm pregnant."

I guess you *can* catch it from kissing.

Now, I've heard of miracles, but this was going some. I mean, things like that happened in the Bible and in the old pagan myths, not in the twenty-sixth century. These days, the family-planning pharmacopoeia looks more like a cornucopia, and my sweet Virginia could have used the Morning After Pill, just in case she'd forgotten her Day Before Pill—or her Just In Case Pill, for that matter. Of course, she could have turned any of them off, and her fertility back on, with the I've Changed My Mind Pill—but that took deliberate planning, not to say scheming. In fact, when you get right down to it, it was just flat-out impossible for her to get pregnant by accident—especially since I had diligently been taking my Foresight Pill.

Which meant that . . .

Ever feel like somebody's out to get you?

I pointed this all out to her with delicacy and tact. "Virginia," I said, "for you to be pregnant by me is not possible, unless you believe in Virgin Birth."

"I've gotten religion," she retorted, "and I was a virgin when I met you."

That wasn't what you'd call a very satisfactory answer, since I knew damn well she wasn't any virgin, and that I had had absolutely nothing to do with it. But I had to let her know I knew, in a tactful way—so I held back a penetrating remark. "Virginia," I said instead, "if you were a virgin, I was the Cardiff Giant."

"I *thought* you were stoned that night." But she reddened. "Anyway, you can't know that!"

Well, no, I can't say I *knew* it, really—not from personal experience. But Rumor speaks, and sometimes it damn near yells in your ear. I have to admit I never caught her *in flagrante delicto*—but she sure seemed to think she'd caught me.

I changed tactics. "Why me?" I said.

"Because," she said reasonably, "you're here. And you *were* there—so you *will be*."

Now I know why they call it "conjugal bliss."

It made sense, in a way—her way. I was here, and I could be pushed into it, when her really significant other had stopped signifying. Maybe he was no longer here—or maybe she knew that he couldn't be bulldozed. Me, I could—I couldn't honestly say that I would have rathered to burn than to marry.

So she may have been full of bliss, but I was feeling somewhat vacuous.

I reined in my panic and tried to be reasonable. "Now, look," I said, "we both know we've never been near the same bed."

"No, I don't," she snapped, "and neither does Daddy."

And there, of course, was the rub—about the only place, too. Daddy would never doubt the word of his darling daughter. Daddy was the kind who would hitch us first and ask questions later; also, Daddy was a very Big Daddy, with a Bigger Wallet, who could afford a Big-Time Investigator to track me down—which Daddy would've done; he had a rather reactionary view of male-female relations.

Not that I blame Daddy, myself—I know there was a time when the little bit Virginia and I had done was counted as an engagement, and more—sort of a promissory note in the wedding march, you might say. But that was another time and another era, several centuries back, and I didn't feel like putting on my paternity suit just to fit in with some nostalgia nut's fad.

Maybe Daddy longed for the era when people couldn't

plan these things too well, but Virginia was calculating for the future.

Just because she had decided to take an excursion to yesterday, though, didn't mean I had to stay home tomorrow.

So what was there to say? "Good-bye?" With a Private Eyeing me before I even got started?

So I dropped out of college (carefully forgetting to tell the registrar), withdrew all my cash (it was the beginning of the month), hopped into the Inter-City Ballistic Missile, and dropped out of sight.

I mean, what would you have done? Really?

2

HORACE

It is an axiom, of course, that you never go to an audition with a friend, for the director will remember only the two of you, and will consequently not remember either. It is less well known that the best time to audition is on a rainy day, when the less hardy (or less hungry) actors are toasting their toes by the electric fire, meditating morosely on their ill fortune. All of which is by way of explaining why I was waiting at the relocated but otherwise unchanged—or so I'm told—Automat on Forty-second Street, just across from the cavernous labyrinth known as Port Authority Bus Terminal. The meaning of the first two words is apparent, though odd; the last two words are blurred by history, and not even translucent. It is difficult to comprehend why a nonprofit corporation that oversees the building and operation of New York City's spaceport should also operate a bus terminal. On the other hand, it is the Port Authority of New York and New Jersey—rather necessary, since the spaceport is in New Jersey's Meadowlands—so presumably it views buses as land-bound ships coming into port, so to speak, and therefore under its aegis.

Be that as it may, I was laying down a discarded hard copy of the local newsfax—nothing but boring drivel about Elector Rudders' ranting that the colony planets were draining Terra's lifeblood, and Elector Undercut's demands for a stronger central government to restrain the anarchic impulses of the lesser races, which, of course, were the nationalists striving for cultural survival in Kazakhstan, Tibet, the

4

Irish Gaeltachta, the Middle East, and the Pyrenees. Depressing, all of it.

I laid it aside and bowed my head in homage to the breath of heat escaping from my coffee mug, in that monument to mechanization that is the modernized automatic food dispensary, centered in that rather gaudy district of travel agencies, cafés, and boutiques, none of which opened before 2:00 P.M.—except, of course, for the Automat, whose robots were on duty in twenty-four-hour shifts, a factor affecting the taste of the coffee.

Its being open all hours, however, explained my presence in that soulless emporium of recycled plankton—that, and a certain shortage of currency common to most of my fellow pilgrims on the road to the temple of Thespis (which is to say, actors; the *artifices scenecis,* or technical staff, make a living, as always—there are fewer of them). I occupied a window seat, to remove myself as far as possible from a gentleman of no visible means of support but a great deal of well-aged aroma who had wandered in, probably hoping to solicit enough coinage to utilize one of the antique dispensers kept on as a curiosity from the Horn and Hardart era—and rather beautiful, in its way; the sculpted spout is worthy of a garden fountain, so it is all the more disconcerting to see it spurt coffee, or a reasonable facsimile thereof. Since he had succeeded in his objective—due to the presence of a gentleman obviously from out of town, no doubt an early theatergoer, if you can call that sort of thing theater—he was now ensconced at a tablette exactly central to the establishment, out of the line of sight of passing patrolmen, but excellently situated to fumigate the total volume of airspace of the emporium.

Accordingly, I had relocated my cup of ersatz coffee to a window seat, affording me an excellent view of the dingy downpour and the sole remaining burlesque theater across the street—rather forlorn, in its way, but subsidized by the city as a reminder of the late twentieth century, when the district thronged with peep-show emporiums, pornographic bookstores, and cinemas and theaters catering to the most prurient tastes of humankind, made obsolete by the advent of three-dimensional television with built-in playback devices (recorders cost extra), yet a monument, in its way, to the enduring appeal of live theater. Since it is maintained more as a tourist trap than anything else, the shows are rather tame by the standards of modern 3DT, glorifying the body beautiful and the art of erotic dance, as well as the tradition of improvised and vulgar comedy—but far more stimulating, in its tawdry way, than the torrid and cheapened spectacles so prevalent on 3DT ROM cubes.

The true testament to the profession of Shakespeare and Lope de Vega was, of course, only a few short blocks away, for the New York theater district is thriving as never before, since it now attracts visiting clientele from a dozen colonized planets, as well as from the ends of the Earth. All come to spend freely in sampling the pleasures of fabled Old New York, so we keep it well restored and in good repair for them—and foremost among those pleasures is the entrancing, magnetic feeling of being caught up in a theatrical performance in which the actors are really, physically *there,* aware of you and responding to your emotions, however subtly. It is a feedback process, a positive reinforcing cycle, and there is an excitement to it that cannot be matched in any other dramatic medium. Oh, they have tried, especially on the colony planets—eschewing all the advantages of the recorded three-dimensional image, with its capacity for close-ups and panoramas, they have made recordings of theatrical performances, then projected them life-size in provincial theaters on New Venus and Falstaff and Otranto, and achieved a totally believable re-creation of the actual performance, visually indistinguishable from the original.

But the sight of the actors is not enough in itself—if theater were merely a matter of visual effects, we would all have been done in long ago by animated features. No, there is a magic to live theater that no other medium can produce. Perhaps it is the actor's awareness of the audience, or the audience's awareness of the actor's awareness, or the actor's awareness of the audience's awareness of the actors—or perhaps it is merely the audience's response to the performance, however guarded, however subtle, and their knowledge that these are real, living, breathing people before them, caught up in the magic of becoming imaginary characters for a brief space of time, in a way that no computer simulation can emulate.

Be that as it may, live theater in New York City is vital and flourishing, and providing jobs for hundreds of actors.

Unfortunately, there are thousands of us seeking those hundreds of jobs.

Tens of thousands, if you count all the excited, enthusiastic young people who come flocking in every year to have their try at becoming rich and famous in a day, or even of securing for themselves a niche in that invigorating, glamorous, wicked, decadent, seedy, weary world of the theater. The majority of them go home in six months, of course, disillusioned to discover that most of an actor's work is auditioning, and hard and disagreeable work it is, too, with the human vampires flocking to feed off the fresh young things and the trudging of miles of crosstown blocks in the rain and the snow—but most of all disillusioned by the horrid, unspeakable realization that they have entered a world in which no one gives a damn about them, in which they are just so many cattle, so much fodder for the bit parts and the chorus lines.

A few of them stay, finding the dirt and crowding bearable as they labor successfully in an advertising agency or brokerage for the weekend delights of one of the greatest cities of the Terran Sphere, for New York City is at once evil and altruistic, enlightened and corrupted, decadent and vital, sleazy and elegant—and many other dualities, with all degrees of intensity between each pair of extremes. New York City can be all things to all people—there is simply so much of it. And if, within it, there are human vultures who feed off the carrion of destroyed lives, there is also the maze of cultural events that uplift the heart and enrich the soul—so a few stay, earning their livings however they can. Most of those move out when they marry and produce offspring, but even then, a few return—if they can.

And, of course, there are always the indefatigable sweet and valiant young things of unquenchable enthusiasm who stay, and do manage to find themselves a life in the theater by sheer determination and diligence, by plodding the endless weary miles of crosstown blocks to auditions, who eke out a living waiting on tables while they toil in the mills of small theaters far from the lights of Broadway—and who do, little by little, manage to earn a living as actors.

Then, of course, there are always the few who strike it rich, are Discovered, and move up to stardom—but I wouldn't know about that.

My friend Barry Tallendar did, once. For a brief shining moment, he was a juvenile with an excellent part, then a leading man on Broadway for three seasons. It was then that Thomas Hyte saw him and was inspired to write *That Kind of Man* with Barry in mind for the leading role of Villehomme, and the rest is history. The critics raved, both theatrical and literary; the public poured in; and the professors required both text and performance for their courses. Barry played for seven years, every performance as fresh as his first, while his fame swelled and swelled. When the 3DT version was released, everyone in every tiniest town knew him by sight; his name became synonymous with culture and sophistication. He was in constant demand for public appearances of every sort; his face beamed at you from newscreens and hard copies; he dined with the glittering and famous—of whose number he was one, of course.

Then the play closed, and something happened. The plays changed or the audience changed—or Barry himself changed, in some subtle way of which not even he himself would be able to tell you. Perhaps he passed the magic age for the urbane sophisticates he portrayed; perhaps he had become too well identified with Villehomme; but, *bon gré, mal gré,* he faded. One production was a flop, he was given smaller and smaller parts, and he aged into a graceful and cultivated supporting player. He was still in demand for a certain kind of secondary part, a sort of mentor in debauchery—and he began to direct. Only occasionally, and only when the play fascinated him, and none of them were ever roaring hits—but they all played well, and made money. So he came to be in constant demand as a "play doctor"—if a show did poorly in its out-of-town tryouts and was in danger of folding, the producer or director called for Barry. He would fly to the scene of the disaster like an angel of mercy and pinpoint the flaws in a single viewing. Even more importantly, he had a positive genius for persuading playwrights and directors alike of the errors of their ways, and he was, of course, immensely influential with the actors.

Now he has aged further, and the parts come rarely, if at all. Oh, he still picks up the odd bit part now and then, sometimes even a strong supporting role, and is in constant demand to fix the play gone wrong and to read scripts before production begins. He is certainly in no danger of starvation, in spite of having lived rather extravagantly in his golden days—but he will never command the spotlight again. He is still invited to read for cameo roles, the sort of ten-line parts that the critics and public alike will remember as a glowing moment in an otherwise dull and tedious performance—but, somehow, he is only invited to read on days when rain is scheduled.

Yes, he is a success, in the theater's terms—which is to say, he earns a living, as I do. Yet he earns his living because of his glorious past, the evocation of the glory of those ten seasons that his name can still command—but I earn mine because I am right for the parts. For Barry is in his late fifties, and I am in my early sixties, and I am a character actor while he is a leading man. My parts will always be there, no matter how old I grow—only three a year, or two, but there nonetheless—and the older I become, the fewer like me there are. Barry, though, is a leading man, not yet old enough in his looks to be accepted in character parts but not young enough for the hero anymore, so he finds one role in a twelvemonth, perhaps two in a good year.

The rest of his time? Showcases, summer stock, off-off-

Broadway workshops, for little pay or none. But he acts. I act. Therefore, we exist.

Have existed, I should say—but the landlords are raising the rent again, and I have never put aside enough to buy a residence. Food is going up in price or down in quality, whichever way you wish to look at it, and a vogue for adolescent dramas has swept the theatrical world, perhaps in response to an aging generation that wishes to stay vicariously young. There are perhaps two or three mature roles in any of these plays, and there are many, many mature actors for each part. Between roles, I subsist on savings, then reimburse the account and fatten it further while I am working.

Now, however, the savings account is lower than in ten years, and never rises to its last level, for there are more months between parts, and the shows close sooner. I am facing the prospect of moving Out of Town or, worse, a retirement in a home for aged and decrepit actors.

Barry, at least, does not need to worry if his account declines. He saved enough in ten good years to last him two lifetimes.

I assume. I have never asked.

His life was rather soggy at the moment, though, as he came hurrying through the rain and into the Automat. The water cascaded off his umbrella as he closed it—and one look at his face was all I needed. That face was composed, but the eyes were too bright, the jaw too firm. I readied myself to show compassion, and pasted a gentle smile on my face as my old friend scanned the few patrons, seeking me. He saw me, and his face lighted up; he came over, shaking the umbrella, then hanging it on the chair back and causing a minor cascade as he removed his overcoat. "How good of you to wait, Horace! But why so near the pane?"

I nodded toward the center of the establishment. Barry glanced that way. "Oh. Well, if you'll excuse me, I'll find a source of heat." He went to the twin spouts, inserted a coin, and returned bearing steam in a cup. Sitting, he said, "A promising audition."

I smiled; that meant the director had promised to call him

if there were good news. "The state of the theater is always promising."

Barry nodded. "We need substance, Burbage! Drama! Character! We must seek new playwrights, new audiences!"

"With a taste for more mature topics," I suggested. "Which off-off-Broadway group are we to join, then, Barry?"

He smiled, eyes twinkling—the valor of the man! "There seems no recourse, does there? Well enough, then, Horace! If we must rebuild the theater from the ground up, let us do so! Let us form our own company, and perform the classics!"

I let my smile broaden, allowing myself to be swept up in his enthusiasm. It was a harmless game, and one that would lift spirits dampened by more than the rain. "Our duty to our Art, Barry!"

"Precisely! Yet the classics alone are not enough, Horace, oh no! We must encourage new talent, we must foster new playwrights!"

"Who write about older characters." I nodded in agreement.

"Must we not deal with the fullness of the human condition? With the whole span of the human race? It is inane and useless to portray life as existing only between people within the same decade of their lives! We need balance! Scope! Vision!"

Do you know, he was actually beginning to stimulate something like hope within me. "Why, Barry—surely you are not suggesting producing plays that are not written for the marketplace!"

"Not written for it, indeed! Only selected for it! If need be, Horace, we shall write them ourselves!"

"Let us not be extreme. But, Barry—how shall we finance this company?"

"Finance? The true artist thinks not of petty pecuniary exigencies, Horace! He creates! He expresses! He emotes!"

"He also eats," I pointed out. "Or is this venture to be amateur, in the highest sense of the term, Barry?"

In itself, those were inspiring words, for the term "amateur" means, literally, a lover—one who does the work out of sheer love for it. It can produce great art—but very little income.

"I would not think of it," Barry assured me. "Let us create a company that shall be professional, Horace, in every sense of the term!"

I frowned, pretending to see obstacles that could be overcome. "Is there really room amid this city's theaters for another company, Barry? For I assume we are speaking of a resident repertory group."

"Repertory? Certainly! But, 'resident'? Ah, no! We must see ourselves as missionaries, Horace! We must carry culture to the benighted plains of the outlands!"

Well, now. Fantasy or not, I hadn't been thinking of leaving civilization, which is to say, New York. "Oh, come, now, Barry! Where will we find actors willing to trek through the wilds?"

"Where will we find actors without jobs?" he countered. "Their numbers are legion, Horace! We shall go out of town with a vengeance, we shall tour the provinces with a company of worthies, we shall develop new plays until they sparkle with brilliance! Then we shall return to triumphant acclaim!"

I must confess that his enthusiasm carried me away—and I was beginning to feel the first inklings that he might be serious. "A noble objective, Barry, but let us return to the question of durance. How could we finance such a company? You cannot be serious!"

"Of course I am serious, Burbage! The more so since my brother expressed interest."

Well, now. That made a difference—and I sat up a little straighter, with even stronger enthusiasm, for Barry's brother was Valdor Tallendar, the financial genius who had risen from a stockbroker's clerk to a commodities magnate in less than a decade—then had gone on to diversify, and now garnered income in scandalous percentages from virtually every sphere of human endeavor. And, since it was whispered that his was the prime interest, both financial and mercantile, in the Venture exploratory mission toward the Lesser Magellenic Cloud, it was possible that he would invest in a project that might yield profits in the future, though not the near future. "Barry, such a company as we are discussing would be doing well to break even. Could Valdor truly be interested in so risky an undertaking?"

"He, too, pays taxes," Barry said—a subtle reminder that Valdor might also appreciate a losing proposition.

"A telling point. How shall we broach the matter?"

"I already have." Barry smiled and glanced at his ringwatch. "Our appointment is for 3:00, and it's just now 2:15. Shall we wend our way toward his office, Horace?"

Well. Of course, I went along. I couldn't let my old friend face such a perilous situation by himself, could I?

But in the cab on the way over, I had to review my priorities, because Barry was most definitely in earnest. There was every chance that he would gain Valdor's backing, too—being a financier, Valdor had to appear to be totally respectable, and I suspect it did his image little good to have his brother a highly visible and notorious actor. He was likely to finance Barry's company just to remove him from the public eye—at least, in New York.

Which set me squarely between the horns of a dilemma, trying to decide which meant more to me—New York, or the theater? Or eating regularly?

The issue had never arisen before. From my undergraduate days till the present, the two had been synonymous—to me, the theater was New York. Now, however, the distinction became suddenly clear, in a way that a mere monthlong out-of-town tryout, or a summer in stock, had never done.

"How long are we to be gone, Barry?"

"Oh, several years, at the least."

Years. That meant giving up my apartment, saying goodbye to friends, and resigning myself to the wilderness of the hinterlands, aching always for the Return.

On the other hand, there was an excellent chance that I would be unable to meet the increased rent on my flat for more than a few more months, and New York without housing doesn't bear contemplation. As to friends, if Barry was assembling a repertory company, most of my intimates would probably be involved.

That left New York itself.

With a tearing inside, I confronted the fact that treading the boards, in front of a live audience, meant more to me than the intimate embrace of a city I loved so well. Farewell, sweet wanton—but the claims of the mistress to whom I am wedded must bind more strongly than the mistress of my dalliance. I reconciled myself, firmly, to quitting New York, if Barry's company came to be. I sat up a bit straighter in the floating teardrop, squared my shoulders, and firmed my jaw. "Just how far out of town did you have in mind, Barry?"

"Oh, I thought we might start with Alpha Centauri," Barry said blithely.

3

I know. You're wondering why I didn't just stay in college and face the music, even if I didn't like the tune. After all, if I hadn't committed the crime, I wouldn't have to do the time, right? Or, to put it more crudely, if I hadn't eaten the stew, I couldn't be hanged for the lamb. A quick gene-map would've proved that the baby wasn't mine—if I could hold out against the pressure long enough for the baby to develop enough to give a blood sample. Even with all the stress, it would have been simpler than trying to make it in a strange city, from scratch. So why didn't I just stay in college?

Good question. I was kind of wondering about that myself, as I faced the pair of punks in the neon jackets and the ankle boots. Their face paint made an interesting collage of colors in the scattered UV from the street lights, and their button earrings winked a message of menace. The biggest one grinned and said, "Hand it over."

Two of them, of course. I tried to remember what Sensei had said when I asked him why they almost always come in pairs or gangs. Something about one being too chancy, so if he has to come alone, he brings a blaster. Get a partner, and you feel brave. "I don't have it," I said. "You're too late. Somebody else got there first."

Which was true. I got off the shuttle in Newark International, and had to struggle through the mob jamming up for the accelerator tube to New York. I was just getting into the car when I thought to touch my hip pocket—and sure enough, it was flat. I about-faced, ignoring the squawks of the people I bowled over, and hurried to the fringes of the

15

crowd, which was very easy, since they were all hurrying past me to get into the cars.

Then, suddenly, there wasn't any crowd, and the tube car was shooting off into the accelerator tunnel. I was alone on the platform, and I knew I was sunk.

Then I had a happy thought. I remembered something about pickpockets not wanting to get caught with the goods, and dumping them in the nearest place. It was awfully smelly digging through the trash cans, but I found it right on top of the mess in the third one—my wallet, suspiciously lean. I yanked it open in a panic, and saw—nothing.

Well, my mementos were there—a holo of Virginia (I hadn't asked for it), the flattened lozenge of a Foresight Pill in its easy-open wrapper (I'm not planning to need it, but better prepared than a father), and my general ID card (not much use to anybody whose retinal pattern doesn't match mine). But spare cash? Gone. My credit card? Gone. And, with my usual lack of foresight, I hadn't thought to write down the number. Which scored that—I was flat.

I tried, of course. I found the nearest pay phone that accepted coins and called the emergency number for Central Credit.

"Central Credit," said the computer-generated face on the screen. "Do you have the number of the card?"

Right to the point, this machine. "No. The pick-pocket . . ."

"Name?"

"Ramou Lazarian."

"*L . . . A . . . Z-A-R-E . . .*"

"I," I said helpfully, "and A-N."

"*I-A-N,*" the face confirmed. It gazed off into space for a second, then said, "Card canceled. Balance was zero before cancellation."

I felt my spirits hit the terrazzo. "Thanks anyway."

"Shall I issue a new card?"

Alarm bells rang in my head. A new card meant a route for the Big-Time Investigator to track me by. In fact, I'd been an idiot not to take it all in cash, and throw the card

away. "No, thanks. I'll call in when I have an address. Bye."
I disconnected before the face could ask questions.

That was that. The thief had already transferred my entire
balance into a transaction number, which would have con-
veniently paid cash. I turned away, reflecting that the pickpockets in New York were real pros—that guy had moved
fast.

Well, at least I was in the tube. I took the next car, found
a hard-copy newsfax, and scanned the want ads.

Nothing.

Well, nothing that didn't require a degree—and I hadn't
quite finished mine. I took a chance, anyway—I got off in
midtown Manhattan and started pounding the pavement.
Every so often, I saw a "Help Wanted" sign. I checked them
all out, but it was the same everywhere—degree or nothing.
That's the way of it—supply and demand. If you want a
skilled job, you look for want ads and "Help Wanted" signs,
but for untrained labor, you have to know somebody.

It was getting dark, and I was getting very hungry, and
very, very angry with the bum who'd pulled my wallet, when
the pair of locals showed up.

The bigger one held out his hand. "Put it there. Or we'll
take it."

"How?" I asked, while within me, the old, atavistic fear
of being a stranger in someone else's territory clashed with
a singing delight. "All I have is nothing. But you're welcome
to all the nothing you want."

He laughed. "Funny boy! Fun, yes. We'll take it out in
fun." And he swung.

The rule in the big city is, "Don't fight back unless you
have to. Buy them off, talk them out of it, but don't try to
fight unless there's a chance they might kill you." It's a good
rule. Fight a big-city mugger, and you might wind up dead.
But when they start using you as a punching bag, there's
always the chance they might get carried away and kill you.

I had run through the rule. And I wasn't about to tell
them what I was—you don't go up to someone and say, "Hi!
I'm a black belt, fourth dan." That's bragging. It also reads

like a challenge, and makes them want to try you out. So I didn't.

I lifted my shoulder and took the punch, rolling with it, then grinned and said, "Thank you," just before his buddy closed in.

They were good, those two. It's true, what they say—the tough ones in the big cities are a lot tougher than the tough ones in the small towns. They were very good.

But so was I. Something having to do with buried anger, the psychiatrist had said—and coming from Detroit.

They were good indeed—I had to feint three times before I hit the big one in his solar plexus. Of course, I kicked his buddy in the knee between the first two feints, and took two punches myself before I could connect and send him reeling, and I had to block the big guy's punches all the while, but when I could get through, I had time to crack a bone before the sidekick got back on his good foot, snarling and with a knife in his hand. Inside I bubbled with joy—the knife meant I could do anything I wanted, and not a court in the land would convict me, not like that principal in grammar school who sentenced me to martial arts class for picking fights. I learned her point very quickly, and very well, because Sensei taught me that it was unworthy to start a fight, and if I did, he'd take it out on me at the next lesson. I hated him for it, but by the time I learned enough not to worry about his threats, I kind of had him on a pedestal, and wanted him to think I *was* worthy. It only took me a few years to learn all he could teach, but that was okay, because he referred me to *his* sensei.

So I learned never to pick a fight. It was so much safer to be a victim. Nothing to it, really—all body language. You hunch a little, you smile eagerly at anything anybody says, you do the best you can to look anxious to please, just generally look like an all-around nice guy—and pretty soon, they figure you're a patsy, and they take a punch at you. Of course, the principal still didn't find it easy to believe I hadn't picked the fight, especially when I started winning so many of them—or when there were so very many. But my sensei did, and told me sternly to stop it.

What could I say? He was faster than I was.

But once learned, the trick is always there—and you know what? I found that I started making friends, just from looking like a nice guy—and having a mean reputation. So I kept it up, and it became automatic.

For the tough guys, too. I grinned at the knife fighter, eagerly and fearfully; I recoiled and he hobbled forward, intent on revenge—and fell back with a howl and a limp arm. I swung around just as his captain was swinging at me; I blocked the rabbit punch with my arm instead of my neck, caught his arm, and swung him face first into the bricks.

Then pain cracked through the back of my head, and all I saw was a lot of stars in an assortment of bright colors that faded, and went out.

Oddly, the notion of leaving Terra disconcerted me for only a moment; once I had bade farewell to New York in my heart, the rest of the planet of humanity's birth failed to move me. There are New Yorkers born, and New Yorkers made, but they are all New Yorkers—and I am just such a one. Romeo remarked that there was no world outside Verona's walls (on the other hand, he may have been confusing the world with Juliet, no doubt due to resemblances in topography). I, in similar fashion, felt that there was no world across the Hudson.

My Juliet? She had sickened of insecurity long ago, and succumbed to the charms and income of an insurance salesman who was now president of his company. I hear from her now and again; her children have children, and her husband wishes to forsake their Long Island manse for a penthouse in Manhattan. She, however, is resisting; what Lola wanted, Lola got.

There have been others of them, down through the years, but none wanted the grinding, gritty life of an actor. No, my only constant mistress has been the theater herself—and my recurring lover, New York. Farewell, Isle of Manhattan—and farewell to the great globe itself.

Ah, well. All the world's a stage, as the Bard said—perhaps it was time to try the universe.

But I had yet awhile before my adieus, and at the moment, I was regarding a spanking-new skyscraper just north of Wall Street.

"It does give me a frisson," Barry admitted, "to walk under letters that say, 'The Tallendar Building.'"

I wondered at the nature of the frisson. Barry had been successful in his chosen profession, of course, and had become financially independent—but he had not moved on to become a Power, and the contrast between the brothers' achievements was too great to ignore. Barry, at least, was still occasionally in the faxes and on 3DT, so he had greater visibility—but when Valdor's name appeared, they were speaking about him, not with him. It might be overstating things to claim he was one of the movers and shakers of the Terran Sphere—but then again, it might not.

The lobby, at least, was not disquieting, being the usual anonymous collection of polished marble and metal. We caught the next car going to the higher floors. It, too, was anonymous, though all its fittings gleamed with quiet opulence. I had been in one of the antiques that they keep for local traffic in the Empire State Building's highest floors, those that date from the building's inception, and I far prefer them to the modern thing. The wood and brass fittings, so economical then, are so ruinously expensive now! It is a matter of stepping back into a more gracious age, when ornamentation had not quite disappeared from human public life, and elevator cars still had a definite "up" and a "down." Impractical now, of course, when the car is hauled over at the top of its arc to begin its descent, since there is a stream of similar cars behind it at regular intervals—but that was impossible when the Empire State was built, of course, since they did not have antigravity tubes or linear accelerators that could increase our velocity during the express range but still stop us without hazard to the cars behind. Still, the feeling that one is in a bucket on an endless belt of excavators, dragging into a mass of humanity, then dumping its load as it nears a drop-off point, is humiliating for those who think. Fortunately, very few of us do.

We emerged from the car and found ourselves facing the reception area of Tallendar, Incorporated. Valdor had the top ten floors of the building, so his reception area was rather large, and sybaritically furnished with carpets of great depth and substance, original paintings by artists whose names were history, the absolute latest in design of chairs and sofas, and the incredible luxury of a live human receptionist.

It was also thronged. I felt incredibly dingy, though my suit was of recent vintage, and the cab had protected it from the rain. We must have looked like a pair of charlatans, Barry and I, wearing suits that obviously cost less than a year's income.

We filed past the crowd of waiting people—no threading through other bodies here; Valdor let his visitors know his wealth and importance by the sheer extravagance of space. We wended our way over to the young man at the console. He looked up with a warm but distant smile. "May I help you, gentlemen?" He said it without the slightest flicker of irony, too.

"We have an appointment with Mr. Tallendar," Barry said.

Was there the faintest trace of sarcasm in the young man's face, or did I only imagine it, as he asked, "May I know your name, please?"

"It is possible," Barry allowed. "I am Barry Tallendar, and my associate is Horace Burbage."

The young man froze for an instant, then looked up at us with new respect—and, I believe, his eyes actually came alive with something resembling excitement as he glanced from Barry to me and back. "Certainly, Mr. Tallendar. Forgive my not having recognized you. Please take the lift behind me to Mr. Tallendar's office."

"Thank you, young man." Barry smiled warmly and led

the way past our single-headed Cerberus—and we walked with lighter hearts and firmer steps, Barry and I, for the young man had conveyed, in his manner, that he was enthralled at meeting the figures that had entranced him on the screen in his boyhood, that only firm self-discipline had kept him from troubling us for our autographs. It would have been no trouble, of course—but one does not importune those who actually have appointments with Mr. Valdor Tallendar.

Still, we would neither of us have minded being importuned, and felt much better for the impression. I had the fleeting cynicism to wonder if the young man's reaction had been genuine, or if he was merely very good at his job. I hoped it was the former.

The lift car was far smaller, but luxuriously appointed, even to the degree of having a definite top and bottom—the lifts for the general public had to have carpeting on both floor and ceiling, since the "up" car turned upside down to become the "down" car. A car that had a real ceiling with a mural, and a floor with hardwood and an Oriental rug, was one more reminder of Valdor's power and importance. We stepped out into view of another—a young woman of such dazzling beauty that even Barry, accustomed to close proximity with the most comely of actresses, stopped a moment in awe.

She did not ask our names, of course—the gentleman downstairs would have signaled her on her screen. "If you and Mr. Burbage would have seats, Mr. Tallendar, your brother will be available shortly." Her voice was low and musical, redolent of scented nights in Paris boulevards and the best in diction coaches. Somewhat dazed, Barry and I nodded to her in mute tribute, then found ourselves a pair of island seats in a sea of cool carpeting that would have done nicely as a mattress. But as Barry sat, he stiffened slightly. Following his gaze, I saw a large canvas with splashes of color that seemed to form themselves into a picture of a man and a woman, hands clasped, gazing out over a glowing plain beneath a velvet sky. The plain was adorned with sharply peaked hills and valleys that were the same shapes inverted—and, at the far side, barely visible in the distance, stood another couple, robed and gowned like medieval royalty. I recognized it, for I'd seen photographs of it on magazine screens, and reproductions in the offices of presumptuous businesses all over the city. I was rather disappointed to see that Valdor Tallendar displayed no more originality than they. "Surely he could have found something less trite than another reproduction of Socorbia's *Continuum*," I murmured.

"He did," Barry assured me. "This is the original."

I stared.

Then I darted covert glances at the rest of the half dozen paintings, loop-screens, and sculptures adorning the room—all discreet, all undemanding but inviting, fascinating, compelling . . . all originals. I inhaled slowly and deeply, somewhat shaken.

"I remember when he bought the Socorbia," Barry murmured, eyes dreamy. "We were having a Sunday stroll through the Village—me giving my struggling younger brother a look at the romantic and glamorous world of the Bohemian, you see; he was an ambitious clerk, and I a hopeful actor, still vying for walk-ons. He found this among Socorbia's other works, and bought it from the artist himself, who was reclining nearby. Cost him more than he should have afforded from his clerk's wages, of course—a week's income, then."

I nodded. I remembered Orly Socorbia—introverted, hostile, and obsessive in his painting, once the Muse struck—but loathe to part with any of his works. I could usually manage to start him talking, though; I learned a deal about painting from him, though never the secret of his fascination for women. Dare say he didn't know it himself.

Gone, now, of course—sucked up into that vacuum that pulls in the financially successful, the famous who become targets for the grasping and the psychotic. Rumor hath it that he dwells in a chateau in Switzerland, when he's not in his penthouse in New York. Sells canvases only rarely, of course, though he has a one-man show every five years or so. He won't sell the originals, but the reproductions keep him wealthy. Rumor hath it that financiers like Valdor pay him to follow his natural bent and keep his originals off the market, thereby boosting the value of their own acquisitions, but anyone who knew Socorbia wouldn't believe that for a minute. Only impending poverty could ever have persuaded him to part with so much as a print.

I leaned back with a sigh, stilling the old, familiar feelings of envy and resigning myself to a long wait. Valdor, of course, like any giant of success, would have to impress us with his importance by keeping us waiting an hour or two before he allowed us to approach the presence.

Then the huge door boomed open, and a stocky, balding man with huge hands and an eerie resemblance to Barry came hurrying out, arms spread. "Ah, brother! So sorry to keep you waiting!"

Barry rose, smiling. He didn't quite make it all the way to his feet before he was enveloped in his brother's embrace and returned it fondly, though Valdor was several inches shorter than he. Valdor was also attired in a gunmetal-gray *complet* with the soft, rich look that only genuine wool can give, and the ring on his finger was diamond—never a wedding band, sadly.

He released Barry and turned toward his office, one arm around his brother. "Come in, come in!" He reached out and caught my elbow. "So good of you to come, Mr. Burbage! My, has it been so long as three years? I'm still thrilled at seeing your face on the screen, of course, and you fairly glowed with goodness as Waffles in that production at the Actors' Institute last spring!"

"How good of you to visit," I said, almost shocked.

"But when will you and Barry appear in the same production again?" Valdor asked as he ushered us over to the sofa and lounger that occupied a small area in the vastness of his office, well away from the glowing wood of his desk. And that was the way of it: he kept the two of us in conversation about our recent doings for a half hour or more, while the financial affairs of three continents waited on our convenience. Any question of Barry's, he would answer briefly but with deprecation, as though mere toiling in the world of trade could not possibly hold any interest for us. I was amazed at the man's tact; never once did he hint that we wouldn't understand a bit of it.

He laughed and nodded as Barry finished the summary of that ruinous production of *Macbeth* we had both suffered at the Drake six months earlier. "No wonder they say the play is cursed! But, really, I thought your Banquo was excellent, Barry, though I suppose I'm biased, and no judge of acting, to boot . . ."

"Your taste is excellent," Barry said sternly, "as every art dealer in the world knows—and I've found your opinions on acting and 3DT to be every bit as incisive." Then he smiled. "Which is by way of saying, I suppose, that your opinions agree with my own."

Valdor laughed. "Then you'll take it in the spirit in which it's meant, Mr. Burbage, if I say that your Drunken Porter was delightful! Really, it was a stroke of genius to realize that Shakespeare meant him to be parodying the Porter of Hell from the Miracle Plays!"

"Only what he'd grown up seeing," I murmured, feeling quite flattered; any other critic would have said I overacted badly—and had.

"It was an excellent production!" Valdor averred. "What a tragedy that it ran only two weeks! When New York is fairly crying for classical theater on Broadway!"

"I'm afraid the handkerchief is too close to the wallet," Barry sighed. "And, yes, I'd agree it deserved a much longer run—though I do notice it attracted very few investors."

Valdor nodded vigorously. "Quite right, Barry! Theater is vital to the welfare of this city, yes, since it's one of the factors that attracts so many tourists, and so many of them transact business while they're here, instead of going to Washington or Houston—so it contributes to the overall profitability of our operations. But it shows very little profit in itself. No, live theater is not a sound investment, and anyone who has to answer to a board of stockholders would be highly irresponsible if he invested in it."

"Surely the tax laws . . ." I said.

He smiled at me. "The tax laws don't allow write-offs for investments that were clearly probable losers, Mr. Burbage. A play that has a chance of being profitable, they would allow us to deduct—and a popular comedy or musical usually does make money, though just enough to make the tax situation slightly worse. They do allow donations to nonprofit organizations, of course, so both I and my corporations make large contributions to the Foundation for the Production of New Plays, the Foundation for the Production of Great Plays, and even the Foundation for the Revival of Great Musicals—they're all nonprofit. But investment? Nothing commercial, no."

I forced a smile. "Which is to say that commercial theater isn't."

He laughed and nodded. "Very true, very true. No, live theater is alive and well—but not profitable. A paradox, yes, but a fact, too."

"I believe I may have a scheme that could prove the exception to that rule," Barry murmured.

Valdor turned to him with a sudden intensity that I found almost frightening. "Really! I'm fascinated! But you don't have to concoct bizarre financial schemes just to . . ." A shadow crossed his face, and he sighed. "Yes, I have begged off from your last three invitations, haven't I? And at the last moment, too."

"You really must take a vacation some day, brother," Barry said gently, "even if you do have to bring your communicator along."

"True, and there could be no better distraction than wandering through Bohemia in your company, Barry. When things calm down a bit . . ."

"You really must." But Barry was smiling, amused. "Till then, you won't mind if I do concoct a business scheme every few months, will you?"

Valdor laughed. "As long as you don't put any of your

own money into them, no. And I apologize again, but it does seem to be the only way we ever talk with one another, doesn't it? Well, what is the scheme this time, Barry?"

"A real one, I'm afraid." Barry turned abruptly serious. "And one in which I do intend to invest a great deal of my capital, Valdor." At the look of alarm that crossed his brother's face, he held up a hand in reassurance. "Of course, there will be no point in my doing so if I cannot raise the remainder of the required capital from other sources."

Valdor's eye gleamed. "Excellent! All I have to do is say 'no,' and you won't be able to squander away your standard of living! But what is the scheme, Barry?"

"Live theater," Barry said, "but not here on Terra." He paused to let it sink in.

But Valdor's eyes struck an immediate glow. "Inspired! Presenting live plays on other planets? But it would be ruinously expensive to ship a whole cast and crew out there, along with costumes and scenery!"

"Not if it were a touring company," Barry murmured.

"Yes, of course!" Valdor slapped his knee, nodding. "Load the actors and scenery on board only once, here on Terra, then have them go from one planet to another! You'd perform several different plays on each planet, of course?"

"Yes, and the more well-established colonies have several cities large enough to support the venture. A short intercontinental hop would be—"

"Even less expensive for them than for you," Valdor assured him. "No, land at one city, then let them make their cultural pilgrimage to your ship. Each colony will pay your expenses for the trip to the next, plus its contribution to amortizing your initial investment! But Barry, it would take decades to pay off a capital outlay like that!"

"Five years." Barry drew an envelope from within his *complet* and handed it to Valdor. "I've taken the liberty of preparing a prospectus."

"You *are* serious!" Valdor slipped the sheets from the envelope and scanned them quickly. It only took him a few seconds, but he frowned and began to ask questions; obviously he absorbed data at a fantastic speed.

"You have actually priced a used freighter, of course?"

"Several. That figure's the average."

"Very good, but I'd want to be sure of your safety. A retired ship from my own fleet might do—or a thorough inspection by my mechanics."

"I wasn't aware you owned ships," Barry murmured.

Valdor shrugged impatiently. "I only invest and sell, Barry, as I've told you again and again. But I do own large interests in some shipping firms, of course, and I have a voice in their policies . . . Now, here's the crux of the whole issue: the audience." Valdor looked up, puzzled. "Are you certain there's no live theater on the colony planets?"

"None to speak of, or we'd surely have heard about it," Barry replied. "I've examined the trade journals, listened to the industry gossip, and spoken with colonials who have come in to see the sights and the shows. They mention the occasional amateur production and the odd strolling entertainer, but nothing more. Certainly there are no permanent companies or communities of working actors."

Valdor frowned. "It seems odd, in an age of hologram-broadcasts and faster-than-light spaceships."

"Perhaps it is because the technology is archaic," Barry offered. "If all you need is two trestles, four boards, two players, and a passion, what challenge is that for the engineers?"

Valdor smiled in millimeters. "Amusing, Barry—but surely there must be a more solid reason."

"Perhaps it is simply the economics of the situation," I offered. "The frontier is the frontier, after all, and pioneers tend to be thoroughly occupied with the process of survival. They have precious little time to spare for cultural pursuits."

Barry nodded agreement. "If they can spare an hour for recreation, they use it as spectators; watching a show takes a great deal less time and effort than producing one."

"That's true," Valdor acknowledged. "Every able-bodied human being is vital, in the early days of a colony; no one can be spared to devote all his time to leisure activities, such as presenting a play."

"Of course," Barry said, "I am speaking of the frontier, not the colonies that have been thriving for hundreds of years."

"Indeed?" Valdor frowned, bridging his fingers. "There *is* live theater away from Terra, then?"

"On the established colonies," Barry admitted. "Of course, they have much larger populations, and a great deal more leisure."

"True." Valdor nodded, still frowning. "On Falstaff or Haskerville, for example, there really is no reason why a few people, at least, couldn't earn a living as actors."

"But why should they bother?" I argued. "They can earn much better pay and be far more secure at an honest job—which are never in short supply, anywhere off Terra."

Valdor smiled, a full centimeter, at least. "There are always more jobs than people, yes—which is why there is still a constant stream of emigration."

"And, of course," Barry said, "there are colonies that are so stiffly prudish that they do not *want* theater—or 3DT, or probably even recorded songs. But we aren't planning to play Prudence—not even its capitol city."

"No theater in Chastity, eh?" Valdor's smile warmed a little, but his manner remained curt; business was business. "Now, tell me, what's your source on these figures for colonials attending theaters here in New York?"

"The Tourist Bureau, Valdor—and the bureaus of London, Paris, Rome, Berlin, Vienna, Moscow, Beijing, Prague, and Tokyo. I'm sure there are others . . ."

"Of course." Valdor had become curt; business was business. "And figures for distribution of 3DT dramas and comedies on the colonial planets, as well as life-style analyses, aspirations . . . I'll hand this to my market research boys and have them come up with a quick estimate. But I'd guess their answer will be the same as yours. This is good, Barry, very good." He couldn't quite restrain his tone of surprise, and Barry smiled, amused. "Why, thank you, Valdor. I've profited from your advice down the years."

"Nonsense!" Valdor slipped the papers back into the envelope and thrust them at Barry. "Merely your own genius, brother!" But he looked pleased. "Yes, your scheme has merit. From the look of it, it's not likely to lose money, at the least—and might turn a handsome profit. I must say I'm surprised at the modest size of the outlay, though."

"Everything is cheaper out of town," Barry explained, "and we don't have to be quite so concerned with union rules. Actors can help shift properties, and the technical crew can be minimal."

"Meaning that they will be adequate, but without featherbedding." But Valdor had suddenly lost his glow; in fact, he was looking very glum.

"You have lost two and three times that amount on business gambles in the past," Barry reminded.

Valdor's lips quirked with temporary amusement. "Ten and a hundred times, brother. No, it's certainly not the magnitude of the risk that troubles me, especially since it offers every chance of a large deduction. My main misgiving is the thought of having you so far out of touch. You're all the family I have, Barry."

"Come, now, brother," Barry said softly, "you know we don't see one another terribly often as it is. We'll touch base at Terra once a year, at least, to renew our material from time to time—and you must admit that the presence of your showman brother isn't exactly good for business."

Valdor laughed and nodded. "True, true—though I haven't let it trouble me in the past, and I've boasted unpardonably of your successes. Still, the question is one of your personal and professional development, so I mustn't let my maudlin insecurities hinder you."

"And is there no possibility of your own personal development?" Barry asked, with an implication that missed me completely.

"Yes, there is that." Valdor laced his fingers under his chin, looking down at his knees. After a few minutes, he looked up. "Your venture might also help me out of an embarrassing personal problem, at that. Very well, Barry— we'll investigate it seriously." He rose, holding out a hand. "Tomorrow at the same time, eh?"

"I'll look forward to it," Barry said, rising with a smile, "regardless of your decision." He embraced his brother, then held him out at arm's length and said, "At least, if I were out in space and you wanted to chat with me, you'd *have* to take a vacation."

Valdor laughed and slapped him on the back as he turned him toward the door.

As we stepped into the "down" car, I murmured, "Your brother must be the most tactful human being I have ever met."

"Oh, he meant most of what he said," Barry assured me, "especially that hint of an embarrassing personal problem."

"Oh?" I didn't dare ask.

Barry said only, "The gossip is true."

Well. The gossip within the trade had it that Valdor Tallendar had, in spite of his brother's warnings, been spending his leisure hours with Marnie Lulala, a former ingenue who had grown into one of the theater's most beautiful leading ladies—unfortunately, also one of the most poisonous, and her vitriol had increased as her looks had faded. She had progressed from leading roles to leading apes, as the more malicious gossip in the trade had it—and the same source held that Valdor was tiring of her, had in fact tired of her some time before, but was not yet willing to summon the cruelty necessary to be rid of her. Something drastic would indeed be required, since Marnie was not the type to take a hint, nor a graceful dismissal, no matter how lucrative. As her ability to attract starring roles had faded, she had clung ever more tightly to her conquest of the moment—which was Valdor, it seemed.

I glanced at Barry, and had the fleeting thought that he just might have concocted this whole scheme as a way of saving his little brother from the dragon lady. Then I dismissed the thought as unworthy—surely Barry would not be so self-sacrificing. Surely he could not feel that blood was thicker than theater.

We stopped in at Blarney's for a celebratory potation, and it may be that I celebrated a trifle too freely, especially since the sun was not yet over the yardarm. But then, in view of the weather, the sun was nowhere to be seen, so I didn't bother to cavil.

Really, we only stayed an hour, then repaired to Carstairs' to dine. Good friends stopped by, as they do at Carstairs'; the decor is pleasantly eighteenth century, and the service, if not human, is at least fully automated; you need only speak your choices aloud, and the table itself presents them to you. So, what with one thing and another, we stayed to chat, and the hour was late enough by the time we came out. Barry bade me good night—he wished to be up early, fully rested, anticipating his appointment with Valdor—so I set off alone toward the loft where some young friends of mine were trying out a new play one of my contemporaries had written. I had promised him I would see it, I had the evening free, and I was suddenly much more determined to appreciate New York to its fullest, every aspect of my life in it, including off-off-Broadway endeavors. I had half an hour till curtain, and it was only three blocks away; no reason, I told myself, to take a cab, though there were several narrow and poorly lighted streets along the route. I was a man over sixty, alone, and it was dark, but I assured myself that I could survive breaking the safety rules just this once more. I set off to find Terry's Theater without a care in the world.

4

I woke up cursing and wincing—each word sent a sprig of pain through my head. The person I was cursing was me, for not having been alert for a backup, a third member of the party lurking out in reserve. He had come up and sapped me on the back of the head. Then they had torn out my wallet—the pieces were there on the ground—and given my inert body a couple of kicks to make themselves feel good; I ached with bruises I didn't remember receiving.

I deserved it. "Always expect everything," that's what Sensei taught me—along with "They go in packs if they can." Two is a partnership, but three is a pack; the biggest one has to have at least two, or he can't feel like the big boss. I was glad Sensei wasn't handy; I would have been ashamed to have him see me.

I started to push myself to my feet, then thought twice—I was going to be very prudent from now on—and picked up the halves of my wallet. I glanced around to see if there were any cards from it lying around, but there weren't. So I tucked it away and, very cautiously, climbed to my feet.

My head stayed on, but it wasn't happy about it. Neither was I. I stumbled down the sidewalk, leaning against the side of the building, looking for a pharm-mart and hoping the punks had left me enough change for an analgesic. Good thing I had dropped out of college—if I couldn't keep my wits about me well enough to handle two punks with a surprise third, what the hell had I thought I was doing in college?

I found the mart and, oh, joy, they hadn't checked all my

pockets. I had a little more than two kwahers in change, and the 'gesic cost a tenth—275 BTU's, though I shouldn't say it out loud. It took a few minutes to scroll through the catalog and find the painkiller, though, then a minute or two more convincing the machine that it really did want to take coins, not the credit card I no longer had. I winced at the noise it made coughing up the tube, and the man taking live orders charged me for the cup of water. That was all there was to his mart, just the machine and his window, in a storefront six feet wide. Talk about low overhead. And minimizing shoplifting.

I gulped the pills with the water, threw away the empty, and slouched down the street waiting for them to take effect. When they did, they came on in a rush; suddenly, the headache was gone, and I was feeling a little more honest with myself. Yes, I had made a dumb mistake, but that didn't mean I was a total incompetent—and, yes, I could have stayed in college, couldn't I? If I could finish off two punks—never mind the gutless wonder in the shadows—I could finish my degree. I should have finished what I'd started, right?

But why bother? My father hadn't.

Of course, I could make excuses. I could say that I didn't think I'd get much studying done with Big Daddy's lawyers dropping little missives under my door every now and then, and I didn't have the money for a lawyer of my own. Why not ask my own daddy, you wonder? Because I didn't have one, that's why. Or, rather, yes, I did, but if I never see that bum all the rest of my life, it'll be better for us both. Much better, for him—he didn't even stay around long enough to see me for the first time. Okay, so the records say Mom divorced him, but it all comes down to the same thing, doesn't it? I wasn't important enough to him for him to be willing to guts it out till I showed up.

Of course, there was Mom, who had scrimped and saved to keep us both going long enough for me to get into college. I would have laid down my life for that woman—until she remarried. I hated her new husband with a ruddy passion, and I wasn't all that happy with her, either. Tell you the truth, I think they were both relieved when I left the house. I know I was. So, no, I wasn't about to go asking Mom for anything, either—and I didn't think she'd take all that kindly to my being up on fatherhood charges.

All of which, of course, is by way of telling you why I didn't do anything with Virginia, other than kiss and grope a lot—but not *that* much. Not with her. Or with any other woman, either.

Well, okay, there was one, whose name shall be withheld to protect the not-so-innocent but delightful in memory—except that I'd been in a mild panic for two months after that, afraid that she was going to come up pregnant in spite of the pills. And, okay, there had been a couple of other wild, drunken, carried-away nights, but the pills had worked.

It still made for panic and chronic anxiety. The pleasure just wasn't worth it. Virginia had had nothing to complain about from me, except having had nothing to complain about.

Which hadn't stopped her from trying to frame me.

What's that you say? What kind of man can I be, if I'm not trying to score with every pretty girl I see? The kind who's not going to be deserting a baby, that is what kind.

So I was down to two kwahers in change, and it was cold. Luckily, a beer only cost one, so I could go in and get warm until the bartender threw me out. I went in, ordered, and took out my wallet, hoping that maybe a miracle would have occurred. Sure enough, there was my good-luck charm, behind Virginia's photograph—a single kwaher bill, worn and frayed, but still with buying power. I liked the symbolism: What really mattered, to Virginia? A kwaher.

Kwaher—short for "kilowatt-hour." 2750 BTU's to the kwaher, 100,000 BTU's to the therm—which makes a therm worth 36.3636 BTU's. The magic number of the third millennium is thirty-six. When Terra finally admitted it was one integral economic whole, it developed a need for a single international unit of exchange, to even out all the seesawing in its hundreds of currencies. Gold was the obvious choice, but too much of it was already tied up in different coins of too many countries, past and present. They could have melted them down, of course, but the antiquarians cried "Foul!" and so did the businessmen, who were sentimental about their old golden eagles and rands. Instead they settled on energy as the international standard that was the same everywhere—very difficult to denature, and measurable in any denomination from joules to horsepower. Of course, it took some haggling to decide which energy unit to use. The BTU was nominated early on, of course, but the rest of the world wasn't too happy about using the British thermal unit—it evoked memories of an empire that hadn't been theirs—so they settled on the kilowatt-hour.

It was very difficult to make a kwaher buy more than an item cost to produce. Services, maybe—the law of supply and demand took over—but food, no. Which wasn't exactly good news, if you were looking at an empty wallet, hoping to find a bill you'd overlooked. I went through it diligently, taking sparing sips of the beer, waiting as long between as I dared. The bartender didn't even notice.

There was still that one kwaher left, slender but fragrant. There was also a deposit slip, for the money I had drawn out just before I left campus and that the pickpocket had extracted before he tossed the wallet into the trash can. There was also another deposit slip, in the sum of 13.5 kwahers; that had been a good month. There was the usual detritus stored away because it was too valuable to pitch, too cheap to file. Had I ever remembered to pick up those pictures? The month-old lottery ticket? There wasn't much chance I would win anything with that—and the anti-parent precaution was to make *sure* I wouldn't.

And that was about it. I folded the wallet and put it away with a sigh.

"This vile song bids fair to undermine the virtue of every fair virgin of the Terran sphere, my fellow citizens, unless we rally to prevent its distribution!"

I winced and glanced up at the wall-screen—only a small

one, three feet by two, the legal minimum, up high above the hero sandwich extruders—but all that was on it was an Assembly debate. Elector Rudders filled the screen in high gear, haranguing as usual against the corrupting effects of the raucous popular music that was, according to him, enervating our youth and sapping the collective will of our future society. I gritted my teeth and looked away, glad that I had the option of canceling the audio on the bar speaker. I did, but someone not too far away had left his on—can you believe it? He *liked* to hear the elector lecturing his colleagues in a style that would have done credit to an ancient revivalist minister.

I knew what he was trying to do, of course, and it almost brought my headache back. He was trying to get the public all lathered up over what he called scandal music—this week; last week, it had been radio talk shows that mentioned sex now and then. He was hoping the voters would spend so much time arguing over freedom to blast out sound and massacre verse that they would ignore what was *really* going on in the Assembly. The Liberals had figured out what he was trying to do, so they had pushed through a law requiring wall-screens in all public places that did nothing but carry the Assembly debates and committee meetings. Nice ploy, but it didn't work—Rudders and the rest of his LORDS party just soaked up screen time bellowing about trivia, and the public tuned him out. Of course, they tuned out the Assembly with him.

It worked. Real well. I knew what he was trying to do, but I reached out and tuned him out, anyway—or at least, his voice. The other patron's speaker was still buzzing, though.

In desperation, I looked around and saw the news terminal. I picked up my beer and strolled over to it, but the first thing I saw was the dark screen; the second was the slot for the credit card I didn't have, and didn't want to use. I sighed and turned back to the bar. The bartender glanced up at me; I took a sip, and he turned away.

As I climbed back on my stool, I noticed a hard copy that some obliging patron had left on his seat. I made a long arm, picked it up, and tried the want ads again. They hadn't changed. Computer programmer, B.E.E. required . . . Dental technician . . . Male nurse . . . Didn't anybody want to hire a dropout?

The bartender looked over at me, then looked harder. I glanced down and saw that my beer had just about hit bottom. I gave him a toothy smile, climbed down off the stool, swigged down the last drop, and strolled out the door, sans newspaper, sans heat, sans job.

It was going to be a long night.

Eighth Avenue by night was pretty garish. The glow signs were glare signs, and each bistro owner had chosen his own taste in colors, making sure they clashed with his neighbor's. It made for some very interesting combinations, which jarred on my sensibilities enough to set my teeth on edge and curdle my depression into something nasty. I recognized the symptoms and looked around for something to distract me—I'd already had one fight today, and I was on a diet.

That was when I heard the yelling.

It was only a single, desperate cry, cut off in the middle, but very obviously that of a soul in distress. I looked around at the other passersby, who were busy passing by—I couldn't believe it. I turned toward where the sound had come from, hurrying to help out—then realized that I had just been given a great excuse for a fight. I started running.

I turned into a side street, away from the lights, and heard a feeble "Help!" and a guttural laugh. I swerved into an alley just in time to hear a voice in front of me say, "This is more fun than his money, anyway," and somebody else growled, "My turn."

Okay, so the rule in the big city is not to fight unless they get violent enough to kill you. But beating up an old man is close enough; he might die. My system shifted into high gear.

They were too old to be punks, too young to be respectable crooks. One of them was holding an old man's arms behind him with one hand, his other over the guy's mouth, and two others were taking turns pounding him.

Only three, and one of them with his hands full. I grinned and stepped up behind the other two without the slightest trace of compunction. The catcher saw me just in time to yell, and the guy I was aiming for twisted aside just enough so that the punch landed in his gut, not his kidney, but it slowed him down enough for me to get his buddy in the chops before the catcher let go and mashed my cheek with a punch like a hydraulic hammer. I rolled back dazed, while the old man sagged away with a groan, and I felt fear stab—this guy might be better than he looked.

Then he was on me, hunched over, punches driving at my midsection like twin jackhammers, and I blocked while my head cleared, much reassured—he was slower than I was.

But his buddies were coming in from the sides. I gave one of them an elbow and the other a foot, and they slowed just enough for me to catch the catcher's punch and slam him into the wall. The third one swung at me then, and he was fast, oh yes, but I was faster, yanking him too far forward and kicking him as he fell. He caught the punch the left-hand one had aimed for me, which slowed him just enough for me to hit him three times. As he slumped against the wall, that hydraulic caught me again, once in the back of the head and again in the shoulder, spinning me around. I groped for the wall, backing fast, trying to recover, waiting for the kick in the head . . .

There was a crack and a howl. I looked up to see the catcher on his knees, head in his hands, and the old guy trying to riposte with his walking stick, to ward off the second thug. He didn't make it in time, but I did.

Then back to the catcher, who was trying to pull himself together as he dug into his jacket pocket and muttered dire threats having something to do with the arrangement of my intestines. I stepped in, caught his hand as it came out, and slammed it back against the stone. He howled, and I caught the cylinder that dropped from loosened fingers. One quick glance, and I felt cold fear shoot through me—it was a tickler. One touch of that blunt muzzle near any of my nerve centers, and I'd be writhing on the ground in agony. But it has a weakness: its insides are largely crystalline. So I cracked it against the wall, then let him watch as the sand trickled out the aperture. There wasn't enough light to see him turn pale, but his eyes widened. He had more sand inside himself, though, and he tried a kick. I blocked it and had to content myself with a blow to his head. He slammed into the wall behind him, rebounded, and went spinning down to the concrete.

I looked around. Unfortunately, they were all out cold, or faking very well. I was tempted to try waking one of them, but my sensei had taught me sternly, so I honored their condition.

The old guy and I stood side by side, looking down at the three thugs and breathing hard. After a minute or so, he rasped, "Safety . . . rules. I thought . . . just this once . . ."

I nodded. "Seat belts always, Pop." Then I looked up at him and grinned. "Hi! I'm Ramou."

"Horace," he wheezed. "A pleasure . . . young man . . . and . . . a thousand thanks."

"You know these guys?"

He shook his head, still rasping. "And I . . . only had ten . . . in my . . . wallet."

"So they decided to take the rest out in trade." I dropped down and went through the catcher's pockets, hoping he'd revive enough for me to take umbrage, but he didn't. I pulled out the wad of bills I found, peeled out a ten, then shoved them back where I'd found them and put the ten into the old guy's hand as I stood. "To the victor go the joules. You're pretty good with that cane, Pop."

"Thank you . . . for the chance . . . to use it. Might I suggest . . . we vacate the premises?"

"Blow?" I scowled down at the thugs. "You really think bums like these might have friends?"

"It is . . . possible. And . . . a policeman . . . might happen by . . ."

"We're clean!" I snapped.

"Yes, but . . . proving it . . . the delay . . ."

And I remembered that I didn't want anything official

going into any computers. "Right." I turned away, offering my arm. "Can you make it?"

He leaned on me, wheezing. "Thank you. Yes, a thousand times, my young friend! But . . . why?"

"It felt good." I glanced back, but our three friends were still decorating the pavement. "Thanks for the excuse. Can I convoy you somewhere? You're not in top shape at the moment." For that matter, I had new aches on top of old ones, and my head was throbbing again. Inside, though, I felt great.

"A few blocks over, there is a bar where I'm known. You must at least accept a potation, my young savior."

"Why, sure, I don't mind." I started to mention dinner, but bit my tongue—it was for him to offer; I didn't charge.

I did glance back a couple of times, in case one of the thugs reconsidered and tried to climb to his feet, but they were taking no chances. Or were genuinely out.

A pity. It made me feel a lot better after losing out to those two morons with the hidden third, but there was a great deal of anger left. Always would be, the shrink had told me. Something having to do with my father . . .

"Sure a few blocks is enough?"

He nodded. "I'll be among friends. As will you, young man—now."

He was as good as his word, and so were his buddies, when they heard his story. That involved introductions, and we found out each other's last names—Horace Burbage, he was. His buddies would have loaded me with booze and banquets, but I still just sipped, even after the food arrived—warmth is worth making last. They would have stuffed me, to show their thanks—but a full stomach makes a slow punch. They stiffened my resolution by swapping mugging stories. I listened, dazed, and refused every ounce of hard stuff they offered me—if it was *that* bad in this town, I had to keep my reflexes fast.

I was really a fifth wheel, so I drifted away a few feet,

found a hard copy lying on a table, and started going through the want ads again.

After a little bit, Horace realized I wasn't part of the party, and came over to join me. I felt an unreasonable rush of gratitude, but I didn't let it show.

He glanced over my shoulder. " 'Help wanted . . .' I take it you're at liberty, Ramou?"

"Only because I moved fast," I said. "Her daddy's got enough to buy himself five private eyes and a judge, without even opening his wallet."

He smiled with that look that means he was holding back laughter, and I felt clumsy and gauche. "No, that's not quite my meaning. In the theatrical trades, 'at liberty' refers to your employment status. I infer you're in need of a position."

"You mean, am I job-hunting? Yeah. But look at this." I turned the hard copy so he could see it and pointed out a few ads. " 'B.A. required.' 'B.E.E. required.' 'M.B.A. a must.' 'C.P.A. desirable.' What's left—alphabet soup? What kind of job can you get if you don't have a degree?"

It must have been an interesting question, because it made him look solemn. "Acting. And free-lance writing, of course."

"Are you kidding? Even the writers have to know something, these days."

"And so do the actors," he agreed, "but they only need the knowledge, not the degree. Admittedly, most people learn far more under the guidance of a professor than they could by themselves, and the names of certain colleges can be of great value when applying for a position. It is even possible to make contacts through some colleges—but in the final analysis, it is the knowledge itself that counts. Surely you have the capacity to learn."

"Oh, definitely." I mean, learning—what does that take? My tests said I was bright, but I never *felt* smart. "I was in college, up until this morning."

"Then go back—" Horace broke off, looking embarrassed. "Uh, no, my apologies. The young lady's there, isn't she? And her father's menials. But surely you learned something during your time there. How long was it?"

"Two years. I was starting on my third."

"In what field?"

"Electrical engineering," I said. "But you can't even be a repairman without a degree, these days. It's all done by big companies, and they want paper."

He stiffened, and his eyes glowed; I thought he was getting an idea, but all he said was, "There are positions. You can still obtain employment clearing tables in one of the better eating establishments, for example."

I frowned down at the fax. "I don't see anything about them in here."

"They don't advertise—it's all done by word of mouth." Horace smiled. "I happen to know several of the mouths. Actors frequently earn their livings as waiters, you see, and some of my friends should be able to tell me the addresses of restaurants that use human labor. If you find the atmosphere congenial, you might even embark on a course of training to become a waiter. And, of course, there are the other branches of the entertainment industry, such as drawing illustrated stories and lettering the dialogue."

I frowned. "I thought those were all union jobs."

"On the contrary, in the modern age, they are generally filled by free-lancers—the pay is execrable, and there are hordes of talented young folk seeking employment therein. There's a remarkably high turnover. You would need some knowledge of computer graphics, of course . . ."

"I've got it! Three-D, too. But don't you have to know somebody before anybody'll talk to you?"

"You do," Horace assured me, "now."

I was beginning to realize I had made a very lucky save.

A trace of concern crossed his wrinkled face. "But you are looking rather worn. Perhaps you should let the issue go for the night and pursue it tomorrow."

He was right; with a full meal and a beer inside me, I was fighting to keep my eyes open. "Yeah, guess I should." I felt that cold, sinking sensation as I contemplated spending the night on the subway and hoping I'd wake up in the morning. But I was hanged if I'd let anybody else know that. I shoved myself to my feet and said, "Well, it's been a pleasure, Mister . . . Horace . . ."

"Just Horace," he advised.

"You sure it shouldn't be Mr. Burbage?" Something about that name nudged at my memory, but I was in no condition to nudge back.

"I am certain," he said.

"It's been a pleasure, Horace. Can we get together sometime tomorrow?"

"Of course." But he looked at me keenly and said, "Where *were* you sleeping tonight?"

The question took me aback—he'd been so tactful about everything else. "Uh . . . well . . ."

"Have you any funds?"

"You mean money?" I glowered. "No. That one didn't stay around to face me."

He nodded. "I had some sort of notion of that. Well, my apartment is small but spacious, and I can only offer you a sofa whose upholstery has seen better days—but you're welcome to it."

"You've got a guest." I sat down again, reflecting that I hadn't done too badly for my first day in New York, after all—two fights, a dozen bruises, and a friend. "Just tell me when you're ready." I fought to keep my eyes open. "Which way, mister?"

"Horace, *please.*" He rose, taking me by the arm and steering me toward the door. "Surely we know each other well enough for Christian names. Shall we go?"

Horace's apartment certainly wasn't anything luxurious—just a bathroom, a food dispensary, a bedroom (I assume that's what the closed door was), and a twelve-by-sixteen sitting room—but it looked great to me.

"Make yourself at home," Horace said, which was maybe unwise of him. I resolved not to take advantage—but I couldn't quench my curiosity about the decoration. The walls were covered with prints and masks—Comedy, Tragedy, some brightly colored Asiatic numbers, and some rather grim-looking ones; the floor-to-ceiling shelves were filled with actual, antique books with titles like *The Booths, The Barrymores, The Empty Space, New Theatres for Old, A History of Theatre in America,* and *Famous Theatrical Designs.* I began to have a notion as to what kind of gentleman I had met—but the collection of posters clinched it, because there was one, with a picture of an apple tree and an old man sitting under it while another guy in evening clothes lurked in the branches—and the old man was Horace! Even his name: "Starring Horace Burbage." So I looked at the rest of them, most of which had half a dozen people or more—and, sure enough, I could find him in each one! I worked my way backward through time, seeing his face get younger and younger, until he was a funny-looking kid about my age falling flat on his prat—and all the while, I was remembering that show I used to watch when I was kid, about the time traveler who lived in the twentieth century and kept stumbling into our time, and every time in between, with his faithful milkman companion who kept getting caught in his capers—and sure enough, it was the same face! *Now* I knew why his name had sounded familiar—I was actually in the same room with Morty the Milkman!

I turned away from the wall, feeling rather numb, and saw Horace regarding me with amusement—and two steaming cups. "Yes, I confess it. I have a vice."

"You're an actor!"

"Guilty. But I'm a rather chilled one at the moment, and I'd guess you are, too. Here." He pressed a steaming mug into my hand.

"But that's great! I mean . . ." I swallowed hard; I was starting to sound the way I've always thought gushing fans do. Horace didn't need one of those invading his private life—and he didn't need to be reminded that I'd been just out of diapers when he was playing Morty the Milkman! I got some thinking time by taking the cup and slurping—

then stood up very straight indeed. "Wow! What did you put in that?"

"Only hot buttered rum." Horace smiled, amused. "It only *seems* to have more authority than usual—because it's hot."

It sounded like something out of a play to me. Tasted like it, too, in fact. To cover my confusion, I turned back to the wall of posters. "These are all really you?"

"I'm in each of them somewhere, yes." Horace stepped up to the wall. "Only the one lead, of course—with a face like mine, one obtains character parts, which are seldom the focus of the play. There were other productions, of course, but I've only just so much wall."

"So these are the pick." I surveyed the gallery, racking my brains.

He saved me. "I'd invite you to my next performance, but there isn't one at the moment. I, like yourself, am at liberty."

"Oh." I felt a rush of sympathy, but it was enough to make me realize I shouldn't show it. "So . . ." I pointed to the poster that I recognized from last year's commercials. "You just got out of this one?"

"No, *Life Alive* closed six months ago, and I'm a bit old for the rigors of a national company—your pardon, that's a touring version of the original production; they pack the scenery in a truck and the actors on a bus, and take the show from city to city." He shivered as he said it, and I wondered if touring was really that rough. "My most recent endeavor was as the Scissors-Grinder in *The Fool Killer*."

"Hey, I heard about that! *You* did that song, 'The Spinning Stone'!"

"I had that pleasure." He turned to me with a bit more interest, as though I had somehow been promoted to a higher grade of humanity. "I wasn't aware that engineers followed the theater."

"No, but I'm as gung ho for music as the rest of us my age—and that song definitely had the most complex rhythm and the best words of the season. I mean, that *never* happens—it's either words or rhythm, not both."

"An astute observation." He nodded; I don't think he'd ever realized it before. "In fact, you may have just hit on the reason why the production folded in its second month."

He had gained a thoughtful look. I figured it was time for distraction. "So what's your next show?"

Mistake. I should have been paying more attention. He started looking grim, but forced a smile. "Ah. At this moment, my friend, that is only a series of possibilities on the glowing horizon."

Talk about an optimist. "Oh." And, "At least it's glowing."

"Why, yes, it is." The smile gained substance. "There is a possibility of a scheme coming to fruition, one which will at least put me before an audience again, in a variety of roles. And, of course, if it falls through, I can always wait, as I have before, until parts are open that call for my talents. There is a long tradition among actors of eking out a living in other areas of temporary employment, so each of us is careful to maintain his skills in high-demand occupations. If the money falls too low, with no prospect of even a 3DT bit part or a commercial announcement, I can always fall back on my record of excellence in data storage operation."

A file clerk? Morty the Milkman, a file clerk? I was astounded. I was amazed. I was dismayed.

But I knew better than to say it. He was looking a little blue around the edges already. Any bluer, and I could have used his mood for a pair of jeans. I tried to think of something that would lighten him up, and remembered that he'd been surprised I'd read one of the classics. "There was that production of *Moby-Dick* on 3DT last year. I heard it was a real whale—but how did they get it to come so close to the actors without killing them?"

"Ah." He cheered up a bit. "I did hear something about that, through the grapevine. It was simply good communication, that's all. Once the whale knew what was requested of it, and that the 3DT company would guarantee a human-free cove for ten years by way of recompense, it was quite cooperative. Highly intelligent, actually—understood direction on the first explanation, executed each take flawlessly; memory like an elephant, that one—and even managed those stupendous effects, such as jumping clear of the water and somersaulting, without the slightest cavil. I've known actors who were more difficult to work with—much more."

"Amazing! But it must have taken jobs away from a whole team of special-effects operators. How did you deal with the unions?"

"Oh, we inducted the beast into Actors' Equity and let the unions fight it out between themselves. IATSE—the stage-hands' union—brought suit against the studio, claiming that the whale could not qualify as a member of any union, since he was not human."

"I remember that case. The judge ruled that he was self-aware, had a moral sense, and could understand enough of human ways to enter into a binding contract, so he was human enough for a union. The environmentalists hailed it as a landmark decision."

"Quite rightly, too—C. Larens d'Arrow, the notorious labor relations attorney, contacted the whales and, for a very modest retainer, laid out a constitution and incorporated them as a nation, so the whalers suddenly found they were committing acts of war. Faced with coordinated attack by schools of whales and lawyers, they decided to diversify and went into partnership with their erstwhile victims. The whales now drive schools of fish into huge weirs—fish traps, you know—and the former whalers net them by the droves. On top of that, the whales warn the dolphins to stay out of the way, so tuna salad is now reliably all fish."

"I remember reading about that! The whalers invested in hundreds of square miles of Arizona desert and filled the market for whale oil with jojoba oil! Then they went into partnership with the Australian drovers, and started selling their customers beef instead of whale meat! Struck me that the human race was suffering an attack of sanity, for a change . . ."

"Well, some race was. Not necessarily ours . . ." Horace

looked up as his communicator chimed. "Ah, a call! If you will excuse me . . ."

"Don't mind me," I assured him, then stood there studying the posters and trying not to listen.

The lad was a very polite representative of his generation, and was certainly doing his best not to eavesdrop. I almost told him not to bother, then remembered that the caller might be a lady friend; there were one or two whose names I'd have preferred not to have used. I clipped in the headset for privacy, just in case, then pressed "Accept"—and Barry's face floated there in my screen.

"Horace! In the flesh! Splendid! I've news—wonderful news!"

"Where are you buying the champagne?" But my stomach was sinking within me.

"The Pleiades! Hang the expense! Horace, Valdor said yes!"

"Wonderful!" I reminded myself that I wasn't fully committed yet—and should be, if I said yes. "But so soon! Didn't he need time to think it over longer? What of the market research?"

"Oh, you know how quickly computers can assemble information! Besides . . ." He winked. "I've a notion that the market was not the strongest factor in his decision, and that he has had ample time to discuss matters with the source from which he really did need an answer."

Marnie Lulala. My heart sank down to join my stomach. "I take it we have a leading lady, then."

"We do indeed! Small enough price to pay for the venture, eh?"

"Oh, certainly." But I wasn't so sure. Anyone who had ever had to work with Marnie would definitely shudder at the notion of virtually living with her for a few weeks, let alone a year—and I'm sure Valdor had. Shuddered, that is. Still, Art was my mistress, and even more demanding than Valdor's. "How soon do you plan to audition?"

"I am entering an advertisement in the trade press tonight, so the agents will find it on their screens in the morning. The young actors will check *Variety* on their screens when they wake up, so a noon audition is feasible."

"Noon tomorrow? But a space . . ."

"The Foundation has given me the go-ahead to use their conference room. I'll make arrangements for a proper rehearsal hall in the morning, of course."

"But, Barry . . . why such . . ."

"Haste?" Barry's eyes twinkled through the screen. "Come, Horace! Isn't this what we've always dreamed of? A permanent company, with the actors in charge of their own destinies? How can I not be eager?"

"How not, indeed?" I agreed, somewhat numbed.

"You will help me on the auditions, won't you, old friend?"

"Old friend"—that did it. That was the nub. Barry was the only friend left from my early days, and was certainly my closest and most constant; not even during the years of his greatest success had he lost contact with me, or patronized me, or failed to assist me in need. How could I refuse him now? "Certainly," I said, more numb than ever. "I will be delighted . . . the prospect is enthralling . . ."

"Stout fellow! Tomorrow, then, at the Foundation! Shall we say 11:30? And the Pleiades now, of course."

"Yes, certainly. Half an hour at the most. My thanks, Barry, my thanks indeed."

The old guy didn't look so good as he disconnected, but he'd certainly been sounding happy enough. Or had it been a bit forced? "Good news?"

"Oh yes, quite good!" He came back toward me and lowered himself carefully into an armchair. "It seems I may not have to be concerned over the matter of employment, after all." But a very bleak look flickered across his face.

"Somebody offered you a part?"

"You might say that. Yes. A variety of parts." With an obvious effort, he wrenched himself out of the mood, forced a smile, and asked, "Are you familiar with touring companies?"

"Like the one you were telling me about earlier, that takes a show from town to town?"

"City to city, rather; Omaha is as small as we go, except for the larger college communities. It has been years since I was in such a company."

"It sounds like fun," I said wistfully.

"Oh, it is—for the first few months. Or at least, it is exciting and invigorating—but it is also tiring." The bleak look again. "And your only social life is with the other members of the company, which can become awkward."

I had an idea what he meant. "After a few months, you start getting on each other's nerves?"

He turned to me with a frown. "An excellent guess. How did you arrive at it?"

"I have some friends who come from small towns, where almost everybody is related to everybody else, and they scarcely ever see anyone new. To hear them talk, they hate each other—but say something bad about one of them, and they all turn on you."

"Ah. Quite." Horace nodded. "Only the relationship is a good deal closer than that, Ramou. Like a family, almost—a 'substitute family,' I believe the sociologists call it. It is a very large family, however, with some very intense rivalries—though your rival one month may be your ally the next. As in a family, you must coexist with some people you don't particularly like in any given week."

"Sounds familiar—uh, pardon the pun . . ."

"No, you said 'familiar,' not 'familial,' " Horace said, with the ghost of a smile. "And, as in a large family, one member may think he's unloved and even hated—but if he's attacked by someone outside the family, or suffers bad fortune, they all rally to help him."

"High price to pay, just to know people care about you."

"Perhaps," Horace mused, "though I've had occasion to think such adversity a blessing in disguise . . . Well!" He slapped his knee. "Enough of an old man's maunderings.

You're surely tired, and will need to be up early on the morrow."

I almost asked why, then remembered that I still needed to be looking for a job. Of course, I could have checked in at the local Government Aid office and taken one of the manual-labor jobs they supply, but that would have meant entering my name and number in a computer, and any hacker could have found me an hour later. An investigator probably would have found me in two seconds; come to think of it, they probably had a tracer program lurking in the network waiting for my number to appear, right that minute. Which meant the loon who took my wallet was in for a nasty surprise when he tried to use the card. I felt better about that, all of a sudden—until I realized that the investigator already knew what city I was in.

So what? Find one person in New York? When he doesn't even have an address? It is to laugh. Talk about Gammer Gurton's Needle.

But that meant I couldn't ever have an address . . .

And that any job I found would have to pay cash—or not insist on proof of ID when I gave them a false name . . .

Suddenly I realized that my choice of jobs was going to be very limited indeed.

I'd been silent too long; Horace was watching me with concern. I felt that confounded rush of gratitude again—what a guy, to be able to worry about my troubles, in the middle of his own! I wondered if I was intruding on his personal grief, or if he was glad to have me there as a distraction. "Yeah," I said, "guess you're right. Sleep it is."

"You'll find it a great consolation," he assured me. He stood up and moved slowly toward the bedroom. "Sleep soundly, young man. We'll try for an early start, eh?"

"Good night," I said, and ducked into the bathroom. When I came out, I found him spreading a sheet over the sofa, with a pillow and quilt on the chair nearby. "Hey, now! You shouldn't go to so much trouble!"

"No trouble at all." He stood up with a smile and clasped

my shoulder briefly. "I find I'm glad of the company. In the morning, eh?"

I grinned. "Early morning. Good night, Horace."

"Good night, Ramou." But he didn't go to the bedroom—he went to the hall closet instead. He took out his overcoat and started putting it on.

I sat bolt upright. "Hey! At this hour of the night?"

"I have a sudden appointment," he said, sounding infinitely weary. "An old friend needs help celebrating."

I started to climb off the sofa.

"No, no." He regarded me with amusement. "I have no need of a bodyguard—I'll follow the safety rules this time."

I paused. "You'll take a cab?"

"Both ways," he promised. "Don't trouble yourself, Ramou."

I sank back—gratefully, if it must be known; I was tired with the kind of weariness that aches in every joint. "Well . . . okay."

"It will be," he assured me. "I have lived in this city for thirty years and more, and tonight was only the second time I've been mugged. It will also be the last. Good night, Ramou."

"G'night, Horace."

The door closed behind him.

"Lights off," I called out.

Obediently, the apartment computer doused the lights. There was still plenty of glow coming in the window, of course. I lay down, warm and massively relieved—by the safety and security of a pillow and blanket and, yes, because I'd had the lurking concern that the old guy might make a pass at me. Not that he looked like it, but you never know— and it always makes for an awkward moment, which I could do without right now. I had troubles enough—almost as many as I would have had if I had stayed on campus. I fell asleep wondering why I'd bothered to run.

5

HORACE

In the morning, I made a few calls to some old friends at eating establishments and illustrated-story companies. They sounded dubious, but agreed to speak to Ramou—so I left the lad sleeping, with the list of potential employers and a note telling him he was welcome for a second night (I didn't commit myself beyond that), and another inviting him to help himself to the food synthesizer; he seemed an honest sort, and I didn't think he'd take a seven-course banquet, especially not upon rising. Of course, a young and healthy appetite . . .

Burglary? Yes, appearances can be deceiving, and though I thought the lad looked trustworthy, you never can tell. Still, I had no valuables—what few I owned were still in my box at the bank—and I did take the precaution of locking the drawers with my mementos; my bureau and desk are steel beneath the veneer, as are most in Manhattan, and the locks respond only to my thumbprint. Not that I didn't think highly of the lad, mind you, but curiosity is a stronger force than dishonesty, and he was probably young enough to remember my stint as Morty the Milkman with the vividness of childhood. No, really, I felt quite safe in leaving him as I sallied forth to meet the world, in the friendly guise of Barry Tallendar.

The reception room at the Foundation for the Advancement of Theater was warm and welcoming, as it always is, and in consequence, there were the usual assortment of unemployable hopefuls lounging about looking through the hard copies of the trades. You can tell them at a glance—the ones who have just arrived, and won't last six months because they wait for Fame to come to them by sitting in the Foundation's reception room reading the trades; the old ones who will never work again because they won't audition for fear of being turned down, but still hope for the Magic Call; and the ones who have no current parts or auditions in the offing, and might as well hang around here rather than elsewhere, since there's always the possibility of a contact that might lead to work.

. . . And, of course, you can always be wrong about what you see at a glance.

Then, over against the wall by the window, sitting prim and properly, with hopeful glows and repressed smiles, clutching their handbags, two young ladies for whom this was certainly the first New York audition, or the second or third—certainly they had not been at it long enough for it to have become routine. I gave them a closer look—they were probably here in response to Barry's notice of open auditions, which had appeared in the morning's edition of *Variety.* Came together, of course, which was a mistake. I resolved to try to remember each separately—which wouldn't be easy; though one was blond and round-faced, the other brunette and overslender, that hopeful glow made them so much alike that it would be difficult to remember that they were two separate individuals, not different avatars of the same soul.

In any case, this was the Lucky Day for all of them—there were auditions ready to hand, no farther away than the conference room next door. I went into it, and must confess that the stir behind me gladdened my heart.

Barry was already there, of course, and already looking harried. He glanced up. "Ah, Horace! Thank heaven! I was an idiot to begin so soon! I need time to prepare, prepare!"

"Oh, stuff and nonsense, Barry." I hung up my coat and sat down beside him. "You've been preparing for this all your life."

That calmed him remarkably. "Yes, I have, in a way, haven't I?" Then excitement built again as he said, "But to have the moment finally arrive, Horace! To think that I am about to step into the footsteps of Irving, Booth, Olivier, Gielgud! And that it is about to happen now, this instant! How can I have the audacity, the effrontery . . ."

"Calm yourself, Barry. Irving was less experienced than yourself when he became actor-manager, and Booth was surely no more so. As for Olivier and Gielgud, they led their companies, true, but were not quite in the same position as Booth and Irving; the distinction between actor and director had been made clear in their time, and they certainly did not have to concern themselves with all the minutiae of management."

"True, true." He was calming again. "Which reminds me; we must hire an accountant, a secretary, a lawyer . . ."

"The lawyer can be retained on a consulting basis, and by link with Terra," I assured him. "The others will have to be able to double as crew or cast, will they not?"

"You are quite right—in a touring company such as this, everyone will have to double in brass . . ."

"Except Marnie."

His face twitched. "Yes. Except." Then the enthusiasm began to build again. "But I certainly should have taken at least a day to select our first season's repertoire! To find at least a dozen options to choose from! To—"

"You mean you have not been mulling over such a bill for the last year?"

"Well, the idle thought did occur to me now and then . . ."

"What are those scripts before you?"

"These?" He looked down at the four stacks before him as though wondering how they'd come to be there. "Oh, Shakespeare's *Midsummer Night's Dream*, Molière's *The Doctor in Spite of Himself*, Wasserman, Leigh, and Darion's *Man of La Mancha* . . ."

"A musical?"

"Why, we must do everything, Horace!" he exclaimed, shocked.

"Delighted to hear it," I assured him warmly, while my

hindbrain wondered furiously about musicians, synthesizers, union jurisdictions, throat lozenges . . . "And the last?"

"Backer's *Didn't He Ramble*. As you see, just the classics. Durable, sure in their audience appeal, edifying and uplifting in their educational and cultural merits—"

"And free of royalties, being in the public domain," I finished. "Surely we could afford the rights to at least one recent comedy?"

"Well, the accountant I mentioned . . . Surely you know, Horace, that I have no head for figures."

I knew nothing of the sort; in fact, I suspected that his investments over the years had been shrewd ones, though that might have been due as much to Valdor's advice as to Barry's shrewdness. Certainly his standard of living had not declined from his days as a star. I glanced at my ring-watch. "Noon, Barry!"

"Oh, how can I begin?"

"In the same fashion as you always have, when you were about to step in front of an audience." I rose and patted him on the shoulder. "Calm yourself, old friend. It's merely stage fright." I turned away to the door, realizing that he really *had* needed me here.

I stepped out, assuming my most authoritative manner. "Ladies. Gentlemen. Who among you is here to audition for—" Hang it, Barry hadn't given me a name for his endeavor! "—for Mr. Tallendar's touring company?"

The two young things by the window raised their hands on the instant, just as though they were in a classroom, bless them. Several of the older actors looked up, nodding, while the young ones already homeward bound (though they did not know it yet) looked at me with blank surprise. And, of course, two or three of the dear older things who spent the better part of their waking hours in the Foundation's reading room—that was one of its *raisons d'etre,* though never stated openly—looked every bit as blank and even more surprised as they said, "Oh," and, "Are there auditions here today?"

"There are," I assured them. Then, summoning one of the

two who had actually come just for the occasion, perhaps their first audition, "Would you come in, please, miss?" After all, it was only fair.

She squeezed her friend's hand for good luck as she rose, and came tripping into the conference room, still clutching her purse as though it were a talisman. As I closed the door behind her, I saw the young idlers begin to sit up straight and look nervous, while the older ones began to queue up at the communicator. By the time this young lady was done, I knew, the room would be jammed. Well enough—half of them would leave when Barry told them what to expect. The other half might even be worth hearing.

By the time I had closed the door, the nervous young thing was halfway to Barry, hand outstretched, and he was rising with full composure, smiling gravely and with the suave authority of a leading man in a drawing-room comedy, head slightly bowed, entirely self-possessed and gracious, even as I had known he would be. "Good afternoon, miss." He touched her fingers briefly before he put a script in them; someone would later tell her that one doesn't shake hands with the director at auditions. I hoped someone would also tell her that she shouldn't encourage closer contact afterward. "May I know your name?"

"Oh! Of course, how silly of me!" She took out her composite holo portrait, with profile, three-quarter profile, and full-length all on one sheet, her credits printed on the back— not completely uninformed, then. "I'm Adrianne Darling, Mr. Tallendar." I could see her restraining herself from asking for his autograph.

"A pleasure, Ms. Darling." Barry gave not the slightest hint of knowing that the name was scarcely the one she'd been born with, or that he'd heard it before; he merely sat down, still with the gentle smile, and took up a noteboard. "Now, would you give us a brief notion of your prior experience and training? We'll have the details from your résumé, of course, but we'd like to hear the précis." It was really just to put her at ease, at least a little. Not many directors would have bothered.

"Oh, I was at Ohio State, I took my B.F.A. there in June, and I was in summer stock in Indiana, at the Rondele Playhouse, for two summers. I played Juliet in my senior year, and I was Mrs. Pearce in *Pygmalion* last summer."

"An excellent beginning. No Equity card yet, though?"

"No, but I have almost half my points."

"Well begun, indeed. Now, please step over to the wall, please, where the lights are focused. I'd like you to begin with Hermia's speech in scene one."

And she was off.

So was Barry. He managed to keep the smile in place. So did I—but Ohio State was obviously not what it had once been.

When she was done, he glanced at his watch, asked her to read one of Titania's lines (so far out of type as to be a clear indication that this was courtesy only), then stood up and said, "Thank you, Ms. Darling. We'll be contacting you if we need to hear you again."

Her smile slipped for just a second, but she managed to hoist it back into place bravely, bobbed her head, and went out clutching her purse for dear life. Barry held the door for her . . .

. . . and stiffened as he beheld a madhouse.

The reception room was jammed; every chair was occupied, every inch of wall space taken up with a leaner. Only one or two had the look of beginners; most of the others, young and old, were obviously veterans.

Ms. Darling recoiled.

Barry supported her with a hand and a smile. "Congratulations, Ms. Darling. You've beaten the rush."

She looked up at him, wide-eyed, then flashed him a smile of gratitude and strode off into the melee, actually looking cocky.

"What shall we do with this mob?" Barry muttered to me.

"Tell them what they're auditioning for," I suggested.

He gave me a growing smile, then turned to the populace and held up his hands. "Ladies! Gentlemen! If I might have your attention, please?"

They quieted.

"I am Barry Tallendar, as some of you may know." One or two of the veterans snickered. "I have the honor of being actor-manager of a new repertory touring company. We will begin rehearsals next week, will depart within the month . . ."

I thought him quite the optimist.

". . . and will be gone from New York at least one full calendar year, perhaps longer if the bookings work out. We will perform continuously, and there will be no chance of visiting this city, or any other not on our itinerary, during that period."

He paused. A startled murmur ran around the room; everyone knew that a ballistic could take you to any city on the globe in a few hours. One of the older gentlemen asked, "Just where are you planning to tour, Bar—Mr. Tallendar?"

"To the colonies," Barry said evenly.

He was answered by an uproar, the gist of which was:

"Jupiter's moons?"

"The asteroid belt?"

"The Martian domes?"

"Yes," said another gentleman—Tony Urbane, we both knew him of old, to our sorrow—"that would make it difficult to pop home for the weekend. Do you really think there's an audience there?"

"We have research that indicates something along that line," Barry said, carefully noncommittal.

Everyone was looking at everybody else, and discussing such topics as:

"Well, of course, my dear, I had no idea . . ."

"The colonies! How barbarous!"

"Do they have shops there? *Real* shops, that is?"

Barry raised his voice again. "You are all welcome to audition, of course. We'll take the youngest first, if you don't mind."

The veterans quieted and nodded; they knew what that meant. They'd been to their share of cattle calls.

Barry turned toward our first young lady. "Ms. Darling, your companion has been waiting quite awhile. May we see her, please?"

There was a startled silence; then the young graduate wended her way through the throng to Barry. He ushered her in with a warm smile and closed the door—just in time to hear one of the older women call out, "Just what is the name of this company, Barry?" Fortunately, the door was already closing, and Barry could pretend not to hear her; he finished the job and muttered to me, "Nice question. What do you call a company that will be traveling to the stars?"

"The Star Company, of course," I muttered back.

He stared at me in amazement. Then the slow smile began, and he turned away to the sweet young thing, nodding his approval. "Now, young lady. May I have your name, please?"

Ten minutes and two short soliloquies later, he ushered her out.

The wall space was clear. Everyone left had room to sit.

Barry's shoulders slumped, but he squared them again and looked about. "Ladies. Gentlemen. I know most of you, except the youngest; I've performed with you, or seen your work. If you are truly interested in joining the Star Repertory Company, we will be glad to hear you. Before we begin, though, are there any questions as to what will be involved?"

He was answered by an echoing silence.

Finally, old Sturdevant stirred himself and growled, "We've all toured, Barry, and for myself, I've not much to leave behind—save the grand old city herself, of course. These others, these young ones, they have family and relatives, I doubt not, and wouldn't want to be beyond reach of their parents, or their fiancés, perhaps."

"Then, too," said an older woman with too much makeup—Juliana never had been able to tell when she was onstage and when off—"they've been yearning to be in New York for ages, poor dears, and aren't about to leave now they've made it here."

"An excellent point," Barry murmured, and turned to a young lady whom we'd not seen before. "How do you feel on those issues, mademoiselle?"

"I have to admit I would rather be able to visit home," she said, "but I resigned myself to missing Thanksgiving and Christmas when I decided to try for a career as an actress, Mr. Tallendar. My parents will miss me, and I'll miss them, but it's a chance to act professionally, to be in front of an audience, and to add several roles to my credits. I need the work."

The other youngsters—under thirty, that is—chorused agreement, all five of them.

"I thank you, young lady." Barry inclined his head. "So long as you understand the nature of the commitment, then. There are few enough of you so that we may dispense with the usual line. We'll hear you one by one, shall we? Yourself first, if you will."

The young lady rose and came toward us with a graceful step that bespoke years of ballet. She stepped into the room, took up a position across the table from Barry's stacks of papers, and proffered her composite. Barry took it, glanced at the back, raised his eyebrows, and handed it to me. I, too, was impressed—if she had really done all this, she was older than she looked. It was surprising we hadn't seen her before.

Or had we? Walk-ons look much alike, and chorus members are indistinguishable. Certainly, if we had, she hadn't stood out. That could be bad, showing a lack of stage presence—or good, showing an ability to yield focus.

Barry handed her the musical. "If you would read Aldonza's speech on page thirteen, please?"

She opened the book—and seemed to change before our eyes. She became coarse, brazen, sensual, and somehow seemed half-dressed, though she hadn't so much as touched her clothing. She read the speech with a raw but seductive vulgarity that fairly seethed with repressed anger.

Barry and I both stared, suddenly realizing she was done. Barry gave his head a slight shake and held out the Shakespeare. "Now Titania, if you would—scene three."

She was imperious, she was queenly, she was every inch a lady—and infinitely desirable.

"Fascinating," Barry murmured. "Page three, please, for Hermia."

He was about to ask for Helena when I nudged his elbow and pointed to the words I had scribbled on his notepad: "15 min." He nodded and stood up. "Thank you, Ms. Lark. We would like to hear you again, on Thursday, at the Trident rehearsal hall. You know where that is, at Times Square? Good. Thank you for coming."

She stepped out, and he closed the door just long enough to say, "She must know how to yield focus," then opened it again to call in the next one.

Half the seats were empty.

Barry sighed. "Ms. Oleo, I haven't heard you in the classics. If you would come in, please?"

As we stepped out into the street, darkness had fallen, and so had Barry's spirits. "Come, now," I consoled him, "Sturdevant isn't truly planning to salve his ego with amateur theatricals while he lives off voice-over commercial revenue."

"I wouldn't put it past him," Barry sighed, "but he didn't have to be so blunt about it. To think, Horace! Only twenty-six stayed the course! And fourteen of those are so abrasive that I would hesitate to commit myself to a week in their company, let alone a year."

"There were five young ones," I pointed out.

"Yes," he sighed, "and Ms. Darling and her friend . . . what's her name?"

"Ms. Darling's friend."

"Quite so. Ohio State must have fallen on evil days, if this is the best they can offer."

"No," I said, "the best already have parts, and the second best stayed for graduate degrees. Poor sweet things, they might as well be on their way home. The other five, though, who are in Equity already . . ."

Barry made a wry face. "Yes, I'd cast them, too, if I were

sure they wouldn't have to say more than, 'Dr. Astrov, the horses are ready.' But for an arrangement where they will have to undertake at least one supporting role? No. Let them hang on the vine awhile longer; perhaps they'll ripen."

"There is the one bright note," I pointed out. "That young lady, Lacey Lark."

"Yes." Barry nodded. "She would do well, in a wide variety of roles. A find, that one, and desperate for her big break—but there is something about her personal manner that hints of trouble."

"I doubt there would be too much, so early in her career. If she were truly vile, you'd have spotted her in an instant."

"I would agree," Barry said, "if she hadn't already proved to be so talented an actress."

"Well," I said, "it was good of Ogden to show up."

"Yes, and I suppose he was relatively sober. Still, we may have to take him."

"I understand he's had to take very cheap rooms," I said. "Surely we owe him a bit?"

"He was a help, when we were fledglings," Barry sighed, "so I suppose we're obliged. Besides, he could draw the poison out of any but the most malicious of youngsters."

"On the bright side," I said, "we haven't heard from Marnie yet."

"We will," Barry answered, with iron resignation.

"Still," I said, "these auditions were premature. Tomorrow will give us a better measure."

"I hope it isn't too finely calibrated," Barry sighed. "Shall we try Blarney's, Horace? I feel my alcohol level subsiding."

Elector Rudders was on the wall-screen as we walked on. "And what have our fellow citizens wrought upon these planets newly born? What have they hewn from the wilderness, what have they built? New societies, in which men are freed from the vices of corrupt traditions of pornographic and blasphemous scribblings, standing tall and clean in the light of new suns, rising in virtue from the dust of moral decay that they have shaken from their sandals! Will we allow these fair innocents to be corrupted by the base and mercenary interests of purveyors of literary trash and musical obscenity? Will we allow these noble pioneers to be exploited by the purveyors of blasphemous icons in three-dimensional images? Nay, nay, my fellow electors!"

We stepped away from the doorway as quickly as we could—the screen was mounted over it. Excellent strategy on Blarney's part—it kept the entranceway clear.

By good chance, Allison and Broderick were there, and between the three of us, we managed to boost Barry's spirits on only two martinis—which was just as well, because that was when I saw young Ramou looking in the window, like a soul without a coin for Charon, gazing with longing across the Styx at Hades. If his face had been any longer, it would have been a dachsund. He only looked in at us solvent ones for a minute, then turned to shoulder his way through the dusk and the chill.

I excused myself and threaded my way through the throng to the door. I came out just before he was lost in the gloom, and ran after him, crying, "Ramou!"

He turned around, startled—and, I thought, apprehensive. Did he really worry so much about Big Daddy's investigator? I began to realize that the lad might not be distinguishing quite accurately between fantasy and reality. I caught up with him, puffing and smiling my rosiest. "Come, you must help us celebrate! The Star Company is launched, and we have completed our first day's auditions!"

He looked a little dazed. "Uh . . . Yeah, sure. I don't mind."

"Stout fellow!" I slapped him on the back, contriving to turn him back toward Blarney's as I did. "And what of your own fortune today, eh?"

An unfortunate mistake—his mouth twisted in a sardonic half smile. "*What* fortune? This time I registered with an employment agency, so I got to hear it from authority—every employer who doesn't require a degree already has all the help they need."

"I feared as much," I sighed. "Well, put it by for the

nonce. There is merriment aplenty; let it catch you up. Barry could enliven even the ghost at the banquet, tonight." I opened Blarney's door.

He paused in the entranceway, startled. "Ghost? You mean Banquo's?"

"Ah," I said, "you've read your Shakespeare."

I could swear he blushed. "Only the major plays."

"It will qualify you for membership in our ribaldry," I assured him, with a gentle shove through the doorway. "Surely you'll have a glass before dining? Here, this way." I took the lead, plowing through the mass to the big round table with the ten actors, the surprising harmonizing of Broadway classics—and the two empty chairs. I ushered the lad into one of them; he was stunned and dazed, looking about him at what were, to him, famous faces. I hoped he wouldn't be too disillusioned at seeing several of them no longer quite sober.

He wasn't. He stared around, amazed and fascinated. "These folks can really sing!"

I took advantage of his distraction to edge a filled glass over to him. "You could swear they do it for a living. What will you eat?"

6

I couldn't believe it. The Great Lamborghini, the evil Mordant Emperor of the Sulfuric Confederation of Planets, Dr. Hansom, Carlo the Cabbie, Suzie Chancellor the Housewife at Law, Madame Bordeaux of the Bronco's Bordello, Dianna Daiquiri the Girl Upstairs, Professor Moebius—all the famous 3DT faces from my childhoood and teen years, there before me in real life! They looked different without their makeup—Madame Bordeaux had crow's feet, Dianna had freckles, the Mordant Emperor was clean-shaven—but they were still them, and I was surrounded by glory.

I looked again and realized that I'd seen some of them the night before, at Blarney's. How come I hadn't recognized them then?

Easy—I hadn't been expecting actors, and between hunger and the confusion of my first day in town, I hadn't been looking very closely. Tonight, though, my mind was a little more settled, and I knew Horace was famous—so I finally realized that his friends were, too.

Of course, in college I'd come to know them all over again, as Trinculo and Caliban, Willy Loman and Blanche Dubois, Bonnie and the Wanderer, Lord Dobrinin and his concubine Zanitska, in 3DT versions of the classic plays—but you remember it better the way you saw it first. Horace was Morty the Milkman, not Falstaff.

And they could sing!

My Lord, I hadn't realized all of them were singers, too! This wasn't any rowdy, off-key caterwauling of drunks—it was the harmonious caroling of people who knew all the different parts the way the composer had written them. I shivered as I realized I was sitting at the same table with the people who had sung those songs in front of an audience, a real audience, not a 3DT pickup—some of them for the first time.

I got carried away. I lost myself. I drifted into an enchanted realm where dirt and slime didn't exist, where everything was song and valor and romance.

Finally, they stopped singing, and I came out of my trance, more or less, hearing them laughing and teasing one another, exchanging bits of incomprehensible gossip about names I didn't recognize. I was just beginning to feel like an outsider when Horace urged me, "Eat, lad! It's grown tepid."

I looked down and, to my amazement, the table had grown a plate with a sandwich as thick as a brick. There was even a glass of some amber fluid. Beer, I decided between mouthfuls. Horace sat back, watching me eat with the smile of a fond uncle, and I managed to mutter, between bites, "Thanks, Horace! You don't know how I needed this!"

"But I do," he murmured. "I was new in New York once, myself. Eh?" He turned, surprised, to the lady on his other side—Madame Bordeaux! And, for a wonder, she wasn't propositioning him, just asking him if Barry was only drunk, or if he was actually planning to take a troupe of actors on a tour of "the provinces" for a whole year. Horace explained that, yes, he was quite serious, and they had already begun auditions. She expressed a low opinion of the mental stability of anyone who signed up with them—why would they be willing to go into exile from all that was worth living for?—while I turned green with envy. To be able to live with people like this, day in and day out, to work with them, and to see what "the provinces" looked like, on top of it all! To a New Yorker, I gathered "the provinces" included San Francisco, New Orleans, York, Marseilles, Quebec . . . Who could ask for more?

Then somebody said, "Rudders," and everyone turned to

face the wall-screen. The whole room went silent, and I could feel their tension.

"A sinful song, a corrupt song!" Rudders ranted, thumping his fist. "This decadent preoccupation with sybaritic sex must be stopped, my fellow electors! We must establish a committee to oversee the music industry, the vultures who . . ."

"Same song, umpteenth verse," someone called from another table, and the tension broke in a tidal wave of laughter. As they turned back to their own table, one of the actors—Carlo the Cabbie—asked, "Why does he bother trying? Everybody knows what he's up to."

"Not the less educated, I'm afraid," Dr. Hansom said, "and in this day and age, that's at least half the population, who can barely read."

"His gambit is obvious, of course," Horace said. "If he can create a great deal of public furor over the more undesirable aspects of popular culture, he can distract the citizenry to the point at which they will become so involved in debating freedom to blast out sound and massacre lyric verse, that they will ignore the duller and more wearisome aspects of the actions of the Assembly."

"Of course," the Mordant Emperor said, "and there's always the chance that such public furor might result in an appeal to the Assembly to abridge freedom of speech in some way."

Everybody shuddered, and he drew some black looks. With a shock, I realized that I was among people who *really* cared about freedom of speech—because to them, words were sacred.

"Perhaps so," the Great Lamborghini agreed. "Perhaps even enough to give the LORDS party the lever they need to cripple discussion of public issues. Then they could, quietly and without resistance, go ahead and put into effect measures such as a Censorship Authority for all speeches, plays, songs, 3DT spectacles—any and every form of communication; the establishment of a State Church . . ."

"Which one?" Susie Chancellor asked.

"Theirs," Lamborghini said dryly.

"And while they're about it," Carlo added, "they might get around to outlawing all personal weapons, including jackknives . . ."

"Yes," Madame Bordeaux said, "and to banning all gatherings of people without special permission from Authority . . ."

"The list goes on," Lamborghini said. "They've been pushing for such an agenda for some time, as we all know—tentatively, with only the occasional mention by an elector or a local politician, just testing to see how public interest lies, you understand, but pushing nonetheless."

"Quite so," Dr. Hansom agreed. "Myself, I have no doubt that, if they thought they could achieve it with impunity, they would cancel the old Bill of Human Rights item by item, which would effectively destroy democracy and concentrate government in the hands of a few wealthy men—themselves, of course."

"Do eat your meal," Horace urged me in a low voice. "Though I'll admit, Rudders is enough to give anyone indigestion. Why are you looking so horrified, lad?"

"Was I really?" I came out of my trance with a start. "It's just . . . I mean, talking about an elector that way . . . So many famous people . . ."

"They haven't outlawed free speech yet, my lad. And I assure you, there's an excellent chance that they are correct in regard to the LORDS party's objective."

"But if you folks know it, don't the Liberals?"

"I'm sure they have realized the goal of this ploy," Horace replied, "and all the others the LORDS have developed to direct attention away from their attempts to consolidate their power. In fact, one of the Liberals' attempts at countermeasures has been the requiring of wall-screens in all public places, and the institution of a 3DT channel dedicated to the broadcasting of Assembly sessions and IDE committee meetings, so that the citizenry will stay informed of governmental workings."

I made a face. "Hasn't worked too well."

"Unfortunately, no," Horace agreed. "The move has backfired—the average citizen, such as myself, resents being forced to witness these proceedings, and has developed an animus to the government that has forced them upon us. We have all developed the ability to block our awareness of them, a sort of heightened ability to ignore—and the LORDS have responded as though to opportunity, bogging the Assembly down in a welter of trivial debate and long-winded speeches about unimportant, but highly visible, items, such as the sexual content of 3DT programs and the occasional iconoclastic play in the live theater. I abhor Rudders and all he stands for, but I must admit that his debates bore me."

There was a general laugh, and Horace looked up, surprised; then, seeing that his colleagues had been listening, he bowed.

"Well said, Horace, well said," Lamborghini said with a chuckle.

"Not that the Liberals have ever managed much of a challenge to the LORDS, anyway," Dianna Daiquiri said tartly.

Which was true; I'd learned it in Contemporary History. Ever since Chako's Rebellion made the United Nations aware that their colony planets had become nations in their own right, the LORDS had acted to keep Terra dominant. That the textbook could tell us, because it was part of the LORDS' official platform. What the teacher hadn't said, my college roommates had—that the LORDS' real goal was to keep a handful of wealthy financiers dominant over Terra.

"How much can the Liberals do?" Lamborghini asked. "The LORDS' efforts have been aided by trade with the colony planets themselves, for they are still economically dependent on Terra."

"Wouldn't go that far, my lad," Dr. Hansom objected.

Lamborghini shrugged. "At least the mother planet still shows a very large trade surplus—even though the United Nations has enlarged itself into the Interstellar Dominion Electorates, and promoted the established colonies to Dominion status and incorporated electors from each of them into the General Assembly."

"Of course," Horace pointed out, "the number of electors depends on population, so all the Dominion electors together are still outnumbered by the Terran electors."

" 'Together' is something they almost never are," Suzie Chancellor said acidly. "After all, each of them has its own agenda of wants and needs."

"Still," Horace objected, "there are issues they do have in common, such as the abolishment of tariffs and the exportation of manufactured goods from colony worlds to Terra— so they do occasionally vote as a bloc."

"And even more occasionally manage to persuade enough Terran electors to agree with them, so that they manage to pass a bill," Suzie retorted. She won a good laugh with that.

"Rumor hath it that such occasions trigger huge victory celebrations on each of the Dominion planets," the Mordant Emperor said. "Celebrations that are steeped in stimulants and lighted by fireworks."

"I'd love to join them," Madame Bordeaux said.

"And they'd love to have you, my dear," Dr. Hansom assured her.

That got the loudest laugh of all, though I couldn't see why, and everybody started discussing the merits of some show on Broadway that they claimed was lampooning Rudders.

"Sounds good," I said, through a mouthful of real beef. "I'd like to see it."

"It's quite good," Horace said. "And very amusing. But laughter aside, Ramou, the facts are rather stark. The LORDS do pretty much as they please on Terra, legally or not. Rank hath its privileges, but wealth hath more."

I made a face. "Rank hath its privileges, and some of them are pretty rank."

Horace laughed and looked up at his companions.

Somehow, they were all going, and I realized it must be later than I'd thought. The Great Lamborghini was telling

Horace he would escort Madame Bordeaux home, for old times' sake, and the Mordant Emperor was strolling off arm in arm with Suzie Chancellor. Dr. Hansom was on his way out with Carlo the Cabbie, and Dianna Daiquiri was going home with Professor Moebius. It occurred to me to ask if any of them were married to each other, but I decided it was none of my business.

Horace glanced at his ring-watch. "Time to drink up, lad. Even Blarney must close some time."

"Oh, yeah, sure!" I seized my glass, but Horace stopped me with a hand on my wrist. "No need to chug it, my boy. We're not in that great a hurry, and there will be more beer in the world. Tomorrow is another day."

All my troubles, and the grodiness of the day, came crashing back. "Yeah."

"Come now," Horace murmured, "buck up your spirits, there's a good chap! Existence can be delightful! There are beautiful women, fast horses, fine wines! You have your whole life ahead of you!"

I stifled a groan.

The lad groaned. He caught himself and bit it back, so it was short, but was definitely a groan—and I decided this case might be worse than I had thought. There was obviously more to Ramou's sadness than a chit mad to marry and an uncaring city; I became aware, all over again, that each of us has a biography, and it may predispose some to despondency. "Surely an opportunity for employment will arise in the near future."

" 'Something will turn up,' eh?" He gave me a rueful smile. I was amazed to hear him utter Mr. Micawber's phrase—most folk his age haven't even heard of Dickens, let alone read him. " 'Fraid not, Mr. Burbage."

"Horace," I murmured.

"Horace. Thanks. Between the want ads and the dozen places I tried today, I am now convinced that a beginner can't get a job in the big city without a degree, a certificate of some sort, or an uncle in the union."

"There are unskilled jobs," I murmured.

"I did find two that were still open, one for a bellboy and one for a busboy—but they said they wanted experience. For carrying baggage—or clearing tables!"

"It does seem unreasonable." I tried to exude sympathy. "Surely, though, there is some task at which you have experience? You've been an engineering student for two years; surely you've acquired some skills."

"Oh, sure, but they're all in the lines that need degrees! A half-trained engineer is about as much good as an inexperienced bellhop. Yeah, I can rig a circuit or troubleshoot a computer array—but I don't have the piece of paper that says I can."

"A computer array?" I pricked up my ears. "Just what sort of program were you enrolled in?"

"Computer structure and systems design."

"Really! You learned to program them, too, I would assume?"

"You kidding? I learned how to talk to the machines in high school! Of course, I got a little carried away, and the planetary government did shoot me a notice to quit poking around outside my own system, or else—but by the time I got to college, there were only two more programming courses I didn't already know."

"Amazing! But you never did it professionally?"

Ramou shrugged. "What do you call 'professional'? I programmed for pay part-time and summers, and the university gave me an assistantship to help out on some of their subroutines."

"Then you *do* have experience."

"Oh, sure." Ramou smiled with bitterness. "But it's in one of those fields that requires a degree. Of course, I'd take part-time now, but they won't pay in cash—and I don't want my name on any computer's roster."

I began to suspect genuine paranoia—but surely the lad knew the network better than I. Far better; I can only do the most modest amount of programming, myself—scarcely literate, as my high-school instructor was at pains to point out. "Still, you have the knowledge, and the manual dexterity. Lad, I suspect I may know of a position for you, after all."

His head snapped up. "I'm all ears."

I nearly said that I hadn't commented on his physiognomy, but restrained myself—his audial appendages weren't truly all that prominent. "If you can be an operator, I happen to know a concern that's seeking a technician. Payment in cash could probably be arranged, and I doubt there'll be need to enroll you in a data base."

"You're kidding!"

"No, but the pay may be a bit . . . erratic. Room and board will be provided, though."

"Room and board?" Ramou frowned. "Hey, what kind of business is this, anyway?"

"A theatrical company. We're about to go on tour and have only just begun assembling our technical staff. Barry had a young designer in mind, but he refused the offer—something to do with a young lady, I believe; she didn't wish to travel, I gather. All our staging equipment will be electronic, of course—holograms and the like. Would you know enough to learn its operation and a bit of routine maintenance?"

"Would I?" Ramou's eyes were wide. "Hey, the illusion boxes were always my favorite!"

Well, there is a substantial difference between a display unit and a theatrical setting—but the principles are similar, and Ramou certainly seemed willing to learn. "And you wouldn't mind traveling?"

"As fast and far as I can, mister."

"Oh yes, the young lady. I'd forgotten."

"I wouldn't call her a lady."

"Perhaps that was your problem. Very well, young man! You'll come home with me again, I trust? You can have my sofa till we can get you on payroll and find you a hotel room. Rather Spartan, I fear."

I shrugged. "I'm used to roaches. When do we start?"

"I'll speak for you to Barry tomorrow." He looked up.

"But at the moment, I see that Blarney is looking at us with a bit of impatience; I believe he wishes to close. Shall we go, Ramou?"

"Yeah, sure!" I finished my beer at a gulp and stood up. "By the way, Horace . . . how far are we going?"

"Approximately one hundred twenty light-years, I believe."

Horace said it as he was walking away from me, and I just stared.

Then I recovered, shrugged, and followed him out. I wanted to get away from it all, didn't I? Besides, exotic colonies on distant planets were even better than New Orleans!

And I'd be living with people like the ones I'd seen tonight! I'd be a part of their charmed circle! Actors, Mr. Frodo, actors!

7

There's nothing like a brisk stride through midtown Manhattan with somebody who knows where he's going. I resolved that I'd have to try it during rush hour, some time—just for the experience. They tell me it's a madhouse. You hear these stories about fist fights at the doors of the tube cars—not between adolescent toughs, but between tired businessmen. You see, the car is so jammed full that they can't squeeze in one more, but the guy who's still trying to shove his way in won't believe it; he's convinced the people inside could jam a little tighter if they really wanted to. So he shoves and throws body blocks, trying to make them fit; and finally one of the guys he's shoving hauls off and punches him. I can hardly wait to see it—must be hilarious, two guys in neat, up-to-the-minute gray *complets,* probably with degrees from first-rank colleges, duking it out like any pair of common Government Assistance workers.

Everybody takes the LinAc Tubes, of course; no private cars are allowed on the streets, just taxis and buses—and limos. I mean, after all, the guys who make the rules have to build in exceptions for themselves, don't they? Though as I understand it, all the limos are officially owned by transportation services, just to keep it legal; the billionaires only lease them, complete with drivers. It does keep the streets nice and clear—but below ground is another matter.

They have a system that's supposed to prevent crowding in subway cars, of course—tube cars every thirty seconds, and each business within range of a given station assigned a different time to close shop. But people hurry, people run, people wait until later so the rush will be over—and they jam up in the stations, same as before. Maybe it's the inborn urge to beat the system, or maybe it's just sheer human cussedness, but the organic realities always come up with new wrinkles that outwit the mechanistic planning. Call it Murphy. Then call St. Vidicon.

Be that as it may, actors work late and sleep later, so we didn't have to hit the tubes until late morning. We got off in Times Square, went one block west, and entered a glossy building that somehow had a well-used air about it. The architects built well a hundred years ago, facing the buildings with materials that are well-nigh indestructible and shed the dirt with every rainfall. The styles date them, of course—Horace told me this one was a century old.

"How can you tell?"

"First, because it has some ornamentation, but not a great deal; secondly, because it has an overhanging second story, then doesn't begin its sweep in until the tenth. The architects had just discovered plasticrete, and the ways in which its structural strength aids cantilevering, so they had begun to be a bit jubilant in their find."

"You mean they were kids playing with a new toy."

"No, that was the next generation—the ones who made the buildings that look like vertical birds' wings, and mountainsides, and frozen waterfalls. They'd discovered the sculptural versatility of plasticrete, you see, and were busy fulfilling one of architecture's older dreams—a sculptural medium that is also self-supporting. Rather expensive, though, so the fad didn't last long."

I nodded, bemused. Seemed there was more to putting up a building than I'd realized.

Inside, Horace threaded me surefootedly through the maze of hallways and lifts until we came to a large double door. One half of it was ajar; he went in, crying, "Barry! Good morning to you! What progress?"

"We can only hope." The Great Lamborghini looked up from a folding desk with a portable area light. He smiled at

Horace and rose to clasp his hand. "Very reassuring to see you, old friend."

"Tosh! You'll sail through this cattle call with scarcely a notion it was there. You see, I've even made some progress overnight—we have an assistant technical director! Ramou Lazarian, Mr. Barry Tallendar."

I started to hold out my hand, but when I heard the name, I froze. I could feel my eyeballs bulging. I hated myself for a callow fool, but there I was, gawking.

The tall, dark, and handsome one smiled, amused, as he took my hand. How in hell did he manage so few wrinkles? He must have been at least fifty; I'd heard he was twenty-five when he played Lamborghini for the big-screen 3DT recording, and my mom said she went to see it when she was dating my father. I felt a surge of anger, and damped it, letting myself glory in shaking the hand of the real, genuine, authentic Barry Tallendar. What happened to Mom wasn't his fault, of course—he wasn't even there. Not in person, anyway.

He was saying, "Oh, yes, Horace's protégé. A pleasure, young man."

Protégé?

Well, I suppose I was, in a way.

Horace was saying, "He hasn't any experience in the theater yet, Barry, but he's well versed in electronics. Two years in an electrical engineering program at a first-rank college." Tallendar began to look a little doubtful, but Horace breezed on. "He's eager to travel."

"Ah!" Tallendar smiled. "Well, you'll learn stagecraft soon enough, I'll warrant. Unfortunately, we have not yet arranged for your tutor. Horace, have you any candidates for technical director?"

I noticed he didn't ask why I was so willing to travel. I was grateful. Of course, maybe it just didn't matter to him—but that made me even more grateful. Where your past doesn't matter, there's a chance that *you* will.

"It would be desirable to have someone with some design

ability," Horace offered. "Not essential, of course—we can go with prepackaged settings . . ."

Tallendar must have seen me wince; he was amused. "No, young man, that's not our objective. I've asked Lamont Morley to come by and have a few words with us. Also Gerri Legafi; I understand they're both at liberty at the moment."

Horace winced. "With reason. Lamont's a genius, no doubt of it—but his tantrums! And his insistence on artistic control!"

"I know, I know, but he's good, and—"

"And Legafi! Why is it his designs always look so splendid on the screen, but so disappointing onstage? In addition, having to live in the same ship with him!"

"Well, yes, I know—but who else is there?"

Horace was silent.

"You see?" Barry asked.

"Margaret Hannischer," Horace said halfheartedly.

Barry shuddered. "How she obtained her union card, I'll never know! Though one might guess . . . surely you would not think of her as pleasant company, either, Horace?"

"No," Horace admitted, "though there was a time . . . a certain evening, several decades ago . . ." He shook off the memory. "What of Robert Edmund Smith?"

Barry threw up his hands in despair. "Certainly a competent technician, Horace, and quite agreeable—but nothing more. And he doesn't claim to be. I suppose, if we're to resign ourselves to prepackaged settings . . ."

"No." Horace shook his head. "Last resort, yes. Well, what of the cattle call, Barry? Are you prepared?"

Barry shrugged and waved at the desk. "A dictation processor, ganged to a screen for your reference, and an Equity card reader, though I'm not expecting anyone already in the union. And I called that young thing from yesterday, Lacey Lark, told her she's in the company, and asked her to come by in case we need to have her read with any candidates. Improbable, but it will give us a measure of her interpersonal skills and willingness to take direction. What more do we need?"

"Nothing," Horace sighed. "And we probably won't even need as much as you've brought . . ."

"Barry?" said an overly cultured voice from the doorway.

"Gerri!" Barry spun about and stepped toward the newcomer with his hand outstretched. "How good of you to come by!"

The man wore glasses. In a day when ocular distortion corrections are a mere office visit, he wore glasses.

Also a fluorescent-green scarf that may have been intended to be an ascot, but overflowed his shock-pink shirt and his pearl-gray *complet*. And a hat! Inside a building, he wore a hat!

He looked around the rehearsal hall as though he smelled a faint but unpleasant odor. "I've heard some gossip about this new venture of yours, Barry."

"All slanderous, I hope."

"Perhaps." He turned to look Barry directly in the eye. "Is it true you'll be gone from New York for a year?"

"At least."

"Well, of course, you can't expect me to subsist among the barbarians!"

"Not even for the chance of designing *Didn't He Ramble*?"

Gerri stilled, and his eyes misted. "A bordello from the heyday of New Orleans, decayed into a mere transient hotel! And to see it staged! What a thrilling opportunity!" Then he frowned, suddenly the realist again. "I was told you were searching for a man who would be primarily a technical director."

"Well, that too, of course, though you would have an assistant . . ."

I began to reconsider the advantages of unemployment.

Fortunately, Gerri was shaking his head. "I, a disciple of Appia and Craig, demoted to the status of common stagehand? No, thank you, Barry. Good of you to think of me and all that, but I fear I must decline. Right, then? Good day, gentlemen!" He twitched something resembling a bow and slid out through the doorway.

Barry sighed, loosening, and Horace muttered, "Praise heaven! Why, I haven't seen so churlish a fellow since Panaloy!"

"Teddy always did have an inflated notion of his own importance, even for a director," Barry agreed. He checked his ring-watch. "The hopeful young ones should begin arriving any minute now. A pleasant—"

"Barry! Horace!"

This one came into the room hips first, and at least he was dressed in earth tones instead of fluorescents—but I glanced behind him to see if he was leaving a trail of oil.

"Why, Lamont! How pleasant to see you!" Barry spun toward the voice, all charm again. "Do come in. I hear your last production at Lake Champlain was quite a success."

"Stock always makes for a pleasant summer," Lamont drawled, sitting in the bigger of the two available chairs. "The critics did me justice, at least. Pity you won't see it mounted here in New York, but the direction was quite faulty, and the actors just weren't up to it. Not to mention that loathsome costume designer . . ."

"Yes, quite," Barry said crisply, and I wondered how closely he knew the costume designer. "Well, as I've told you, Lamont, we're assembling a touring company—"

"A year in exile," Lamont sighed, "but we must endure any trials that may arise, for Art's sake, eh, Barry?"

I wondered how long he'd been out of work.

"There would, of course, be an assistant to execute the humdrum chores?" Lamont said severely. "You can't expect an artist of my caliber to dirty his hands arranging platforms and pounding in loose nails, now, can you, Barry?"

Tallendar's smile almost slipped. His voice sharpened just a little as he said, "There would be some actual physical dexterity involved, I'm afraid, Lamont. In a touring company such as this, everybody must serve double functions."

Lamont just stared at him.

Barry stared back.

Then Lamont said, in a tone that could have frozen mercury, "Just how far away from New York would you be going, Barry?"

"Several hundred light-years, Lamont," Barry said evenly. "We plan to tour the interstellar colonies."

"Colonies!" Lamont was on his feet with a roar. "Not content with the barbarities beyond the Alleghenies, you would doom me to the outer darkness of the waste and wilderness? How dare you even *think* of me for such an undertaking!"

"Why, for the excellence of your designs, of course," Barry said smoothly.

Lamont turned red, tried to say something, but choked on it. I wondered what I had missed. Then he snapped, "Good day, Barry Tallendar!" and was out of the room so fast I half believed he was scooting on the lubricated track he had left on the way in.

"Ah, well, a pity," Barry sighed, "but we can't all be friends, can we?"

"Certainly not when some of us are more neurotic than others," Horace agreed.

"Ah, but who am I to point the finger?" Barry turned back to the table. "Still, I must confess, Horace, I am somewhat relieved."

He was relieved? I was ecstatic!

The door edged a little farther open, and a girl with a face that would have given me nightly dreams in high school peeked in. "M-Mr. Tallendar?"

Barry rose, straightening slowly, and turned to her with a smile on his face. "Ah, yes, young lady, do come in! Have you come to audition for the Star Repertory Company?"

"Y-Yes, I have." The girl stepped into the room with a tremulous smile. "May I read?"

"Why, of course, dear lady! The hour has arrived; auditions may begin!"

"Oh, I'm so glad to hear it!" She turned and called out the door behind her. "We were right, girls! This is the place."

With a joyful shriek, they surged in, chattering and caroling.

I plastered myself against the wall and just stared. Forget about high school—that face would have made my nights sleepless in college! And that one, and that one, and that one . . .

Horace lined them up at the end of the room as fast as they arrived, handing out single sheets of hard copy. I just stood there, dazed by the sight of so much feminine beauty in one room. Every one was a winner! And not just faces, either! The lowest I saw was a clear eight hundred on the milliHelen scale, at least!

Then the guys started coming in, and I bristled. I don't know what it is, but when you realize you're homely, the sight of a handsome male face rouses all sorts of resentments. It helped a little that most of them walked like the dandies in *The Scarlet Pimpernel,* but not much—those *complets* were cut to reveal the contours of shoulders, chests, and biceps, and if there was a single guy there who hadn't spent most of his adolescent free time in a body-building boutique, he must have slid right by me. Each one of them paused just an instant as he saw the lineup of girls, but kept on going—hardened cases, I guessed, used to too much of a good thing.

"Mr. Tallendar?"

I turned and looked at the owner of the contralto that had stepped over to Barry, and promptly forgot the plethora of pulchritude at the end of the room. If those girls had been beautiful, this one was dazzling. I knew in an instant that this was the face that would haunt my dreams for the next century, that would have launched a thousand ships if it had been born just four thousand years earlier, that maybe *had* launched a thousand ships, and this was just its latest incarnation.

And that was just the face—the body would have ruined the discipline of an entire army. The dress seemed to be cut demurely, though—it was just an accident that it revealed every contour of hip, thigh, and bosom, and the owner

certainly seemed to have every attractive contour that had
ever existed. I realized I was staring—realized it primarily
because my eyelids tried to blink, but grated like sandpaper.
I forced myself to look away—say, at Horace—and tried to
swallow. Tried. Not too successfully, if the truth be known.

"Ms. Lark!" Tallendar inclined his head gravely. "So
good of you to join us!"

Lark. What a beautiful name. The skylark, the *alouette,*
the bird of dawn! I remembered something Horace had told
me last night, about the day's news, something about an
ingenue named Lacey Lark. I knew the name was branding
itself on my memory forever.

"I tried to be early . . ."

"And you succeeded," Barry assured her. "It is merely
that the vanguard of the thundering horde attempted the
same. If you would take a chair, and watch till we need
you?" He unclipped a folding chair from the side of the desk
and spread it open, off to Horace's left. She floated over and
into it as gently and as gracefully as a gazelle, while the faces
of all the girls at the far end of the room curdled with envy.

Other girls? No, forget it! This was no girl, this was a
woman! In every way! To say that she was blond is to say
that crystal is glass. Her hair was gold, the gold at the end
of the rainbow that every man aches to own. Her eyes were
huge, blue, and luminous, like the depths of the pond that
beckons to you at the end of a long hot day in the fields. Her
mouth was a rose, only just burst from the bud; I longed to
see it blossom to its fullest. Her cheeks were the clouds
before the sunrise, and I ached to be there to see the dawn.

I could go on, and lower down, but what did it matter? I
was entranced. I had to speak with this divine creature, I
had to learn to know her, deeply and intimately. For the first
time, I was absolutely sure I had done the right thing in
leaving campus and Virginia.

Horace had finished handing out the single-page scripts,
and Barry was saying, "The young lady on the left end of the
line. Would you begin reading at the top of the page,
please?"

Horace stood back to watch, and the girl began. Even I could tell she was horrible. I mean, I've heard a more lifelike delivery from a band saw. But Tallendar, bless him, sat listening to her gravely, with total and undivided attention, just as though she were the foremost actress of her age. Somehow he ignored the muted snickers and muffled titters coming from the rest of the lineup—but I'd be willing to bet you dough against nuts that he remembered every face that was managing to let a smothered laugh escape.

For Tallendar, I learned, was that rare commodity among directors—hell, among any men of any age or class: a real gentleman. His conduct was always impeccable; he knew the rules of behavior so well that he never thought about them anymore; and the most important of them, he told me on a certain tense occasion some years after, was consideration, thinking of the other person's feelings. I never forgot that— and I never forgot how courteous he was to that poor talent-less star-struck college dropout, either.

She only had one short speech, and it couldn't have lasted a full minute. Personally, I thought the chick was a real clunker, but if she was, Barry never let her know.

Only, when she was done, he nodded gravely, made a note on the back of her head shot, and said, "Thank you, Ms. Arstru. We won't need you any longer today. We'll notify you if we need to hear you again."

He said it nicely, but even the veriest beginners know what that means. Even I had heard about it, and I'm an engineer. It was a polite version of, "Don't call us, we'll call you," and it meant she had flunked. She stepped out of the lineup with her chin down and her spirits sagging. I ached for her, but there was nothing I could do—and after Virginia, I knew better than to try.

"Next, please?" Barry took the mug shot on top of the pile, glanced at it to make sure it was the right one, then flipped it over. "Miss Chirpster? The Juliet line, please."

She threw everything she had into it—including the kitchen sink. Me, what did I know about acting? But at least it had some life to it. Too much life—she could have bottled the overflow and sold it at a premium. When she was done, though, Barry only nodded gravely again, thanked her, and assured her he'd call her if they needed her. Her smile slipped for a second, but she hoisted it back into place and marched out, chin high, shoulders back. I had to admire her spirit—or her experience; and I began to wonder why anyone would ever try to get into a business where you spend most of your time humiliating yourself in front of other people.

I found out that other directors actually would have made scathing comments that they thought were witty. Why not? The poor kids couldn't fight back.

"I think we need a gentleman next, just for variety," Barry said. He picked up a composite portrait off the other pile, correlated the image with the reality, flipped it over, and said, "Mr. Corinthian? The Cervantes speech, please."

And the kid was off, detailing the fictional Cervantes's faith in dreams, like a stock boy reading from the inventory. Okay, maybe I'm just jealous—the guy wasn't much older than me, and had the kind of looks that tighten bodices, with every muscle well defined. Me, I can lift like a robot, but I have all the aesthetic appeal of a vault door. Still, I thought the guy's reading would have been much better if he'd measured it with a tape, marked it every two feet, and run it through a buzzsaw.

"Thank you," Barry said. "We'll call you if we need to hear you again. Mr. . . . Laram?"

"La-*rahm*." The kid was thin, with a pointed nose, eyes set too close together, and a forced smile that was all laminated teeth.

"Quite so." Was there the slightest hint of frost on Barry's syllables? "The Shakespeare, please."

Hey, it would have been a great reading, if the character had been a villain—filled with repressed hostility flaring into open anger at key moments. Trouble was, the guy was reading Bottom. But Barry listened gravely, nodded at the end, and assured the kid that he'd call him if, et cetera. Then back to the girls—and on, and on. Barry began to look a little frazzled. Finally, in the middle of another guy's reading, he called out, "Mr. Lazarian?"

The kid stopped, startled.

"No, no." Barry waved. "Do keep on—please."

I recovered from my surprise and stepped up to his elbow. "Yes, Mr. Tallendar?"

"I really must have a cup of coffee to sustain me, Mr. Lazarian. Would you be so good as to bring one in?" He pressed a coin into my palm.

Well. Now I knew what technical assistants did. "Sure."

The kid had stopped reading again, turning pale.

"No, do go on," Barry said instantly. "I am listening, though it may not be apparent." I guess he knew he didn't need any kids who looked like handsome ferrets.

The actor started reading again, his tone tightening.

"I'll have one too, Ramou." Horace gave me a coin. "And a loaf sandwich, if you will?"

I nodded—and on the way down, saw Her eyes. Lacey Lark was gazing at me with wide and soulful orbs. "Coffee would be wonderful," murmured a voice like the undertone of the tides.

"Yes, please." Horace pressed another coin into my hand. I smiled at Lacey Lark and headed for the door. Behind me, I could hear the kid finish reading, and Barry saying the usual formula.

Hey, directors have to eat and drink, too—and there were a *lot* of kids to get through.

There was a food synthesizer just two doors down.

While the first cup was filling, I heard a voice behind me say, "We now present the noon summary of events of the General Assembly."

I listened with half an ear while I removed one cup of coffee, punched for another, and set the first one into the double-decker carry-tray. Then the announcer said the word "Rudders," and he suddenly had both my ears, and most of my brain, too. I watched over my shoulder.

The IDE announcers couldn't strictly be called newscasters, since all they did was give you the high spots of the government's morning (and, at seven o'clock, the afternoon) and ignored anything else that might have happened in the world or the colonies. More to the point, they gave you the government's version of those events; the commercial and independent stations usually had a different slant, and sometimes different facts. Not that we're accusing the IDE of propaganda—just summarizing. After all, you can't include everything, can you? It's just that the independents and the IDE announcers disagreed as to what was important.

Rudders himself I wasn't interested in—too much bombast, and too many words wrapped around his basic meaning. But a summary was another matter—if I could find out what he was trying to do without having to wade through the verbiage, I would. And since his little manifesto yesterday, I was very interested.

"Yesterday," the announcer said, "Elector Rudders called for an examination of the morals and loyalties of the professional theaters on Terra. The Liberal party responded with a restatement of its classical principles of freedom of speech."

That sounded pretty lukewarm to me, and I wondered about the *announcers'* loyalties.

Elector Valencio was there on the screen now, saying, "Milton said it best: 'Though all the winds of doctrine were let loose to play upon the earth, so Truth be in the field, we do injuriously by licensing and prohibiting to misdoubt her strength. Let her and Falsehood grapple; who ever knew Truth put to the worst, in a free and open encounter.' "

The announcer was back. "Elector Rudders, however, seems to have less faith in the marketplace of ideas, and more in the interstellar government."

Now it was Rudders's face on the screen, ranting. "It is a Gresham's law of entertainment and public information, my fellow electors—and, though Gresham may have framed his law to describe currency, we must consider that it may apply to all media, not just to the medium of exchange alone. In currency, Gresham tells us, the bad will drive out the good—and that is the case with popular music, 3DT programs, and theatrical shows, too. The bad will drive out the good—the obscene and blasphemous will drown out the discourse of morality and piety, and we will be left with nothing but those performances that appeal to the most prurient aspects of our natures. It is not sufficient in itself to express faith in the innate goodness of humanity, or in the innate good taste of the average man; it is not enough to state that the audience should have what it wants. Indeed, the audience only wants the prurient and shocking because the same media that offer such performances have convinced the audience that such debased content is what they do want, what they should want; they have corrupted and twisted the natural morality of mankind into depravity, when they could have lifted taste and morals alike, up and up, in a steady progression toward human excellence. But since the marketplace of entertainment has proved that, left to itself, it will do just the opposite, it remains for us, my fellow electors, to not leave it to itself. There must be some form of government regulation of the businesses of entertainment, or they will drag us all down to debasement and depravity."

I hated to admit it, but part of what the man was saying almost made sense.

He sat back on the picture, and the screen didn't cut away from him until after we'd heard a second or two of wild applause.

Then, finally, the announcer was back. "Broadway's producers, however, responded today to the elector's call."

And there was a tall, Savile Row suit with a man inside, looking distinguished and serious, and somehow totally respectable. He was the businessman incarnate, and nobody could think of him as a purveyor of trash.

"We insist that the liberty to know, to utter, and to argue freely is most vital, above all other liberties, and that to restrain the freedom of speech under any pretext will slowly erode that freedom. It is the cornerstone of all our other liberties; without it, our rights will slowly be eroded, until we end in shackles. Yes, some will take advantage of the liberty to express ideas; some will use this liberty as an excuse for prurience and bad taste. But this right is so important that we must endure the risk of abuse, rather than risk our freedom."

Personally, I thought he made a damn good appearance—but Barry would have done better. Couldn't have it, of course, because everyone knew Barry as an actor, and the producers were trying to represent theater without making it seem like show business, if you follow my drift.

Now the announcer was back. "This morning, however, Elector Rudders responded with a call for a boycott."

I stared, feeling electrified.

There he was again, Mr. Pit Bull himself, saying, "The producers of these lewd theatricals not only flaunt their arrogance in our faces, my fellow electors, they actually have the audacity to claim that they are behaving morally! Such moral turpitude deserves no reply of discourse alone—they have shown themselves to be impervious to sweet reason. The time has come for action, my fellow electors! And I urge each one of you to contact your constituencies this very evening and urge them all, all, to abstain from attending professional theatrical performances, but most especially those offered in New York City, in that haven of godlessness that calls itself 'Broadway'!"

I stared. I couldn't believe it. The man was actually using the government telecasts to call to the general public and tell them to cut the producers' throats.

"Tomorrow," the elector said, "I will introduce legislation proposing to restrict content in all public performances to that which is wholesome and patriotic. I know that many of you will contend that I oppose freedom of speech, but that sacred right applies, and should apply, only to public speeches, not to sordid portrayals of indecency."

The heck it did! Speech is speech, whether it comes from the pulpit, the lectern, or the stage—or the music box, for that matter. The old bastard knew that, and was deliberately trying to impose his own definition on it for his own purposes—which had nothing to do with the survival of democracy or even of morality. He knew damn well that if he could get the public to swallow censorship on the stage, it was only a matter of time before he'd be trying to censor conversation between friends, and enforcing it with wiretaps and *agents provocateurs*.

"We must resist, my fellow electors!" Rudders wound up. "We must resist the incursions of the godless and anarchistic wherever possible!"

And the announcer was back, but not before we'd heard the bare beginning of the booing mixed in with the applause. "The news agencies have issued a statement of protest," he informed me, "and Elector Rudders has assured them that he does not intend to limit freedom of news reporting in any way, so long as it is done responsibly."

And he was the one who defined "responsibly." Which meant that any news agency that disagreed with him was apt to be accused of sedition and obscenity, too.

Rudders was setting the stage for a wholesale assault on freedom of expression. So much for his pious mouthings about the future of democracy.

"That concludes our noon summary," the announcer said. "We now return you to the General Assembly."

The famous room was there, and I turned away, shaken, to find myself staring at four rapidly cooling cups of coffee. I started punching buttons again, deciding that I would have to take Horace aside and tell him about this as soon as I could.

I filled the order, sorted out whose change was whose, and brought it back. I handed Horace his cup and loaf and muttered a quick summary of the news story to him. He looked shaken, but muttered back, "Mere rhetoric, Ramou, empty rhetoric. He knows such a program doesn't stand a chance in the Assembly; in fact, it will die in committee. He's just after publicity." He summoned a smile and clapped my shoulder. "Put it behind you, lad; it's not worth your concern."

But he looked worried as he turned back to watch the next neophyte read.

Barry was looking really frayed, and thanked me without bothering to lower his voice at all. Ms. Lark murmured her thanks in a voice that would have sent me up a tree if she'd been out on a limb. I stepped back to watch some more.

"Ms. Souci," Barry called. "The Titania, please."

The next girl in line began to read—and suddenly, she was the only thing in the room. Her face had become unique, not prettier than the others, but more fascinating; her posture, her slightest body movements, hinted at censored pleasures even as her words rang with an angry denunciation that somehow made a man want to grapple with her. Her bosom seemed more full, her hips more curving, her lips more inviting even as she snapped out hot words of denunciation.

Barry looked up and didn't blink once during her entire thirty seconds.

Then she was done, and the magic was gone, and she was only another beautiful girl again, even sweet and demure, waiting her turn.

Barry made a note on her data sheet. "Fascinating. Would you return at three o'clock, please?"

A murmur of indignation swept the hall. The Souci girl said, "Thank you, Mr. Tallendar." It was normal, maybe even formal, and I found myself disappointed—I'd been wondering if she could say so much as a "good morning" without making it sound like an invitation. She went toward the door like all the others, though—but as she passed me, she gave me a look that went right through my brain and down to my groin. I felt like a heel, betraying my true love Lacey Lark so soon, for this total stranger; I felt like a two-timing, fickle idiot, the worst of the cads—but I knew I would have gone anywhere that look led me. I watched her as she went out, but her walk was normal, none of the enticing quality Lacey Lark's had.

Then I looked back at Barry, and saw Lacey looking at me. Then she glanced at the door, her mouth flattening with

sarcasm, then back to me, with a slow, heavy-lidded smile.
I stared. Then, belatedly, I realized I should smile. I did.

Finally, the last arrogant kid had swayed out the door,
and Barry rose slowly, as though every joint hurt. As he
stepped aside, Horace collapsed into his own chair with a
weary sigh. "Not bad for a cattle call, Barry. May I compliment you on your courtesy?"

"Thank you, Horace. Still, I shouldn't have called for
coffee in the middle of that young man's reading . . ."

"After his first three words, we knew you wouldn't miss
anything. You know we've both suffered far worse."

Lacey Lark caught my furtive glance and nodded slightly
in agreement. She'd known much worse, too. I wondered
how many directors had had her come back at three o'clock.
Then, with a shock, I wondered *just what* Barry wanted her
to come back for. Then I squelched the thought, angry at
myself—surely I did him an injustice.

Surely.

"I think that Souci lass may have possibilities," Horace
offered. I stared at him—I'd thought he was a little old for
that.

"An electrifying reading," Barry agreed. "In fact, with
that sort of talent, one wonders if, in all fairness, one should
not counsel her to stay in New York for a year longer; she
might find her Big Break."

"Let's see . . ." Horace leafed through the pile of head
shots, then pulled hers. I was astonished; he'd alphabetized
them as they went along. "My heavens! She's been in the
business five years!"

"Five years?" Barry stepped over, staring down. "Why on
earth is she still coming to open auditions?"

"Three years in dinner theaters and provincial reperto-
ries," Horace summarized. "Two years in New York, but
only three showcases, and a dozen off-off-Broadway productions, plus stock every summer . . ."

"You mean she doesn't have her Equity card yet?"

Horace shook his head. "Now that you mention it, no.
She must have enough points . . ."

"But not the initiation fee? It isn't *that* high!"

"She may have made an unwise choice," Horace said slowly. "She may have thought Equity would not condone her continuing in so many off-off-Broadway productions." From the way he said it, you knew he meant "amateur."

"Unwise, indeed." Barry frowned. "Does she want to work in this business, or doesn't she?"

"Misadvised, I would say."

"Then let us advise her properly!" Barry straightened, eyes snapping, a white knight out to save a fair maiden. Privately, I thought that any fair who could look like that on cue couldn't be a maiden.

Then Barry looked over at us young 'uns. "Enough. Half an hour for lunch, friends. Ms. Lark, you noted the ones you'll be reading with this afternoon?"

"Yes, Mr. Tallendar. Mr. Callow, Mr. Tallow, and Mr. Couth."

"Quite right." Barry seemed gratified to know she'd been paying attention. "We'll have at it again at three, shall we? Each to his own comestibles, then."

It was a polite dismissal; Barry and Horace wanted to have lunch by themselves. I had a notion they had a lot of discussion to do about those three-line auditions. I nodded affably and turned to go. Horace had already given me my first week's pay—I guessed it had come out of his own pocket, and I was damned well going to make sure it stayed in mine.

Lacey Lark stepped up to me as we moved toward the door. I looked down, into the hugest pair of glowing eyes I'd ever seen. "I hate to dine alone," she husked. "Will you escort me?"

I tried to ignore the fibrillation in my chest and the tingling throughout the rest of my body, and swallowed. "Yeah, sure! My pleasure." I meant it, too.

I watched the two young ones go out the door, her hand already possessively touching his arm. I wondered what she wanted from him—just lunch? Or more? Would it be his pocket that was impoverished, or his soul?

I had my doubts about Lacey Lark, none of which could affect Barry's decision to include her in the company—she was a talented and promising actress, and would mind her manners as long as we made it clear to her that she had to. I wondered if Ramou fell under Barry's aegis in such a matter, then decided that his emotional life was his own concern—but that I should perhaps give him some gentle warnings about the ladies of the theater.

Many of them are wonderful, you understand, with hearts of gold that ache for others and seek to assuage their pain, no matter how often their own hearts have been broken—but others seem to feed on that breaking of hearts, and see every man they meet as a challenge. They nourish their egos off the emotions of the males in their lives and feel compelled to try their strongest to enslave every man they meet. The world of the theater is filled with pitfalls waiting to entrap young men, and one of them was Lacey Lark.

I could not believe that Ramou meant anything to her, other than as an amusing diversion, a puzzle to be solved, a trophy for her collection. In fact, she might not even have noticed him as a man at all, if it had not been for the way he had looked at the Souci girl as she left the hall.

No. I do her an injustice. She had already realized that he was a member of the company, and as such, certainly worth swaying to her side. What side? Oh, rivalries were sure to arise—her sort always find them. And, too, she was observant, and quite intelligent; surely she had already realized that Ramou was close to me in some way, and that I was close to Barry. Therefore, by winning his affections, she would be ingratiating herself with the powers of this embryonic company.

She had not yet learned to allow for the experiences of others, or to think that any but a misogynist might suspect her motives. I hold the females of my species in high esteem, but I have learned to suspend judgment as to the motives behind any human deeds, male or female. Some thrive on politicking—they are born to it—and feel the need to develop a power base wherever they go. Frightfully insecure, of course, though they hide it well. Very well. Lacey Lark seemed to be full of self-confidence, completely independent, and a power to be reckoned with—all of which she was, or might become. However, she knew herself to be hollow within.

Nature abhors a vaccuum—feminine nature most of all— and Lacey meant to fill hers with the devotion of unsuspecting males who had a deficiency of judgment and an excess of hormones.

Let us be fair. I've known the same to be true of men, in regard to women, at least as frequently. It is merely that I try to avoid such persons, and have an easier time avoiding them when they are male. Easier than when they are female—when I was young, I gravitated toward such women as a compass needle toward a lodestone. It happens much more rarely now, of course. There are advantages to age.

8

What do you say when you're taking a beautiful girl to lunch, and you're total strangers?

Anything, as long as it's not insulting. And I didn't mind showing my ignorance—I wasn't *supposed* to know anything about theater. So for openers, I tried, "That was bizarre!"

The limpid blue eyes looked up at me, ready to be offended or amused, depending on the next stop of my pinball. "The audition? But why?"

"It was dehumanized! He just lined them up like ducks in a shooting gallery, and didn't let anybody speak for more than thirty seconds! How can he tell anything about their acting that way?"

"Just by listening." She was deciding to be amused. "He's had lots of experience, and he can tell whether or not the person's any good by the time they've said ten words."

"What if you're having a bad day?"

"You don't dare," she said simply.

I felt a chill. I was about to ask if she'd ever had a bad day, then thought better of it. "So it's all a charade! Tallendar's just going through the motions—he isn't really expecting to find anybody for the parts they need to fill!"

"No," she agreed. "The real auditions happen separately, in smaller rooms and with only a few people, and they're set up by the agents."

"Then why bother holding the auditions at all?"

"Because Equity says they have to," she explained, "and if the producers don't follow Equity's rules, no actor who belongs to Actors' Equity will work for them. Since that includes all the big stars and the important, established actors, the producers follow the rules."

"Oh." I chewed that one over. "But why does Equity insist on the open auditions?"

"So that the ones who aren't in Equity yet have a chance at roles that might help earn them their union cards—and so that the young ones who do have their cards can have a chance to be noticed."

She didn't seem to be including herself in that. I was obviously talking to an old hand. "But if the directors know they're just doing it because they have to, and the actors know they're not really going to have a chance to show what they can do, why do any of them bother?"

"Because sometimes the director will find someone for a small part," she explained. "Sometimes somebody stands out."

"When they only let them read for ten words?"

She nodded.

I shook my head. "Then why did Mr. Tallendar let them read for more?"

"Because he's nice." She smiled, and the sun came out. "Most directors don't let you talk for more than a sentence, maybe two—and they don't even pretend to pay attention. They talk with a friend, laugh, say nasty things about you to someone else . . . You have to win their attention. They'll look up if they hear something really dazzling, but it doesn't happen often. But they *will* look over the line and come up and ask you for your phone number and address."

"But they have that anyway, on your résumé!"

"No, they have the number for your answering service. If you give the director your home number, he knows you're willing to play ball."

I was appalled. "You mean you have to go to bed with the director to get a part?"

"No. If you're good, and the director needs you, he'll cast you anyway."

"Then why does he bother?"

"Because sometimes it works," she said acidly. "There are always kids who don't know how things really work. Sometimes the director will even give them a part—in the chorus. But they'll never get very good roles, because everyone will figure they can't have talent or they wouldn't have gone to bed with the director."

"How about if they really *do* have talent?"

She grimaced. "How about if they're really in love with the director?"

Fair question. "I didn't notice Horace or Mr. Tallendar propositioning anybody."

"No. I was surprised. As I said, Mr. Tallendar's very nice."

I was beginning to understand that the word "gentleman" might still have some meaning.

"How long have you known Mr. Burbage?" she asked.

Here was my chance to impress—but I decided to stick to the truth. Lies have a way of snapping back at you. "Only a couple of days, really. But we've done a few favors for each other."

"Favors?" She looked at me sharply. "What kind of favors could you do for him?"

I decided not to take offense at that—she probably hadn't realized how belittling it had sounded.

Then I realized that she probably had. I was dealing with a very smart cookie, and I had to assume that she knew exactly what she was doing. I heard my emotional armor clank shut, but I pretended not to notice. "Muscle stuff. He has furniture that needs moving, likes to take walks at night—you know."

"Yes." I could see she was trying to figure out whether I was gay or a charity case. No, strike that—I don't think she believed in charity. "I take it you're new to the theater?"

I nodded. "Saw a few plays in college, and I don't mind telling you, it was really electric, after a lifetime of 3DT."

"Yes, I know." Still amused, but with a glint that said she remembered. "So you became stagestruck?"

"No, I became a father—or so she said. Me, I knew there

was no way, so I lit out before she could call the cops. Then I met Horace, and I was hard up for a job, and he steered me to the Star Company."

Well. That settled one of her questions. But she looked a little dazed; I don't think she was used to so much honesty. Looked faintly repulsed, too.

I found that to be true with most people. They don't expect people to be honest about themselves, or with themselves. I don't expect it, either, which is why I try so hard. I mean, I grew up in the ruins of what happened when two people lie to themselves about how they feel, so I was bound and determined not to lie to me.

Impossible, of course. We all need our illusions, we live by illusions. I lie to myself all the time, and it takes me months to realize I did. Years, sometimes. It's a brutal process, and it's never done—but it'll keep me from wrecking my life, and somebody else's. Love can be an illusion, too. That's where the phrase "true love" came from—to distinguish the real thing from the phantasm. If there is a real thing.

True love? I don't know. I guess I still believe in it. Not that that was what I was feeling for Lacey Lark, of course— but it was well above simple lust.

Simple lust. You notice how they say that? "Simple" lust—as opposed to complex lust. There's a moral in there, somewhere.

We turned into an Automat, but a nice one—tasteful decoration, curtains, a rug. Me, I was just following—it was her town. "So I don't really know anything about the theater—but I'm sure having one hell of a lot of fun learning."

That won a smile from her again. "What were you doing before this?"

"Going to college." I pulled out the chair on its swivel and held it for her. She sat down, looking faintly surprised. I stepped around and sat down across from her, then pressed the patch that lit the screen in the middle of the table and scrolled the menu. "What's good here?"

"Everything and nothing," she answered.

I looked up, frowning. "What is this, philosophy?"

"No, food preparation." She smiled, and I was enchanted all over again. "In an Automat, everything's cooked well enough to be tasty, but nothing's really excellent."

I nodded. "That makes sense. And here I was afraid you were getting mystical on me."

She laughed and glanced at the menu. "I like the broiled chicken. You know the rule—never eat meat unless you can recognize it."

I didn't, but it made sense. I mean, with chili, who can say what's in it? Only the cook. I nodded. "Chicken it is." I punched in two chicken dinners.

"What were you studying?" she asked.

It took me a second to realize that she didn't mean herself, or the menu, either. "Electrical engineering. That's why Horace thinks I stand a chance learning stagecraft."

"You mean technical theater." Amusement, but the nice kind—I could live with it. "I had to learn a little bit in college, but it was just running packaged sets and setting sound and lighting cues."

I was appalled. For college? That sounded like kindergarten! But I tried not to let it show. "How do you set the cues? Just go through with a copy of the script?"

"Oh, no! You can't really set them till tech rehearsal, because the director has to see each scene and tell you how to make the fine adjustments. That's why I had to learn at least a little bit—so I'd be able to talk to the tech operators if I ever wanted to direct."

"Do you?"

Lacey shrugged. "Not yet—but I may, some day. I've only been in the business six years, but I've already worked under two dozen directors . . ."

I was later to learn that, at her age, that counted as bragging.

". . . and some of them were so inept it was infuriating. It does kind of make you begin to want to see how well you can do—anyone could do better than some of those idiots I've worked with in stock and rep."

"But not yet?"

"No." The smile dazzled me. "First I'm going to become a star."

Somehow, right then, the only question I had was, *How fast?* "I don't doubt it," I said. "But how will it help to go traveling with a company that's really heading out to the boondocks?"

"I'll come back with a string of very good credits," she explained, "and all of them will be working under Barry Tallendar. He's very highly respected in the profession."

I stared, wondering just how much of a good deal I'd fallen into. "But I thought he was history!"

"Only as a star." She smiled. "Producers still go to him for advice, if something's wrong with a show. He has a reputation for being able to say in a moment how to fix what's not working. He's merciless, though."

"I thought he was a nice guy."

"No, silly—merciless to the show! He's always courteous to the people. Well, of course, there are always a few people in the business that even he has to be deadly with—but except for them, I mean."

I understood—I thought. "So when you come back, you'll get better parts, just because you worked under Tallendar?"

"Yes. It's worth being away from New York for a year."

Somehow, that rang false; a girl with her looks, and talent enough for Tallendar to have cast her already, probably could have done at least as well by staying in New York. There had to be some other reason why she was willing to leave town.

Of course, what did I know?

The bill. She ignored it when it came chuckling out of the slot—and after all, I had been the one to punch the orders in. I fed bills into the other slot and followed her out, reflecting ruefully that one good resolution was already shot.

While the young folk were dining at the Automat, Barry was waxing enthusiastic over lunch at Blarney's. He obviously was feeling optimistic about his brainchild. "That young lady should make an excellent soubrette, Horace. Really, it's amazing she hasn't done better in New York!"

"Very," I agreed. "Of course, she could have found good advice, if she had really wanted it."

Barry frowned. "What are you saying?"

"That she has talent and dreams, but may lack ambition."

Barry leaned back, nodding thoughtfully. "Not an entirely unattractive attribute, in a lady who will be living and working with a group of rather temperamental and difficult people." He looked up at me. "Of course, we can't really know that."

"No," I agreed. "It could just be bad luck."

"Or that she wants to act, but not in New York." Barry smiled. "This is where she has to be based, though, to attend the auditions."

"Or that she wants to *act*," I agreed, "more than she wants to *be an actress*."

Barry nodded. "Yes, quite right! Again, a very attractive quality! That young man we've netted, though . . ."

"Which one? We're calling back three."

"Larry Rash, the one who seemed to be made of wood till his turn came. His résumé is scanty, to say the least."

"Fresh out of college and two summers of stock," I agreed. "Promise, but not much else. Certainly he stands to benefit from a year with the company—but do we?"

"Two summers of stock does not exactly testify to his character," Barry reflected. "Let's see—which companies was he with, Horace?"

I referred to my notes. "The Woodstock Playhouse, and the Summerfun Company across the Hudson."

"Ah, yes! I've seen some of their work." Barry took on a very thoughtful look. I didn't wonder he'd been over to Montclair to see them—during the year, they rented their theater and shops to New York producers who wanted to try the show out of town, but also wanted to keep it in range of the critics. Barry had been called over there several times, to doctor ailing plays. "I know their managing director, Horace. He might be able to lend us some insights."

"Why, yes, you introduced us, that night when you dragged me along to see their revival of *The Black Crook*. Astounding production, that. The chap's ingenious."

He bent an eye on me. "Are you offering to have a little chat with him?"

"Certainly. A brief vidcall should do it, eh? While I'm at it, I'll ask if he knows anyone fit to be a technical director; since he's already out of town, he might have a better lead on someone willing to go farther out." I was amazed at how quickly I had found myself adapting to the notion of leaving Earth—but then, out of town is out of town. Once you've made the decision to leave, it really doesn't matter how far you're going—across the Hudson or across the light-years, it's all the same.

"Yes, the technical director." Barry frowned. "That may prove to be our most difficult problem, Horace."

"There isn't exactly a horde of qualified people eager for work," I agreed.

Barry nodded. "Men who know both theater and mathematics are very difficult to come by."

"And, of course," I said, "they can name their own salary."

"Well, not quite that," Barry demurred. "The show must show a profit, after all. But anyone who is truly qualified as both a designer and a technical director can make half again the salary I can offer, and that without leaving Terra."

"But surely the challenge of the unknown . . . the longing to see new and different worlds . . ."

"The spirit of adventure doesn't seem to count for much, against a good salary and the blandishments of New York," Barry sighed. He patted his lips with a paper napkin and rose. "Well, back to the audition hall. A few of the people that I've asked for should be showing up."

"Out of curiosity, if not the thrill of the challenge," I agreed, rising.

* * *

We had a surprise in store. On our return to the hall, there was indeed someone waiting for us—but he wasn't an actor. Or, rather, I should say that he wasn't a member of Equity, though he was as able to carry a role as three-quarters of their membership. Acting was not his forte, though, nor his métier.

We stepped out of the lift, and Barry stopped short, staring through the open doors at the tall, burly figure who strode about like a caged panther, thwacking his palm with a rolled-up hard copy.

"I don't believe it," I said, staring.

"But it must be him," Barry countered. "Who else could it be?"

"A sound point." I took the lead and strode forward, hands outstretched and calling, "Merlo! Merlo Hertz!"

The young, and not-so-young, actors sitting around the edges of the room in instant chairs looked up, startled.

The tall man looked up, too, and his frown ameliorated into a guarded smile. "Hey, Horace! How've you been?"

It was one of Merlo's affectations that, although he had degrees from Carnegie and Yale, he spoke like a tradesman—no doubt to facilitate his dealings with stagehands, or perhaps from a secret desire to have been one. I say "have been" because, from hints he has dropped at one time or another, I have gained the impression that he secretly wishes he had been a stagehand in the days of vaudeville, when all flats were built to a width of five feet nine inches, so that they could easily pass through the doors of railroad boxcars.

He could not have passed through that door upright, of course. Merlo was well over six feet. He had curly red hair with a receding hairline—Merlo was one of those people who could never take the time to have an implant done—a round face with a stubby nose above a large chin and hard eyes that always seemed to be angry, until tech rehearsal, or unless he was constructing a set. He was one of those people who always seemed to be in a rush, as though life couldn't possibly last long enough to contain all the things he wanted to do.

"Well enough," I assured him. "Merlo, you do remember Barry Tallendar?"

"Yeah, everyone in the business knows Tallendar." Merlo pointedly dropped the "Mr." "Question is, does he remember me?" He held out a hand. "Good to see you again, Mr. Tallendar." After all, now it was a form of address.

"*A Long Day's Journey into Night* at the Odeon, and *The Comprador* at the Champlain Playhouse." Barry shook his hand. "Of course I remember you, Mr. Hertz. I've always wondered why you never undertook design in the city."

"Because they won't hire me," Merlo said bluntly. "Summer stock, yes, but not Broadway. They're glad enough to just let me run the show here in town, but I want to design, too."

"Well, Merlo," I said, "if you insist on attempting to actually touch the staging console controls yourself here in New York, you can't expect IATSE to countenance your designing."

"Look, I'm IATSE too, right? And the Designers' Guild is all politics these days, anyway. So if a fumble-fingered stagehand reaches for the 'chroma' knob when I told him to boost the modal level, what am I supposed to do?"

"Anything other than reach out and touch the knob yourself," I said.

"Call the shop steward," Barry suggested.

"He *is* the shop steward!" Merlo pointed out.

"That does make the issue problematical," Barry sighed. "Of course, The Star Company will be union, but the rules are looser out of town . . ."

"I can get leave, anyway," Merlo snapped. "Would you let me design?"

" 'Let'?" Barry smiled. "Hardly the word for it. 'Require' might be a bit more to the point. Though I would stipulate that the sets you design don't have to be used on the first few nights of a run, if the director isn't enthusiastic about them, and if I prefer to use a prepackaged setting—and I would also stipulate that we would not be obliged to use the set you design for more than three performances in toto."

Merlo glowered, and for a moment I thought we'd lost him. I wondered desperately why Barry insisted on such a stipulation when we were ourselves in no position to cavil—then realized that he was merely making certain Merlo would work within the director's concept and earnestly try to achieve something in harmony with the whole, rather than going off on his own and designing something that was an artistic marvel in itself but had little to do with that particular production.

Grudgingly, Merlo said, "Yeah, all right. It's more designing than I'd get to do in New York, anyway."

"Of course, you would have to work within the director's parameters . . ."

"Yeah, sure." Merlo shrugged impatiently. "I've done my share of directing, too, Mr. Tallendar."

"And of acting," Barry reminded him. Merlo winced, but Barry added, "Of course, a director must know how to act, mustn't he, Mr. Hertz? Yes, certainly. We may even need to press you into service for a bit part on occasion."

Merlo turned thunderous, and I thought Barry had indeed pressed the issue too far. But Merlo's face suddenly cleared, with a diabolical grin. "Well, if we're crossing union lines that much, there sure wouldn't be any fuss about my running the board myself."

"None at all—in fact, you'd have to take charge of buying it," Barry assured him. "I would expect you to have a decent catalog of prepackaged sets and scenic pieces to hand, though."

Merlo frowned. "What for?" I could see he was thinking that Barry intended sabotage, a means of guaranteeing that Merlo's designs would be used only for the stipulated three nights.

"Just in case," Barry explained. "We might have to mount a show so quickly that you wouldn't have time for a full design."

"Oh, yeah, well, sure!"

"Very good." Barry shook his hand again. "You're hired."

Merlo stared. "Just like that? You don't want to see my résumé? My portfolio?"

"I saw your designs that summer in Lake Champlain, and I've seen several shows for which you were technical director," Barry assured him. "I've no reservations about your abilities, Mr. Hertz. You do know, though, that we'll be gone at least a year?"

Merlo shrugged. "I spend a lot of time out of town, anyway."

"Yes, but it will be impossible to return for the weekend. Our first stop is Alpha Centauri, and we expect the midpoint to be Haldane's Star."

Merlo nodded. "I'd heard the gossip."

So. The rumor mill was in its usual fine shape. How long had it been since we'd made the public announcement—thirty-six hours? Forty, at most?

"I don't mind traveling," Merlo was saying, "and I kind of like the idea of seeing new planets." Unexpectedly, a grin broke through.

Barry responded with a wide smile. "We'll have the papers for you tomorrow. For today, though, I'd like you to visit the supply houses and choose the equipment. Nothing elaborate, I'm afraid—we can only afford to spend sixty thousand therms on staging equipment and supplies."

"That's a pretty small board," Merlo said with a frown, "and a smaller inventory."

"If the company succeeds according to my expectations, we'll be expanding a bit every year."

Merlo shrugged. "I can't ask for better than that. What do I use for payment?"

"Have the accounts billed to me, at the Star Repertory Company, Tallendar Building, Wall Street."

"*They're* handling your accounts?"

"My brother will refer the matter to one of his clerks, yes."

"Oh." I could see Merlo revising his ideas about the

company's chances; he hadn't connected the two Tallendar names, the actor with the magnate. Not many of us do; they belong to separate worlds.

Just then the lift door opened, and out strolled Ramou and Lacey, arm in arm, she looking smug and he looking elated. Obviously lunch had gone well. Perhaps too well—I decided the lad needed a distraction. "Nicely timed, Ramou! I'd like you to meet your new boss!"

"Boss?" Ramou's head came back down out of the clouds so quickly that I almost heard it strike ground. "You hired a—what did you call him?"

"Tech director," Merlo snapped. "And designer. What kind of stagehand are you, if you don't even know the names of the jobs?"

"A brand-new one," Ramou said right back, "who doesn't know anything about the theater at all. I've had two years of electrical engineering, and I've done a lot of maintenance and programming for pay, and holo work for fun. Other than that, my only qualification is that I'm eager to learn."

His frankness rocked us all, I think, but Merlo's interest kindled. He grinned. "Hey, good enough! At least I don't have to unteach you a lot of fool notions about art and self-expression that you picked up in college. Come on, boy, you're about to get your first lesson! We've got some shopping to do." And he caught Ramou by the arm as he strode off toward the lift.

To say that Ramou was surprised would be the veriest understatement. He managed to look back long enough to wave at Lacey and, I hope, at me. I raised a palm in reassurance; then the lift door closed, and I could only wish him well.

9

The elevator door closed behind us, and Hertz said, "How long you been with the company, boy?"

I decided I was going to have to do something about that "boy," but this wasn't the time or the place. "About twelve hours."

He looked at me with a glint of amusement in his eye. "Long enough to start something with the ingenue, huh?"

I goggled—I had thought *I* was forthright. There's a distinction, though, between being forthright and being rude, and Lacey was none of his damn business. "I wouldn't say that. Not for lack of trying, though."

"Don't. She's poison."

Fortunately, I hadn't stopped goggling. "You've had an affair with her?"

Merlo shook his head. "Never even been in the same company with her. I know her type, though—she has a hobby."

He waited. I didn't bite.

"Men," he amplified. "She has this compulsion to try to make every man she meets fall in love with her. Likes to keep them in the bank, never knows when one of them might come in handy."

I felt the anger surging, but I kept my face wooden. I also felt my armor going up—he'd been around theater a long time, maybe he knew what he was talking about.

Maybe he didn't, though. I knew I wasn't in love with Lacey, because I wasn't sure I was—but I did get a very pleasant feeling just from being with her.

111

"Women are addictive," he advised me, "and there are an awful lot of 'em around a theater who can bend a man's fancy like modeling clay. Don't get hooked."

I thought of asking him how he knew, but decided it was none of my business—which raised an interesting point.

"I appreciate the advice," I said, "but it's none of your damn business."

He surprised me; he chuckled. "Sure, go ahead, don't believe me! But if you're gonna be my assistant, boy, I don't want you mooning around because some ingenue has taken to batting her eyelashes at someone else. That's the kind of thing that makes an operator miss cues."

I had a feeling I was missing a whole bunch of 'em, but he was coming up with ones I couldn't miss. "Private life is private, Mr. Hertz. You're going to be my boss, not my warden."

"Oho! So it does have some spirit! But listen in, boy—"

"No."

He frowned. "What?"

"I said, no. I won't listen if you call me 'boy.' " I had the sinking feeling that my job was going down the tubes, but some things you don't stand for. After all, I could always walk out of New York.

His face went wooden. Then he nodded. "Fair enough. You're a man grown, even if you're still young enough to do a lot of dumb things. What was your name again?"

"Ramou," I said. "Lazarian."

"Ramou." He nodded. "Not that I'm taking back anything I said about that girl—what was her name?"

"Lacey Lark."

"Lark, yeah. Believe me, I've seen girls like her foul up young guys like you so fast they never did figure out what shot 'em. But they're one of the hazards of the trade, Ramou. If you want to be a stagehand, you'd better start becoming immune to them."

I thought of asking if he had been one of those young men, but just because he was being a donkey was no reason why I should. "Just how do I manage that?"

"Easy." He grinned. "Start caring more about staging consoles than you do about women."

I just looked at him for a second. Then I grinned back. I mean, after all, he may have been old and sour, but he was an engineer underneath it all. "Only trouble is, I've seen women, but I've never seen a staging console. In fact, I've scarcely ever seen a stage."

Merlo shrugged. "Don't need 'em anymore. You can stage any play in the middle of a big room, the way they used to do in the Middle Ages—but it makes it more fun if you've got scenery and lighting. Costumes too, of course, but they're not our worry, much. And with a staging console, you can go right back to that big room and have the actors perform there, but put the scenery right behind them."

"Wait a minute." I stared. "I've seen a couple of plays. Are you telling me that the scenery wasn't real?"

"Of course it was real." Merlo frowned at me. "What's the matter with you, kid? It came out of a staging console, same as any."

"I mean, it wasn't built out of real wood and paint?"

Merlo chuckled and shook his head. "Scenery never has been real, kid, even back in the days when it *was* cloth stretched over wooden frames—they called 'em 'flats.' But they didn't cover 'em with real wood or brick, just painted 'em to look like it."

"Well, of course. I mean, you couldn't build a brick wall three times a day, and tear it down for the next scene."

"Okay." Hertz spread his hands. "We're doing the same thing. Only we're painting with light."

I thought that one over as he led me down the stairs into a tube tunnel.

As we came down onto the platform, a train was just coming in behind the clear wall. The cars slowed to a stop on the other side of the transparent plastic, and the safety wall between the platform and the tracks slid open in synchronization with the car doors. People began to pile out. There wasn't much noise—only a few of them were talking to each other—but I had to concentrate to figure out when I was supposed to get on, and I didn't want to miss my jump.

Hertz, though, did it by second nature, talking all the time. "So the console just makes the projection strips along the floor generate coherent light beams to whatever height we set them at, then fills between 'em with spread light and ties them together to generate the hologram. After that, it's all just programming individual points."

"Like the illusion boxes kids play with," I said, entranced.

"Damn big illusion boxes! And the projections are a lot more solid-looking. Sure, we have to put up door frames, so the actors can go in and out, and sometimes a window frame, too—but the rest is light. You want a grotto? No problem. Show me a picture, I'll add a bit of my own imagination and program it in looking better and more magical than the real thing could ever be. Want the inside of a cathedral? No sweat. The outside? Easy. The Rocky Mountains? Okay, that takes a bit longer, but we'll have it for you tomorrow." He flashed me a smile. "You're hooked, kid."

"Yeah! When can I see one?"

"In about ten minutes." The car hissed to a stop, and the door slid back. Merlo strode out, and I hopped to keep up with him. "So the only reason you're still ga-ga over women," he finished, "is that you've never seen a console."

What could I say? He could be right. An engineer is an engineer, after all, and a woman is only a set of hyperbolas and parabolas. But I'd reserve judgment till I'd actually seen the thing in action.

Merlo led me up the ramp, outside, down a block, and over half a block, telling me one thing after another about what his consoles could do and how they did it, eyes glowing. I began to recognize the signs—it was like another man telling me all about his girl friend. Merlo was in love, and any woman who wanted into his life would have to resign herself to being second. I wasn't sure I wanted to be like that.

Then Merlo led me through a doorway into a shop, and

I realized it wasn't a matter of what I wanted to be, but what I was.

It was dingy and crowded, the walls lined with racks from floor to ceiling, filled with great gray consoles and little blue ones, components in boxes and components out of boxes, bins of spare circuit cards and cables. But the center of the floor was clear except for a grid of rails, and on them stood a model of a theatrical setting, two feet high and five feet wide, a castle dungeon so real you could see the chips of mica in the stone and swear you smelled the damp. You could certainly see the trickles of water from between the blocks.

I swallowed. "That's light?"

"More elaborate than you had in college, hey?" Merlo gestured toward the set. "Of course, spread the rails and we can enlarge the scale, life-size or bigger—though your power requirements go up as your scale does."

"Not that much," I protested. "This is all low-level stuff."

"The consoles are, but the lights take juice. Not as much as they did when I got into the business, but still more than you can run off a battery. We've got it down to what a small generator can handle, though, for companies that want to perform out in the open."

I glanced back and forth from the dinginess of the walls and the room itself, to the glamour of the setting before me. It seemed incredible that the wonderful, colorful, magical world of the theater could really come out of dumps like this.

But it did.

Up came a fat old guy with his jacket off and a grin on, hand outstretched. "Hey, Merlo! How was Connecticut?"

"Coulda been worse, Carl." Merlo shook his hand, then waved at me. "This is my new assistant, Ramou Lazarian."

"Good to meet you," said the smile, wrenching my wrist as he did. Didn't manage to crunch my hand, though, which I think surprised him. "Been in theater long?"

"Since sunrise," I said.

He stared, then turned to Merlo. "A rookie?"

"He's willing," Merlo explained. "And we're heading for outer space."

"Oh! You signed up with Tallendar, huh?"

"Just." Merlo grinned. "Word travels fast."

"Brother, with a nut idea like that, it practically gallops." Carl frowned. " 'S true, then? You're gonna tour the colony planets?"

"For real," Merlo confirmed. "So we need the whole system, Carl—console, light rails, set cubes, prop protos, form synthesizer, costume generator . . ."

"Costumes is over at Hook's, but I can give you everything else, Merlo." Carl frowned. "Who's paying?"

"You send the bills to Barry Tallendar, Star Repertory Company, Tallendar Building."

Carl's face went immobile for a few seconds; the mention of the Tallendar Building did it. Then he smiled, eyes glinting. "Okay, sounds good! What'd you want, Merlo?"

"Sixty thousand therms' worth."

Carl frowned, losing energy. "That won't buy much of a system."

"We'll start small and grow—so everything has to be expandable."

Carl nodded, perking up again at the thought of future profits. "New or used?"

"Used, of course," Merlo said, "but not too used."

Carl grinned and turned away with an expansive wave of the arm. "Right this way."

I hurried to catch up with Merlo. "Are you crazy? Won't Barry squall if he hears you bought used?"

"Nobody buys new these days," Merlo told me, amused at my ignorance. "Not when they're going on tour. How'd you like to be setting up for our first show on Centauri's New Venus and have a chip blow? And find out we don't have a backup?"

"Well, of course not . . ."

"That's the way it is with every component." Hertz nodded. "Even with the best quality control, the damn things are just so complicated inside that even with integrated rings packed tight, there's plenty of room for Finagle and his gremlins. Let the big houses in the cities break them in for us. They sell their boards every two years now, so they can stay abreast of the technology. I'll make do with two-year-old gimmicks, if it boosts my chances that they'll all work right."

"Will Mr. Tallendar understand that?"

"If he doesn't, he can hire a new T.D.! Besides which, yes, he will—he's been around stages long enough to know what's going on. And he's a man of the theater, if you know what I mean."

"No," I said, "I don't."

Merlo sighed. "I see I'm still overestimating you. Well, Ramou, there're actors who're just actors, and don't know a damn thing about the scenery, especially not to slam the door too hard—and there're stagehands and tech directors and designers who know everything they possibly could about putting sets together, but don't have the faintest idea what goes on inside an actor's head. Then there are directors who used to be actors, and figure that gives them the right to scream at the tech director every time something technical isn't working exactly right, even though they don't know a damn thing about programming a set or projecting it . . ."

"Sounds rough."

"You should only know," Merlo growled. "It makes you get prickly. Sometimes I think the stagehands' union got started just to muzzle the directors, not to give us better pay."

"So that's the theater?" I asked. "Actors, stagehands, designers, and directors?"

"And costumers, and makeup artists, and electricians. And the actors sneer at the stagehands because they're just laborers without any creative soul, and the stagehands sneer at the actors because they're total incompetents, and the costumer thinks they're all crazy because they don't realize clothes are wonderful things that have to be treated like jewels—and the director yells at everybody."

"Very pretty." I began to reconsider the upcoming year of living with these people. "Sweet, even."

"Oh, you better believe it. Believe me, you've never heard a bigger racket than clashing egos. But every now and then, you'll find one, a very rare one, who went to a school where they made him learn a little about tech, and made him work on the crew for a few shows—and made the techs and the designers take a few acting courses and act in two or three laboratory productions, and made them both put in a few hours in the costume shop and learn a little bit about why the outfits tell something about the characters. And a few of them, a very few, actually started respecting what the other guy is doing, and kept learning about it in odd moments. If he was an actor, he started asking the stagehands about their jobs, and if he was a designer, he started asking the actor some intelligent questions about how he was developing his character."

"You mean there are people out there who know something about every part of the theater?"

"A few." Hertz grinned. "Still a few. And Tallendar's one of them. Drop him in the middle of Nebraska without anything but the clothes on his back and a fat bank account, and he could have a whole theater running in a month, just by hiring locals and teaching them the absolute minimum."

It occurred to me that maybe that was just what Barry was doing, but I didn't say so. "So that's a 'man of the theater'?"

Merlo nodded. "And Tallendar is one of 'em. The last of a dying breed."

I dropped behind him a few paces as he bulled ahead to listen avidly to what Carl was saying about the big gray chunk of machinery he was bending over. I wanted to get a look at all of Merlo, because if he was so big on Barry being a "man of the theater," it followed that Merlo probably was one, too—and his remembering that Mr. Tallendar had said something about it meant that he had done some acting in his time. It could explain why the two of them got along so well—at least, as well as Merlo could get along with anyone.

On short acquaintance, I doubted that anybody could, much. Least of all, me.

"And the price?" Merlo asked.

"Fifty thousand therms," Carl answered.

I was appalled. You could buy a house for fifty thousand—pretty nice house, too. But Merlo just nodded and sat down behind it. "I don't want new, you know."

"Sure, sure, but this is the one I've got set up at the moment. Why not try it before I reconnect it to the one you wanted to look at?"

Merlo shrugged. "It's your demo." He touched something on the board, and the dungeon disappeared. It was so sudden, and it had been so real, that I nearly cried. But before my tear ducts could do more than think about it, a glowing cloud appeared over the rails, colors appearing and swirling within it. Then they settled down into different areas, and Merlo grunted, "Nice effect."

"The latest," Carl assured him.

Then individual shapes began to grow out of the cloud, like lampposts and trees appearing out of a fog—only these were the walls and ramp and floor of a very ordinary-looking living room. The cloud melted away, and Merlo nodded. "Not bad." He punched at the board again, and the living room broke into a thousand fragments and came raining down on the rails—except that they never got there; somewhere in between, they melted out of existence. I don't know where they went; I was too busy watching the rain.

Then lances shot up from the rails, lavender, gold, pink, scarlet, and a fairy-tale castle sprang up, painted in sharp bars of color with darkness in between them. More color percolated up between the bars until the walls appeared completely solid and real. Merlo did something else, and a robin's egg–blue sky appeared behind the castle, with grass in front of it and to either side, and a few small fruit trees here and there.

And then, so help me, the castle let down its drawbridge. I stared—I'd been staring for some time—and wondered what would happen if an actor-knight tried to ride across that drawbridge. Would Merlo chuckle?

It would depend on who the actor was.

Squares of brown appeared, and the castle, block by block, was replaced by what had to be the throne room inside it—hung with tapestries and captured shields, with a huge double throne on a dais at its center, under canopies of gold. I had just barely decided it was all there, when jagged streaks of lightning stabbed down through it while thunder boomed all about me. I think I jumped, but Merlo was just saying, "Nice. Nice." Then the after-glare cleared, and I found I was staring at a vast landscape, with mountains towering far beyond a forest, and a Brothers Grimm cottage in the foreground. Streaks of color lanced through it, the mountains and forest faded, the cottage turned into a nine-teenth-century Midwestern farmhouse, and all around it stretched vast plains, green with crops under an enameled sky. All of this was three-dimensional, mind you—it looked perfectly solid, so it was very disquieting to see the land begin to ripple underneath it. The ripples grew higher and higher until they hid the house, and the whole scene went through a giant convulsion, then settled down bit by bit into a view of a Chinese pagoda with a scene straight off a lady's fan, complete with river and old peasant poling a barge. He moved and looked totally real, and I wondered what the actors' union would say about him. But that scene grew hazy even as I was watching; new shapes began to appear; for an instant, everything was a murky, foggy neutral ground with every color in the spectrum someplace within it; then shapes started clarifying, the one set dissolving into the other, and I found myself looking at heaving waves with a ship's rail in front of them, the deck boards broken here and there by hatches and funnels, tilting in time to the waves, and Merlo saying, "Good. Very good."

And it all faded away, just like that.

I stood wide-eyed, feeling devastated; now I knew how Ferdinand must have felt when Prospero made the masque disappear.

"How about add-ons?" Merlo asked.

Carl shook his head. "This is the basic board, mind you. It's self-contained. What you see is all there is."

"It's good for what it is, but it's got a lot of things I don't need, and it's missing the ones I do."

"Like what?"

"Color controls."

"They're preset."

"That's the problem. If we're doing a Molière, I want tints; if we're doing an O'Neill, I want everything grayed."

Carl shrugged. "Your choice. Me, I like primaries."

Merlo gave him a narrow look, then turned to me. "It's good for a beginner, though. Sit down, kid."

I didn't need a second invitation. I was in the seat before he finished the sentence. I was even thinking that, anyway, "kid" is a promotion from "boy."

"This bank is scene A." Merlo swept a hand across a row of pressure patches. "Each button is a different scene, stored in memory from a ROM cube. See the jewel lit next to the bank?"

"Yeah."

"That means that whatever's punched up on this bank is what you're looking at. See the button that's highlighted?"

"Yeah."

"That's the scene. Press another button."

I did, and something blinked out of the corner of my eye. Looking up, I saw the dungeon there. "Hey!"

Carl chuckled.

"That's all there is to it," Merlo said, grinning. "But if you want to be a little less abrupt, push this button here." He pointed to a patch that said "Fade"; like the rest of the patches, it glowed dimly.

"Okay." I pressed, then looked up quickly to see the scene fade slowly into darkness. "Great! How do I get it back?"

"Press 'Fade' again."

I did. The dungeon appeared slowly from the darkness. "Terrific! How do I do all those other ripply comings and goings?"

"The other patches next to 'Fade,' in the transition cluster."

I looked. They were all there. One said "Statics," one "Lightning," one "Ripple," and so on. One even said "Dissolve." "Great! But how do I get it to go into another scene?"

"Punch one of the buttons on the 'scene two' bank."

I hesitated with my finger over a patch. "But not the same one as on 'scene one'?"

"Of course not—unless you want to see it covered with snow." Merlo pointed at another cluster of patches. "If you want to do that, press 'Outline.' "

I looked; "Normal" was lit. I pressed "Outline," and it lit, but "Normal" went dim. Not out, just dim—it was designed to be operated in the dark, I guess.

"Not 'Dissolve,' " Merlo cautioned. "Anything else, though."

I looked up at a bunch of patches that had strange patterns on them, some with arrows. "Like these?"

"Yeah, but then you want to punch 'Wipe' on the transition cluster."

I did. Then I punched the patch with all the little stars on it. "Now what?"

"Punch the 'Go' patch."

It was halfway between the two banks, right next to the "transition" cluster, but set off by itself. I punched "Go" and sat back to watch.

Pinpoints of light appeared, grew into stars, then grew to meld into each other and push themselves into nonexistence.

I stared, enthralled. The rush of feeling that swept me was unbelievable. I felt like a god—or at least an archangel.

Merlo chuckled. "Try going to another scene."

I looked down and saw that a jewel had lit next to scene two, no doubt to remind me what I was looking at. I punched a different button on scene A, then punched "Go." This time the stars had different colors inside them; then, as they grew, they revealed shapes until, when they were gone, so was the dungeon, and the mountains towered where they had been.

I grinned and punched another button, then "Multi-squares," and "Go." The whole scene turned itself into blocks that shuffled around with blocks of other colors, like a checkers match gone crazy. When it settled down, I was looking at the living room. I punched another scene, another transition, and watched lightning strike and change the room into the fairy-tale castle. The grin was so wide it was beginning to hurt, but I couldn't get it off my face. I punched, and punched again, and again, and again.

Finally, I leaned back with a sigh and looked up at Merlo.

He was grinning like the cat that swallowed the canary. "Beats anything, doesn't it?"

He meant women. I wasn't sure about the console winning the race, but it was in the running. "How do they make the scenes themselves?"

"Same as you make pictures in an illusion box, only a lot more so." He pointed down. "Leave the keyboard at the bottom alone; that's for programming, and I don't think he's got the cube hooked up."

"Sure I do," Carl said.

"How much?" He meant memory capacity, not price.

Carl understood. "Ten gig."

Ten gigabytes? I was disappointed—that was good for a high-school illusion box, but surely not enough for something like this!

Merlo didn't think so, either. "Expandable?"

Carl shook his head. "This is for schools, Merlo. All they want is buttons for the kids to push, and a reason to get 'em started programming."

I stared. *This* was for schools? Where had it been when I'd been going through?

Probably right there in the theater, now that I thought about it. All I had been interested in was the physics lab and the computer shop.

Merlo nodded. "What else you got?"

Carl sighed. "Nothing used, just now—you're hunting in the wrong season, Merlo."

"I know—all the road shows just went out." He pointed at a huge console in the corner. "How about the Taillefer?"

"It's an antique, Merlo."

"Yeah, well, let's give the kid a history lesson. Come over here, Ramou."

For once, I didn't mind taking orders.

Then I stared. It was huge; it was gargantuan. It had more button patches than a fusion power plant, more jewels than the queen of Sheba. "What does it do?"

"A little more than the board you just saw, but not a whole lot." Merlo pointed at a bank. "You can preset two scenes, but that doesn't do any good unless you've got three scenes or more, and you only need the middle one for a line or two. Maybe that tour sequence in *Around the World in Eighty Days*, where they're supposed to go to five different countries in the space of one song—but even then, two banks will do it with some fast reflexes. And it's got resident memory for fifty scenes, where that baby board you just used only had ten." He pointed at a cluster of five patches. "That's how you select which scenes you're going to load into the active banks. But those fifty scenes are all you get—you can't add on any new ones, so you can't keep up with the catalog."

I frowned. "That mean you can't build any new scenes yourself?"

He looked at me with an appraising eye, but all he said was, "No. It has a laser slab built in for cutting new designs—but if you want to buy anything prepackaged, you have to get a separate unit to convert it from ROM cubes to slab. You also have to convert the programming system, and that's a pain."

I sighed. Ten years is really antique, in electronics. "How about programming?"

"None of the new tricks built in," Merlo said, "and the memory's only a hundred gig."

I frowned. "You know this board pretty well, huh?"

Carl chuckled, and Merlo's face stiffened enough so that I knew he was stifling a smile. He just nodded, and said, "I ran a road show with this board ten years ago. Set it up, run for three days, pack it up, and move on, two towns a week. Yeah, I got to know it pretty well."

Ten years. What had I been doing, ten years ago? Just entering fifth grade. Rocket Rangers. Junior Null-Ball. "And didn't like it?"

"Oh, no! It was beautiful, ten years ago. I still get mushy thinking about it."

His mush must have been frozen.

"And I'd still take a Taillefer hands down, all else being equal," Merlo went on, "but it's not. The price is five times anyone else's." He turned to Carl. "How much is the new Taillefer?"

"How big?"

Merlo frowned, considering. "Ten scenes loaded, expandable, five hundred–gig memory."

"One hundred twenty-five thousand therms."

Merlo spread his hands. "See? More than twice our total budget. Thanks, Carl. We'll be back for extras, when we know what board."

"Hey, why fuss?" Carl protested. "You know you're going to buy a Taillefer, and they all take the same ROM cubes."

Merlo shrugged impatiently. "I might have to settle for less."

"The new Ferrette model is only forty thousand therms."

Merlo frowned. "I said, don't tempt me. I've got a hell of a lot more to buy; I can't blow four-fifths of my budget just on the console."

"I'll throw in the rails."

"And the costume fabricator? And the set-prop maker?"

"Well, of course—you can't expect—"

"I don't. And I don't buy new, either, Carl, not when I'm going out of town."

"Yeah, I know," Carl sighed, "no sale. Well, come back when, Merlo."

"Bye." Merlo was on his way out the door. He reminded me of Lot leaving town.

I caught up with him. "That board was a lot of fun, though."

"Good." Merlo nodded, walking fast. "You've got the makings of a tech, then. Let's see if we can't find something you'll like even more. One thing is absolutely essential, Ramou: it's got to be adaptable for any form of staging—proscenium, thrust, even full arena. You never know what you're going to find for a performance space, on the road."

I didn't have the faintest idea what he was talking about. "And that little board wasn't?"

"No. It was for proscenium only. Like I say, it was made for schools. Maybe community theaters, too, but they make do with less."

That seemed very odd to me. It made sense later, of course. Sort of.

The rest of the day kind of blended into a gestalt impression. The big thing I learned was that when you've seen one theatrical supply house, you've seen them all. Merlo did pick up a few items along the way—he found a prop fabricator he liked, and he detoured into a costume house and picked up a used Fabric-cator, then ordered a dozen drums of cellulosludge. The seller looked doubtful, told him that was scarcely enough to mount even one musical, but Merlo said they'd recycle. She still looked doubtful and said, "Are you sure your costumer will like this Fabric-cator?"

"Why not?" Merlo said. "It's cheap, rugged, and adaptable—it'll take any pattern you sell, won't it?"

"Well, of course—it's a Fabric-cator, not like the other brands. But it's scarcely the latest . . ."

"But it's cheap," he finished, "for a Fabric-cator."

She sighed and offered to show him the pattern books, but he said he'd leave that to the costumer, he was only supposed to take care of the hardware. When we were out the door, I said, "I didn't know we had a costumer yet."

"We don't. That's why I got saddled with buying it. Let's see—Proxy's is next."

So on to another staging store, where he bought all manner of lamps in your basic three colors—he tried to explain to me about additive and subtractive color theories along the way, and I listened gravely, not letting on that I'd learned it in high-school physics class. Then another staging store, where they only had three consoles, all demonstrators, all new—but they had racks and racks and racks of scene cubes. Merlo flipped through the catalogs, found the basic fifty designs that he liked, and told me to try them out. The salesman told me where things were on the biggest console, and I went to it with a will, getting slightly dizzy as I made mountains merge into forest into underwater city into Lunar landscape. Merlo pronounced himself satisfied and told the salesman where to send the cubes and the bill. As we came out, I said, "I thought you couldn't buy the cubes until after you'd bought the board."

"I stretched it a little. There was a chance I might buy something besides a Taillefer. Not now, though. We've tried fifteen consoles, and none of the other brands are worth half the price of a used Taillefer. I'll take the grade-school model if I have to, but I want the Tai."

We squeezed in the door of Nogawa's just as he was closing it. He didn't look happy to see us. "Look, I like to go home at five, Merlo." Once again, I was amazed that Merlo seemed to know at least one salesman in each shop. "The wife's expecting me for dinner."

That was rare enough these days, when husbands and wives have not just separate beds, but usually separate apartments, too. I felt for the man.

"I'm shopping for consoles," Merlo said. "The best I can get for thirty thousand."

Nogawa sighed and turned back into the store. "Taillefer, right?"

"Got to be."

Merlo looked around like a bird dog scenting pheasants. I was amazed—Nogawa's was so neat, without being glitzy! The racks lined the walls, but they were full of cubes and components; all the consoles rose from the middle of a polished hardwood floor, like rocks from a sand garden.

Merlo homed in on a board no bigger than the one we'd started our day with. Nogawa said, "I'll patch it in," and went to punch buttons on a rack at the back wall.

Merlo sat at the board. "How much?"

"The thirty thousand you said," Nogawa sighed, "for you."

Merlo must have given him lots of business in the past— either that, or the grapevine had already told him about Merlo's new job.

Merlo didn't even offer me a chance; he sat down at the board himself and started punching buttons. The shop lights dimmed, and a castle sprang up. I gasped. It wasn't from a fairy tale—it was real. The blocks were real stone, they had to be, and there was none of that translucency at the outside edges. The definition from this console was high, very high, more than I'd ever seen—and I could see why we'd need it, if this scene was expanded to life-size, as it would need to be to have actors in and around it. It looked just as real as they would—the drawbridge wasn't just wood, it was old, and it had a rotting board in the middle. The moat had scum. I decided I didn't like whatever lived there.

It dissolved in a shower of sparkles, and an arid plain stretched far away with the legs of a huge statue rising up in the background. Next to them lay a very ugly head with an uglier expression. Then the sun swung down the sky to a glorious sunset, night fell, and the moon rose—no, it wasn't the moon, it was too big, too blue. It was Terra itself, and that wasn't a desert, it was a moonscape. A rocket blasted out of a crater, its exhaust filled the whole scene with fire, and when it faded away, I was looking at an English manor house in the middle of a broad, flat plain that could only be a moor. It was early morning—I could see the new leaves stirring and hear the bird song. Then the whole scene rippled as though it were painted on a piece of silk that a dancer was waving, and it *was* a piece of silk, and the graceful hands waving it showed just at the edge of my vision, then whisked the scarf away to reveal a Siamese palace that grew larger and larger until its portal filled the space, then expanded out of it, and we were in the throne room, its pillars adorned with precious stones, its windows open to the tropical air. But those precious stones sparkled more and more, until the sparkling filled the screen, and . . .

On it went, but only to four more locations. Then the staging area darkened, the store lights brightened again, and Merlo gave a satisfied grunt. "I was right. There's nothing like a Taillefer."

"We both knew that," Nogawa said, sounding bored. "Why didn't you come here early in the day, Merlo?"

Merlo shrugged. "Everybody else does. I figured you'd be out of stock, Frank."

"I'm never out of stock. Shall I wrap it up, or will you eat it here?"

"Send it over to the Tallendar Building." Merlo rose, stretching. "Send the bill there, too, care of Barry Tallendar."

Nogawa nodded. "So the rumor is true. Bon voyage, Merlo."

"See you next year, Frank. Save me some good stuff."

"Only if you get here before noon."

I had edged closer to the console; now I stared. "Merlo! It's only got a ten-scene memory!"

"Yeah," Merlo said, "but it'll connect to an exterior memory unit. We'll buy that next year. And I can load in a different ten scenes every day. Also, it's got fifteen-hundred-gig RAM, and some options on the keyboard you won't believe, that make a week's programming doable in a day. Also, I can put any of those pre-packaged scenes into RAM and modify them any way I want, save it on slab, and load it in on five minutes' notice."

I stared, awed. "You mean I can turn that Lunar rocket into a flying saucer?"

"You can," Merlo said, "when I say you may. You've got a few more items to learn about programming, kid."

Nogawa laughed. I gathered Merlo had just made an understatement.

As Nogawa locked up behind us, I said to Merlo, "What next?"

"A beer and a steak," he said. "Sure, there's a little more to buy, but I can do that on lunch breaks, and they're luxuries, not necessities. It's time to start designing, kid."

10

"So the venture is proceeding well, Barry?"

"Quite well, Ogden, yes." Barry shook the hand of the huge old actor. He had to look up at Wellesley's face, and certainly could not have seen around him. "We're still lacking a costumer, but we have the necessary minimum of actors, a technical director who can also design, and a technical assistant. It will be good to have you with us."

"My pleasure, I'm sure," Ogden wheezed, and gave me a dramatically hearty clap on the shoulder that was, unfortunately, rather feeble. "Be like the old days, eh, Horace?"

"It will indeed, Ogden." Actually, "the old days" weren't quite as old to me as they were to Wellesley—but I knew what he meant. "Touring from town to town with the old Globe Repertory Company." Actually, "town to town" had meant summer in Woodstock, autumn in New York, winter in San Francisco, and spring in Chicago; but we had done a deal of traveling nonetheless, and it had been the entry to the profession for Barry and for me—all due to Ogden's good efforts. He had sponsored us for the company, impressed with our trouper spirit in summer stock, when the juvenile lead had canceled out at the last minute and Barry had taken the role, while I had filled in for Barry as well as filling out my own role in the chorus with some very quick changes indeed. Ogden had been directing, and had invited us to join the company of which he was a member. We did, and played three wonderful years before Barry landed his first leading role, and I broke into Broadway character parts. "The last of the old touring companies, and the first of the new, eh?"

"Quite, quite." Ogden tried to clap me on the shoulder again, then turned his bleary gaze back to Barry. "It does seem to be something of a minimal company, though."

"It is indeed," Barry agreed. "Mass counts for a great deal, when you're attempting to transport it from one solar system to another. Not that we intend to short anyone on personal effects, mind you—but we do have to retain the minimum number of actors and technicians."

"Hire local talent, eh?"

"If we can find any, yes—for the chorus, and for the technical crew, if we need more than we have. Oh, it will be very lean for the first season, Ogden, very lean."

The phrase was perhaps inappropriate in the company of an actor in his seventies who still stood well over six feet, but nonetheless tipped the scales at nearly four hundred pounds. Ogden took it as it was meant, though, and rumbled, "Who else have you signed, eh?"

"A neophyte named Larry Rash for the juvenile, and a young lady who's nonetheless had several seasons in New York, a Lacey Lark, for the ingenue. We've found another young lady who promises to be an excellent comic actor, a Susanne Souci. They are the only new ones, though."

"And only the juvenile sounds to be really inexperienced." Ogden nodded his huge head in satisfaction. "Who are the more seasoned members?"

"Winston Carlton has agreed to join us for a season—"

"Winston!" Ogden opened his eyes wide—a rare occurrence. "But he's been doing so well, in 3DT! Why would he exile himself to the outer darkness?"

I could see the phrase nettled Barry, but Ogden couldn't.

"He does work consistently, but he still longs for the excitement of live theater," Barry said.

" 'Course. Don't we all?"

"Certainly. But Winston has found difficulty persuading theatrical directors to take him seriously. It isn't as though he had starred in a 3DT series and was a certain box-office draw."

"No, no." Ogden stroked his beard, musing. "Seems to be in the wall-screen whenever I turn it on, playing one villain or another, but he does a different series every week."

"Quite. So he expects to reestablish his theatrical credentials with us. He does a marvelous Claudius, Ogden, and is superb as Richard III. Unfortunately, we're not doing either this first season, but he is so effective as virtually any villain—and I don't mind telling you, I've high hopes for the artistic quality of this first season."

" 'Course, with so many old hands, eh?" Ogden said heartily, and clapped Barry on the shoulder.

Barry withstood the aroma of alcohol and smiled in return. "I will take the mature male leads, of course, and Horace will take the older character roles. We will be looking for a costumer who is also a capable actress, and she can take such female character roles as may become necessary—"

"Costumer acting!" Ogden stared, scandalized. "Barry! The unions . . . Oh."

"Precisely." Barry smiled. "The rules are considerably looser, out of town—and there's always the draft."

Ogden smiled from ear to ear. "Theater as it should be! Ah, this will be such a delight, Barry!"

I withstood the wave of stale Scotch that wafted past me and returned his smile warmly. Whatever his shortcomings, his enthusiasm alone would fuel the company spirit—if his spirits didn't act as fuel first.

"But you haven't mentioned the leading lady."

"Ah." Barry laid a finger aside of his nose. "There are several candidates, yes."

He was overstating the case. There were only two ladies in their thirties, both of whom were charming and a delight to work with, both quite attractive and very talented, each willing to leave New York for a year, each for her own reasons. Barry was finding it very difficult to choose between them—difficult because, if Marnie Lulala appeared even at the eleventh hour, we were obliged to take her rather than either of the others. Marnie was beautiful, if fading, and was unfortunately aware of both. Her talent was mammoth, but not as an actress; still, she could do an excellent performance in contemporary parts, if you didn't mind the character being Marnie under a different name.

But she was impossible to work with.

To say that Marnie was arrogant is to acknowledge the limits of the English language. To say that she was a prima donna is accurate, but only because the term leaves wide its scope—it virtually has no limit for selfishness, pettiness, arrogance, conceit, insulting behavior, self-admiration, lack of consideration, expectation of special privileges, or any of the other manifestations of insecurity. She was, in short, a spoiled brat grown up and free to express herself as she wished. The thought of having to work with her, let alone live in the same ship with her, for a full year, was rather horrifying—but for Barry's brother Valdor to continue a more intimate relationship with her would be impossible. My heart went out to the man. I could understand how he could have become involved with her in the first place—she had been, as I've said, very beautiful in years past, and could be extraordinarily charming when she wished; she was, after all, an actress and a professional, no matter how limited. Besides, if she was the price of Valdor's cooperation, we would have to endure it.

Oh, I don't mean that Valdor would not have invested in the company if we hadn't agreed to take Marnie. It is simply that, by doing so, he had done us a favor; now we owed him one. Unfortunately, in our case, that favor had a name.

Barry was seeing Ogden out the door with a clap on the shoulder, a laugh, a reminder that we would begin rehearsals within the week, at 10:00 sharp—and was making sure the old man didn't topple over before he came to the lift door. Once inside, he would be all right—it had tastefully designed handholds. I turned back to tidying up the office, which Valdor had so kindly leant us for private auditions—

not in the Tallendar Building, of course; it was a hotel suite on Forty-second Street.

Barry came back to join me, putting his hard copies in his portfolio and packing away his notebook computer and cubes. I held up a copy of the company register. "It will be good to work with old friends again, Barry."

"It will indeed," Barry agreed. "We are going to be spending a great deal of time together, living in each other's pockets aboard a cramped ship, so we have to be certain that we will all be compatible as well as capable—or as much so as actors can ever be."

I nodded. "If they all get along well enough with us, there is an excellent chance that they will get along with each other. But what of the youngsters?"

Barry nodded. "Larry Rash and Lacey Lark are unknown quantities, of course. I've talked with people who have worked with Lacey, and they say she's pleasant enough, but have their reservations. Still, she has experience and talent, and is willing to undergo our voluntary exile. The Souci girl, though, is a gem, at least according to Waldo Woeful; he directed her in stock last summer. And Julie Jolie played with her in Syracuse last year, in a musical; she says Souci is one of the ones with golden hearts. Her only liability is that her prime pastime is flirting, but she seems to regard it with a playful air, manages to keep her young targets from becoming serious or, if they do, lets them down easily . . . Well. So says report."

"So it says," I agreed. "Have you been able to learn anything of that Publican chap?"

Barry shrugged. "What can you learn about a man whose only credits are college theater twenty years ago?"

"You did check with Morton's Tavern?"

"Yes. They say he has been tending bar with them on weekends these six years, and has a rare gift for distracting drunks with his conversation to the point at which they stop being troublesome. Indeed, they say that he has managed to abort several brawls by joking and camaraderie, finally managing to persuade them all to join him in a song."

"That bespeaks some talent as a performer."

"It does indeed. But if he has been laboring all these years as a hopeful actor, why hasn't anyone in the industry heard of him before this?"

I sighed. "There are many who cling to Manhattan and the vain struggle for a part, Barry, even for decades after it has become clear that they have no hope."

"True, but those folk are usually without talent, and Publican is quite adept. All technique, of course—we'll have to work with him on characterization and motivation, on immersing himself in the role . . ."

"Haven't you just indicated sufficient reason for his never having been cast? Certainly if one also accepts his claim of a tin ear and two left feet."

"He would never have been acceptable for a chorus, that's true. But you would think *someone* would have remembered hearing him audition!"

I shook my head. "The chap's so self-effacing that I can believe it easily. Be honest, Barry—would we even be giving him a second look, if he didn't have such an excellent portfolio for building properties?"

"True," Barry admitted. "He must be a genius at programming, in a small way, and I've no doubt he has supplemented his barkeeping income with odd jobs in the computer industry, with cash payments and no tax records. Still, one is tempted to think of Haroun Al-Raschid roaming the streets of Baghdad in disguise . . ."

"What, an elector infiltrating our ranks, to make certain we are no threat to the mighty government of the Terran Sphere?" I smiled. "Come, Barry! Even if the Interstellar Dominion Electorates did take notice of a fledgling theatrical company, an elector would hardly come to investigate us in person!"

"No, of course not," Barry said, with a small, self-conscious laugh. "There's nothing of the look of the politician or the policeman about him, after all. But a professor, now . . ."

I frowned, gazing off into space. "You have a point. His

manner of speech . . . the hint of the unconventional in his bearing, his style of dress . . ."

"Only the hint," Barry agreed. "If he were truly a man of the theater, it would be flagrant—but to only hint at being unconventional . . . Yes, he could well be a professor on sabbatical."

"But why would he not tell us?"

"Excitement, perhaps? The wish for greater involvement in life? The conviction that we would not cast him if we knew he had a Ph.D.?"

"Barry, you're constructing a character again, and the man isn't even on the printed page! Besides, if he were on sabbatical, he would need a guarantee of being back by a specific date. No, early retirement would far more easily fit the case."

"Quite right." Barry nodded. "A professor who has taken early retirement, because he has developed regrets that he never truly lived. So he has cast away his prior identity and come to involve himself in the flamboyant and glamorous lives of a troupe of strolling players! Do I make my man, Horace?"

"Excellently," I assured him. "So well that you should write a play around him. The only anomalous datum is the tending of bar on the weekends."

"Yes, there is that." Barry frowned. "Odd leisure-time pursuit for an academic, isn't it? On the other hand, what I've heard of professors' pay . . ."

"Except that they usually supplement it as consultants, not purveyors of alcoholic beverages. Still, a man used to restraining drunks from overintoxication might be very useful, with Ogden aboard."

"Yes." Barry frowned. "Ogden is a liability, of course, but he will do well enough, if we can limit his alcohol intake and the scope of his roles."

"Except for Falstaff," I noted. "He'll never forget a word of that part—and he does it so superbly."

"True. A pity we're not doing *Henry IV* this season—but after we've dazzled our rural brethren with contemporary comedies and comedic classics, we can return for a second year with the occasional more elevated offering."

"A consummation devoutly to be wished." I glanced at my watch. "Well! It's almost five, Barry."

He nodded, allowing himself to hope. "In another three minutes, we can declare auditions done and walk out free of Marnie. Of course, even if she decided to join two minutes before lift-off, we'd have to take her—but two minutes before the end of auditions might indicate that she has decided to accept whatever other sort of separation agreement Valdor might have in mind."

"He is so much the gentleman," I sighed. "Why doesn't he just tell her to be gone, weather the blast, and be done with it?"

"There is publicity," Barry offered.

"The gossip sheets? No one in the business community would accept them as meaningful—except to enhance his status, possibly. And she certainly has no grounds for legal action, considering the roster of her former beaux. No, Barry, if Valdor is allowing her this means of saving face, it must simply be to his own generosity that we must ascribe the blame."

"The ladies always have been his weakness," Barry sighed. "He cannot bear to hurt one of them; still thinks of them as fragile, vulnerable things. Memories of Mother, no doubt."

"Two minutes," I noted, watching my watch. "One minute and fifty seconds . . . One minute and forty-five . . ."

The door opened.

In came a Vendici dress with a sable wrapped about its collar, and Marnie inside.

She was forty and aging fast, but the way she moved still pulled my eye about so fast I almost heard it click. Her chestnut hair was coiffed in elegance, adorned by a hat in the epitome of fashion; her large brown eyes were half-lidded, perhaps in contempt; and her full red lips were pressed tight in annoyance. Inspected individually, each feature of her face was quite ordinary; but put together and infused with the magic that was Marnie, they somehow became intensely desirable.

"So good to see you again, Barry." Her tone indicated a longing to attend his funeral.

"Ah, Marnie, what a pleasure!" He swept off his hat in a bow, caught her fingertips, tested the resistance and decided not to kiss them, and rose with a sparkling eye, all without the slightest hint of dismay. "You are resplendent, as always."

"Of course, and it takes a deal of time. I hope this interview will be worth it, Barry."

"Interview?" Barry's eyebrows shot up. "Marnie! If you are willing to grace this company with your presence, you know you have but to indicate it in the slightest, and the reception will be rapturous!"

Laying it on a bit thick, I thought—and so did she. Her eyes glittered with antagonism, but she knew the situation even better than we did, so she said, "Of course I wish to join you, Barry. How could I resist a chance for such adventure?"

She certainly had a way with words—or with the tone in which she said them, at least. She had progressed from implying a wish that he drop dead, to the implication that she was immersing herself in a year's residence in the Outer Hells. I had to admire Valdor—if the rumors were true, he had put up with her for three years.

"It is settled, then," she sighed. "When do we depart, Barry?"

"In a month, Marnie. The date isn't exact yet, but it should be just after Christmas."

"An excellent gift," she drawled.

"And an excellent celebration of the new year." There was sudden irony in Barry's tone, and a glitter in his eye. "The birth of a new year, and of a new company, eh, Marnie?"

Her glare was silent fury, but, as I've said, she had no choice. "Of course, Barry! A celebration, indeed!" Her tone indicated that it would be a wake, preferably his. Valdor had sent her into exile, and had the means to enforce it. Not that he would be violent, of course, but he could ensure that she would be refused entry to the social circles she most craved and would dwindle in forgotten solitude.

The swords had been drawn. It promised to be an interesting bout. I only regretted that it would last so long and might injure a dear friend.

"Now if you'll excuse me, I have an urgent appointment." She swirled out without waiting for an answer.

"She knows how to make an exit," Barry sighed.

"Pity she didn't make it more thoroughly," I opined. "You are ever the gentleman, Barry."

"Of course, Horace—especially since manners can cut more sharply than knives, eh?"

"A pity," I sighed. "I had almost begun to let myself hope for one of the others. Surely she did not intend for me to feel such disappointment, Barry?"

"Of course she did." Be it said to his credit, Barry enjoyed a good fight. This one, however, did not promise to be good. "Please excuse her ignoring your existence, Horace."

"Of course. It gives me leave to ignore hers. I was quite fearful she might insist on reading for us, Barry."

"That would have been a trial," Barry admitted, "especially since I brought a cutting from *Hedda Gabler* just for her."

"Barry! You know she would have done abominably!"

"Precisely. It struck me as a good opportunity to remind her of her own shortcomings."

"Surely you did not think to induce humility in her."

"No, not really," Barry sighed. "Fortunately, she does well enough in anything written after 2200."

I shook my head. "Amazing that you were able to treat her with such courtesy."

Barry shrugged. "She *was* a star, after all."

"Unfortunately," I said, "she thinks she still is."

Barry shrugged. "Who knows? She may make a comeback—when *we* come back, to Terra. Well, we're all packed up, Horace, and she has had the courtesy not to require us to unpack our scripts and noteboards. Shall we go?"

"Blarney's awaits," I agreed.

We had just ordered when Ramou shambled up to the table. "Ah, Ramou!" I reached up to clasp his hand. "Do sit down and join us!"

"Yeah, thanks." He sat down mechanically, staring at the tabletop.

Barry frowned. "What's the matter?"

"Consoles," Ramou mumbled. "Components . . . Miracles . . ."

Barry looked at him in amusement. "I think our young friend has just had his first exposure to the wonders of modern theatrical scenery."

"Scenery!" Ramou exploded. "That was no scenery, it was a set of alternate realities! It was stupefying! It was echoic! It was enchantment!"

"And you are still stupefied and enchanted," I interpreted. "Do you believe you can come down from the clouds long enough to place an order for some food?"

"Food?" The trance was gone, and Ramou was back in the here-and-now. "Yeah, sure! But I can pay for myself, this time."

"Not with your producer present," Barry said firmly. "We'll call it a working meal. Did Merlo find anything, Mr. Lazarian?"

Ramou's eyes glazed again, and I feared we were in for another recitation of wonders—but we were saved by the bell.

Or by the sound of the 3DT, rather.

I frowned, looking up, irritated. Here I'd been about to tell Barry and Horace all about the wonderful gadgets Merlo had showed me, when the noise from the wall-screen interrupted. Horace frowned, looking up, and I suddenly realized the conversation had died. Well, not died, but it was definitely ailing.

I looked up, too. Elector Rudders was back on the screen again, his craggy face yawing with its pitbull bite. "So, my fellow electors, it is absolutely vital that we restrain the covetous urge to sexual decadence that besets our society! Only when the producers of these obscene theatricals—pornographic in their very liveness, in the lewdness of actresses' actual fleshly presence, fairly begging to be stroked and caressed—yes, and of the immediate and intruding presence of male actors, too, churning up emotions of turbulent lust in the breasts of our wives and children . . ."

"Why, he is talking about us!" Horace stared at the screen as though the elector were a cobra, which may not have been too far off.

"Only when these insinuating and provocative theatricals have been banished, and the rulers of the theater have sought a regeneration of moral fiber, will our society be safe from them! Only when the producers of these ominous spectacles have removed all elements of decadence and sexual innuendo, when they have purged their stages of the unprovoked and disruptive violence which they portray . . ."

"What violence?" I snorted. "The gun in *Hedda Gabler*?"

Horace looked up at me in surprise. "Yes, I'm sure he would include that weapon—but, hush, please, Ramou. I must hear this."

All of them had to, in fact. Every actor in the place was silent, though I saw some beet-red faces and some mouthing of words I wouldn't want to repeat.

". . . when their violence has been restricted to that which is real, such as friendly fistfights and battle scenes that show the selfless and gallant valor of the men of our armed forces in glorious strife. They must no longer undermine the traditional values of our culture; they must refrain from questioning the rightness of Christianity, of heroic men of the past such as Luther and Calvin—indeed, the rightness of religion itself! They must cease to stir up sentiment against the established order and the rightfully ordained government of the Terran Sphere! Such seditious and traitorous language must not be tolerated!"

Somewhere in the background of the Assembly, a few voices were shouting "Here! Here!" and some odd words which I took to be the same thing in other languages. It shook me, but the elector fairly seemed to swell at the sound. "Therefore, my fellow electors, we must rally the forces of tradition, of duly constituted government, to restrain the excesses of these immoral play-actors!" He sat back, done for the moment, and the crowd in the bar erupted into Babel.

"What does he think he's doing?"

"He can't mean it!"

"Are we moving back to the Dark Ages?"

It went on like that for a while, everybody talking at once, and I couldn't for the life of me figure out who was listening, especially since none of them seemed to be talking to me. Finally, it began to calm down a bit, and somebody got around to asking the key question:

"Why us?"

A woman of impeccable grooming and uncertain age shrugged and said, "Why not?"

"Because we don't have a mass audience! How many voters are they going to reach by trying to squash live theater?"

"A point," Horace said, "but it has its converse: How many votes will they *lose* by going after us?"

Everyone got quiet and thoughtful at that, and a well-groomed man in his forties said, "That's right. He did raise quite a backlash to his attack on 3DT, didn't he?"

"Only when he attacked the top-rated series," Barry qualified. "People were delighted to hear him rant against the immorality of 3DT in general—made them feel better for overlooking the issue, I suppose—but when he tried to leach their favorite comedy, they rose up in vociferous protest."

"Not that he heard them," a fat and somewhat sloppy man with a red nose said. "Only the pollsters did."

Barry nodded. "But Rudders hears the pollsters."

"But," said the Sweetheart Upstairs, who couldn't have been as young as she was trying to look, "but isn't the whole point of his attacks to gain him publicity? Before he attacked the music industry, he waited to see which recordings sold well enough so that people would pay attention when he ranted—and when they complained too loudly about him, he shifted to the 3DT as a more visible target, if you will pardon the pun."

"I won't," Horace said, "since it was unavoidable. Then by attacking the top-rated series, he gained even more publicity—but now he needs to convert that notoriety into support, and he has the masses feeling guilty about enjoying a show that authority has told them is immoral."

"So," the woman said slowly, "he offers them a target they don't care about, and tells them it's even more immoral than any of the 3DT shows . . ."

"But we're not!" a man at the end of the table protested.

"Of course not," Horace agreed. "Who said he had to tell the truth? It's never been a qualification for public office before."

"But he tells them we are," the Mordant Emperor said, "and they turn in righteous wrath upon the theater, thereby expiating their guilt while preserving the innuendo-filled 3DT comedies and violence-prone detective shows they so adore."

"Which means," Barry said gravely, "that he may very well succeed in censoring the professional theater."

"Surely New York won't let him!"

Barry nodded. "New York City is well aware of the theater's contribution to attracting tourists. Elector Rudders seems to have ignored their importance to the gold flow, but Manhattan certainly hasn't. Yes, I think we can count on the support of the mayor and the council."

"At least the borough council," someone qualified.

"That much, at least," Barry agreed. "Still, it behooves us to minimize his cause for complaint."

There was a deathly silence. Then the well-groomed woman said, "You're not thinking of capitulating!"

"Not really, no," Barry agreed. "We must reinforce that by urging the producers to present a solid front, and to issue a refutation to the news services. Still, we would strengthen that position by showing some sign of . . ."

"Compliance?" someone gasped. "To mere rhetoric? To empty attempts at pressure?"

"They may not be empty soon," Barry said, with some irony. "Still, I was about to say 'responsibility.' "

"I consider my productions to have been quite responsible, Barry," said a jowly man with a scowl and a diamond.

"As they certainly have been, Leander," Barry assured him. "But we are not the only producers on Broadway, and some of our colleagues, lamentably, have pursued titillation without regard to its moral context."

"All right, so they've gone for cheap thrills," the fat man in the green coat said. "But if the audience wants to see it, who is Rudders to tell them not to?"

"The elector for Eastern North America," Barry replied, "and the head of the LORDS party, which happens to include nearly every plutocrat and magnate on Terra."

There was an uncomfortable silence. Everyone knew what that meant in terms of influence, and just how silently but legally that influence could be brought to bear.

"Just what kind of 'responsible behavior' were you thinking about, Barry?" the jowly man asked.

"We can't really afford to bring along a full chorus in our first season," Barry sighed. "I was planning to drop *Man of La Mancha* from the bill anyway."

There was a chorus of shocked protest.

"But Barry," the grande dame said, "*Man of La Mancha*! Who could possibly protest to a classic drawn from a classic!"

"Elector Rudders," Barry answered. "Aldonza's 'I Was Born in a Ditch' is just the kind of stuff out of which he could brew a tempest in a teapot. And the rape scene is . . ."

"Never mind." The grande dame shuddered. "I take your point."

"As do I." The jowly man looked distinctly unhappy. "I

had been considering a rather innovative venture, but I'll have to speak with the playwright about it."

"If it's Sandy," the sweetheart said, "he won't speak."

"I know how he feels," the man sighed, "but we may have to wait till the climate is more propitious."

I think he meant, until the heat was off.

"Time to revive the classics again," Barry said, "and only the ones that have convincing moral arguments behind them." He stood up. "But fascinating as the topic is, I fear we must leave it for this evening. We have rehearsal in the morning. Mr. Lazarian?"

"Uh . . . Yes! Mr. Tallendar." It took me a second to realize he was talking to me.

"Could you take charge of having an urn of coffee and some Danish ready at the rehearsal hall?"

"Of course, Mr. Tallendar!"

"Then let's depart, lad," Barry said, with a flourish toward the door. Horace rose, too, and turned to follow Barry out. I trailed along, waiting for a chance to ask Horace where I was supposed to find an urnful of coffee.

What can I say? That a coffee urn was more important to me than Rudders? Darn right it was—politics is vital, but making a living is pretty important, too.

11

So all of a sudden, we were starting rehearsals. I thought Barry was panicking without cause—but when we got home that night, Horace punched up the news channel, just in case we'd missed anything that day, and there it was, the third story in.

"Elector Rudders . . ."

We both stopped what we were doing and swiveled to face the screen. Amazing, how the man could command our attention.

". . . introduced into committee today a bill which would set up a commission to oversee the production of new plays, and would require a license from that commission before the play could be presented to the public. The bill also includes a list of types of content the elector deems to be against the public interest."

Horace groaned. "Not the Licensing Act again!"

I was curious, but my question could wait. I stayed riveted to the screen. There had to be more.

There was. "While the bill is under discussion," the announcer went on, "the elector asked for precautions."

Suddenly, Rudders was there, his face filling the whole screen, as solid and alive as though he were a real presence in our lives—which, in a way, he was. "During the discussion of my Licensing Bill, we must take care that prurient and vested interests do not seize the moment as their final opportunity to thresh their profits from the souls of our young and our decadent. I therefore call upon all the cities of Terra, but most especially on the metropolises of New

York and London, to issue temporary executive orders demanding that all theaters close their doors and cease to do business."

Horace moaned more loudly, and the announcer was back. "We asked the mayor of New York City if he would consider cooperating with Elector Rudders's request."

Mayor Sanchez was there on the screen, proud and hungry for battle as an Aztec warrior, his eyes flashing into the cameras. "With all due respect to the illustrious elector, the city of New York has a long record of defending the rights of freedom of expression and freedom of assembly, and will continue to do so as long as I am mayor. Our theaters will stay open. In fact, tonight I'm seeing a production called *The Boys in the Back Room*. I invite the elector to join me."

They cut back to the announcer the instant Sanchez had finished saying "me," but not quite quickly enough, because some people out of the camera's range had begun to laugh. Good reason: *The Boys in the Back Room* was a story about political corruption in New York, back in the heyday of Tammany Hall—only Boss Tweed bore an astonishing resemblance to Elector Rudders, and his cronies behaved just like the LORDS party in the Assembly, and the issues Tammany Hall was pushing for were the exact same as several of the laws passed in the General Assembly last year. It won a slow smile from Horace, and he killed the screen before the announcer was quite done with his tag line.

"That," he said, "is the sort of production Rudders is really out to eliminate—and is the true reason for the freedoms of speech and press guaranteed by the old Bill of Rights."

"The right to make fun of politicians?"

"That, but more generally, to criticize them and their policies, and present the alternatives. Open public discussion of the issues, my lad—if you can persuade the audience to listen. That was what was happening in England, before the Licensing Act was passed in the early 1700s."

"Licensing Act?" I frowned. "This isn't the first time?"

"Oh, no, only its latest appearance! You see, my boy,

everyone really approves of censorship, underneath it all— as long as it's our enemies who are being censored. We all want to keep our opponents from saying things we don't like. *Our* opinions, however, should be free from the slightest vestige of censorship. But the only way to protect our own right to free speech is to protect everybody else's, and the people in power always forget that. So once they've gained office, they begin to try to silence the opposition— and if they're in the government, they may actually be able to do it. So there is constant pressure to limit open discussion, and it always comes in by decrying the immorality of the opposition's statements."

I frowned. "But can't they eliminate the really putrid stuff without touching the political and cultural criticisms? There has to be a point of balance, after all, some range of moderation."

He looked up at me, surprised. "Why, wherever did you learn such a vital philosophical concept?"

"From Sensei. Can't they set some kind of sensible limits?"

"To be sure, they can—the social scientists have shown us, time and again, which kinds of content damage the minds and behavior of the audience. But the politicians won't accept their findings, because some of them always inhibit what the politicians want to do—or the special interest groups they represent."

I frowned. "Can't they set some sort of minimum principles? Sort of a fence around a great big wide corral?"

"To be sure, they can—but who's to set them, and who's to implement them? If I wished to, I could ban *The Boys in the Back Room* on the grounds of immorality—it is rather open about the ways in which the nineteenth-century politicians spent their leisure hours. Any sort of valid code rests on the responsibility of those who use it—but that responsibility can be just as well exercised by the artists and the producers, as by the politicians."

I frowned. "But they don't."

"Who? The politicians? Or the producers?"

"Yes."

"Ah." Horace gave me a wide, sad smile. "There is the nubbin of it, lad—there will always be those who take advantage of their position, who abuse the media of communication. But once the politicians gain the power to restrict those freedoms, it's almost impossible to make them give it up. The producers are much more flexible." He shook his head, sighing. "However, there is always the danger of the people willingly giving the government that power if, once waked from the spells of our theatrical illusions, they find themselves impoverished or damaged. That is the specter that will forever haunt us—and therefore must we always be wary of our limits." He looked up at me with a smile. "Which brings us to our rehearsal tomorrow, doesn't it? For the expression is in the work, and if we do not do the work, we forfeit the right. So let us each find his bed, and arise vigorous and eager—for as Carnegie said, 'My heart is in the work!' "

I was there the next morning, bright and early and with a whole urn full of coffee. They began to straggle in about ten o'clock, looking bleary and feeble, and I was the most popular guy in town. They each picked up a doughnut and a cup of coffee, except for those who preferred tea, and I had that brewed and ready. Lacey choked on it and accused me of brewing substitute coffee.

"I'm sorry," I said. "Never done it, myself. It's just the catering service."

The catering service was twelve feet wide and eight feet high, was two doors down from Tridement, and accepted coins, but it preferred to have a credit card in the slot.

They sat around the wide, flimsy-looking table in chairs that looked even more flimsy, trying to make conversation that nobody really felt up to. It was my first encounter with a theater morning—too little sleep after being up too late the night before. But what the hey, that's show biz.

Then Barry came in, looking fresh and dapper and earning the instant enmity of every single member of his cast, though of course they couldn't show it. In fact, they all perked up and looked fresh and dapper themselves—after all, they were actors, weren't they?

"Good morning to you all." Barry tried to sound sympathetic but couldn't quite keep the triumph and excitement out of his voice as he went on. "Welcome to the first rehearsal of the Star Repertory Company. We are met to commence our life together, though in no manner greater than rehearsal, at the moment. This morning, my companions, we will rehearse Swathe's *Filters and Phyltres,* one of the best of the comedies in the modern repertoire. Now, you should all have found copies of the script at your place at the table; I don't need to remind you to write in your name . . ."

Everyone slipped out an erasable stylus and began personalizing.

"There are, of course, several other members of our company who will not be attending rehearsals for this play," Barry added while they scribbled. "They will join us to read through the rest of the plays in our first season's bill, and we will rehearse with them all *en route* to Alpha Centauri's New Venus."

They finished writing and looked up, the young ones with polite attention, the older ones with affable boredom.

"Now then—our cast is as follows: Ms. Lark will play Nancy Naif, Mr. Rash will play Colin Callow; Ms. Souci will take the part of Flora Flirt, and Mr. Wellesley will portray Codger."

" 'Course," the massive old actor chuckled. "Type casting, eh?"

Barry looked up, mildly surprised. "Glad to see you in such good spirits, this morning, Ogden."

"None but the best," the veteran assured him.

I believed it. I'd seen him pour a generous dollop from the flask hidden inside his jacket, and the hair had grown into a full-sized dog and bitten him again. He definitely had the most aromatic coffee in the room.

Barry smiled, nicely hiding his misgivings, and went on.

"Mr. Burbage will play Adage, and Mr. Carlton will take the part of Sinister."

"My public would be disappointed if I were anything else," murmured the Mordant Emperor and all-purpose villain.

"Just so, though I certainly shall cast you against type in at least two productions," Barry promised.

"Two!" The famous eyebrows went up. "My contract only stipulates one."

"Which was good of you," Barry agreed, "but that was indeed one of your reasons for joining our enterprise, and I intend to fulfill it past the letter. You shall play Lodar in *Alchemy,* and the Sad Man in *Didn't He Ramble.*"

A murmur went around the table, and Winston beamed, if a face that diabolical can be said to. "Ingenious, Barry! A touch of the sinister, but not a true villain! Shouldn't the part by rights be Ogden's, though?"

"Not in my interpretation of it," Barry returned, "and Ogden deserves the same one-show rest that I am trying to accord the rest of the company." He turned to look around the whole table. "We are producing four plays for our first season—four nights will certainly be enough for any colonial city; I doubt the population will support more. Out of those four, I shall try my best to see that each of you appears in only three, so that you may each have a day's rest."

"Why, that's very considerate of you, Barry," Ogden rumbled, but Lacey and Larry didn't look so sure.

"Ms. Lulala will play Majesta." Barry glanced at his watch. "She has a late entrance, so she should be joining us at an opportune moment."

Another murmur went around the table, though I could have sworn I didn't see anyone's lips move. They were uncertain as to whether he was being sarcastic, or trying to cover for Ms. Lulala—at least, *I* was. So we didn't know how to react.

" 'And here, I hope, we have a play fitted,' " Barry misquoted. "Now, this is a twenty-second-century comedy, ladies and gentlemen, so try to put yourselves into the mindset of an actor of three centuries back. Let us begin with act one. Ms. Lark?"

I found out later that the neophytes were still holding back, waiting to see what kind of a director Barry was. The old hands, however, were relaxed and open—they didn't have to impress anybody, since they all knew each other's faults and strengths, and already knew what kind of director Barry was. There's the supermarionette director, the absolute dictator, who has it all worked out in advance, down to the finest inflection in the smallest character's voice, and tells each of his cast what to do and where to go—and they wish they could tell *him* where to go, if he's a really sarcastic and belittling sort, which some of them apparently are. At the other end of the scale, there's the Arthur Hopkins–style director, who lets (in fact, demands that) the actors make it all up themselves—characterization, blocking, interpretation—and just sits back and watches and occasionally says, "No, that isn't working, let's try this," and takes each of the actors aside for a chat about his character and how he's playing it now and then, and the actors are going crazy wondering, "When is he going to start directing?" Then, suddenly, they realize that opening night is only a week away, but son of a gun, that whole play has suddenly pulled together and is positively glowing like a finely cut jewel that's waiting to be polished.

And, of course, there are all sorts of directors in between—it isn't a polarity, it's a sliding scale. I got the impression that most of them are somewhere near the middle, telling the actors how they want the show to look, but open to the individual actor's creative input. The only questions are "How open?" and "How bossy?" That's why the first few rehearsals are always a matter of feeling each other out, so that director and actor know how to respond to each other—and to the other actors, too, because the director pretty well establishes the context within which the actors have to interact.

So Lacey started out with life and energy, but far from her fullest spate. "Well, this is pretty ridiculous! He told me he'd be here at seven o'clock—I timed it carefully to be ready at seven-fifteen—then I stalled as much as I could, but there's just so many times you can take off your lipstick and put it on again, and wouldn't you know it, here I am, all ready, and not a sign of him! Seven forty-five, too—I just hope he told the restaurant to put back the reservation!"

It sounded pretty contrived to me, but in Literature 103 (required, engineers), the prof had told us that this scene was a model of exposition. If that was the model, I'd hate to see the real thing.

Barry knocked on the table.

"Oh, there he is!" Lacey did a nice blend of Righteous Indignation and Gloating Anticipation of Slow Torture of Hapless Victim. "He's going to spend the rest of the evening being sorry he tried this!" She pantomimed opening a door as she caroled sweetly, "Oh, good evening, Colin dearest! How nice of—"

The real door hissed open, and Marnie paraded in, complete with fur stole, dark glasses, and small nervous dust mop of dog. "I'm dreadfully sorry to be late, darlings, but you know how tediously cautious these chauffeurs can be. Really, Barry, you ought to contract with a service whose drivers know the meaning of the term 'hurry!' " She looked around with a smile of slow and malignant relish. "Good morning, all."

The younger actors molded their faces into carefully pleasant and properly respectful lines. Ogden grunted something neutral, and Winston rose like the true gentleman he was, nodding his head in greeting. "Ah, Marnie, still your old self! How appropriate to see you."

The malice flashed into pure anger that was gone almost before I could be sure I'd seen it—but if I had, she'd meant me to. She was a pro, after all. Then, all syrupy sweetness, she crooned, "What a delight, Winston! Really, you're looking amazingly well, after all those 3DT epics."

Winston's smile deepened with amusement, but the younger cadre seemed nervous. Before he could try for another thrust, though, Barry was on his feet, all courtesy.

"Good morning, Marnie. Mr. Lazarian, would you take Ms. Lulala's wrap? Have a seat, my dear. Coffee? Tea?"

"Coffee, black." She shrugged out of the wrap without waiting to see if I had it and shoved the nasty little varmint at me. I caught him, surprised, then recovered and swiveled him around so that the end with the teeth pointed away from me. He looked back over his shoulder at me with two angry yaps ending in a growl, wriggling furiously, but he couldn't reach me. Barry gave me a quick look of apology, and I found myself smiling to tell him it was all right—me, who two days ago would have turned my back on anybody who tried to treat me like an object! The man had magic.

I held the dog like a football in one arm while I found an empty chair for Ms. Lulala's fur, half expecting it to turn and try to bite me, too. Then I drew a cup for her and slid it in from her right. The dog yapped furiously and wriggled, trying to reach his mistress, but she was already buried in the script, and the two of us could have been chartreuse elephants with mayhem in mind for all she cared. I took Small-and-Nasty over to a corner to try to set things straight with him, wondering why on earth she had brought the little monster to rehearsal.

To prove she could get away with it, of course. Rank hath its privileges—and hers, as I've said before, were pretty rank.

I set the toothy dust mop on the floor, and sure enough, he lunged for my hand, jaws gaping an inch or so. I snatched my hand out of his way, stroked him twice on the back, then scratched behind the ears as he writhed around trying to bite. That made him angrier; he snarled and snapped, no doubt under delusions he was a wolf, and Ms. Lulala looked up in midline to do some snapping herself. "Don't you dare hurt my Wing-Ding!"

I was tempted, but I only said, "Just petting him, ma'am."

"He doesn't like to be petted!" she cried in anger, but just then, Wing-Ding closed his eyes and slumped down, succumbing to the pleasure of the ear rub. She stared, then clamped her mouth shut, giving me a glare of fury—but she couldn't very well tell me to hurt him and make him angry again, could she?

She turned back to her script, giving the next line some added vehemence, and Barry said, "I don't quite think that's the subtext we're looking for here, Marnie, though the energy level is excellent." She gave him a quick glare, then went back into the script.

Hey, I like dogs—and cats, and canaries, and ferrets, and . . . Well you get the idea. I've always had a way with animals—and it looked as though I'd need it.

"But you can't mean that I have to move out in five days!" Lacey whinnied, or rather, I should say, Nancy did, and Marnie—or maybe I should say, Majesta? No, I decided it was definitely Marnie—pursued relentlessly. " 'To the landlord belongs the door latch'—and if you're not out of this apartment by midnight Friday, my dear, I'll change the lock on it!" She slapped her hand on the table, no doubt to indicate a door closing—I knew the play from class, but also from 3DT.

And the door shot open, and a rotund voice boomed, "Here they are, in their nest of sin!"

We all looked up, startled, then on the verge of panic—for there he was himself, jowls, eyebrows, and all—Elector Rudders, with half the New York City news corps behind him.

In the forefront, of course, were the two guys with camera-bumps on their shoulders, servoed to their helmets—and those helmets read "IDE PIA"—the Public Information Agency for the Interstellar Dominion Electorates. The elector had brought his own flacks, including the sharp-eyed guy without a camera but with a dictation mike next to his lips, giving himself a running commentary on our reactions to the elector. He'd oversee the editing of the camera ops' recordings, adding his own voice-over interpretation of the event, which, to say the least, would be as unfavorable to us as it could be. Then the PIA IDE would offer the finished story to every network in the world—all the worlds, in fact, though the colonies would get it months late—and if Rudders was involved, it would be important enough to make the evening newsfeed. That meant that every station would have to show it, or lose viewers— whether they liked him or hated him, the people at home loved to watch Rudders; he always put on a good show. Which meant that, wherever he went, the news services had to send their own crews to shoot and present their own story about the event. If they didn't, they'd have to feed us *his* version of the event, which they would rather have died than do. Professional jealousy, more than anything else, I think—but the upshot was that, where Rudders and his trained flacks went, the news services had to follow.

How do I come by that opinion? Well, the media have always fascinated me, all the media—but especially 3DT, probably because of the gadgetry. The gimmicks got me interested enough to read a few books, and I added that to what I saw on the screen, and drew my own conclusions.

Rudders wasn't depending on the audience to draw *theirs,* though. He was in full spate already, turning to the cameras and orating. "Here, in this haven nestled amid the decadent luxuries of New York City's Times Square, these actors have met to plot the latest corruption of the Terran public." He turned on Barry, who had risen to meet him with a polite smile. "You, sir! The notorious Barry Tallendar! Are you not the leader of this crew of cultural subversives?"

"I have that honor," Barry said gravely.

Rudders reddened; somebody was resisting him, and that was not to be tolerated. "There can be no honor among thieves, and surely you steal the cash from the pockets of the good souls who flock to the magnet of your perversions!"

"Not at all," Barry murmured. "Most of them use credit."

There was a laugh among the press corps, quickly smothered, and a short and strangled chuckle from somewhere among the actors. Rudders calmed, instantly cool, eyes narrowed and gauging as he realized that he wasn't up against somebody who was going to try to refute him with logic, but against a master showman who was threatening to upstage him and make him look like a clown. He cut the rhetoric and got down to business. "And what is the latest depravity you seek to foist upon your audience this season?"

"Swathe's *Filters and Phyltres,* a farce three centuries old," Barry said easily. "We intend to open on—"

"Corruption!" The elector cut Barry off as soon as he realized the director was going after free publicity—after all, that was supposed to be *his* prerogative. "And what would you say is the theme of this piece of moral sedition, Mr. Tallendar?"

"Why," Barry said, "that one must never confuse lust with love, but the young are in great danger of doing just that."

Rudders was actually speechless for a few seconds, turning pale as he realized that Barry had just made a sex comedy sound moral.

And come to think of it, it was.

"Lies!" the elector erupted, and whirled about to orate into the cameras again. "You see how these actors pervert even the noblest of intentions, how they can twist the meaning of even the most stringent of examinations into the semblance of pure intention! We must never make the mistake of underestimating their ability to seduce and lead astray! Nay, let us leave them in their den of iniquity, and shut the door upon them!" He suited the action to the word, marching toward the doorway with his flock of cameras retreating before him, and punctuating his final sentence by slamming the door. I was amazed; one of his men must have disabled the automatic control while none of us was looking. It was supposed to be unslammable.

The room was quiet for about two heartbeats. Then, as one, every actor around that table rose to his or her feet, applauding wildly—even Marnie.

Barry turned back to them, bowing, a glint in his eye and a smile of amusement on his lips—but of something more, too, some gleam of wild excitement that I recognized. It was the way I felt in the middle of a good fight.

"Thank you, my dear friends," he said as the applause subsided, "but I fear we have won only the set, not the match, and that even this shall be presented as a defeat to the mass of viewers at home."

"If it's presented at all," Marnie retorted. "He did not leave, Barry—he fled."

"But saving face as he went," Horace qualified.

"Quite true, quite true," Ogden wheezed. "Knew you'd steal the show from him if he stayed a moment longer, what? Oh, well played indeed, my good fellow!"

"Why, how kind of you, Ogden." Barry resumed his seat. "But let us not underestimate the fellow. He is still quite a danger to us."

"Yes, quite," Winston said, with a diabolical smile. "He's going to have to get rid of us one way or another, now— we're too likely to show him up as the ass he is."

A shadow crossed Barry's face, but all he said was, "Then let us be ready to perform at a moment's notice. Take five, my friends—Mr. Lazarian, the coffeepot, if you will? Then we will regather to continue act one."

I glanced at my ring-watch and felt the stirring of concern. I had invited Ramou to join us for dinner at Blarney's, an invitation I had been sure he would accept—but dinner was past, and so was the post-prandial liqueur, and there was still no sign of him.

"Surely there is no cause for anxiety, Horace."

I looked up, startled. "Is it that obvious?"

Barry hadn't quite been at his most ebullient this evening, himself. He had sat quietly while the laughter and repartee went on about him, only interjecting the occasional comment and giving an amused smile where ordinarily he would have laughed quite loudly. It was the measure of the man that he could notice my anxiety in the midst of his own.

"Obvious only to one who knows you well," Barry assured me. "It's the lad, isn't it? Ramou Lazarian."

I turned away. "I know—it's none of my affair."

"He is a man grown," Barry agreed, "and from what you

told me of your meeting, more than able to take care of himself."

"True enough," I agreed.

"But you have this avuncular streak in you," Barry sighed. "Adopting stray kittens isn't always good policy, Horace."

"I know," I said, "but I can't stand to see the poor things suffer alone, if I could have prevented it. I never let them come too close, though, Barry. Besides, who are you to speak? I could mention a charity case or two on your own record."

"True enough," Barry agreed in his turn, "so I know whereof I speak. Besides, Horace, I had hoped for your company this evening. I have a meeting that I would like you to attend, as my assistant."

"Oh?" I looked up, surprised. "What meeting would trouble the director after hours?"

"Not the director, but the producer. Those of us with more than a few years' experience are having a quiet conference tonight."

I felt the first breath of danger; it enlivened me considerably. "The topic?"

"A response to Rudders." Barry stood up. "Can you leave word for the young man with one of our friends, Horace?"

"Surely." I turned to Harry. "Harry, you know that young chap we've taken on as assistant?"

"The one who has been going home with you?" Harry gave me a knowing smile.

He *would* see it that way. "Entirely innocent," I assured him. "Tell him to have supper and put it on my tab, will you? And to wait for me here."

"Why, surely," Harry said easily. "Glad to oblige, old man."

"Good of you, I'm sure." I stood up. "And, Harry—*don't* offer to take him home yourself. Believe me, he's not braced for that sort of thing." I turned to Barry. "Shall we?"

* * *

Barry and I stepped through the doors and back into the nineteeth century. The ceiling was low, the beams were blackened with decades of tobacco smoke, and the walls were hung with a vasty collection of clay pipes, varying from short stubby Irish models to long-stemmed Dutch churchwardens. The maitre d', at least, was live and human. He managed something between a nod and a bow. "Good evening, Mr. Tallendar. Your party is waiting. If you would step this way?"

"I know where the private room is, Joseph," Barry said with a smile.

The maitre d' glanced at the mob behind us. "It would be a kindness, Mr. Tallendar. I regret that there is only myself to conduct our patrons tonight."

"Not at all. Shall we, Horace?"

We did. I followed Barry past the arch and into the smaller chamber, shutting the door behind us.

The room was richly appointed, and the table was almost filled; I had to squeeze a bit to get my chair in. "Gentlemen." Barry nodded at them all. "A pleasure to see you again."

"Odd seeing you sitting with the producers, Tallendar," a lean man said with a gray smile. "I'm more used to negotiating with your agent."

"Kind of you to say it, Clement. Still, I have ventured to enter your realm, and with a repertory company—I trust you're aware of it?"

"Yes, and you're mad," a stocky man in a suit worth a month's living said. Cornelius; I recognized him from Equity negotiations. "Idea can't possibly show a profit. Have any idea of the cost of starship fuel?"

Barry nodded. "Water is indeed at a premium, once we're off-planet; fortunately, fusion engines don't need anything else. Still, I expect that the cost of maintaining human beings in relative comfort will be considerably more dear—which is why I'm dropping the musical from the bill."

"Oh, *that's* why, is it?" Dandor smiled, amused. "The fact that the musical in question just happens to be the sort of thing that Rudders can make hay out of is just a coincidence."

"Certainly," Barry said, with a return smile of his own. "After all, he could mow an even greater crop from *Didn't He Ramble,* couldn't he?"

"If he had the wit to understand what its content truly is," Clement demurred.

"Now, gentlemen," Barry murmured. "After all, the fight is certainly the sort of wholesome fistfight he was discussing, isn't it?"

"Oh, quite," Cornelius agreed, "especially since authority wins."

"And Bonnie is scarcely as sympathetic as Aldonza," Leander concurred.

"It also has no need of a chorus." Barry's smile was still in place. "So some action is, of course, laudable . . ."

"Don't worry, old man," Frederick grumbled. "We're all going at our scripts with a blue pencil. But the principle, hah? We must assert the principle of free expression!"

"I heartily agree," Barry said.

"Still," Dandor interjected, "it wouldn't do any harm to condemn irresponsible conduct, scenes of questionable taste being included for sheer titillation . . ."

"Stuff it, Dandor!" Cornelius growled. "You know I make sixty percent of my profits from shows with sexy lyrics!"

"I wasn't intending to mention any specific subgenre— but we could indict the presentation of plays solely for profit, mention that there are more noble motives."

"What are we, public theater?" Cornelius grunted. "Besides, government-funded companies have proved to be even more susceptible than we are to political pressure."

"Still, profit as the *sole* motive for purveying scurrility . . ."

"We'd hoist ourselves on our own petard," Clement said dryly. "Why are any of us in this business, except to make money? No, don't mention ideals to me, gentlemen—I don't like to admit to them."

"Let's get to some outright proposals," Cornelius grumbled. "Can't spend all night bickering over the fine points if we don't have the bold ones, eh? Barry, you're the outsider here—how does it look from your perspective?"

Barry smiled and began talking. Inside of one sentence, they were hanging on his every word. He told them the gist in two minutes, and they spent two hours arguing over it—but in the end, they all endorsed his rough draft. After all, he was the one among them who best understood theater.

12

Well, it was a New York paper—what would you expect? There it was, the headline of the day, above even the civil war on Vega II and the economic strife between Zaire and Madagascar: "Producers Answer Rudders." That concerned me, so I paused by the newsfax, even though I should have been hurrying to get that coffee urn filled and those pastries up to the rehearsal hall. I dropped in a coin and caught the hard copy as it came out. There was the flat picture, Barry just left of center, beside a shorter man in a dark *complet* and manicured hair with a very serious, businesslike look about him. I would have thought I was looking at the class portrait of the alumni association of the Harvard Business School, not a band of Broadway producers. I would probably have been right, too—most of these men were businessmen first, and theater men second. Except Barry, of course, and the jowly guy I recognized from the night before—but in Barry's case, at least, the business was in the blood: Valdor's, if not his own.

I scanned the text. It was pretty good, all things considered. They reminded the good elector (presumably they had sent him a copy) of the sacred need for free speech in a democracy; that without the free exchange of ideas and information, the electorate couldn't make wise decisions to write to their electors about. They acknowledged the potential for abuse of that right, but noted that all rights can be abused, just as power and position can be abused, or used irresponsibly—I liked that; it wasn't quite a return attack on Rudders, but close enough that everybody knew what they were talking about. They also pointed out, however, that such abuse can be countered by responsible behavior and concern for truth and morality, especially on the part of competing speakers or, in this case, producers; that for every porno show, there's a serious play condemning promiscuity, and for every play about Billy the Kid, there's one glorifying Pat Garret. I thought that last was a nice dig, myself, reminding the elector that theater doesn't really do much violence, since 3DT can do it so much better. Privately, I wasn't too sure Barry had the ratios right; I suspected it might be more like one play about sexual ethics for every ten porno shows—but the principle was there.

I tossed the hard copy in the corner recycler and went on about my day's duties with a firmer step and a lighter heart. It was reassuring, just knowing that the producers weren't about to take Rudders's attack lying down. Of course, I was waiting to see how he'd lash back.

Hey, what can I tell you? I always did like a good fight.

They straggled in, bleary-eyed and groggy, but I was experienced now—I had the urn ready and the cream and sugar dispensers filled, and I tried to make my smile warm and cheering, but not too bright. Last came an older man, a little past plump into chubby with a fringe of hair around a bald head—I wondered why he hadn't had an implant, then realized it might be useful for character roles. "Good morning, good man. This the rehearsal hall for the Star Repertory Company?"

"Sure is." I tapped the urn. "I'm Ramou Lazarian, tech assistant and general gofer. How do you take it?"

"Regular, like myself. I'm Charlie Publican."

"Pleased to meet you." I held the cup under the other spout and pressed for cream and sugar.

"You been with the company long?"

I looked up sharply, but his eye was twinkling. I grinned. "Since its very first day. Been acting long?"

"No, not as a pro, no. My fling at fame 'n' fortune, y' see."

"Really?" I tried not to look too astonished—he was forty-five at least, maybe more.

"I know, I know." He smiled. "At my time of life, eh? But that's the why of it, lad—mid-life crisis, and all that. Go ahead, ask it."

"Uh—okay." I swallowed. "A little late to be going into a chancy line of work, isn't it?"

"Not really, no. A little money put by to tide you over, a sabbatical, a leave of absence—and if it doesn't work out, there's always the salt mines to fall back on."

I held out the cup. "What kind of mines?"

He took it. "The minds and hearts of young people, lad!"

"Oh." I frowned. "You're in the music business?"

He smiled, amused. "Nowhere near, worse luck. Wish I could grab them the way it does, though. No, I've been a teacher all these years—and that's half the reason, you see."

"No, I don't."

He shrugged, looking resigned. "Why did I labor so long to uplift and enrich their souls, eh? When the moment the bell rang, they were out the door with their players plugged into their ears and damn near right into their brains. Oh, what I told them went in the one ear and out the other, but the music stayed."

I felt sheepish. "Must be tough."

He grinned. " 'If you can't beat 'em, join 'em.' Only I've a tin ear."

"So you turned to acting?"

"They watch 3DT, too," he assured me. "And, who knows? In years to come, they may see me on the screen, and suddenly—"

"—believe what you were teaching was worth learning, after all." I nodded with chagrin. "Yeah, I catch you."

But I missed him, really, because just then the door opened and in came Lacey, looking bright, alert, serious, and beautiful. I turned to tend to her cup, and Publican drifted away, understanding that she was prettier than he was, and I was a hormonal basket case. I stretched out filling her cup as long as I could, and she gave me the glittering eye, knowing what I was up to and playing along—until Larry came in the door. Then she shut up and stepped back, and I handed him black coffee and turned back to Lacey.

"Cream and sugar!" he snapped.

I looked him up and down, taking in the sticklike figure. "Well, I guess you can afford it." I added a healthy dose of both and handed it back. Just then Winston came in, and Horace, the two of them walking very close to Ogden on either side, so I was busy for a little bit, and they turned away, neither of them drinking his coffee but saying things like, "Drink it down, now Ogden, there's a good chap," and, "It's organic, Ogden, it really won't hurt you."

"But it's not distilled," he rumbled.

"Believe me, you wouldn't want it to be," Winston assured him. "Have you ever tried espresso? No, of course you have. Do drink it up, Ogden, or we'll send Ramou for a double cappuccino royale."

Ogden sipped hastily.

"Another," Horace urged. As soon as he lowered the cup a half inch, Winston was saying, "One more, now," and before I knew it, Horace was handing Ogden his own cup and taking away the empty. They steered him to a seat that way, and I turned back to see a young guy with a mile-wide grin that looked really odd coming out of a long face with lank black hair and a long jaw—but somehow it all fitted together, the way Abraham Lincoln's did, after he grew the beard. Only this guy didn't have so much as a mustache, just thick black eyebrows and a nose that was a little too big. Somehow you liked him the second you saw him. I hoped it wasn't just good acting.

"Hi." I reached for a cup. "I'm Ramou Lazarian, general handyman. How do you take it?"

The grin vanished in a stare of total surprise. "So soon?" Then it came back. "Oh, you mean the coffee! Regular, thanks. I'm Marty Kemp."

I valved in some of the sweetness and light, wondering what he thought I'd been talking about. "You weren't in *Filters and Phyltres,* then?"

"No, I was in Men's Wear at Bloomingdale's."

I looked up, startled, and caught the grin full blast. My own grew slowly; I couldn't help it. "What were you doing there?"

The grin widened; there's nothing a comic likes better than a straight line. "Just trying things on. Until the floor-walker caught me. No, but really . . ."

"I doubt it."

"What are you doing, trying for *my* job?" He tried to look outraged and almost succeeded. I just barely kept back a laugh.

"Don't," he urged.

"Don't what?" I stared.

"Keep back the laugh. Let it out; it's good for you. Not bad for me, either, now that you mention it."

"I didn't," I said. "You don't mind if people laugh at you?"

"At me, or my jokes?" Before I could answer, he went on. "Hell, no. That's what I want them to do."

"How about if they laugh when you *don't* want them to?"

He shrugged. "That's show biz. Every audience is different. As long as they laugh, that's all I care."

I frowned. "Aren't you worried about being a clown?"

"Are you kidding? Who do you think steals the show?"

"Don't they make you give it back?"

His eyes gleamed with delight. "They can try, but it hasn't worked in nine hundred years."

"Nine hundred? How do you figure that?"

"Because Shakespeare has Hamlet telling the players, 'Let not your clowns speak more than is set down for them.' Good advice, and the directors still need it. Give us half a chance, and we'll take over. We did, in the Middle Ages."

I stared. "The comics took over?"

"Sure. Why do you think they kicked us out of the churches?"

"I didn't know you were ever in them."

"Not if we can help it," he agreed.

"Oh, I don't know." I grinned. "You've got to watch the ladies."

"I do," he assured me. "Every chance I get."

"Well! I see you lads have met."

We looked up, and Marty did a quick stumble over his own feet, ending in a bow, and all without spilling a drop of coffee. "Mr. Tallendar! Sir!"

"A sir upon my character," Barry said with mock severity. "Let this be a lesson to you, Ramou—never cross horns with a comic actor."

"Sir, I resent that!" Marty drew himself up. "I am neither cross nor horny."

"Nor under any compulsion to tell the truth," Barry noted wryly.

Marty spread his hands, which is a good trick with a loaded coffee cup. "What is truth? Compared with a good punch line, that is."

Revelation struck, and I cried, "So that's why they called him 'jesting Pilate'!"

They both turned to me as though I'd lost my mind.

I shrank back. "It's a quotation. ' "What is truth," said jesting Pilate, and would not stay for an answer.' "

They both relaxed; Barry sighed with relief. "Thank heaven! I thought you were speaking about the prospective captain of our spaceship!" He turned to look out over the hall. "Well! I see I'm the last to arrive. Shall we begin, then?"

"Catch you later, Ramou," Marty said as he turned away.

"Only if you linger overlong," Barry advised me, and followed the comic to the big table.

I took it as some kind of warning and resolved to heed it—but warning about what? Of course, any time I was with Marty, I'd have to count my mental change, but aside from that?

Barry went to the empty place at the center of the big table and looked around with a warm smile. "Good morning, ladies and gentlemen!" In response to the obligatory groans, he amended, "That is a wish for the future, not a statement of the present. We are meeting to begin rehearsals for the one original play in our repertoire, which shall be having its out-of-town tryouts—"

Smothered laughs came from several points of the table.

"Oh, do let the laughs out," Barry urged them. "It's good for the soul—mine, as well as yours. Our play, my friends, is *Vagrants from Vega,* by Manuel Cant—No, Marty, don't try for it . . ."

Marty closed his mouth with a martyred sigh.

"Which brings us to the matter of the cast," Barry went on. "For those of you who have not met them—which is all of you, since they were not with us yesterday—I would like to introduce to you Ms. Margaret Oleander, who will be playing mature supporting roles with us; Mr. Charles Publican, who will be playing second character roles; and Mr. Martyn Kemp, who will be our low comic."

"And they don't come any lower," Larry sneered.

Marty grinned up before Barry could stop him. "How low can you go, Larry?"

"I see you two have met," Barry noted.

"Since college," Larry snapped.

Marty nodded. "It was a passing fad. At least, *I* was passing."

"I'll have you know I graduated!"

Marty didn't say a word—he just looked very, very surprised, and Larry started getting red in the face.

"Now, gentlemen," Barry purred. "I would ask that you keep your private rivalries very private indeed." But there was steel under the velvet of that voice, and I felt a little chill at the thought that one of them might be left behind on Terra. I mean, I scarcely knew these guys from Adam, especially since neither of them looked like an australopithicine—but I'd liked Marty at first quip, and even though I couldn't help feeling that Larry would look better in a trash can than in a suit, I suddenly didn't want him gone. I was surprised at myself. Had I already come to think of us all as being part of some whole, integrated entity that would be wounded if any one of us were cut away?

Yes. I was a member of a company, now. And so was Larry. Somehow, that seemed to be much more important than his having all the charm and grace of a piece of sandpaper.

"Now, since I have introduced our new colleagues," Barry went on, "let me introduce the play. *Vagrants from Vega* is a small-cast musical, about a group of tourists en route from Vega to Terra, who begin to argue with the captain about the navigation and become totally lost."

There was another smothered laugh.

"Oh, let it grow." Barry's own smile spread.

"A play for the tired tourist, eh?" Ogden rumbled.

"Really! I thought it a cautionary tale," Winston said, smiling.

Marty raised his eyebrows. "I can see I'm gonna have some competition here."

"That wouldn't take much," Larry sneered.

Marty only gave him a goat's eye. "I should cry union— jurisdiction, you know."

"What," Horace said, "have the comics set up a separate union, then?"

"That's the hell of it," Marty admitted. "We have to go for in-house arbitration."

"Then we might as well do it within the company as within the union," Barry said firmly. "In any case, you'll find that, once we have slipped the bonds of Earth, union rules will be considerably more flexible—the committee decided ten years ago that the farther you are from New York, the looser the rules will be."

This time the laugh was only a little smothered.

"At that rate," Winston said, "by the time we set up for our first performance, there will be *no* union rules at all."

"Still the minimum," Barry assured them. "Scale will apply, though that scarcely affects you, Winston—and jurisdiction between Equity and IATSE, of course."

"But with everyone subject to the draft at the slightest need," Horace qualified.

"I'm afraid so," Barry agreed. "Nonetheless, we are founded as an Equity company, and I intend to remain so. Now, if we may return to the play?"

Marty gave a loud, theatrical sigh, but everyone else obediently opened his script.

"Our tourists, trying to instruct the captain in proper navigation, about which they know nothing, will nonetheless have the good fortune to land on liveable planets—"

"Stretching credulity a bit there, aren't we?" Winston asked.

"Not really; the playwright has thoughtfully given each planet an FTL radio beacon, and the ship itself homes on whichever is nearest."

Larry frowned. "But faster-than-light radio doesn't exist."

Marty started to say something, but caught himself in time.

"That's right." Lacey frowned. "I thought this was supposed to be a contemporary comedy, Mr. Tallendar."

"It is science fiction, at least nominally, Ms. Lark—I assume the playwright wished to protect himself from the wrath of the Navigators' Guild. Therefore, our action is set three hundred years in the future, in 2807."

"Convenient." Winston smiled. "Does the IDE survive?"

"The playwright is tactfully silent on the issue of interstellar government, and nicely evades it by having the host planets each inhabited by a different alien species."

"Isn't that going to require a rather large costume budget?"

"Not when we amortize it over two years' run and keep the costumes as part of a permanent repertory. Now, the parts are as follows: Mr. Wellesley is Captain Fuddle; Mr. Kemp will be his assistant, Otto Hand; Mr. Carlton is Mr. Malfeasance, the leader of the tourists' mutiny; Ms. Lark is Bess Etopon; Ms. Souci is Sausa Ness; Mr. Rash will be

Dash Enoff; Ms. Oleander will be Hedda Strong; and Mr. Burbage will be Vox Logos."

I glanced up at the new woman. She was nowhere nearly as stunning as Marnie, but definitely handsome, though she looked too kindly to be her understudy. She nodded with a happy smile.

Ogden frowned. "No part for Marnie, Barry?"

"I have endeavored to give each of you a one-play rest in the bill, Ogden, as I mentioned yesterday." Which was by way of explaining why he was giving himself a rest from Marnie's temperament. "Now, let us begin. The scene opens on shipboard, in the passengers' lounge. One by one, they straggle in, looking a bit shaken; after all, for many of them, it's been their first lift-off. Otto Hand is the first to arrive, and dispenses medicinal beverages to those who are unable to steady their fingers long enough to punch the dispenser themselves. First among them is Vox Logos. He steps up to the bar and says—"

"Is it always that rough?" Horace asked. I blinked, surprised; he didn't quite sound like himself, all of a sudden. Oh, the same voice, of course, but a little deeper, a little rougher, and the words sounding a little flatter, somehow.

"Oh, no," Marty answered, sounding just like himself, only more so. "It's usually a lot worse."

Larry spoke up, sounding completely like himself. "A large one, bartender!"

"Officer Hand, to you," Marty sniffed. "A large what?"

"Of whatever will make me feel better!"

"We're not allowed to give out that kind of stuff, Mr. Enoff, unless you're in pain."

"I'm in pain! I'm in pain! Oh, all right, give me whatever *he's* having."

"Um, Mr. Rash," Barry interrupted, "I'd like that with a bit less indignation and a bit more arrogance, if you please."

Larry looked up, wide-eyed. It must have been the first time in his life that anyone had told him to be *more* arrogant. Then his face slipped into neutral, and he nodded with icy politeness. "Of course, Mr. Tallendar." And he looked back at his script, every line of his body expressing outrage. I guessed he'd been top of the heap at his college, and wasn't adapting too well to being at the bottom of the *real* pile.

Barry watched him as he reread his line, all director for the moment, thoughtful and contemplative. I have a notion Larry almost got fired from the company right then. But Barry held off for a few days, until it was too late to change his mind.

"He's having trouble getting used to lift-offs," Marty said, "and I'm praying we don't have a gravity failure. How about just some seltzer, sir?"

"Only if it's a tincture of Scotch—about half and half, my man." Larry fairly sneered it, and Barry looked up at him again, still thoughtful, but let it pass.

"Wow! What a rush that was!" Susanne caroled. "Happy lift-off, everybody! Wasn't that a thrill?"

"I suppose," Larry said in withering tones, "if you like having an elephant sit on your chest. But I suppose you're familiar with that, aren't you, Miss Ness?"

"If you're referring to yourself, Mr. Enoff, don't bother. Mr. Hand, may I have a whiskey sour?"

"That's a little strong for right after lift-off, Ms. Ness."

"That's okay, I could use something strong." The way Susanne delivered that line sent a ripple through my every extremity; I wondered how Marty could stay tranquil while she said it. Of course, he was an actor.

Barry was nodding with approval, and Horace said, "Not while he's on duty, Ms. Ness."

"All right," she said agreeably, "when are you *off* duty, Mr. Hand?"

"Only when I'm sleeping, Ms. Ness," Marty/Otto sighed, "at least, until we get to Terra."

"Well, while you're sleeping . . ."

"Thank heaven! An outpost of civilization!" Winston/ Malfeasance gasped, like a desert traveler suddenly sighting a night club. "Bartender! A double martini, quickly! For pity's sake!"

"That's a little strong for right after lift-off, Mr. Malfeasance," Hand said again.

"Don't tell me what's good for after lift-off, you monkey-suited juvenile," Winston snarled, and I shivered as my blood ran cold; the Mordant Emperor was in top form today. "I've ridden out more lift-offs than you have molecules in your anatomy! A double martini, at once!"

Marty stuck out a hand. "Glad to meet you! I've always wanted to shake the hand of the Flying Dutchman!"

"What colossal impudence is this?" Malfeasance snarled.

"Just the usual sort," Hand replied. "If you've been through that many lift-offs, you must have been sailing for centuries. Well, here's your martini—it's your stomach. Barf bags on the wall, over there."

"Impudent puppy," Malfeasance sneered. "I'll have your stripes!"

"Why? Planning to turn into a skunk? Just take a sharp left at the corner there, sir—that'll take you direct to the brig. Save us both a lot of trouble, if you're going to keep on insulting a ship's officer."

"The brig? Hah! I've met your captain, young fellow! He wouldn't dare!"

I was amazed. There it was, the mutiny in miniature. How had *that* happened, all of a sudden?

"Come now, Mr. Malfeasance," Horace/Logos said, "there'll be time enough to settle our differences on Terra, and it's only two weeks in H-space."

"Yes, if our retread of a captain aimed the ship correctly," Malfeasance snapped; but there was a flag on the play, or at least Barry's hand. "Horace, a bit of iron under the geniality, if you will."

Horace nodded and repeated the line—no outrage, no body English—and Winston picked up his line exactly as he'd first said it. No fuss, no muss—but there was tension in the room as Barry nodded easily in approval. Everybody knew that Larry had just been given a lesson in how to take direction.

Except, maybe, Larry. He didn't even look up, didn't really seem to notice.

The scene went on; Ms. Oleander came in; then Lacey's character started playing up to Enoff, who was having a verbal dual with Hand, and Ms. Ness reacted to the competition by competing, flirting with Enoff, too, ostensibly because Hand couldn't let himself respond for the next two weeks.

Barry slipped out a pocket audio recorder/player as Horace's character made a final appeal for order: "Now, please, my fellow passengers! I'm sure our captain knows his astrogation, and even if he didn't, his computer certainly would!"

"Yes, but does he know which keys to press?" Malfeasance snapped.

"Doesn't have to," Hand put in. "It takes oral commands."

"Which you do not, I see."

"You're out of the chain of command, mister. I answer to the captain only."

"Who will, I am sure, see us safely to Terra," Horace pleaded.

"You're sure of more than I am, Mr.—" Winston broke off. "Barry, just what is this character's motivation for trying to stir up trouble like this? Does he have an old grudge against the captain, or an illegal shipment of contraband that he's trying to divert to an interdicted planet, or what?"

"Why, whatever you please, Winston," Barry said easily. "The playwright gives us quite a few hints, but nothing definite."

"I see." Winston nodded. "A vice."

The younger set looked blank—I knew I must have—so Horace slipped in easily, "I don't suppose we'll be doing a medieval morality play, will we, Barry? Where the vice is a character that delights in stirring up trouble, just so he can tempt people toward the path to hell?"

"And needs no excuse for his misdeeds—it is simply his nature." Barry picked up on Horace's lead right away and filled in what our professors had left out. "Perhaps next season, Horace, if we can find one that isn't interminably preachy."

"Surely *Othello* would do," Winston said with his diabolical leer. "He's the vice taken one step farther, after all, into becoming a believable human being."

I stared. "You mean all that arguing about why he did it is nowhere near?"

That gave the actors a face-saver; they could all look disparagingly at the ignorant engineer. To do them credit, though, only Larry did, with maybe the slightest of grimaces from Lacey and Oleander. But Horace gave me a warning look, and I shrank inside; I had obviously spoken out of turn. Gofers are to be seen and not heard. I decided not to try to help out again.

But Winston was nodding. "Precisely, young man. Iago needs no excuse for his betrayal and machinations; it's his nature. Though, of course, Falstaff is the more pleasant side of the vice . . ."

"Yes, merely tempting people into debauchery instead of murder," Barry said, amused. "So you have full license, Winston. Play it as you will."

"Put in what the playwright left out, eh?" Winston smiled. "Very well, Barry. Have at it! 'You're sure of more than I am, Mr. Hand!' "

"And here," Barry said, "as you can see, we have our first song. Mr. Burbage will serve as musical director, leading you in this . . ."

There were startled glances from the young folk, mentally revising their opinion of Horace's standing in the company.

"But for the moment," Barry went on, "we'll hear the composer's version. Mr. Arbuthnot will not be traveling with us, of course, and may open another production of this play on Terra while we're gone—but I expect that he will wait, and rewrite according to our experiences on the road."

The tantalizing promise was there—to play on Broadway, when we got back from the colonies. Everybody settled into close attention as Barry pressed the flat block of the recorder.

I sat back, amazed and delighted by the effects that Arbuthnot was getting out of his synthesizer. It changed voices for each character, and the diction was better than mine. In fact, it made you wonder why composers bothered with living singers.

Because there was a thrill to them that you couldn't get from machines, of course. That's what our company was all about.

It was a driving, fast-paced exchange in dialogue between the passengers and Hand, then between themselves, then back to Hand again, punctuated by occasional lines in full chorus. I was amazed; during a five-minute song, the lyricist managed to take the whole cast from more-or-less friendly squabbling into full polarization of all the passengers, swayed into line behind Malfeasance's accusations, with all of them on one side and Otto Hand on the other. Logos, though, was squarely in between—or standing aside and neutral, if you prefer.

The song ended, and Barry said, "So that's what we'll be doing. Ogden, if you will?"

"Shouldn't it open with a chorus number, Barry?" Ogden rumbled. "One of the unwritten rules, after all."

"Not so unwritten, either," Winston contributed.

"An excellent point, and Mr. Arbuthnot will be glad to hear it." Barry punched a note into his notebook. "I shouldn't be surprised if he is at work on it already. Onward, if you would, Ogden. The captain enters . . ."

"Avast there, me hearties!" Ogden boomed. "Heel about on the starboard tack!"

"Uh, Captain," Hand murmured, "this is a spaceship, not a clipper."

"Water, vacuum, what matter? A sea's a sea! The captain's greeting to you all, me happy passengers!"

"Not so happy as all that, Captain Fuddle," Malfeasance snapped, and we were off into another rattling, staccato number coming out of Barry's recorder, a mutiny with meter. By the end, the passengers, led by Malfeasance, had the captain thoroughly cowed, and were trooping off to the bridge, despite Hand's objections that it was for officers only, and Logos's protestations that the rule had good reason behind it.

"As I said, a cautionary tale." Winston was smiling with amusement. "Pure drivel, of course, Barry, but a romp."

"Not so pure as all that," Ogden rumbled. "How's for I play Fuddle like Rudders, Barry, eh?"

Everyone looked up, startled. Nobody had thought to take this silly comedy as anything but the nonsense it appeared to be.

"Worth a try, certainly," Barry said slowly. "The rest of you look for similar correspondences, eh? On to scene two."

Scene two was on the bridge, with Malfeasance dictating a course to the computer, and the computer objecting that it was impossible for a number of reasons. Finally, in a rage, Malfeasance ordered it to execute his commands anyway, and Fuddle, thoroughly cowed, bade it go ahead.

"Lighting effect here," Barry murmured, "and everyone will stagger about with the disorientation of transition into H-space as you all sing."

The number compressed a week of H-space travel into three minutes, and brought quick howls of laughter from the whole company, chopped off quickly so they could hear the next line. Finally, it ended with a chorus of "All fall down!"

"And they do," Barry said. "Then the lights come back up, and they troop off with glad cries to the passengers' lounge again. The air lock opens, equalizes pressure, opens both hatches, and in comes . . ."

"Illian the Alien," Marty hissed, "at your service." Then in his normal voice, "I take it Hand stayed behind on the bridge, Mr. Tallendar?"

"Oh, yes! We must have Arbuthnot add a line about his remaining on watch!" Barry punched a quick note. "Thank you, Mr. Kemp. The rest of your line now, please?"

And on they went, through the planet of Foible, in which nothing worked and the natives gloried in their disorder, except whenever the earthquakes came, which were growing larger every week. Foible, it turned out, was about to disintegrate from lack of molecular cohesion, and just after every earthquake, the natives did worry about it a bit. Logos managed to persuade them to try manufacturing gluons and dispersing them into the planet's crust, which they promised to try—but they were already back to partying as the Terran ship took off. Lousy science, of course, but hilarious dialogue and musical numbers that knocked the company into laughing fits for minutes at a time. Barry rode it all out with only a smile, but looked immensely reassured—he was taking quite a chance with this one.

Then the passengers argued with the captain again and managed to get Malfeasance the right to set course, of course—and landed on another planet that was anything but Terra. Ostensibly. Now that I was alert for political satire, I nearly fell off my seat as I found out that they had reached the planet of Satiety.

This time Captain Fuddle stayed on the bridge, and Ogden played Brinker the Thinker, who expounded a philosophy of seeking danger as the only way to give life any excitement, in a utopia where everyone had not only everything they needed, but everything they could want—or at least, that they could think of. So he led our glorious passengers up knife-edged mountains, with Hand just barely managing to save the ones who fell, and Logos managing to talk them out of the most dangerous paths. Finally, though, they all stood at the edge of a cliff with a rockfall closing off the path behind them and only a slender, antique, swaying rope bridge before them. Brinker sang a solo exulting in the vividness of life in such a situation of danger, and the whole company sang a chorus of dismay.

"And, blackout," Barry said.

It made one hell of a first-act closer.

"I think we might break for lunch now," Barry said, smiling around at everyone. "Only half an hour, if you please—I'd like to finish the read-through, then go back to work on a few trouble spots. Restore yourselves, my friends."

Marty managed to make it out the door before Larry could get close enough to start tossing insults.

13

The impoverished younger folk went to the food dispensary on the corner, and the old pros went to Blarney's. I hesitated, not really feeling welcome with either group, but Marty saw and reached out a hand to snag my arm. "Come on, Ramou! Planning to starve?"

I grinned, by way of thanks. "Not really. Thanks, Marty."

"Don't mention it—unless they ask, which Larry'd better not. On second thought, I can tell them Barry sent you to keep the peace."

"Pieces of whom? No, don't tell them that—it might be too close to the truth."

Marty gave me a better laugh than I deserved, and set me a fast pace catching up with the others.

We joined them just as the wall slid aside and they went in. We punched up our sandwiches and drinks, and sat down at the same table as Larry and the ladies. He looked up indignantly, but Marty just gave him a big, wide grin. Larry looked daggers at him, but I guess he wasn't feeling really rude today, or the presence of the ladies inhibited him, because he just shut up and sat down, unwrapping his burger.

"Is it always like this?" I asked, to break the silence.

"What?" Lacey looked up, surprised—she'd heard the same question two days before.

"Rehearsals. Do they always read through all the plays before they rehearse them?"

"No, and it seems simply idiotic to me!" Larry glared. "How am I to keep straight which role is which?"

"Mnemonics," Marty suggested.

"What do you mean, 'mnemonics'!"

Marty reddened a little at his tone, so Susanne chimed in, "You know, things like, 'This character's a tourist, so it must be *Vagrants*?' "

"Well, yes," Larry allowed, since it was a pretty girl who had said it, "but yesterday's lines are so similar to today's. How am I to remember which go with which character?"

Marty suddenly became very intent in studying his sandwich. Larry noticed and turned on him. "Oh, don't give me that—"

"Shh!" I held up a hand, turning to the screen. For once, I was glad Elector Rudders was shooting his mouth off.

I wasn't glad for long, though.

I was just slipping a fork into my crab salad when Barry clasped my forearm. "Horace—he's at it again."

I looked up at Ogden in alarm, but he was staring up at the wall-screen. I was suddenly aware that Blarney's had taken on that ominous quiet again, and we could all hear the wall-screen. Worse, we could see Rudders's pugnacious face as he was saying, "My fellow electors, it is with great sadness that I must inform you that, our discussion on the issue notwithstanding . . ."

Discussion! It had all been his windiness, with a few hoots from the gallery!

". . . there has been no indication of heightened awareness of responsibility from the theater industry, in New York, London, Beijing, or anywhere else on the planet Earth. Therefore, with great reluctance, my fellow electors, I am introducing into committee today this bill." He held up a thick sheaf of papers. "It is a proposed law, which will set forth strict limits for what may be said or done on the stage of any theater on Terra, or within its colonies."

A hubbub swept the Assembly. Rudders looked up and

waited it out, the tragic look firmly in place, but a glint of satisfaction in his eye.

When the hubbub had almost finished dying down, he leapt into oratory again. "Some may cry 'censorship,' and I cannot deny it. The press, the news services, public speeches must be sacrosanct, their freedoms never infringed upon— but the entertainment media have too much influence for depravity and degradation of the human mind and soul to justify such license. I came to this conclusion only this morning, my fellow electors, when I learned that a troupe of Godless actors is preparing to spread their lewd and seditious influence beyond the boundary of Terra's atmosphere. Not content with corrupting the morals of the citizens of our home world, they have determined to take ship and launch themselves into the Void, to infect the pure and noble colonies themselves with the seductions of live actresses and actors!"

The hubbub broke out again, but more startled than shocked; the intonations were, "Did you know about this?" "No, I didn't. How about you?"

I did. And I was shocked.

"This agent of infection calls itself the Star Repertory Company, led by none other than that arch-Cassanova, the notorious Barry Tallendar, well known to all of you as Mr. Arachne, the corrupter of innocence and seducer of virgins in that 3DT classic of obscenity, *The Scalphunter*."

Hubbub again. These fellows hadn't been reading the trades. More to the point, most of them had never seen Barry do more than one or two roles, so his biggest hit was the one they could all identify. Never mind that *The Scalphunter* showed the aging playboy Arachne as a total cad and despicable heel; never mind that its very clear message was for young girls to avoid the blandishments of such romantic-seeming but decadent figures as Arachne, and for young men to reject the notion that a man's masculinity is measured by the number of his seductions. Never mind that the thrust of the show itself was definitely moral, or that Barry had done an excellent job of showing just how completely selfish and flint-hearted such Cassanovas were—on the surface, it looked like titillation.

Rudders let the reaction reach its peak and start to decline, then roared into the noise, "Are we to let the innocence of our beloved interstellar electorates be despoiled by this agent of corruption? Are Terra's fair daughters to be seduced and demeaned by this thief of virtue and his minions? Nay, nay, my fellow electors! We must firmly curb the excesses of these players, and we must do it now!"

I wouldn't exactly say that his fellow electors met him with enthusiastic applause, but it certainly was a noisy reaction of some kind.

I turned away, incredulous and shaken. "He means it! He really means it!"

"But why?" For once, Winston looked nonplussed. "You don't for a second think that he really cares about the colonies, do you?"

"Certainly not," Barry said. "After all, he was the one who introduced law after law designed to limit Terra's support for the colonies, both with money and with matériel."

"A moment." I frowned. "That does fit some sort of pattern. The Star Company is one more thing he could deny to the colonies."

"He really doesn't want anything decent going to the colonies!" Susanne cried.

"Just what does he think we're *really* carrying to the distant lands?" Marty wondered. "It sure isn't pornography or obscenity—the 3DT programs they're sending out to them already, year after year, are a lot worse than than any play we've got scheduled."

"Or anything we're likely to schedule in the future," Lacey agreed, "considering how Tallendar and the other veterans talk about art."

I decided to sit down and do some analyzing of the plays we were putting on next season. Did they contain ideas that were a threat to Rudders?

But then, what ideas weren't?

"He can't mean it!" Lacey was pale.

" 'Fraid he can." I remembered what Horace had been saying the night before. "Let's finish up, folks. I think we'd better get back to the rehearsal hall."

Larry transferred his indignation from Rudders to me, but Susanne said, "Who's got any appetite, after that?"

"Then bring it along." I stood, wrapping my sandwich. "We'll have a break, won't we? And the doughnuts are stale."

"Hey," Marty protested, "they were stale when you brought them in this morning."

I turned, ready to be insulted, then saw the grin. It was Marty's specialty, I found out—or one of them; a big, wide, rubber-mouthed, loose-lipped smile full of orthodontists' specials, and it was always infectious. I couldn't help grinning back. "Okay, I'll run out and get some cheese and crackers while you folks are rehearsing—but I can't guarantee what'll be in the cheese."

Larry started to say something, but Marty stopped him with a forefinger. "Never argue with the guy who brings the food, Larry—and I'm bringing mine. Let's go see what Mr. Tallendar says about this."

Larry shut up, finally, and we went.

But Barry had more immediate problems than Rudders. We arrived to hear someone roaring out "Mack the Knife" in German, sounding very authentic—which is to say, as though he'd just chugged a liter of gin.

"Oh, no." Lacey rolled her eyes up. "Who let him at it?"

We came in, and there was Ogden, swaying and gesturing wildly, with Horace propping him up.

"We were distracted by the elector," Winston explained, "and he slipped in three martinis while we weren't watching. Then he was so upset by what Rudders had said that he ordered three more. We managed to hide the third, but five are more than enough."

So was Ogden. He swayed, threatening to crush Horace in his fall, so I raced over and shoved my shoulder in under his. My head, more likely—that guy was *tall*. I got him back up vertical, of course. Then I had to throw my weight against his, to keep him from leaning over to the other side. He didn't miss a beat the whole time. I yearned for one of those mythical instant drunk cures you always hear about in college bull sessions, but they're as much a part of life as the Easter Bunny and the tooth fairy, and just as real. If they do exist, nobody outside the family is giving away the recipe. Probably couldn't get past the Medicine Inspection and Regulation Enforcement department, anyway.

"Thank you, Ramou." Horace looked a little shaken. "I can manage him now."

"You and your cardiac," I told him. "Try, and you'll both be under arrest. You talk him down, Horace—I'll keep him up."

"Say mmm?" Ogden blinked down at me as though he'd just discovered a cat clinging to his coat. "Oh. H'lo there, young fella."

"Good afternoon, Mr. Wellesley." I pointed to a chair, then made a quick grab to keep him from toppling. "Would you like to sit down?"

"Sit down?" Ogden swirled an arm in an expansive gesture that nearly knocked me off my feet, not to mention him. I pushed with all my might. "What matter wounds to the body of a knight errant?" he roared. "For each time he falls—"

"—he crushes his squire," I finished. "Sink, and we sink together."

"Float, and we float a loan!" he added, with a roar of laughter that could have fueled a spaceship. "Ha! Well said, young man! Onward, my faithful squire! Onward to glory!"

"How about rehearsal instead?" I suggested.

"Rehearsal? Marvelous idea! Let's do *Threepenny Opera*!"

"No, it's *Vagrants from Vega* today, Ogden," Barry reminded, but he was looking at me. "Are you up to it, Mr. Lazarian?"

Now, there was a notion—holding this ton of lard up while they read act two.

"We tried the Sobriety System Pills," Winston told me in an apologetic tone, "but they only made him more intoxicated."

"Murphy," I sighed. "Oh, well, what the hell? I needed weight-lifting practice, anyway."

"Very good!" Barry shoved a script into Ogden's hands. He promptly fumbled it, and I caught it, handing it back. "Now, if you'll just sit down, Ogden?"

"Down? Nonshenshe! We were about to crossh the bridge, Barry!"

"All right." Barry sighed. "Everyone around behind Brinker the Thinker, ladies and gentlemen. He is about to lead you across the rickety rope bridge."

"Yonder it lies!" Ogden roared, pointing out over the script and glancing at it out of the corner of his eye. "Four cables and a path of planks! Onward, my gallant visitors!"

"I really question the wisdom of this move," Winston said with an icy sneer.

"Yes, but the rockslide buried the pathway back," Susanne snapped. "It's a little late for questions, isn't it, Mr. Malfeasance?"

"In any case," Horace said, "the slide has given us our answer. We cross, or starve. Lead the way, Brinker." Then, to the rest of the passengers, "If it will hold him, it will hold the rest of us."

"Well, that's pretty cold-blooded!" Lacey said.

"Not really. I did a rough calculation from the thickness of the cables, and if they're not too old, they should hold all of us together. The planks, however, might be rotten." He turned back to Ogden, who kept trying to take the first step, while I kept holding him back. "Do watch your step, Brinker!"

"Sure-footed as a cat!" Ogden roared, and plunged. I hauled back, but he managed the first step anyway. The result was that he swung about, so when he started crossing the bridge, he was going sideways. That had its advantages—now I only had to brace him front-to-back. "Reminds me of the time back in Ought-Six!" he roared, taking a large step with his right foot. He put his weight on it six inches too soon, and I had to hurry and push it down, then push him back as he tried to fall on me. "I and my mate sought danger and excitement in the mountains of Monolith!" Brinker bellowed as he took another step, then windmilled his arms, a look of horror on his face as he leaned too far back. I raced around to his flip side before he flipped, and shoved hard. He swung back up to the vertical. "We were on holiday in Peril!" He went past the vertical and started to sway forward. I leapt around to the front, pushed him back up—and he took another step to the right, overbalancing. I pivoted around and propped him up. "She took fright at the sight of the rope bridge," Brinker orated, "so I had need to carry her over!"

"Oh, that must have been very reassuring," I muttered from somewhere under his armpit. All of a sudden, I was *really* hoping he'd get to the other side. I knew this was a bridge with suspense, but I didn't want *that* kind.

"There!" Ogden took one more triumphant step, threw up his arms, and overbalanced. I caught him at seventy degrees and shoved hard, but the floor was slippery, and I was losing ground. Barry leapt in beside me, and we propped him back up. Ogden didn't even notice, just cried, "And the great crossing is completed!"

"Excellent." Barry pointed at a chair. "And there is the rock on which Brinker now sits!"

" 'Course, 'course." Ogden slouched toward the chair, almost pitched forward onto the table, then lurched back as Barry and I pulled. I shoved the chair forward. It caught him right behind the knees, and he sat with a suddenness that jarred the whole room.

"Thank heaven," I sighed. "The robot who manufactured that chair did a damn good job."

"And so have you." Barry wiped his brow. "You can go for coffee now, Ramou."

"A gofer's job is never done," I sighed. "How many, Mr. Tallendar?"

"One, for yourself." He pressed a bill into my hand. "As large as you want, and take as long as you please. You deserve it."

I was back before the end of the scene, though. I hate to say it, but I didn't *want* to be away.

"Did they agree to support you?" I asked as Barry came back from the comm unit.

"Well, yes and no." Barry sat down and accepted the glass, forcing a grin—but it came out as a rictus. " 'Oh, we're right behind you, Barry lad, we won't budge an inch'—but it was definitely 'we,' the respectable businessmen, talking to the scandalous actor-outsider." He took a sip—a long one. "They all agreed to the statement I'd prepared, and voted unanimously to endorse it—but on the condition that I would present it to the news services myself. And I do mean 'myself,' Horace—when the vote was over, they all came up with one excuse after another for why they couldn't come with me." This time the smile gained strength, though from sarcasm. "So I've spoken with the New York bureaus, and they asked me to come in right away. I did, and they recorded my statement—with nothing in the background but a plain gray drape. No other producers, no businessmen." The smile became sardonic. "They're cutting us adrift, Horace."

I felt my face sag and fought to pull it up, to smile. "Do you mean that we must sink?"

"Not at all! We shall swim, we shall cavort in the seas of space!" He held up his glass for a refill. "We shall persevere, Horace, and we shall triumph! We shall continue our rehearsals—and I shall meet Valdor tomorrow to discuss a preliminary engagement on Broadway."

"On Broadway!" I pushed my jaw closed, caught my breath, and objected, "But, Barry . . . the unions . . ."

"Oh, none of these plays is going to run long enough to make a profit on Broadway, of course, but having played there will make excellent publicity when we perform in the Colonies. 'Fresh from a triumphant season on Broadway!' Could there be better publicity, for the culturally starved and pretentious provincial? We will show a loss on Terra, but may expect to recoup it at the box office on New Venus, Otranto, Nova Nova Scotia, and Falstaff."

I nodded slowly. "The overall profitability, eh? And the current loss, to keep our subcorporation from taxability, since a successful Broadway season would show that we are not a sure loss. Perhaps it's well that we are trying out a new piece, after all."

"For New York, yes," Barry agreed, "but not for the colonies. We're playing revivals and classics, generally; the folk on the frontier want to see the hits from Terra, not new stuff that may or may not be good."

I nodded. "Of course, we were originally planning on returning to New York for a run *after* a 'successful season' in the Colony Planets; we are only placing Broadway at the beginning of the run, instead of its end."

Barry smiled. "It would be a shame to waste all the free publicity Elector Rudders is providing for us. Who knows? We might even show a profit on Broadway!"

"Or at least off-Broadway," said I, ever the voice of caution. "Then we would at least break even."

"If we can run while we're still in the headlines," Barry agreed, "thanks to the good elector."

14

We left rehearsals more or less in a bunch, of course, and Horace and Barry lingered behind to tell the lights to turn off, and to lock up. I hung back, too, just in case they should dream up any extra little jobs—and because Lacey had missed the first lift car.

"You could have caught it, you know," she said, with the amused smile again.

"So could you," I pointed out.

"I'd rather not be in the same car with Ogden Wellesley," she confided. "I prefer my gin firsthand."

Then the doors opened, and Barry and Horace came up, so we kept the conversation to more discreet topics, such as the weather and Elector Rudders, and broke it off as soon as we could to listen in on the old pros.

The door opened, and we stepped out into a jammed lobby.

"I thought I declared rehearsal done for the day," Barry said.

The whole company was there, even Ogden.

"Reporters, Barry," he said. "Lurking in hiding—but young Kemp here saw one peeking out with that telltale bump on his shoulder. We decided to wait for you, so we could confront them en masse."

"Or look for the back door," Marty qualified.

"You would look for the duck-out," Larry sniped.

Marty frowned, then remembered himself and grinned. "Better part of valor and all that, Larry."

"Quite so," Barry agreed. "We mustn't forget, ladies and

gentlemen, that we are in the public eye. We must show no sign that could be construed as being ashamed of what we are, or what we do, especially now with the elector attempting to cast us in just such a light. We must also be mindful of the opportunity for publicity. United we advance! Onward, troops!"

And, like any good commander, he led the way out the door. We whooped and followed.

The reporters sprang out from around the corners of the doorway and jabbed their mikes into his face. There were two of them, but the woman got her question in first. "Mr. Tallendar! Elector Rudders has called for you to break up your company! Are you going to do it?"

"Certainly not," Barry said. "We are a profit-making enterprise, and intend to continue as any business would."

"Then you're going to go on with your salacious act?" the man demanded.

"There will be nothing salacious in our bill, Mr. Quacketer."

"But I heard you were running *Man of La Mancha* . . ."

"The play is perfectly moral," Barry informed him. "It deals with the redemption of a fallen woman, in spite of the brutalizations to which men put her."

"Then you're not going to let the elector buffalo you," the woman inferred.

"Not at all. Unfortunately, we discovered that we could not afford to hire a full chorus, so we may have to drop it from the bill . . ."

"Then you are capitulating!"

"Certainly not." Barry smiled. "We may yet run with it; we'll just have to see about the feasibility of some very rapid costume changes."

Somebody laughed—I don't think it was one of us.

"How do you feel about the elector's attempts to keep you from touring the colonies?"

"I find his attitude lamentable. There is certainly no reason to keep our fellow citizens in the gloom of cultural deprivation," Barry said. "We intend to bring them enlightenment and elevation, and hope for the active cooperation of the IDE government."

The reporters really looked surprised. "You don't mean you're asking Rudders for help!"

"Not Rudders, no," Barry said with an amused smile. "There are other electors, after all—more than a hundred of them, if I'm not mistaken."

"You mean you're going to ask the Liberals for help?"

"I wasn't intending a direct petition," Barry said thoughtfully, "though now that you mention it, the idea has merit."

"And you're sure these plays of yours won't corrupt the colonials?"

Barry's smile deepened, obviously squelching a laugh. "I sincerely doubt that our brothers and sisters of the far-flung dominions would be surprised by anything in any of our plays."

One of the cameramen had to stifle a snicker, but the reporter bored on relentlessly. "You don't think *Filters and Phyltres* is immoral?"

"Not at all," Barry assured him. "In fact, it shows the consequences of immorality, and its conclusion, I think, is quite clear—that deluding ourselves about love leads to misery."

"And you think that'll stand up to public scrutiny?"

"I am so certain of it that I invite the public to scrutinize our work," Barry said, suddenly intense. "We shall open at the Winter Garden on New Year's Eve, to add to the festivities; curtain will be at 8:00 P.M. Tickets will be—"

"Thanks very much, Mr. Tallendar!" The reporters swung around to face their individual cameras, each saying something to the effect of "That's Barry Tallendar, managing director of the Star Company, with his reply to Elector Rudders!"

I glanced up at Barry for permission to plow through them and start home, but he held up a cautioning hand. I sighed and waited.

"Okay, that's it!" The reporter turned back to Barry. "You know we don't give free publicity, Mr. Tallendar."

"Quite so," Barry agreed. "Merely full disclosure of information."

"Yeah, sure," the lady reporter snarled, then tried for a smile. "Well, we'll be seeing you." And she marched away, her camera op and audio op behind her.

"I'm sure we will," Barry murmured. He gazed after her a moment, pensively, then turned to us. "If they should try to pester you, my friends, you need only tell them that we are performing as scheduled, and refer them to me for all other information."

It wasn't just a protection and way out, it was an order, no matter how politely phrased. Only Larry looked even a little nettled, but he joined the chorus of assent.

"Very well, then." Barry nodded, satisfied. "Shall we wend our way to Carstairs', friends? Those of you who wish, of course."

We all wished. Barry picked up the tab for the first round. Though I would have felt better, all around, if I hadn't heard him murmuring to Horace, "I do hope the cameras didn't show all their faces . . ."

Elector Rudders, though, didn't think it was such a bad idea. We all went to dinner together, which meant Blarney's, that being the medium level for the pocketbook, and we went looking over our shoulders all the way. We didn't find any reporters, but as we walked into Blarney's, Elector Rudders was looking over his shoulder at us, from the wall-screen over the door.

"It has come to my attention, my fellow electors . . ."

"Meaning his spies," Horace said with a grunt.

". . . that the infamous Star Company of actors, rather than heed my call for responsible behavior, has instead reserved a theater and declared its intention to present its plays on Broadway itself, prior to their departure for outer space!"

A hubbub of disbelief swept through the Assembly.

"But isn't that what he wanted?" I said. "For us to come up with a bill that we wouldn't be ashamed for the public to see here on Earth?"

"One would think so." Horace frowned at the screen.

"Such a display of impudence, my fellow electors, must be met with drastic action! Since they have shown themselves unwilling to respond to the concern of the public . . ."

"Public?" I yelped. "Only him!"

"Yes, but Barry has proved that he will not be intimidated by an elector," Horace explained. "The other electors will naturally find that unacceptable."

"Therefore, my fellow electors," Rudders rumbled on, "I have introduced to committee today this bill, which prohibits the emigration of any group of Terran actors for purposes of propagating their immorality in the form of plays of any sort, to any planet or star, other than Terra."

The hubbub broke again, but Rudders orated over it. "Moreover, this bill will be retroactive, requiring the disbanding and dissolution of any company that has formed with the intention of such emigration!"

"He's going to break us up by *government edict*?" Marty bleated.

I spun to Horace. "Isn't that in restraint of trade, or something?"

"Quite," Horace assured me, his face grim. "But since few or none of the electors own stock in theatrical enterprises that are planning to tour the colony planets, none of them have anything to lose by voting for his bill—and it will allow them to avoid the general issue of freedom of expression."

"You mean outlawing live theater off-planet would get them off the hook?"

"Precisely." Horace nodded. "It would nicely remove them from the dilemma of seeming to care nothing for public morality, while defending freedom of expression. No, it's a very neat maneuver indeed, Ramou—I would admire the man for his deftness, if I didn't abhor him so for his politics. It's an excellent gambit, and I don't doubt he'll receive quick action."

I turned back to the screen, feeling numb, seeing the waving and gesticulating throughout the Assembly, and hearing the roar of furious argument. "Then maybe we'd better start some quick action, too?"

"Oh, nothing precipitate," Barry soothed. "Even if he disbands us as the Star Company, we can re-form as a New York organization and play on Broadway as we've planned. With the publicity he's giving us, I don't doubt we'd have a successful first season, even showing a profit. No, I think we will continue as planned."

I wondered why Horace looked guilty.

To my shame, I found myself secretly hoping that Rudders's scheme would go through—for if it did, I would not have to leave New York.

That was when Rudders pulled out the mug shots of us all, very large ones, crying, "These are the reprehensible originators of this foul plan, my fellow electors, and their minions! The archseducer himself, Barry Tallendar . . . the prime villain, Winston Carlton . . ."

He went on like that, ostensibly showing our pictures to his fellow electors, but the camera saw them, of course, and pasted our faces out there for everyone in the world to see—all the worlds, on time delays from one month to twenty.

But it was the New York audience that really mattered.

The screen cut back to the overview of the huge chamber, and the president of the Assembly began the ritual of adjourning for the day. Rather numb and unfocused, we turned away to find a table.

"Hey, any publicity is good publicity, right?" Marty insisted. "Look—I'm famous, and they haven't even seen me act!"

"You mean," Larry said, reviving, "*because* they haven't seen you act."

"That could only make things better." Marty pulled something out of his pocket and pressed it over his mouth; when he took away his hands, he was wearing a black beard that blended perfectly into his hair. He stood up, grasped his lapel, and orated. "My friends, my very dear friends throughout all the planets, though I am cognizant of the good elector's concerns, I must demur. He is overly concerned about a very minor, and self-correcting, problem."

We let out one unanimous hoot of surprised laughter, then broke up into chuckles.

"Why, it's Counterhand, Elector Counterhand to the letter!" Ogden rumbled, well into his third Scotch. "Excellent mimicry, lad."

"Try this one on for size." Marty whisked away the fake beard and pulled out a huge nose. He jammed it on, bent over a little, thrust his jaw forward, and declaimed, "Immorality, my fellow electors! It creeps upon us everywhere, it lurks in every corner!"

"Rudders himself!" Barry cried amid shouts of delight. "You've captured him perfectly!"

"How about this?" Marty tucked the nose away and, without any makeup at all, twisted his lips and pulled in his jaw, suddenly looking just like Quacketer, the reporter who had ambushed Barry. "Have you stopped beating your wife, Mr. Tallendar?"

"I don't have one," Barry cried with delight, amid hoots of laughter.

"See? I knew I could get you to say something incriminating!" Marty threw his chest out, lowered his eyelids, and looked down his nose at us. "Barry, dah-ling! How rude of you not to invite me when the press came calling!"

Everyone laughed, with an edge this time, and two or three shouted, "Marnie!" "Lulala, to the life!"

But Barry sobered. "I'd rather you didn't mock other members of the company, Mr. Kemp. We must stick together, you know."

"Oh," Marty said, abashed. "That include you, Mr. Tallendar?"

Barry gave him a slow smile. "No, of course not. It's open season on me, within the limits of courtesy."

Nothing definite you could say Marty did, except to suddenly have perfect posture—but he was so good a caricature of Barry that he must have been practicing. "Welcome to you all, my dear friends. And may I congratulate us all on having met our nemesis and advocate, the electronic press, and having prevailed!"

This time the hoots of laughter turned into a round of applause. Marty sat down, applauding himself and turning to Tallendar. Barry stood, smiling gently, eyes shining, and took his bows to the ovation of his colleagues.

Marnie hadn't been left out of it, though. Right after the evening newsfeed, they caught her walking her dog—and from the look on her face when the reporter asked, "What do you think of Elector Rudders's charges?" she hadn't been watching.

Either that, or she was doing a great job of acting. I was really surprised to see Marnie walking her own dog. I thought stars had services to do that kind of thing.

"I think the elector's charges are untrue, unfair, and un-chivalrous," Marnie said with a toss of her handsome head.

"You really think the Star Company's list of plays isn't immoral?"

Marnie laughed. "Immoral? My heavens, no! If you'd seen some of the plays my agent brings in, dah-ling, you'd know just how puritanical Barry's bill is!"

"Puritanical?" the reporter fairly yelped. "You call *Filters and Phyltres* puritanical?"

"Of course it is, dah-ling. The sex in it may begin as good clean fun, but it ends in mutual pain. If anything, I'd say it's too preachy."

"And what's it preaching?" The reporter sounded a little numb.

"Why, that sex is never just for fun," Marnie said. "That there's always some deeper part of yourself involved, a part that gets hurt."

"Would you say that's true from your own personal experience, Ms. Lulala?"

Marnie gave the guy a glare that would have shattered the camera's lens, if it had been made of glass. Then she gave him her most cherubic smile. "All I owe the public is a good performance, dah-ling. 'Night, now."

She turned away toward her building's door, but the reporter bleated, "So you think Elector Rudders is right to call for the Star Company to break up?"

Marnie whirled about, looking totally appalled for about half a second. Then her eyes narrowed. "The Elector is a know-nothing busybody who loves meddling in businesses that he knows nothing about—and believe me, my sweet, he knows absolutely nothing about the theater!"

Then she turned on her heel and stalked away into her lobby, dust-mop dog yapping over her shoulder.

Nobody stumbled into rehearsal *that* morning. They just grabbed their coffee on the fly, already chattering away, comparing notes on how they thought we had all looked on the screen, and how Marnie had looked just moments later.

Finally, Barry came in and held up his hands. "My friends! May we begin the day's work?"

They all turned toward him and let out a single unanimous cheer.

Barry stared, surprised. Then he smiled, holding up his hands for quiet again. "Thank you, thank you all, my friends—but the accolade you gave me last night will certainly suffice. I, at least, had time to prepare—but Ms. Lulala was caught completely off guard."

"Was she *really,* Mr. Tallendar?" Lacey asked.

"Completely," Barry assured her. "She was on the comm to me minutes after I reached home, a recording on my answering system really, scolding me in no uncertain terms for not having told her about the elector's activities, or warning her about the imminence of the electronic press— and, no, don't tell me that 'electronic press' is an oxymoron."

"The electronic press is an oxymoron, Mr. Tallendar," Marty said obligingly.

"So are the reporters," somebody answered, and the whole room erupted in far more laughter than the joke was worth. As it faded into chuckles, they took their seats around the table, still comparing notes on the festivities.

"If we could remove our attention from the Rudders Follies for a few minutes," Barry said, passing out new scripts, "I'd like to return you to the Play of the Day Club."

"Dashed confusing, all these scripts coming at us one after another, Barry," Ogden rumbled. "Why don't we rehearse each one at least halfway before we take up another, hey?"

"Because I'd like you to be working at memorizing them all, Ogden, while we're rehearsing the first. I'm anticipating that we'll open on Broadway with *Vagrants from Vega* in a month's time, and rehearse *Filters and Phyltres* while *Vagrants* is in performance. We'll open it after the third week of *Vagrants,* then play *Filters* for two weeks—I don't think it'll bear more traffic than that, being a revival—and go on to open *Didn't He Ramble.* Then the Shakespeare two weeks later, and the Aristophanes two weeks after that—"

"If Rudders gives us that long," Winston reminded him.

"If he doesn't, Marnie'll go in and eat him alive," Marty told him, and the whole cast erupted in laughter.

And so, of course, right into the middle of the laughter, in came Marnie. She stopped and stared, the color going out of her face, thinking we were laughing at her—but Marty caught sight of her and shouted, "Our heroine!" and the whole company leapt to its feet, applauding.

Marnie glanced quickly from them to Barry, then back to us all, face going rigid as she thought she was being mocked, then smoothing out as she realized we meant it. Finally, she began to smile and stepped forward to take her bows. As the applause died, she said, "Thank you, one and all. It really was nothing—only honest answers to dishonest questions."

"I'll mind my manners," I assured her, stepping up to put the cup of cappuccino I'd been saving next to her place at the table, then turning back to take her hat, dog, and coat.

"Why, thank you, Mr. Lazarian," she said with a gracious nod. Horace stood up to hold her chair, and she sat on it as though it were a throne, head high and eyes sparkling as she looked about the table. "I think I may enjoy this season, after all. What play is it today, Barry?"

But when we finished rehearsal that night, Barry and Horace and I came down in the elevator to find the lobby jammed again.

"More reporters?" Barry asked as he moved toward the front.

"Something a bit more grim, Barry," Marnie informed him. "Larry went out and caught sight of a few rough-looking men lurking down the block with a bottle and some ugly muttering."

I was sure Larry had dodged back in so fast he could've qualified for the track team. I started grinning and edged my way to the front.

"They saw me and let out a cry like hounds sighting a fox, Mr. Tallendar." Larry was pale. "I thought I had better wait for your direction."

Which was more than he had done in rehearsal—but what the hey, we all learn humility somewhere. I felt my eyes widening in innocence, my grin loosening in a pathetic, eager-to-please look.

"The police, Barry," Ogden suggested.

"I think they'll be rather slow in answering tonight," Barry said slowly. "All things considered, my friends, I think a sally in force . . . Horace, what's the matter with Ramou?"

"Oh, he gets these spells from time to time," Horace assured him, and turned to me. "No, Ramou! The idea is to avoid an incident, not create one!"

"I won't start anything," I promised.

Barry gave me a narrow look. "Don't finish it either, Ramou! We mustn't fight back if we're attacked, unless they break through our line to the ladies."

"Oh, we're to stay back here and let you be decimated?" Marnie demanded.

"Only for appearance' sake, my dear. I assure you, it's

vital that we be unquestionably seen as nonviolent. Ready, everyone? Sally forth!"

I was about to object to his taking point, but he was out the door, and I couldn't do anything about it except to hurry after him. So did everyone else; we marched out, heads high, steps firm, Horace muttering at me, "Remember, Ramou, no fighting! None!"

"Aw . . ." I began, but that was when they hit us.

Suddenly it wasn't just the one bottle, it was a dozen, and they were all being waved aloft and swung down at us by a bunch of bums in duroplex jackets and jeans, just off the late shift at the Government Assistance office, faces red, eyes glaring, breath stinking, bellowing such choice compliments as:

"Buncha faggot creeps!"

"Whores of Babylon!"

"Death to the effeminate!"

"Porno queens!"

"Lousy pimp hustlers!"

. . . and other cheery slogans demonstrating a high level of culture and an open mind. It hit me like a sledgehammer—we were being swamped by the Fundamentalist Brigade!

"No, Ramou!" Horace wailed.

"Just blocking, Mr. Burbage," I called back. Pain shot through my forearms as bottles and fists glanced off them—but from the outside, it only looked as though I were jogging my arms like a cheerleader. One of the bums tried to jump past me to get at the girls, but I stuck out a foot and he fell flat on his face.

"No fighting!" Horace wailed.

"Buncha faggot cowards!" a bum yelled, swinging his bottle roundhouse at my head—then whirling around and crashing into his buddy, 'cause at the last split second my head wasn't there.

"We are men of peace!" Barry cried. "We must not strike out!"

"I didn't," I shouted. "He tripped!"

Then, suddenly whistles were shrilling all around us, police were moving in and hauling the bums off, and bright lights were shining in our eyes. There was another crowd around us, and somebody was orating. "There it was, folks, a spontaneous demonstration against the immorality of the Star Company! Mr. Tallendar, what did you do to start this brawl?"

"We came out the door," Barry answered. "But you know how it is."

"No! How?"

"Muggers will be muggers," Barry sighed. "This is New York."

15

They couldn't bear to edit that out—it made such a great tag line. "Muggers will be muggers," Barry said again from the screen. "This is New York." Then the camera zoomed out to include the reporter, turning to face his audience—with all of us in the background. We all looked wonderful, on the screen in Carstairs'—but not in real life. Lacey and Susanne were still a little shaken, and Marnie was still making reassuring noises to them—she had decided to join us, for once. Larry wasn't looking any too good himself, had a bruise or two—but I saw on the screen that it was *him* Barry had been telling not to fight, not me.

The anchor came back, saying, "In spite of his nonchalance, though, Mr. Tallendar has cause for concern. Unconfirmed sources tell us that he has hired bodyguards for his actors."

"What?" several voices said, all faces turning to Barry.

"Unconfirmed indeed," he assured us, "because it's not true. However, if you feel the need . . ."

"Oh, come now, Barry!" Marnie scoffed. "For a rabble like that? I wouldn't lower myself to it!"

"Surely taxis will suffice," Winston protested.

"I should think so," Barry said, "if you will all promise me to use them. I shall reimburse you in advance, of course."

"Sure, if you're paying," Marty said. "But you might try *telling* us some things in advance, too, Mr. Tallendar."

"Why, Marty," Barry murmured, "whatever could you mean?"

"You knew those reporters were laying for us, didn't you?"

"Not *knew,* no . . ."

"Oh, spare us the epistemological question, Barry," Ogden rumbled. "You made a damned accurate guess."

"Well, since you mention it, Ogden, yes," Barry admitted. "I had a notion someone might have tipped the news services to the fact that there was a small mob assembled near our building."

"Just who did you have in mind?"

"Well, considering that, over dinner last night, we saw Elector Rudders on the screen, displaying large holos of each of us, one by one—"

"And the Assembly's Rules of Order powerless to stop him," Horace interjected.

"And that he derided Tridiment for renting us a rehearsal room on Times Square—well, his more unruly supporters were bound to take it as a hint, especially the ones who happen to be out of work at the moment and spend their time watching screens in public places . . ."

"You mean he didn't even have to issue orders?" Ogden rumbled a laugh. "Dashed good! Henry II, rolling on the floor and ranting, 'Will no one rid me of this meddlesome priest!' Eh!"

"The technique is well known," Barry agreed, "and the news services are aware of it, too. They were also aware that the end of our rehearsal day would probably give them just time enough to have an exciting clip for the evening feed."

"But, Mr. Tallendar!" For once, Lacey looked surprised, maybe even shaken. "You mean it was all just a show?"

"That's what it amounts to, my dear—but a show with no producer, and no director. Not that it mattered—the actors knew their paces."

"Oh, no! I can't *let* that go!" Marty was on his feet, sticking the false nose over his own mass of schnozz, hand on lapel, orating, "Now, my fellow goons! There is no need for me to show you their pictures—I did that yesterday, on 3DT. And there is no need for me to tell you your places—

but just to be on the safe side, you three hide behind the left-hand side of the building, you four over at the right, and you five across the street. Now, here are your bottles—oh, all right, empty them first, if you must . . . Right, let's run it through, then . . .

"But, Mister Rudders!" A high nasal voice, as he yanked the nose off and hunched over a little. "What's our cue?

"C-u-u-u-u-ue?" Nose on, hand on lapel. "You've been playing pool all these years, and you don't know how to take a cue? Right, now, remember to play to camera—what is it, group two?

"Duh, hey, uh, Mistuh Rudduhz." A deep husky voice, no fake nose—and, somehow, Marty looked like a beetle-browed Neanderthal. "What's our, uh, motivation?"

"The eternal thanks of the LORDS party, Mr. Blow, and a little extra in your Government Assistance check. Now, all together . . . One . . . two . . . cue! No, no, group one, you're supposed to cross toward the doorway! Downstage, group two—don't block group one. Group three, counter when you're crossed . . ."

And on and on, going from Rudders, to Hophedder, to General Secretary Pohlola, fake beard following fake nose, fake cigar shooting a jet of water at a glass on the table, fake blaster whipping out to hold up the government for extra Assistance checks (it popped out the time-honored red flag with "Z-Z-Z-Z-Z-T!" on it in golden letters).

Finally, Barry managed to stop laughing long enough to rein him in. "Enough, enough, Marty! Any more, and I'll need abdominal surgery! Oh, my aching sides! But thank you, dear friend, for this priceless performance."

"Oh, it doesn't have to be priceless." Marty held out a cupped palm. "You can always slip a bonus in my pay envelope."

"You would get my check in the morning, but I'm afraid nothing would check you." Barry glanced at his watch. "Time, dear friends, time to call it an evening. We must be up betimes, to rehearse. Let us all repair to our cabs, thence to our beds. Good night!"

He stood up, and Horace, Winston, Ogden, and Marnie stood with him. But Larry called, "Just one more round!"

"Perhaps just one." Barry turned back, suddenly serious. "But do keep it to just that one, won't you, Mr. Rash?"

A somber mood settled down—one that hadn't been hovering very far away, after all.

Barry realized, and tried to shrug it off. He forced a smile. "After all, the ladies need their beauty sleep—and Marty needs it more than any of them."

Marty tipped an imaginary hat. "I could pull a Rip Van Winkle, Mr. Tallendar, and it wouldn't help."

"It certainly wouldn't help rehearsal tomorrow morning," Barry countered, smiling. "And so to bed, my friends—early, eh?"

They gave him a loud promise with raised glasses, and he turned away, still forcing the smile.

Horace lingered. "Ramou, won't you join us?"

I glanced at my own generation, then stepped over to Horace, walking with him after Barry and saying, low-voiced, "I think I'd better stay with this crew, Horace. Something tells me they're not going to be good little boys and girls and go straight home."

Horace glanced back with anxiety.

"Even if they do," I said, "somebody's gotta keep Larry and Marty from braining each other."

"Well, that's so," Horace allowed. "There's nothing to spur on male antagonism, like the presence of young and pretty ladies. Though I hadn't thought Marty particularly susceptible to the fair sex . . ."

I looked up, startled. "You mean he's gay?"

"Only Marty knows for sure, and perhaps not even he. Do take a cab, though, won't you, Ramou?"

"As soon as I've seen them safely home, Horace," I promised. "You sure you want me barging in, even at such an unseemly hour?"

"Of course!" He seemed shocked. "Where else would you sleep? And so late due to your efforts on our behalf, too! Have no fear, Ramou—I'll be glad to wake up at any hour to let you in. And Ramou . . ." He grasped my arm. "No fighting, eh?"

"I promise I won't start anything," I said.

But he knew me too well already, and the grip didn't loosen. "Not just 'not start,' Ramou—not lure anyone else into starting anything. Promise?"

I sighed. "You're a hard man, Horace Burbage—but all right, I promise. Only real, genuine defense of myself—or that troupe of young actors in there."

"Ah." Horace looked back briefly, anxiety furrowing his face. "So that's your reason. You don't depend on them to be prudent, eh?"

"Would you?"

"I suppose not," he sighed. "But do come home as soon as you can, Ramou. I'll be awaiting your report with bated breath."

"Then I'd better bring a cat. All right, I promise I'll come by your place as soon as all of them are inside theirs."

"I'd appreciate it." He smiled. "Break a leg, Ramou."

Well, after all—he didn't say whose.

I saw him out to the curb, where Barry was waiting by a cab and the others were just pulling away in shiny plastic teardrops with robot drivers. I waved as Horace climbed in, then turned back into Carstairs' to find my colleagues, whether they liked it or not.

Just in time, too—Larry was looking a little too ruddy, and Marty was saying, "Prostituting my art? Rash, if I'm a prostitute, you're a cast-iron virgin!"

"That's just your virgin of the story," I said, sitting down.

Larry transferred his furious glare to me, and Marty protested, "Hey! No undercutting my punch lines!"

Susanne looked relieved, but Lacey said, "It really was *under*cutting, too, Ramou. Where did you ever find such a weak pun?"

"Ramou." Larry's eyes took on a nasty glitter. "Where did you ever find such an asinine name?"

I felt the surge of grade-school embarrassment—how many times had I had to suffer that question? And from somebody who was nominally adult, too! The old responses came surging out; I could feel the wolfish grin pulling at my lips; but I had promised Horace, so I kept a poker face and said, "Comes from an ancient and honorable name, Lawrence—well, strike the 'honorable.' Comes from the middle, in fact—'Scaramouch.' "

They all stared. Then Susanne said, "Really, Ramou?"

"Really." I frowned around at them. "What's so spooky?"

"Nothing at all," Lacey said, "especially not in Carstairs'. It's a theatrical name, Ramou."

"From the commedia del l'arte." Larry smiled, feeling safely superior again.

"Oh." I said. "So that's where my father got the name from."

"Was he in the theater?"

"He was a traveling man," I said, as noncommittally as possible, and reached for the pitcher. "Ah, one final round! How nice of you to save one for me!"

Marty yelped, and Lacey said, "You might pour it in a glass first, Ramou."

"Yeah, I suppose it could go around one more time," I sighed. I poured and passed it on; Larry topped off his glass, then the ladies', and Marty finished it. "To health!" I said, lifting my glass.

"To health," they chorused, but I got some funny looks, and Lacey said, "Odd toast, Ramou."

"Okay," I said, "to youth!"

Well, they drank to that one.

"To beer!"

They drank—and drained them.

"To bed!" I set down my glass and stood up.

The girls looked surprised, and Larry smiled. "Perhaps *you* need an early bed time, Ramou—but we don't."

"We promised Mr. Tallendar," I reminded.

They all sobered a little, and Lacey said, "Oh. You were appointed." And Larry said, "The techie is our watchdog."

That term "techie" bothered me, somehow—maybe because of the diminutive tacked onto the end. But I forced the smile and said, "It's eleven P.M. as it is. I'd rather not have to bring *two* urns of coffee tomorrow."

"Oh, all right!" Lacey sighed, standing up and picking up her pouch. "I'm coming, Mama."

The rest of them got up, too, with a little more good-natured grousing, and we headed for the door.

I tapped Marty as we followed the girls and Larry. "Hang back a bit, okay?"

He slowed, letting the others get a step or two ahead of us. "What's up, Ramou?"

"Can I borrow your beard and nose for a while?"

He frowned. "Well, sure, but it's not as easy as it seems." He pulled them out and handed them to me. "Just be careful, okay? They took a lot of hours."

I stared at them. "You mean you *made* these?"

"Well, sure." He looked pleased. "Every actor should be able to put on his own makeup. Though I do like to think I have a touch for it."

"A touch? You're a genius!" I pressed the beard against my face; it clung like a baby. "What holds it on?"

"It latches onto your beard stubble, the way burrs hold onto your pants. That's right, the nose just presses on . . ."

"How come I can still breathe?"

"Skill," Marty assured me, then covered a chuckle. "I take it back—it does come easy."

"I look pretty stupid, huh?"

"No, no, really! You look comical—I mean, as though you're trying to make people laugh! Just a real nice guy who looks like a scream! It's not the makeup, Ramou—you've got the talent."

"Thanks for the compliment." From him, it was one. I guessed all those years of looking friendly and eager had left their mark. "But doesn't the nose look like it's stuck on?"

"Yeah, but leave it on for a few minutes, and it'll adjust to your skin tone. Before, I was just yanking it off too fast to give it a chance. Believe me, you'll look real."

"Dumb, but real," I interpreted. "Okay, let's catch up."

"Oh, yeah!" Marty looked up, taken aback. "They'll be in the cab and out of sight by now!"

"I don't think so," I said—and sure enough, we came out to the end of a breezy argument.

"But we promised Mr. Tallendar," Susanne was saying.

"Pooh! There's no danger, as long as we stick to the main streets and follow the safety rules! How far is it—two blocks to the tube, and how far from your stops?"

"A couple of blocks," Lacey admitted.

"Three," Susanne said grudgingly.

"There, you see? I'll escort you each to your doors before I go home! No danger at all!"

"Well . . . okay."

They turned and walked away.

"I don't like the sound of this," Marty muttered.

"So are you going to let them walk into danger without protection?" I gave him a nudge. "Go be gallant, Marty! I'll be right behind you. You won't see me, but I'll be there."

He gave me a frown. "How'd you know this was going to happen?"

"Because I've met Larry before," I said. "He wore a dozen different faces and bodies, but they all had the same mind. Go protect the maidens from distress, pal!"

"Maidens, my eye," he muttered, but he turned away and caught up with them.

I waited a few minutes, then crossed the street and followed. It wasn't hard—they were making enough noise for a dozen. Whether it was the festive mood from Carstairs' carrying over, or whistling in the dark, I didn't know—but it didn't matter. They were a magnet.

I was watching for iron filings.

They made it to the tube stairs without any trouble, and went on down with twenty or thirty other people. It was eleven P.M., and the theater crowds were on their way home. I slipped in among them, one more unobtrusive face and certainly not the only one wearing a beard, keeping my eyes and ears wide open.

The car sighed to a stop on the other side of the clear wall.

It slid open, and everyone stepped aside for the passengers to file out—this wasn't that kind of a rush hour. Then in they streamed, and I went with the flow.

I began to hear occasional words—"Rudders" and "actors," with "immoral" and "indecent" thrown in—but I couldn't get a fix on them. The voices sounded rough, but they were buried in the crowd. My happy quartet roared on, though, laughing and trying to top each other's lines, sounding a little hysterical by now. They might as well have been wearing signs.

The third time the train stopped, my happy campers got off. There was a sudden rush and surge; someone jostled me, hard, as he hurried for the door. Several people called out in protest, but the hounds were already out the door, and I had to slide and sidle pretty fast to keep up with them.

They were better dressed than the ones this afternoon had been, and looked to be working, at least. Some of them wore blue collars, some of them wore cheap *complets*, but they all had the same fanatical, self-righteous set to the jaw. A couple of them were pretty big. Fear seized my vitals, then surged up in elation—I wasn't even going to have to try.

"Where'd they go?"

"Up there—the escalator!"

"We could jump 'em before then."

"No. Too public."

An empty tube station, too public? What did they have in mind? I decided I should cut them in on reality right then—but I remembered my promise to Horace. It grated, but I followed along at the back. They didn't even notice I was there—or if they did, everyone assumed someone else had invited me.

Then we were on the escalator and out onto the street. Fifty feet ahead of us, my partying party was just passing out of the light, into the pocket of darkness between two street lamps.

"All right, get 'em," somebody deep and hoarse said up front, and we all started running.

I had just a glimpse of Larry and the girls looking up,

starting to look scared, and Marty looking terrified, before the toughs hit, yelling, "Whores!" "Desecrators!" "Blasphemers!" "Seducers!"

Lacey screamed, but Susanne saved her breath and started kicking. She caught a goon on the shin, and he howled, jumping up just long enough for me to catch his collar and yank him off his feet. Then I noticed Larry, white as a sheet but making a few punches before a fist slammed into his jaw. I pushed on the shoulder, kicked in the ankle, and the guy stumbled forward; he and Larry went down in a tangle.

Lacey was screaming; some Bible-shouting sickie was ripping her dress off with a gloating laugh. His attention was pretty well fixed; he didn't even notice me, just the sudden pain in his back. He straightened up, and I pulled back, kicking forward, then spun aside fast, so that he staggered back into one of his buddies. He turned with a roar of rage and started slugging. Buddy yelped, "It wasn't me, it was him!"

The bodice-ripper was too angry to hear him, but the other two looked up, startled, and I knew I'd been fingered. That was okay—I didn't have to be discreet. I stepped in, catching one of them in the solar plexus, then the jaw, spun to kick the other on the kneecap, turned back to the first just in time for his fist to graze the side of my jaw—graze or not, it *hurt*! But I doubled him over with two quick chops and a punch, then whirled back to the bodice-ripper and his grappler, who were just now realizing I wasn't on their side.

Oh, it was glorious! Five toughs left, three of whom didn't know anything more about fighting than they'd grown up with—and from their style, I'd say they hadn't been reared in New York. I kicked and punched and lashed and chopped, catching punches on my shoulders and arms, but stepping aside in time to make them glancing blows, spinning from one to another in a *kata* drill that would have made Sensei proud.

Then, suddenly, three of them were down and groaning, and the fourth was advancing on me, a sidling step at a time, one arm outstretched with a fist on the end, the other cocked and ready.

I was tempted to step back and bow—the guy knew some kind of martial art. But I didn't think he was in the mood to honor the etiquette, so I feinted a kick, punched as he started to block, slammed a real punch, and felt it connect— just before a large rock slammed into my jaw, and I saw stars. I fell back, bricks rasping at my back. I couldn't see much in the star glare or hear anything through the roaring, so I punched and kicked by sheer instinct. Somebody was yelling, and I heard a Valkyrie scream, but I kept on punching and hoping I was facing the right way.

Then I could see again, and the big guy was down on one knee, curled around an agony in his midriff. One of my blind kicks had connected.

I stepped forward, feeling as though I was swaying and hoping I wasn't.

Susanne stepped in with a lifted high heel.

"No!" I yelled. "He's *mine*!"

She looked up, startled—I don't think she'd recognized me. But the big guy grunted and came up in a rush, lashing out with a kick that would have broken my hip, if I'd been there. I managed to sidestep just enough, then jumped in before he'd quite recovered, and hit him in the sore stomach again. He gagged, doubling over, but I knew the trick—I bent over him, fist swinging back, and he straightened up hard and fast, trying to hit me in the face with his head. But I leapt back, then in again to shove him on up and back, hard, into the wall, and hit him three times before he could recover. He slumped to the ground, out cold.

I spun around, breathing hard, looking for someone else to beat on . . .

. . . and nearly laughed my head off.

Two of the toughs had pulled themselves to their feet and were hulking over Marty—who had his "blaster" out, and was stammering, "Not—not an-nother st-step! Back off, b-back off! Or I'll sh-shoot!"

Larry was trying to pull himself off the ground long

enough to be of some use. Lacey was trying to help him, so of course he couldn't get his feet under him.

Susanne was stepping in with shoe lifted and blood in her eye.

One of the toughs made a grab for the gun.

Marty jumped back, but the big hand clamped down over his, and the gun made its little sizzling noise, as out came the banner proclaiming, "Z-Z-Z-Z-Z-T!"

For a second, everyone was frozen, outrage building in the two apes.

That was long enough. I kicked the first one out of the way, punched the other one twice, rocked back from a punch of his—he caught me just wrong, and pain blazed in my shoulder—then caught him with a kick and two more punches. He slumped, out cold.

I spun about, to find that Larry had managed to pull himself together just enough for the last tough to trip over him. *"Y-a-a-a-h!"* the guy yelled, arms windmilling before he slammed into the concrete. He tried to lever himself up on his forearms, shaking his head, and Susanne stepped in, slamming down with that shoe. The guy bucked, then fell back still.

"Oh!" Hand at her lips, eyes wide. "I didn't—is he . . ."

I dropped down beside him, wheezing and panting, and felt for his jugular. Then I shook my head, climbing to my feet. "No. He's—just fine—or will be."

Larry was climbing up Lacey, with Marty's help. "I—thank you, stranger . . . I—"

"Don't mention it." I pulled off the beard and popped off the nose.

Oh, it was worth a lifetime of labor, just to see the look on their faces.

I grinned and handed the makeup back. "Thanks, Marty. They would have recognized me from the news, you see. This way, they thought I was one of them."

"But—Ramou!" Larry exploded. "You *knew* they were going to try this!"

I shook my head. "Didn't know a damn thing. Just

trusted what Mr. Tallendar said." I turned back to Marty. " 'Fraid the beard's a little the worse for wear."

"Oh, it can be fixed." The rubber grin beamed up at me again. "Easier than I can, anyway. Thanks, Ramou. Thanks a lot."

"I'll say!" Susanne grabbed me and planted a huge kiss on my cheek. "Thanks is the least of it!"

Desire sizzled through me, leaving an imprint of flame where her lips had been, where her body had touched me for a moment.

"Yes . . . thank you, Ramou," Lacey said, more slowly, and "Thanks," Larry muttered, as though a dentist had pulled it out of him.

"Glad to oblige." I looked around at our groaning but erstwhile enemies. "Let's get a block or two away from here, okay?"

Nobody argued.

Two blocks farther on, I flagged a cab. It swerved over, top swinging up. I bowed Lacey in and said, "Anybody mind taking a cab?"

They didn't.

I tapped at the door, wishing I could get some of Horace's makeup to cover the bruises. Maybe he'd be so sleepy he wouldn't notice . . .

"Who is it?" the door grid asked.

"Ramou," I answered.

Locks clicked and the door shot open. "Ramou! The most desperate—my heavens, man! What happened?"

"We won." I grinned at him. "I kept my promise, Horace—I didn't start it, and I didn't con them into it. On top of that, I got our team home safely."

"Thank heaven for that!" He went loose with relief. "Come in, come in at once! We must get some bruise plasters on those horrible disfigurements!"

"Horrible?" I said as the door closed. "You'd praise Marty to the skies, if he made any that looked this good!"

"Only if he made them with makeup, Ramou. Come along, now."

As he was applying the plasters, I asked, "How come you're still wide awake and dressed? No confidence in me?"

"I have every confidence in you," he assured me. "It's merely that Barry just called. He had received a message from Merlo—it was left on his machine—and is now checking with Valdor, to confirm it. I'm waiting for him to call back."

I tensed. "Message? Merlo? What about?"

"Elector Rudders."

I groaned. "Do we have to take him seriously?"

"I'm afraid we do. He's been talking about *us* again, you see."

I frowned. "Us, actors, or us, the Star Company?"

"Us, the Star Company. He has told the Assembly that his staff will file tomorrow morning for an injunction to prevent our leaving Terra with our 'repertory of timeless shame'!"

16

So, all of a sudden, Horace and Barry decided we should leave for space, *now*—and they didn't seem to be too picky about which space they left for.

I got to hear them when Barry called a few minutes later. "Rather a compliment," he said, "if you look at it the right way."

"I don't," Horace snapped. "The man has enough influence to kill our dream aborning. But—why us, Barry?"

"Why not?" Barry shrugged. "More to the point, who told him what about us? This isn't his standard modus operandi."

"A good point." Horace frowned.

"Hey, hold on!" I yelled. "The guy's a nut! Worse, he's a nut in office! He doesn't need any more reason than he's said." Then I shut up, looking from one to another as an awful realization dawned. "You don't believe that's his real reason, do you?"

"Not for a moment," Horace assured me. "The LORDS never do anything for the reasons they say—their deeds are always just ploys, gambits in a larger game. Their pattern is to attack highly visible productions, not small fry who won't guarantee them a headline. Rudders is the worst of them—I've heard the gossip."

"What gossip?"

"That he instigated a boycott against the recording industry because one singer had refused to grant him her favors," Barry explained. "That he slandered a production on Broadway that was only slightly earthy, really quite moral—because he was having a quarrel with a friend who owned stock in it. No, rest assured, my young friend, if the estimable Elector Rudders has chosen us for a target, he definitely has either a personal reason, or a partisan one."

I frowned. "What personal reason? Who does he hate?" Then I remembered Virginia, and I began to feel sick.

"No, no," Horace said quickly. "I'm sure he doesn't know your young lady's father. What was her name, by the way?"

"Virginia Clapstick," I said.

Horace shook his head. " 'Clapstick' doesn't strike a bell, and there's no particular reason to think he'd have any animus against you."

"But there's no reason for him to have it in for any of us!"

"Reason or not," Barry said briskly, "I think it behooves us to lift off as soon as we can."

"Lift off? We don't even have a *ship*!"

Barry nodded. "Buy one."

I fairly felt my eyeballs bulge. "You don't just run out and buy a spaceship!"

"Why not?" Barry said reasonably. "It's in the budget."

"We can but try." Horace stepped over and clasped my arm. "Can you find Merlo?"

"Uh . . . yeah! Sure. Where did he call Barry—uh, Mr. Tallendar—from?"

"He was at home," Barry said, "trying to find a costumer. Priceless fellow! I hadn't managed to find one yet."

"And he'll wait for me there?"

"He may, or he may already be gone. But he told me where he would be—one of three bars out by the space-port."

"Bars?" Horace looked at Barry, appalled. "Has Merlo turned to the bottle?"

"No, no! He said something about trying to find a pilot he knows."

"Of course." Horace relaxed. "He's one step ahead of us—and you do have to have a pilot before you can lift ship, don't you? Good enough, Ramou. Go tell him we said to hire the man and buy the ship. Begin with his apartment, and if he's not there, search the bars. Is that as you wish, Barry?"

"Quite right," Barry said, "and send the bills to—"

"The Tallendar Building." I nodded, aglow as quickly as I'd been a-sink. "Right, chief! I'm off!"

The door closed behind the boy.

"Chief?" Barry said to me.

"Just accept it," I advised him. "As long as he's referring to you with respect, we're doing well." Somehow, I didn't question whether or not Barry was serious; the threat was real, and I suddenly found that this new-fledged company did matter to me. "I will ring up the members of the company and get us all packed."

"No, Horace, you can't take that all on yourself! I shall call half of them."

"No," I said. "You take Marnie. She's easily as great a problem as all the rest put together."

He looked stricken.

"She won't listen to me," I explained.

Barry frowned and nodded, his faith in me restored. "Certainly, Horace. Besides, I couldn't ask that of you."

I disconnected, reflecting that the ghost of Oliver Cromwell never ceases to haunt the theater. Of course, the spirit of prudery and repression goes back much farther than that old Puritan, but it was he who succeeded in closing the theaters, where most others only tried, and failed. His secretary Milton defended freedom of the press most zealously, but didn't seem to notice what was happening to the playhouses.

Of course, Milton was a writer, not an actor. Even so, he may have noticed that the plays of Marlowe and Shakespeare established a profoundly moral environment, which more than redeemed their moments of earthiness; but his employer Cromwell saw only the earthiness and none of the morality. Either that, or he resented a competing, and more effective, preacher.

Charles II rescued England from his clutches, of course, and gave theater a new lease on life—but Puritanism had already been exported to the New World and managed to gain a stranglehold on the cultural spirit of America, possibly by dedicating the colonies to the accumulation of money, of which they were careful custodians, being master merchants. So Cromwell died in England, but his ghost lived on in America.

Not that my brethren of the Thespianic Art have ever been above reproach, mind you, nor the ladies, either—but I have always wondered if the true motive of Cromwell and his ministers had been to silence a dissenting voice. Actors and playwrights tend to be liberal, partly because they are seldom wealthy, and partly because comedy implies criticism of the pompous and self-righteous and requires the freedom to take a jab at anyone in sight. Governments loom larger than individuals and are always the most obvious targets, and fairer game than most, as are politicians and other highly visible people—but visible people tend to have influence, and seek ways to silence the voices of conscience. The targets become the gunmen.

Elector Rudders was only the latest in a long line of critics of the followers of the Muses—and as usual, his motives were suspect, being ostensibly moral but primarily political, aimed at increasing the power of himself and his party.

Of course, one of the LORDS' primary efforts was to prevent the entertainment media from spreading to the newer colony planets—they were quite well entrenched on the old. This was only one more gambit in the LORDS' attempt to control the dissemination of information; they knew that the I.D.E. would never consent to controlling which plays or songs would be exported to the frontier, and that opening it to private enterprise would result in an indiscriminate, chaotic barrage of all sorts of programs, most of which would be inimical to their goals. The only alternative was to prevent the export of 3DT, audio recordings, and, yes, even of books. They could not succeed entirely, of course, but they were trying, and between the astronomically high cost of interstellar shipping, which prevents all but the wealthiest pioneers from affording luxuries such as 3DT cubes, and the machinations of the LORDS party, the flow of information to the colonies was being kept down to a trickle. Rest assured, if Rudders really thought there were any significant amount of money to be made by marketing recordings or cubes on the outlying worlds, he would have done it himself—or if he really cared at all about the welfare of the colony planets. His goals were power and wealth, as were those of the other members of his party; I cannot honestly believe that any of them cared about the happiness of the people of the Terran Sphere. Instead, he viewed all but the oldest (and most lucrative) of the colonies as being burdens on the shoulders of Terra—by which he meant that they were an economic drain that was costing more than it brought in, and were therefore of no use to him, since they were not yet markets for the companies in which he owned stock.

But let us be fair to the man. To do him justice, he had been grinding his ax against *all* the media, and most especially against freedom of speech itself; he had not targeted 3DT or theater alone. If he had mentioned live theater, it was presumably because the actresses could be touched after the show was over—or were not willing to be touched, by him.

These musings had taken me over to the food dispenser and through the compounding of a tall drink. I now returned to sit down by the communicator with a sigh. It was going to be a long evening. I had to call my neighbor, Borgio, and ask him to keep an eye on the apartment for me. One doesn't give up an apartment in Manhattan lightly, or simply because one is going to be gone for a year. I would ask the Tallendar clerk to pay the tab; perhaps I could arrange a sublease by mail.

Which meant that I had to tidy up a bit more than usual, to leave the apartment ready to be viewed by strangers. And pack.

But, first things first. I referred to my company roster and started punching numbers.

Ogden was at home, which was good, but he was drunk, which was usual. I was braced for it; Ogden is so rarely fully sober that one is quite shocked if one finds him in full possession of his faculties—almost as though one were meeting a stranger, as it were.

"Horace! Good to see you again so soon! Come over and share a bottle, why don't you?"

"Sorry, Ogden. Press of affairs, you know."

"Affairs?" He gave me an owlish look through the screen. "What affairs could concern you at this hour of the night, Horace? . . . Oh! Pardon the indelicacy." He leaned back from the screen, far enough for me to see the glass of amber fluid in his hand. "Well, let's not keep the lady waiting. What did you wish to tell me?"

"There's no lady at the moment, Ogden. The affairs are purely those of business. I'm afraid we're going to have to move the departure date up a bit."

"Ever at your disposal!" He waved the tumbler in a grand gesture, spilling half the contents, which was probably just as well for both him and it. "Ready at a moment's notice! By how much are we moving it up?"

"By a month. That moment you spoke of?"

Ogden paled. "You don't mean it!"

"I'm afraid I do. Dawn tomorrow, Ogden."

"Dawn! But I won't even have time to hunt up more than a half-dozen cases of good Scotch!"

"I'm afraid we must all rough it," I soothed. "See if you can't make do with bourbon, there's a good chap."

"Bourbon! Horace, please! Spare me the obscenities!"

"My apologies."

"Can't put this off a week or two, eh?"

"Afraid not. This is a chance at earning an income, you know, Ogden."

The great man nodded his shaggy head across the screen. "Understood. Oh, yes, all right, tomorrow morning, then."

"Very good. We'll send a car." Actually, I had in mind a

small bus. "Can you have everything else packed in time, Ogden?"

"*What* else? Oh. My makeup and costumes. Yes, they're in trunks already."

"Delighted to hear it." I sighed. "You might wish to bring some rehearsal clothes, too, Ogden, and a *complet* or two, for meeting the natives at local festivities."

"Really! Didn't know they wore more than skin. Well, if you say so, Horace, I'll throw something in a suitcase."

"Underwear might be a good idea, too," I advised. "And socks. Don't forget socks."

He nodded, scribbling down a list. "Underwear . . . socks . . ." He looked up. "Toothbrush, I assume?"

"Yes, and the usual toiletries."

"Quite." Ogden glowered down at the list, then up at me. "Horace—you're sure this trip is necessary?"

"Well, Ogden, it is a chance at an income." I didn't mention it was possibly his last chance; we both knew that. "And Elector Rudders is fulminating against us, trying to have a court order drawn to keep us from lifting off."

"Rudders!" Ogden stared at me, shocked sober. "Bastard would do it, too—lost a starlet to me when he was just a clerk, and was a damn poor sport about it! Probably sulks about it still, when he's alone. No, Horace, I'll be packed and ready by dawn!"

"Your apartment . . ."

"Own the blasted place. I'll leave a year's advance for the maintenance—if you can forward it to me, Horace?"

"I'll have them bill our account at Tallendar's." I made a note. "If you'll excuse me, Ogden, I've several others to call."

"Certainly, certainly," the old man rumbled. "Sunrise, eh? Must've lost a week or two somewhere . . ."

I sighed. "No, Ogden, we had to move the date up."

"Date? Quite so, quite so. When's opening?"

"In about four light-years. Good night, Ogden." I disconnected, paused for a sigh, then punched in Winston's number.

On the second ring, he answered. "Hello, this is Winston Carlton."

"Winston," I began, but he went right on talking. "I'm afraid I can't come to the phone right now, but if you'll leave a message when you see the green screen, I'll call you back as soon as I may."

I gnashed my teeth. I hate recordings.

"If it's truly an emergency," Winston's image said, "you can reach me at the following number. Good night, now." He disappeared into a wash of green that filled the whole screen. Over it, in yellow numerals, appeared a call number. I sighed, jotted it down, disconnected, and punched it in.

A suave face over a formal collar appeared, with a tapestried background behind. "The Pleiades. May I help you?"

The Pleiades! Well. But I shouldn't have been surprised—Winston was one of our more affluent members. "I believe Mr. Winston Carlton is having a nightcap at your establishment," I said. "I'd like to speak with him; this is Horace Burbage."

"Ah, yes, Mr. Burbage! Your last visit was quite pleasant; you should honor us more often. I regret to say that Mr. Carlton is with friends; is it truly an emergency?"

I ground my teeth and forced a smile. "I'm afraid it is. If you would be so kind?"

"I will see if he will accept the call. If you would hold for a few minutes, please?" He smiled politely, and the screen filled with a brocaded background behind the word "Pleiades" in ornate script, while Beethoven's Seventh filled the speakers. I took a deep breath and forced myself into calmness; I was feeling anything but pastoral. Then the screen cleared, and I found myself looking at the villainous face that I had known from its youth, when Winston was a neophyte and I an old hand of five years' experience—but the picture was very fuzzy and kept shifting about. "Hello, Horace! Is there a difficulty?"

I frowned. "Is something wrong with your set, Winston? You look rather murky."

"No, no! It's my pocket commset. Here, I'll ask the waiter to bring a full one."

Well, that explained it. Being so affluent, Winston carried a portable comm. It gave quite good sound, but the picture was of very low definition. After all, what can one expect from an optical pickup the size of one's fingernail? "No, don't bother, Winston—I won't be that long. I'm afraid we've come up against a bit of a snag."

"You don't mean the company's not going to happen after all?" The famous villainous features tightened in a glower that would have struck apprehension even into me, if I hadn't known him for the most gentle of souls.

"No, no," I said quickly. "We're going, and going quite well. In fact, immediately—it's become imperative that we lift off at dawn."

"Dawn! But what's gone wrong, Horace?"

"Elector Rudders," I said. "He—"

"Say no more." Winston's face tightened; he shared my views of the worthy elector (but worthy of what, I won't say). "What's he doing, Horace? Trying to keep us home?"

"Why, however did you guess?"

"It fits his logic. Which one of us has antagonized him?"

"I really couldn't say, Winston. It may be that we're a part of a larger picture that we can't see just yet."

"You're generous."

"Am I really? At any rate, we have to lift off at dawn."

"Yes, of course." He looked unutterably sad. "Ah, that events should come to such a pass! But if Rudders is about to pounce, it behooves us to make a dash. Newark Spaceport, of course?"

"Of course," I agreed. "I'll call when we know which gate. Freight section, I suspect."

"Of course. We're the smallest part of the cargo, aren't we?" He managed a bleak smile. "Six A.M., then. In fact, I'm sure I'll be packed and ready by two. Anything I can do to help then?"

"Not at the moment," I replied, "but that could change."

"Do call me if anything does come up," he urged.

"I will," I assured him. "Good night, Winston." I disconnected. Then I took a moment or two to set myself—I was about to speak to a stranger. And, though he had seemed very pleasant in our interview after the call-back audition and during our one rehearsal, he was largely an unknown quantity. I referred to my notes and punched his number.

The screen cleared almost instantly, and I found myself staring at the bald head with the fringe of brown hair and the soft, round face that was beginning to show jowls. The image was muddy, and with rather poor definition. I sighed; another pocket unit—and, from the look of it, one much cheaper than Winston's. The background wasn't very clear, but I thought I could make out rows of books.

"Charles Publican," he said, his tones low. "Oh! Mr. Burbage. Pardon my softness, but I'm in the public library at the moment. If you'd like to hold on, I'll go to a pay comm."

I stared; then I remembered that the library had begun to stay open twenty-four hours a day, as soon as they had finished transcribing even their oldest books to computer text.

"No need," I assured him. "I've some news, Mr. Publican. When you hear it, you may not wish to join us after all."

"And miss the chance I've been yearning for all these years?" He smiled. "I doubt it. But tell me, Mr. Burbage."

"We're moving our departure date up a bit, Mr. Publican."

"Oh?"

Wasn't giving me much to react to, was he? "Tomorrow morning. Six A.M. Can you be at Newark Spaceport?"

"No problem," he assured me.

I was amazed; he might have been talking about a luncheon engagement.

"May I know the reason?" he asked.

"Certainly. Elector Rudders is seeking a court order to keep us from leaving Terra."

"No surprise," he assured me. "I heard him at the Automat over dinner. I'm still trying to digest it."

I wondered if he meant the dinner, or the elector.

"I'll be packed in an hour," he said, "if you need help organizing the company to go, Mr. Burbage . . ."

"I'll call if we need you," I assured him. "Otherwise, we'll have a car pick you up at six."

"My hotel might not understand," he said. "I'll meet you at the spaceport."

I understood—he was going to have to leave his lodging by an indirect route, possibly without paying his bill. I decided that he had been living on the edge, trying to work his way into the business all these years, after all. "I'll call as soon as we know the gate number, then."

"I'd appreciate that. Well, I'd better finish my notes and go pack. Good night, Mr. Burbage."

"Good night, Mr. Publican." I disconnected with the odd, unsettling feeling that I had just finished speaking to a rather strange man, though I couldn't have told you the reason. On the surface, he seemed to be entirely ordinary.

Perhaps that was why. In the world of the theater, an ordinary person is an anomaly.

I leaned back and drew a deep breath. So much for the character actors. Now for the hard part . . .

17

I shot into the lift as though I had a meteorite stuck to my seat. I punched for the ground floor, but it seemed to take forever for that car to reach the lobby. I was just as hot to trot as they were, maybe more so. You see, I had stopped into the employment agency I had registered with that second day, to tell them to forget about me—and they told me that a very polite gentleman in a very quiet gray *complet* had been in to show them my picture and ask if they had seen me.

For once, I was grateful that people in New York don't want to become involved. They had told the nice man that they had never seen me, and they now told me that they never wanted to see me again, either. The nice man had asked if he could see their records, and they had told him, "Not without a court order"; apparently his wasn't the first such request they'd had. He had smiled and thanked them and gone out, and they had dug out my registration form and slipped it into the atomizer. They hinted they might do the same to me if I stuck around, so I thanked them nicely and left the premises, hopefully not too quickly.

I didn't need to be told who the nice man was, of course. Big Daddy had been just as quick to hire his Big-Time Investigator as I had thought he would be, and they had loosed a man from their New York office to check the usual contact points for strangers who had left in the night.

Why New York?

Why not?

Also possibly because of that pickpocket who had used

my credit card—but I wondered if the investigator's firm had men checking Chicago, Los Angeles, San Francisco—yes, this could be very expensive. I resolved to make sure it was wasted money.

Since then, I had been very careful to watch my back trail, and had gone to great lengths to lose anybody who just happened to be going in the same direction I was for more than a block. I hadn't seen anybody follow me as far as Horace's apartment building, and I double-checked as I came out, and checked again at the street corner, but as far as I could tell, I didn't have any unwelcome company. So, all in all, when Barry told me to go tell Merlo to buy a spaceship, I was all too happy to oblige. Lifting off at dawn tomorrow sounded like a fine idea. I wondered why they had to wait so long.

I took a few shortcuts on the way to Merlo's block of flats; they must have added at least half a mile to the route. The two subways involved had very few riders so what with one thing and another, I was pretty sure that when I arrived at Merlo's door I didn't have company.

The bolts shot back, one after another, and he pulled the door open, head turned away from me and calling, "So the old hands are good people, Grudy, and the young folk are trainable."

"Oh, dear," said a sweet little voice that sounded like my maiden aunt, if I'd had one. "This is such terribly short notice, Merlo."

"I'd have told you sooner, Grudy, but they didn't tell me I could hire the costumer. They still haven't, but if they do . . ."

"They do," I assured him.

"They just did." He was walking back to the commset as he said it. I peeked over his shoulder and saw the perfect grandmother's face on the screen. Her hair was gray and tied up in a bun; her face was wrinkled but kindly, and she wore real honest-to-goodness glasses, presumably being one of those people whose eyes have such a rare conformation that they can't have their natural lenses corrected. Either that, or she was insecure.

Very much so, at the moment—but which of us wasn't? "We lift off at dawn," I said.

Merlo nodded, unsurprised, and the face on the screen said, "Well, they've always called me in at the last minute, anyway. Who is the young man, Merlo?"

"My new assistant, Grudy. Ramou, meet Grudy Drury, *costumière* extraordinaire. Grudy, this is Ramou Lazarian. He doesn't know anything about theater, but he's eager, and a good kid."

"Dear me. Can he fix a Fabric-cator?"

"Sure, if I give him the manual. I wouldn't say you'll have the latest or the best, Grudy, but not far from it."

"And it's been so long since I worked with real actors," she sighed, "at least, in person. All this rental-house design has been without ever seeing the people who wear them, Merlo—you know?"

"I can imagine. But it does mean leaving New York, Grudy—and at dawn tomorrow."

"Well, I know a perfectly lovely young actress who needs an apartment, so I'll have no problem making the arrangements," Grudy said.

"Send your flat maintenance tab to Tallendar," I offered.

"Barry?" She looked doubtful; then her face cleared. "Oh, you mean his brother. So that's where Barry's getting the money for this."

Barry? Did everyone in this business know him?

"It's so sudden," she sighed, "but I can't resist it. Very well, Merlo. Where am I supposed to be, and when?"

"We'll send a car," he assured her, "at six A.M." Then he grinned. "It'll be good to work with you again, Grudy."

She smiled, dimpling. "And with you, dear boy. Good night, then, Merlo."

Dear boy? Just how far back did they go, anyway?

The screen went dark, and Merlo spun around in his chair to face me. "So Tallendar said yes?"

"Both of them." I nodded. "Buy the ship and send the bill, et cetera."

"Great!" Merlo surged to his feet, his eyes gleaming, and I decided I'd lucked into the right boss. "Glad he did the wise thing and let me take care of the spacing. But what do I know from spaceships, huh, kid? First we find us a pilot— one we can afford." He grabbed his jacket and turned to the door. I followed.

He hesitated with his thumb over the pressure patch. "We're going into some pretty rough territory, kid. You can bow out if you want . . ." He didn't finish the sentence; I had catalogued my bruises, weighed them against the thrill of another fight, and started a grin. Merlo answered it with one of his own. "Oh, it's that kind of day, is it?"

"Too early for breakfast," I assured him. "We'll have to use our muggers for a late-night snack."

He laughed and clapped me on the shoulder. "Okay, kid! Off to the strip!"

I followed him out, deciding I could definitely put up with "kid."

When interstellar traffic started up on a commercial basis in the early 2200s, New York wanted to make sure it stood to gain as much thereby as any Terrestrial city. Of course, the main spaceport in the western hemisphere was in Florida, but it was rather far removed from the business centers, which each grew ballistic missile ports, then quickly realized that a missile port is not so terribly far removed from a spaceport. New York cast about for undeveloped land by the square mile, not too far distant from Manhattan, and finally realized what it had been saving the marshes of New Jersey for all those years.

Private houses had tried to grow there, but had developed an alarming tendency to become houseboats, so development had died. Commercial establishments tended to wish to be near housing, so they had let the wetter Meadowlands persist as the natural habitat of small furry animals, large broadcast towers, and a sports complex. The coming of space travel changed all that. Once recognizing that it was losing out on a potential bonanza, New York City authorized the Port Authority of New York and New Jersey to develop facilities. The Port Authority looked about, discovered that Newark International Airport had weathered the transition from air travel to missile travel quite nicely, and extended its facilities, including gantry towers, repair and refitting hangars, and a road straight to Manhattan.

So the Spaceport Turnpike became the main road to New York City, partly as a result of the efforts of developers who had bought tracts of land to either side—and, with visions of the wealth brought in from the colonies, methods of firm footing and waterproofing were gleefully developed. The result was a strip city running from Manhattan to Newark Spaceport, and a ring of chandlers' shops, warehouses, and seedy bars all around the spaceport itself, uncharitably referred to as the Blight Belt.

Merlo and I stepped out of the tube stop into a world of garish overhead lighting and roaring traffic. Before us, pools of semidarkness alternated with the bright sickly lights of arcades and taverns.

I shuddered. "People actually live here?"

"No," Merlo said. "They live a couple of miles away, where there are official towns. The only dwellings here are cheap hotels that cater to spacehands. Well, let's start, Ramou. One bar's as good as another."

We sauntered past a darkened cavern, lit only by a single dim light over the lintel that illuminated a sign informing us that this was the Transformer Transporting Company. As we passed, three thugs stepped out of a three-foot space between the warehouse and the arcade next door, holding blades that gleamed in the darkness. Their leader stepped in front of Merlo while his buddies moved up to flank us on either side.

"Your money, man," the leader said, grinning. "Not worth your life, is it?"

"They're careless, kid," Merlo said, sounding thoughtful.

"Only one more of them than there are of us. What do you think?"

I knew what those "blades" could do. They were monofilament; the light was just a glow-bulb at the base of the strand, lighting it up so that the guy using it could see where it was. If they wanted to get really mean, they could turn off the lights, so that you never knew for sure where the "blades" were.

But that took skill. If a punk turned his light off, you knew he'd had a lot of experience, and maybe even training, no matter how informal. A genuine slice-artist was a very dangerous customer indeed.

If Merlo wasn't scared, he was crazy. On the other hand, knowing Merlo, that was a distinct possibility. Of course, he was also trained as an actor, so maybe he *was* scared, but just didn't show it.

Me, I *knew* I was—but I didn't show it, either. I'd been trained, too, but *not* as an actor. I gave each of the toughs a quick up-and-down glance and nodded. "They do have a slight edge, Merlo. The blades."

"So," Merlo said, "take *away* the blades."

The lead tough laughed; he thought we were crazy, too, but in his favor. "You try it, gringo, and you're dead." He had red hair and green eyes, Irish as they come, but the new season's big 3DT hit, "Street Talk," came out of Televisa in Mexico City, and the hero was Mexican. "Just give us the wallets now, and no one gets hurt."

The main point is to get out of it without fighting, if you can. Fight, and someone could get killed. Even if they're just maimed, that's very wrong, if it could have been avoided. Reluctantly, I said, "I don't know about you, boss, but they can have my wallet." I'd taken everything out of it except the change from the bills Horace had given me. "Money you can always get more of, but you can't give a guy back his leg."

"You chicken, kid?" Merlo bleated, but I tossed my wallet over and said, "Damn right I'm chicken."

"I never figured you for it," Merlo growled, and reached for his hip.

But the lead tough snapped his head up, glaring at me. "What kind garbage you handing me, man? Nothing in here but twelve BTU's!"

"What do you mean, 'nothing'?" I said in indignation. "That was supposed to last me the rest of the week!"

The tough gave a high, thin whine of a laugh, and the one on left flank said, "*Esta loco,* man." He looked Italian.

"We don't like guys who try to cheat us, man!" the leader said. "We take it out of your hide!" He threw the wallet at my face and followed it, coming in fast with his blade.

I batted the wallet back into his face, my heart singing within me, and went for his knife arm. Filament knives have a weakness—they can only cut, not stab. Get behind them, and they can't hurt you. Which is what I did.

How? Don't ask. If you've been trained enough, you already know. If you haven't, and try to do it, you'll wind up on a slab. Ask a sensei.

Merlo roared and tried to jump the guy, but I was already there, and the tough howled as the knife dropped. The blade light went out as it hit the concrete. Then it crunched under my boot. He howled again in anger as he heard his treasured toy go pop, then howled a third time because his arm wasn't supposed to bend the way I was trying to push it.

His buddies shouted and jumped in, and Merlo came to his senses and realized I didn't need help. He turned to catch the left-hand punk, and I had to admit that what he lacked in finesse, he made up for in brute strength. The tough howled and kicked, five feet off the ground, but he couldn't do Merlo any damage with his back to the big guy, and he couldn't get at Merlo's arm with his blade.

That left the right-hand one. I knew I couldn't take chances here, so I gave the leader's arm a nasty twist as I threw him at his buddy. The leader made a noise halfway between a scream and a shout, then screamed again as he collided with his partner's blade. I was right on top of them, picking the blade handle out of the mess and stomping on it. Then *I* howled as the flanker caught me with a kick from below, not quite where it would do the most damage, but close enough for a lot of pain. Not enough to disable me, though, so I picked up the flanker and threw him against the wall, hard. He hit at the same time as Merlo's kid, and the two of them slid down into a jumbled heap together. I jumped in, kicked at a jaw—and the leader shouted as he grabbed my leg and twisted. I went with the motion, whirling with the twist but a little faster, and landed with my knee in his belly. Then I cracked his head back against the pavement with a quick punch. His eyes rolled up and I jumped back, panting, glancing to either side, just in case they had backups.

They didn't.

"You okay?" Merlo asked.

I nodded, panting, and glanced at him, then glanced again. "He got you!"

"He did?" Merlo held up his arm, saw the blood welling through the cut in the sleeve. "Son of a gun! I never even noticed."

"That's the trouble with filaments—they just part the molecules, and you don't feel anything." I helped him out of his coat, then ripped the lower half of the shirtsleeve off and inspected the wound.

"Just a scratch," Merlo grunted, but I could see it was beginning to hurt.

"A little more than that, but still just a flesh wound," I said. "Time to get you to a hospital."

"Time?" He gave a brittle laugh. "We don't *have* time—Rudders is seeing to that. We'll pick up some bandages at a mart. I'll last, kid."

He probably would. It wasn't much more than a shallow cut. But I resolved to have it checked as soon as we were out of this. "Fair enough." In the meantime, I bandaged the wound with the cloth I had torn away.

"Thought you were scared of them," he grunted as I bound the bandage.

"Of course I was," I retorted. "They were experienced,

they had weapons, and this is their home turf. Of course I was scared. I would have been an idiot if I hadn't been."

"No, no! I mean *scared!*"

I shrugged impatiently. "Look, Merlo, the first thing my sensei taught me was that you never fight unless you have to. If you can walk away from it, you do. If you have to apologize, you do. If you can buy your way out, you do." Then I grinned up at him. "But if you can't, then you have a good time."

He just stared at me for a minute, then grinned back. "Didn't know you were a pro, kid."

I shook my head. "Never did it for money."

"All right, all right! Trained, then."

"Oh, yes," I said softly. "Not that I don't think I still have a lot to learn—but trained, yes."

His eye glinted. "How much trained?"

I shrugged. "Enough that I'm obligated to teach, if the occasion arises—which it won't, here. Hold on a sec." I stepped over to scan each of our erstwhile victims, making sure they were all out cold, and they were. I peeled back eyelids, checked pupil sizes, and felt limbs until I was satisfied. The leader began to wake up as I was probing him. He moaned.

"It's only a sprain," I told him. "We both lucked out; I let go before it broke. But get to a hospital, huh?"

He stared at me as though I were crazy. "Yeah, sure," he muttered.

"Your buddies will be all right, aside from bruises and headaches. You'll all need new knives, though. Dumb thing to carry, but I suppose you think you need them."

He didn't say anything, only made a croaking noise, looking at me as though I came from another planet. Well, he was half-right—I was on my way there.

I straightened up and went back to Merlo. "They'll be okay, more or less. Let's get going." I helped him back on with his jacket.

"Yeah, right." He flexed his hand. "Everything still works. Yeah, let's go, kid." And we went on down the strip.

* * *

The purpose of business is to make a profit. That is done by bringing in as much as possible with as little risk as possible. This applies to those who seek to make money by mugging, too. Having proven ourselves to be a high-risk venture, Merlo and I had very little further trouble as we swaggered down the street. I did my best to look friendly and encouraging, but the word seemed to be running along the strip faster than we did, and no one gave us more than a few shouted insults.

We turned into a bar that called itself The Mataxaman, and entered an ambiance of bazouki music and Mediterranean aromas. About half the clientele looked to be Greek, and they all looked to be tough. It was obviously a hangout for the heavy-equipment operators who pass for stevedores in our enlightened age. Loud, hoarse laughter echoed about us as we shouldered our way toward the bar. One patron of bloodshot eyes and devil-may-care mien stood up and disputed our right to pass with the eloquent phrase, "What'cha think y' doing here, lubbers?"

"Lubbers," indeed! When the man himself had probably never gone closer to space than the hold of a ship he was unloading. I grinned, anticipating fun.

Merlo noticed; I think it made him nervous. "Looking for a man," he told the local.

"Oh, yeah?" said that overintellectual individual. "What man?"

"I'll know when I find him," Merlo said. "I need a spaceship captain. Cheap."

The stevedore threw back his head and guffawed. From his sandy hair, I guessed him as an honorary Greek, at best. "You want your atoms spread all over H-space, Charley?" The "Charley" is an insult, coming from a proletarian; I had reason to know, given the school I went to. Apparently the man had mistaken the cause of Merlo's nervousness. "You hire a captain who'll work cheap, it's because he's no good."

"I'll worry about that when the time comes." Merlo's

voice roughened. "Know anybody with master's papers here?"

The man turned surly all of a sudden. "Nobody with captain's papers comes in a bar like this, bozo! And no hoity-toity guys from Fifth Avenue, neither! They get out! Got it?"

Several of his friends were crowding around us now, with the kind of grins that people get when they're looking forward to a good show. I started a slow smile of my own and waited for the first punch.

But Merlo noticed. "Well, if there's nobody here of officer rank, we won't hang around. C'mon, kid, let's go." And he fairly yanked me toward the door.

A couple of large and beefy ones slid into his path. I gave them my friendliest smile, but Merlo said, real fast, "ScusemeIgottagetoutahereFAST!" and slammed between them and through the doorway. A couple of angry shouts rose behind him, and I turned back to grin encouragement, but by the time they got done jamming out, Merlo had me ten feet away and going fast.

"Aw, come on, Merlo," I pleaded. "Just one?"

"It wasn't just one, it was five at least," he retorted. "What's the matter with you, Ramou? Isn't one fight enough for one night?"

"That wouldn't have been a fight," I complained. "Just fun." I glanced behind me and became hopeful—one mug had separated himself from the clot in the doorway and was prowling after us.

"What happened to your rule about walking away from a fight?" Merlo demanded.

"Brawls are different," I explained. "No hard feelings."

"Yeah, just bruises. Well, I'm sorry, kid, but we're on an emergency errand tonight, and there's no time for fun." Just to make sure, he hustled me through the next door. It called itself a cocktail lounge, so presumably served a higher class of clientele.

I suppose it was, in the social hierarchy of the spaceports. These guys looked just as rough and greasy—machine grease, that is, in the pores and wrinkles of the hands; they didn't wash it off completely until they got home. But they wore the sleeves of their pullovers rolled up high, to display their collections of tattoos: little hearts that said, "My Heart Belongs to Venus," banners blazoned "Ceres City Soaked Me," banded globes that read, "Ganymede Gonzo," and ringed spheres that wore the legend, "Titan and Tight." They were spacers, all right, but the ones who load and unload cargo from the inside, go crawling out on the hull to fix broken antennae, and spend the long weeks between planets going over the ship with fine-toothed combs, making sure everything mechanical still works. One out of three savvies electronics better than the others; he's the captain. They travel in groups of three, on the ships and off them; they are shallow-spacers, cargo haulers who work the routes between Terra and Mars, Terra and the asteroid belt, Mars and the Jovian satellites. The outer planets they leave to the miners, who come in every few months to bring back ores.

Consequently, each trio tends to be very tightly bonded, and sticks together in the face of trouble like protons to neutrons. Sometimes there are two men and one woman, or two women and one man, and you have gluons. Sometimes they even marry. But wedded or single, together for one voyage or a lifetime, they come off their ships overcharged with tension and isolation, hungry for company, fun, and fights.

My spirits lifted the moment I walked in.

Heads came up all around, and a long, drawn-out sigh of satisfaction seemed to echo through the room. Surely it was my imagination; it couldn't really have said, "Fresh meat!"

Merlo read the signs and stopped five feet inside the doorway, glancing to either side, but mostly at me. I swear he wouldn't have been worried without me. "We're looking for a man with master's papers," he said.

"Sexist!" a woman snapped.

"Unemployed," he qualified, "and willing to ship out tomorrow at dawn."

"What you got against women, Bonzo?" It was one of the

biggest, ugliest gorillas I had ever seen, with a two-day beard, bloodshot eyes, and two hulking females right behind him.

"Nothing," Merlo said. "No officers, right?"

He meant "in here," but someone else decided to misunderstand. "Of course there are women officers!" Another female stepped up to him, her head coming to his clavicles, with two orangutans behind her.

This was great. Two trios was just right—one for Merlo, and one for me. I gave them my friendliest grin.

The gorilla saw me, picked me out as Merlo's weak point, and responded true to form. He prodded me with a thick forefinger and said, "Gonna wait for this one to grow up?"

Well, now. Muggers you give in to, but barroom brawls are another matter. A mugger is out for money or blood, but a barroom tough is looking for recreation. He needs to release some aggressions. So did I, so I grinned.

"No, Ramou." Merlo stepped between us. "We don't have time. Out." He curved an arm around me, not touching, and I gave in with regret.

"Ramou," the tough called after me. "What kind of sissy name is that?" His girlfriends cackled.

"Original," I muttered. "Very original. Please, Merlo? Just a little?"

"No such thing as 'a little,' when he's got half a dozen friends who're itchy, too. I promise you a real great time at a bar I know on Ceres, Ramou—but right now, we have to make every minute count."

"That's what I was wanting to do," I growled, but I let him lead me out.

Ceres? What would Merlo know about the bars in the asteroid belt, anyway?

We went on down the street, ignoring catcalls and smart remarks that had been original no longer ago than the invention of the steam engine. I glanced behind every block or so and was delighted to notice that the gorilla from the first bar was still shadowing us. But alas, Merlo pulled me into another establishment before he could catch up.

This one was named The Three Oranges. The bars had been improving as we got farther and farther away from the terminal buildings. This one had leather chairs, indirect lighting, real wood veneer for the tables, and red-jacketed waiters. Prokofiev's opera echoed about us as we came through the door, then cut off as we stepped past the hat-check stand—a novel idea in sound curtains. I felt out of place in my canvas and cords, and hoped somebody would notice.

Unfortunately, the clients were all very courteous. They glanced at us, looked surprised, then went back to their conversations, politely ignoring us. This might have had something to do with the stripes sewn on the sleeves of the *complets,* and the quantity of brass insignia adorning the collars. The ladies were smartly dressed, some in uniform, some not, but none looking like professionals at anything that didn't require a desk and a computer. Over against the far wall, a few couples moved in slow, lazy dances to the strains of a keyboard operated by a lady who had set it to sound like a twelve-piece acoustic orchestra, complete with strings and reeds. She crooned a tale of love and woe in a voice toned down to a discreet but gland-stirring murmur.

One of the red jackets stepped up to us, head slightly bent. "May I help you gentlemen?"

"We're looking for a man with master's papers, who might be amenable to a job on short notice," Merlo told him.

The red jacket looked faintly annoyed. "You might try the officer's registry in the morning, sir."

"I'm afraid we don't have that luxury." I was surprised at how genteel Merlo was sounding. He really was a good actor—but was he in character now, or usually? "We have to lift at dawn, and we've just developed a personnel emergency." He made it sound like appendicitis, instant cancer, and terminal pregnancy all rolled into one.

"Surely the registry's emergency desk . . ."

"They have no one available on such short notice." Merlo

sounded so sure that I wondered if he had played this scene before. "You see, we're independent . . ."

The red jacket drew back as though at an offensive odor. "I can understand your plight, sir, but I must insist you not annoy our patrons."

I grinned.

"No, Ramou!" Merlo made it sound like "Down, White Fang." That roused the mule in me; I was determined to prove I was human. I stepped forward, crowding Red Jacket. "I see a gentleman alone, by the band—"

That was as far as I got. Red Jacket had already snapped his fingers, and two boys in shorter red jackets picked me up by the arms, turned me about, and took me out the door. Somebody bellowed behind me, and I knew Merlo was getting the same treatment. I wondered where they had found two men tall enough.

They set me down hard, but not hard enough for me to take reasonable offense. "Get out and stay out, cull," one of them snapped.

Out of the corner of my eye, I saw Merlo stagger as they shoved him. Anger soared—Merlo *was* my side, now—but I throttled my temper and growled, "I'm going, I'm going."

"You bet you are," a short red jacket sneered, and slammed a punch into my belly.

I shrank back; his fist drove my forearm against my midriff, so most of the impact was soaked up—but it was enough to be legal. I came up grinning and said, "Thank you."

He stared, taken aback. " 'Thank you?' For *what*?"

"For making it self-defense," I said.

Merlo moaned. So did Short Red, as I batted down his guard, squeezed a pressure point, and snapped his head back with a quick right. He folded, and I felt a pang that the fight should be so short, but his buddies shouted and leapt to his defense. Merlo roared and leapt to mine. So the next few minutes were very confusing, and a punch sent brilliant pain through my head, another made my gut ache, and a third sent a shower of hurting through my shoulder—but I got in four kicks, half a dozen punches, and two throws.

Then, sadly, it was over, with four red jackets rolling around the pavement moaning, Merlo staring down appalled, and a strange guy in a peaked cap standing beside Merlo, rubbing his knuckles and laughing.

I felt indignation. "Sir, this was a private fight!"

A siren howled at the terminal end of the street.

"Be glad he helped us out!" Merlo grabbed us both by the arms and hustled us away from The Three Oranges. "We're short on time, remember? And a hell of a lot shorter, now! Let's go!"

"Wrong way," the stranger snapped in a tone of authority. "I know a place to hide, close."

Merlo glanced at him, once quick up and down, and decided he was on our side for more than convenience. "Okay, but it's got to be close!"

"Two blocks," the man promised. He led the way, walking fast for two blocks, then turned aside into a dark side street. I braced myself, still feeling good, but he pulled me up alongside him and said, "One thing you got to learn about barroom brawling in spaceports, kid—don't pick on officers. They call cops."

"But I didn't," I protested. "Only waiters. Besides, I waited for him to punch me first."

"Cops don't understand the fine points," he explained, and hustled me in under a glow sign of a municipal map with "The Four Oranges" blazoned across it. No, not Prokofiev—East, West, and South, with Orange in the middle. They were all towns, not far away.

The patrons looked up with the usual grins, anticipating some relief in the routine, and I answered in kind, but our guide said, "They're with me, boys and girls," and they all turned back to business with loud sighs of disappointment. We waded through shuffleboard, loud conversation, blaring 3DT sports screens, a muted Elector Rudders who was declaiming something about immorality paraded shamelessly on stages, and a small dance floor crowded with couples and trios gyrating in motions that reminded me of planetary libration and the precession of equinoxes, to the accompaniment of a keyboard that seemed to be set mostly on drums, going to three different time signatures that seemed to interact with an intriguing resemblance to music.

Our guide gestured to a small but clear—if not clean—table and said, "Sit. Cops won't think to look here, and nobody on the strip will tell them."

I sat with a disappointed sigh.

"Another time," he advised me as he sat. A waitress was already there, looking bored and dye-blown—what was luxury in Manhattan was simple economics here; family worked cheaper than automated machinery. "Grog," he told her, and nodded at Merlo.

The big guy sighed. "Gin. You might turn the vermouth bottle in its direction."

The eye under the peaked cap cocked itself at me. I thought of playing coy by only ordering a cola, then decided to be honest. "Short draft."

She nodded, punching buttons on her tray, and drifted away.

"I hate to take the time tonight," Merlo sighed, "but I guess we'd better relax for a few minutes. Thanks, mister." He cocked a stern eyebrow in my direction.

"Yeah, thanks," I sighed, then perked up. "Always feels nice having somebody come in on your side."

"I may, if you tell me a good enough story," the man said. "Call me Gantry. Who're you?"

"Ramou Lazarian," I said.

"Good to meet you." He turned to Merlo.

"Merlo Hertz," the big guy said.

The blown blonde drifted up again, setting drinks down. "Here y'are, Captain McLeod." She set a clear tumbler in front of Merlo. "Too much vermouth?"

"Fine," he said without touching it, staring at Gantry. " 'Captain'?"

The blonde frowned down at our host. "Wasn't I supposed to tell?"

"You timed it just right," he assured her. "Yes, gentlemen. Captain Gantry McLeod, at your service."

Three swallows later, with the waitress paid off and McLeod done chuckling, Merlo exhaled sharply and asked, "Where did you come from?"

"From the first bar we went into," I told him. "I saw him come out and follow us, and I was hoping he'd start something."

McLeod shook his head. "Never start. Only finish."

"But why didn't you tell us sooner?" Merlo exploded.

McLeod shrugged. "Wanted to see if you were worth it. I'm retired, Mr. Hertz. You'd have to be a rather special case to bring me out to active status again."

"How come you were hanging out with the stevedores?" I demanded.

"They're good company. I started as a cargo walloper myself, you see." He looked at me with a pair of clear blue eyes that nonetheless had quite a few red veins in them. "But I got curious about where the ships I was loading were headed, so I went and took a college admissions test. Turned out I had more brains than I knew."

"So you went to officers' school?" Merlo asked.

McLeod shook his head. "Mechanics' school. Officers have to pay their own way."

I nodded. The government pays for mechanics and electronics techs—anything to keep commerce going. I had considered the option myself, before I found out I had enough aptitude to qualify for a scholarship.

Merlo was staring. "You worked your way up from elec and mech?"

Gantry nodded. "Not that I wanted to, of course—but the master came down with food poisoning, and the second was laid up with flu. I had sense enough to subsist on K rations, and brought the ship in on the master's instructions when she was conscious, and ground control's advice when she wasn't. It was such a kick that I wanted to do it again, but they won't let you without a ticket—so I plowed my savings into college, and came out a second."

"And from there, it was just time to master." Merlo nodded.

He seemed to know an awful lot about it.

The blonde showed up again and put a full glass in front of McLeod. I wondered about that, but it turned out her timing was right again; McLeod said, "Thanks, love," drained the last inch from his last glass, and handed her the empty with a bill stuck to the bottom. He put down another bill for a coaster, sipped the new drink, and set it down on the bill.

"But why'd you retire?" Merlo asked.

"This new Klein-flask control system," McLeod explained. "It sets my teeth on edge—something about my being able to perceive extra-low-frequency electromagnetic waves."

Merlo nodded. "I've heard of that. Doctors're stumped—it's not hearing, and it's not visual."

"Nor tactile," McLeod agreed. "But Interstellar Lines converted all its ships to it, so they pensioned me off."

"But you could have found another position," I protested.

He turned that bloodshot gaze on me, and it wasn't quite so clear anymore. He was shaking his head, and Merlo agreed, "Not over fifty, Ramou. That's when they start pressuring you to retire."

I thought about asking how he knew, but McLeod was nodding and saying, "It's just superstition, something about the reflexes slowing down after forty."

"Garbage," Merlo agreed. "It's the computer's reflexes that matter, not yours."

"It is that." McLeod smiled. "But you two look interesting. What's the berth, boys?"

Merlo looked at me with hope in his eyes, then back at McLeod. "Actors," he said.

McLeod stared.

"A company of actors," Merlo explained. "A whole traveling theatrical troupe, going from planet to planet performing live plays."

McLeod just sat there a moment, wide-eyed. Then he sat back slowly. "What a blessed mad fantasy!"

The waitress set a new glass down in front of him, took up the empty and the bill, and moved away. McLeod started on it and asked, "What kind of ship are you flying?"

"That's part of the problem," Merlo said. "We don't have a ship yet. Kind of thought the captain should choose it."

McLeod's eyes gleamed, but all he said was, "Why the rush?"

"Elector Rudders," Merlo explained. "He seems to have—"

"Rudders!" McLeod spit. "A name to conjure by—conjure the worst sort of demons in the human soul, that is! Prudery masquerading as piety! One word from him, and all the ravening monsters of human insecurity surge forth to ravage their more productive brethren!"

I couldn't help but agree with the sentiments, though I did think he could give Rudders a run for his rhetorical money. Merlo was nodding, though, with enthusiasm. "He's picked us for his latest targets. Says our theatrical immorality shouldn't be exported to the colony planets."

"Says *nothing* should be exported to the colony planets, you mean!" The empty glass thumped on the table. "He'd cut off all traffic to the newer planets if he could, leave them to root for a living or die—and not much better for the older, nearer colonies! If he could figure out a way to get their money and resources without sending anything out from Terra, he would! And be damned to space travel, that's what he'd do!"

The blonde had made another drink appear, and McLeod was performing the impossible feat of downing a swallow at the end of every sentence. "The most timorous, shrinking spirit in the human gestalt, that's what he appeals to! The fear of the dark, the fear of the unknown! The ones who want to zip Terra back into its tight little womb and pretend progress ended in A.D. 1500! Except for modern medicine, of course, and food synthesizers, and automated housekeepers, and private cars."

"If the spirit of adventure isn't totally dead, he'll be willing to kill it," Merlo agreed. "Is your master's ticket still good?"

"Hum?" McLeod brought up sharply against the speed bump of the change of subject. He finished the last swallow in the glass. "Of course, why shouldn't it be?" I was amazed at how little his pronunciation was slurring. He unzipped a pocket inside his jacket and pulled out a thick, official-looking leather wallet. He opened it and unfolded a sheet of parchment. "Yeah, it's still valid."

Merlo craned his neck around to see.

"Haven't renewed it, of course," McLeod went on, "but the renewal date's still a year off. Six months, anyway. Only been six years I've been outa shpace."

I had been amazed too soon. The booze was beginning to make itself felt. That is, I assumed he was feeling it—he was finally showing it. At least, his diction was. " 'Spose I oughta check it, now that you mention it," he went on. "Never heard 'bout any blot on it. Been awhile, though . . ."

"Well, you're the man we need." Merlo seemed blithely indifferent to McLeod's condition; he didn't even seem to notice as the waitress set yet another grog in front of the captain. "Are you up to piloting another ship?"

McLeod considered it, now that the proposal had been stated outright. He stared down into his cup, then took a long swallow, came up for air, turned to Merlo, and shook his head. "Not with a ship made in the last ten years. Those new Klein-flask control systems prodush a shubshonic that sets m' teeth on edge an' give me the heebie-jeebies."

I nodded; he'd said it before, and we'd covered it in one of my classes. For a few, a very few people, the Klein system had stimulated acute anxieties, which was one reason the space industry had started crash research on an even newer system. "The system that just came out last year," I said, "the double-helix control systems—do they bother you?"

Merlo looked surprised, but McLeod only took a thoughtful sip—well, gulp, really—and said, "I've heard about 'em, but I don't give 'em much hope. Concept's off. Look what double helix's done in our genes. Give me the old Moebius system any time. Why, one time when I was out toward Aldebaran on a cargo run—"

"Yeah, I know what you mean," Merlo sympathized. "You could make a ship turn corners with a Moebius—not that you'd want to, of course . . ."

" 'Cept round a shun," McLeod chuckled, "to get extra velocity, when you're low on fuel. Did that twice, youngshter . . ."

Merlo managed to derail the reminiscence a second time. "Pilot the Star Company, and you can pick the ship of your choice. You want a ship with a control system that won't produce subsonics, you've got it." He didn't mention that, with our budget, a ten-year-old ship would probably work out better, anyway. "Will you take the job?"

McLeod's gaze lost focus, not that it had much left anyway. "Be nishe to be in shpashe again . . ."

Merlo slipped a folded hard copy out of his pocket. "Just sign here, and you will be."

McLeod peered down at the paper, but he was distracted by the arrival of the latest glass. He drank a third of it at a swallow.

"Distant suns," Merlo murmured. "The feel of a ship's controls under your hands again . . . Beautiful actresses . . ."

"Where'zha dotted line?" McLeod owl-eyed the paper.

"Right here at the bottom." Merlo pressed a pen into his hand, accidentally guiding it toward the line. McLeod leaned closer, then leaned back, then closer again, and laboriously moved the pen. Of course, he had such a heavy cargo of alcohol that his signature was a little hard to read, but Merlo wasn't one to be picky. He glanced at it, decided it was recognizable enough to be legal, and turned to the waitress who had showed up with another tumbler. "Just bring the bottle—he'll need something to keep him company."

She looked doubtful, but she headed back to the bar. Merlo nodded to me and stood up, hauling on McLeod's arm. I did the same, and the old captain came unsteadily to his feet, blinking. Merlo stuck his head under McLeod's arm. I did the same, and we half carried, half walked him toward the door. A dozen or so of his buddies stood up, looking angry, but I perked up, looking interested, and they started to look uncertain. Then McLeod started to sing, "Shpace again . . . Into shpace again . . ." and, slowly, they sat back down.

The waitress materialized right next to the door. "Here's the bottle, sir."

"Oh, thanks. Just stick it in his hand, huh?"

She did.

Merlo said, "I can't reach my wallet, but if you reach inside . . ."

"No, I'll just put it on his bill," she said. "He does this all the time."

Not the most encouraging comment in the world, I decided.

"Have a smooth time getting him home, boys," she added. She really seemed to care.

"I hope so." Merlo didn't mention the slight detour we had in mind—about 120 light-years' worth.

We got him out the door, and Merlo waved. A sled-cab swerved soundlessly over to us. The door opened, and the mechanical voice asked, "Destination?"

"Chandler's Refitting Yard," Merlo said. "Just wait till we're in, will you?"

So we folded McLeod into the cab and drifted off, me reflecting that for a man of the theater, Merlo Hertz seemed to know the spaceport district awfully well.

18

Once we had poured McLeod into the cab, Merlo was ready
for the touchy ethical question of whether a contract signed
in an altered state of consciousness is binding. Well, not
quite ready—he had the cabbie stop by a mart first.

"The meter will continue to run," the mellifluous synthe-
sized voice warned him.

"I'll be quick."

"Where's that young man going?" McLeod wanted to
know.

"Just needed to pick up a pack," I assured him. I didn't
say of what, because I didn't know.

Then Merlo slid into the seat next to him again, calling
out, "Continue to destination."

"Complying," the cab confirmed, and drifted off again.
There was no sensation of motion, really—the acceleration
was that smooth. But you could see the lights outside the
bubble beginning to move backward, then faster and faster.

Merlo broke the seal off a bottle of water, dropped in two
fat pills, and waited for them to stop fizzing. Then he said,
"Another drink?"

"Don' min' if I do," McLeod slurred, and reached for the
bottle. He started to chug it and broke off with a splutter.
"What kind of poison is *this*?"

"Gran'ma Horvhee's Sobering Syrup and Home Hangover Remedy," Merlo answered.

I stared, then realized I was gawking and tried to look
nonchalant. The fabled drunk cure? Did it really exist? Had
I maligned the fabled rabbit?

McLeod came up glaring. "Youngling, I've just spent an hour and a considerable amount of brass trying to achieve this condition. I'm not in a hurry to get rid of it." His diction had tidied amazingly; the remedy was as good as its label, for a wonder.

"I thought you might want to check on the item you just signed," Merlo explained, "so you won't claim we tried to kidnap you for a year."

McLeod stared at him. Then he chugged the rest of the bottle. He tossed it away with an oath. "Terrible! Sweetened mint has to be the vilest taste in the universe, unless it's in a julep . . . All right, I'm sober. What did I sign?"

Merlo handed him the hard copy, then slipped the penlight from his pocket and held its cone over the paper. Like the little yellow-handled screwdriver, that penlight was always there in his breast pocket, along with a stylus or two.

McLeod flipped through the contract, nodding at familiar paragraphs. "All seems to be in order; nothing unusual. You sobered me up for *this*?"

Merlo let out a sigh of relief. "Just wanted to make sure you really did mean it when you said you'd pilot the Star Company's ship."

"Command, you mean." McLeod folded the papers and slipped them inside his *complet*. "There's authority that goes with the position, remember."

Merlo nodded, though he looked as though he'd like to forget it.

"And I seem to remember some mention about a ship that doesn't have Klein-flask controls," McLeod said. Obviously, he remembered as well drunk as he did sober.

Merlo nodded again. "You get to choose the ship. I didn't write that in, because we're on our way to do it right now."

"Ah." The blue eyes were clear again. "Then maybe you did have reason to sober me up."

"Right. You might be able choose a good ship by its skin, but I can't."

McLeod shook his head vigorously. "No one can, young

fellow. Choose a bad one, yes—but a good one takes some hunting inside."

"Oh, come on! Let's say a brand-new Equator-class freighter . . ."

"Thought you were taking a whole theatrical company," McLeod snapped.

"We are."

"Equator couldn't possibly be big enough, then. Need a Jovian, or bigger. And brand new? Don't make me laugh. Brand new, you don't even know what weak components slipped through quality control!"

I seemed to remember Merlo saying something of the sort about consoles, but I decided it was my turn to keep my mouth shut. I was beginning to have an inkling of what Merlo was doing here.

The cab pulled up by a locked set of Crystalok bars. "Fifty kwahers," the cab purred.

"Highway robbery," McLeod grumbled as Merlo pushed a bill into the slot. "But at least you don't have to tip them."

"We have not traveled on a highway, sir."

"Well, if you can tell the difference between Ring Drive and the toll road," McLeod snorted, "your discrimination circuits are damn good." He shoved himself out before the cab could answer, so I was left with the brunt of hearing it say, "Discrimination is prohibited by IDE Act 194736, specifying equal access to cabs by all . . ." I shut the door in midsentence, and the cab took off with somewhat more acceleration than it needed.

"Don't need any smart-mouth machine," McLeod grunted.

I had to agree. Somebody had tinkered with its programming, allowing it to change the context of a phrase in order to reply.

Merlo was pressing the call-patch next to the bars. We waited, chafing in the chill.

"Got that bottle, young feller?" McLeod demanded.

"I passed it on down," Merlo answered. "Ramou, one shot all around."

"You can trust me with my own bottle, you know," McLeod snorted as I filled the bottle cap.

"You're the captain now, sir," I said as I handed him the shot. "You're not supposed to have to do your own fetching and carrying."

"Never did put up with that snobbish nonsense," McLeod grumbled, but he looked pleased as he accepted the shot anyway. Merlo caught my eye and gave me an approving wink.

"Who's calling at this time of night?" grumbled a voice from the speaker by the gate.

"Captain Gantry McLeod," our officer barked before Merlo or I could get our mouths working. "We've developed a sudden need for a used spaceship." He glowered up at Merlo. "What kind of terms?"

Merlo was taken aback for a moment, then shrugged. "Cash, as far as I know."

"Cash on the barrelhead," McLeod amplified into the box.

There was silence for about fifteen seconds, then the voice said, "Give me five minutes." It sounded much more cooperative.

"What are we looking for?" McLeod demanded. "Deep space only with launches, or atmosphere-capable?"

"Atmospheric," Merlo said immediately. "We have to be ready to do one-night stands; we can't take a whole day shipping things down from orbit by launches."

McLeod nodded, satisfied. "Take just as much fuel, when all's said and done. Never mind that it's just water—it still costs. Of course, that puts a size limit on your ship, you know. Can't go above Jovian and still get off the ground."

Merlo nodded. "Jovian will do."

I hoped he knew what he was talking about. Either that, or he had an unholy amount of faith in McLeod.

A man in a dark *complet* and a big grin showed up on the other side of the gate. "Yes, sir, good evening, gentlemen, good evening!" He touched both thumbs to the lock, and the gate swung open. "Welcome to Chandler's Refitting Yard! I'm Harry Chandler, Jr., at your service."

McLeod frowned. "Where's the old man?"

"Oh, Dad retired two years ago, Captain . . ."

"McLeod," Gantry snapped. "Gantry McLeod. No business retiring—he was still a young snapper."

"Well, yes, but he figured that, at sixty, he'd paid his dues and had a right to enjoy life. And your companions, Captain?"

"This's Merlo Hertz, technical director for the Star Company," McLeod said gruffly. "This's his assistant, Ramou."

As youngest, I figured it fell to me to do the courtesy. "Sorry to wake you up, sir."

"Glad to, glad to." Chandler gave me a piano grin. "First thing Dad taught me, is that you do business whenever it comes, any time of night or day."

Especially, I thought, when you were talking about a million therms.

"Jovian class," McLeod was saying. "Moebius control system. What've you got?"

Chandler frowned. "You're talking about something twelve years old, or more. Sure you want a ship that's that long out of warranty?"

"Wouldn't take anything else," McLeod snapped, and Merlo looked relieved—he couldn't afford anything else. "Of course," the captain went on, "we'll want to see the service records."

"Sure, no problem, no problem! Well, most of our ships are up in orbit, but if you'll come this way, I'll show you their pictures and data in the office . . ."

McLeod shook his head. "Atmosphere-capable. Jovian class."

Chandler spun about, staring. "You want an inter*stellar* ship that's atmosphere-capable? Where're you planning to go—pioneer planets?"

"Anywhere we have to," Merlo assured him, "with a whole theatrical company."

Chandler frowned at him as though doubting his sanity,

then shrugged and turned away. "If that's what you want, that's what you'll get—though I have to tell you, nobody uses Jovians for interstellar work these days. Interplanetary, some, but mostly for cargo hops within single planets."

"I flew 'em to Wolmar and back, youngling," McLeod growled. "I'll swear by 'em any time."

Just the word *Wolmar* chilled me. If that military prison planet was half as bad as the 3DT epics and the magazines made it look, it was the torture pit of the universe, inhabited by perverted and depraved human beings who thought of murder as a misdemeanor. In fact, rumor went that you had to be a sadist just to qualify for entry. If McLeod had flown out there even once, he'd had a human cargo aboard, and of course they would have wanted an atmosphere-capable craft; every time they had to load their criminals from one ship to another, there was a chance of escape.

Chandler piled us into a small floater. We lifted off the ground a foot or so, and he drove us weaving through a landscape of tall, gleaming skyscrapers. It was eerie to think that each one of these huge buildings could actually lift off and go up to the station in orbit, and that some could go farther.

McLeod looked at the great crane structures surrounding the ships. "We're still in the repair yard. Where're the ones for resale?"

"Out there." Chandler pointed ahead. I looked, and saw seven sleek shapes like porpoises standing on their tails, straining and eager to be back in their natural element, swimming the sea of stars.

"Oh, where are you going, and what do you wish?"
    the old moon asked the three.
"We have come to fish for the herring fish
    that swim in this beautiful sea!"

I shivered with the thrill of it. A childhood dream, about to come true! What kid doesn't fantasize about being a spaceship pilot and going to exotic and distant planets? What kid ever gets the chance?

Me. Ramou Lazarian. Kid, grown up.

Almost.

The buggy slowed, then moved slowly around a silver cliff. "Now, this is a great little item. Only ten years old, yeah, but it does have a Moebius, just as you ordered, and the last model they ever built, so it's—"

"If that ship has a Moebius, it was grafted in after it was built," McLeod snapped. "That's a Ronlin, and the first model they ever built had a Klein. So did the last—they went out of business in five years."

"But this ship gave good service for ten years!" Chandler protested.

"Yes, but what happened then? Look at the striations on its aft end; the planetary drive's so far out of adjustment it's never coming back. Don't try to foist off your junk on me, young man!"

"Sir, I take offense at that! We repaired this ship ourselves, we guarantee—"

"And if the planetary goes off, who's ever coming back to collect?"

"I'd like to see the spec chart," Merlo said thoughtfully.

Chandler sighed and punched patches. The buggy's screen lit up with a schematic of the ship. McLeod grunted and punched. I craned my neck to see over their shoulders.

Sure enough, there was a convoluted mass of lines and, beneath them, the notation, "Planetary drive scrapped; new Bolyon drive installed."

McLeod shook his head. "I'm going to have a human cargo, young Mr. Chandler. I can't be giving your new drive its shakedown cruise. Besides, Bolyon makes its planetary drives for the Klein system. The only way you could have gotten it to match Moebius was to have taken it out of a junked freighter—and either way, I'm not up for trying it."

"It's really a fine old ship," Chandler sighed, "but I can see you've made up your mind. Well, we do have two more Jovians in inventory." He nudged the controls, and the little buggy launched itself out of its orbit around the Ronlin and headed past two smaller ships to another giant. There it slowed and started circling the base again.

"Now this," Chandler said, "is our most attractive item. Interior's luxury, absolute luxury! She was made for the Terra-Centauri run, and I don't have to tell you the oldest colony is also the richest. Lotta people come in from there on business, yes sir, and to see the sights. With the prices they're paying, they don't want to feel cramped or aching, no sir, they want fun every parsec of the way—yes, they want getting there to be half the fun, and it was in this ship, oh yes, friends, been some really high times on the old *Centauri Filly*! Cost ya a megatherm and a half, but worth every BTU of it! Ten years old, but only used for a dozen trips in all that time! No more than twenty-four entries and lift-offs, and only twenty thousand light-years on her! Engine's in fine tune, couldn't be smoother, swear it just came from the factory! Except, of course, it's been broken in, tried and true. Look at that skin—scarcely a single meteoroid pit!"

It certainly did look as though the ship was in wonderful shape. It gleamed like diamonds all the way until the curve of the prow hid it from sight, every line a designer's dream, a work of art that could leap the solar system. I especially liked the marvelous crinkly texture, and was amazed that any shipbuilder would go to the expense of putting a finish like that on anything so large.

So why was McLeod plastered back into the upholstery, shaking his head as though he were staring at Dracula, and muttering something fearful?

"Looks beautiful," Merlo agreed, "but one and a half million is past my limit."

"Well, we might be able to shave a few therms . . ."

Merlo finally took his dream-clouded eyes off the tall ship and glanced at McLeod, then stared. "What's the matter, Captain?"

Chandler had seen, too. He had a sinking look about him.

McLeod pointed. "See that pebble-grain texture on the

ship's hull that makes it look like metallic pigskin? I've only seen that once before, and it was on a ship that almost didn't make it back out of H-space. Something was bad wrong in the isomorpher; it was shuttling its load into another reality, then pulling it back into this one, back and forth like a yo-yo. The crew and the supercargo were all insane; only the ship's computer was whole enough to tell the tale, and that only because it was a real cheapie, didn't have enough circuits to do much more than compute a course and retain a journal. Xenologists and physicists had a field day with its log-cube, though . . ." He frowned at Chandler, who had turned gray. "Who's selling this—Puritan Interstellar Insurance?"

"Well, now that you mention it . . ."

"Mighta known!"

"They replaced the isomorpher, though! Gave it a test flight and everything!"

"How far—two light-years and back?" McLeod shook his head. "Ship's jinxed now, young feller. No captain in his right mind will sign aboard her."

"It's perfectly safe," Chandler protested.

"Says you, who doesn't have to ship out in it. Your daddy never would have put a thing like this on the block."

"But it's been repaired! Thoroughly! Even a new computer, the latest and the best! It's totally illogical—"

"So are spacemen," Captain McLeod snapped.

"How come the Astronautic Authority's letting it be sold?" Merlo asked.

"Probably don't know about the earlier case; Terra's Authority is snooty, tends to ignore what happens in the pioneer worlds, and this was out toward Betelgeuse, was kind of hushed up even there. But word gets around among the guild." He turned to Chandler, shaking his head. "Nice try, youngling. I hope your last one is a better bet."

"Not really," Chandler sighed, "but I'll show it to you anyway."

Yes, sir, I was really glad we had Gantry. Not that I'd

stopped worrying about the drinking—but if Merlo could take it in stride, so could I.

We drifted over to the next ship in line. It was huge, it was gargantuan—or was it only the pitted hull plates and dullness of sheen that made it look that way? My stomach sank—the last time I saw something as battered as that, the cat finished it off and had it for lunch.

But McLeod could see things I couldn't. His eyes lit up and he crowed, "Now *that* is a ship!"

Chandler looked up at him, startled. "Are you cra— I mean, really crazy about it, Captain?"

"You bet I am! That's a genuine Peregrine, best ship Atlas ever made, and I know those lines! It's fourteen years old, not a month more or less!"

"It's been through the wars," Merlo said, frowning.

"Probably has, m' boy, probably has! Allernon and Haldane IV got into an argument ten years back, and I wouldn't be surprised if this ship got caught in the cross fire! But she kept her passengers safe—see that one single patch way up high, there?"

"No."

' "Course not, it's melded in so well only an old eye could see it. And she'll keep her passengers safe for many a trip more, mark my words!"

Merlo intended to. "But the way the metal's been blued toward the stern . . ."

"Pooh! Just shows the planetary drive's been used a lot. If we get in and find the machinery's all been refitted and updated, we'll know it's as good as it looks."

Privately, I didn't think that would take much.

Chandler was looking at the ship as though he hadn't seen it before.

I pointed. "Way up high—those pits."

McLeod nodded. "Empty bays, where the FTL and subether sensors used to be. Probably put in new ones; they're only half the size."

"No," Chandler confessed, "not yet. Y' see, it looks like such a piece of junk, I just never got around to—"

McLeod snorted. "Mean it was something that was here when your old man retired, right?"

"Well, yeah . . ."

"He knew what he was doing, not having it junked. Yes, sir, old Harry knew a good ship when he saw one. Have new sensors in there by five A.M.?"

"Oh, yes sir, Captain! I'll get the crew out of bed and have 'em on overtime."

"You're sure this is the ship, then?" Merlo let his doubts show in his tone.

McLeod nodded. "Sensors can be swapped, engines can be fixed or even replaced—the important thing is the ship itself! Peregrines were built to last a hundred years—probably why they stopped making 'em; nobody really needed to buy new, except to keep up with the latest in gadgets." He looked up at Chandler. "Still got the original computer?"

"Why . . . uh . . ." Chandler punched up the spec chart on the buggy's screen. "Yeah."

McLeod nodded with satisfaction. "Then it's a SAG-LOC."

I frowned, finally recognizing something I knew about— but the wrong thing. "Isn't the SAG-LOC kind of, well, ancient?"

"Only as computers go, sonny. Developed it twenty years ago, yep, and phased 'em out ten years ago—but it's a holistic model that's damn near indestructible." McLeod nodded, satisfied. "I've shipped with SAG many times, and I'd trust it with my life."

"Me, too," Merlo muttered, but I don't think they were talking about the same SAG.

"Buy a ship like that, and you can't go wrong," McLeod said. "Might have to replace a few spare parts, but it's worth doing. No, young man, this is a mighty fine vessel. Why, she's even got exactly the same silhouette as my last command!"

"Nostalgia?" I murmured.

"Maybe." He grinned. "But more to the point, it means I already know this ship. She'll stand on her nose for me, if

I ask her nice. Besides, she'll have a Moebius control system."

"Now, of course," Merlo was saying to Chandler, "you wouldn't be asking us a million therms for a ship you thought was a piece of junk."

"What? Oh, no, of course not!" Chandler was looking green around the gills. "Just nine hundred thousand."

"Seven fifty."

They agreed on eight fifty. Then Chandler said, "Of course, there's the new sensors to be figured in, and the overtime for the boys I'm going to call out of bed . . ."

"You can—" Merlo stopped, feeling McLeod's hand on his arm.

"Give the man his money, son," the captain said. "Just so he does a real nice job." And, without waiting for an answer, he said to Chandler, "Five percent bonus if it's ready by five and I pronounce it sound."

"Done!" Chandler looked triumphant and turned the buggy. "Want me to call you a cab?"

"No, we'll go over the specs and the prints in your office while you're getting the work done," McLeod said easily, and settled back next to Merlo, murmuring, "Don't take it so hard, young feller. It ain't as though you haven't got the money for it."

"Well, no," Merlo muttered. "I just hate to lose a haggle."

"Believe me, you didn't. Would you bet your life on this ship?"

Merlo began to realize what he was talking about. "I just did, didn't I?"

"Not quite yet," McLeod allowed. "We haven't accepted delivery."

As we pulled up at the office, I protested, "But Captain McLeod—don't you need to do any packing?"

McLeod stopped, half in and half out of the buggy. "My flat will take care of itself, young man." He looked up at Merlo. "You'll have the maintenance paid?"

"Sure." Merlo whipped out a keypad. "Just give me the address, and Tallendar will pay the freight."

Chandler looked up wide-eyed at the name of Tallendar.

"But," I said, "personal effects . . ."

"I can buy what I need at Marsport. There's a small chest in the closet that's always ready to go, though."

19

I had the good sense to get a note from the captain, and the commcode from Chandler, before I left; everybody else seemed to have kind of overlooked the fact that I couldn't get into McLeod's flat without his thumb to print the lock, and I didn't think he'd want to part with it. Of course, in special cases, the building's security computer can overide the lock, which was exactly what I was going to have to do.

I fed the bills into the cab's meter, telling myself that Horace would give me more when I found him, then realizing that I wasn't going to need much after this morning. Well, I expected to have to have some pocket money whenever we made planetfall, but I was beginning to see that I wasn't going to have much time to spend it. I began to have visions of returning to Terra with a very fat savings account. I decided to write to the college for course withdrawals and a leave of absence, after all, as soon as I figured out how I could do it without danger of being traced.

I surveyed the neighborhood; it was ten-story buildings with lots of little windows, and spaceships towering behind them—not far from the port. Apparently the captain had never been able to bring himself to be too far away from his work. I began to realize that Merlo hadn't just sweet-talked a drunk into doing something foolish; McLeod had never really resigned himself to being planetbound. For an instant, I wondered about his private life, if he had had any. Wife? Kids? That struck a nasty note, and I put the subject behind me. None of my business, right?

I went up to the captain's building, and, for a wonder,

there was a human inside the armorglass who gave me a speculative glare when I tripped the alarm by coming up to the door. She keyed a mike and snapped, "Go away!"

"Errand for Captain McLeod!" I called, hoping there was a mike out here as well. Just to be on the safe side, I unfolded his note and pressed it against the glass. She squinted and peered at it—hadn't kept up with her lens corrections, probably. At her age, they'd need to be done every year. She was sixty if she was a day, with a glare that could have chilled Eskimos and sent their dogs howling. She wore the security uniform like the sails on a ship—with the trousers at half mast. Her hair was gray, her face had so many lines it could have done duty as a weather map—and the weather was stormy. She nodded, half-satisfied. "I'll have to have that confirmed by comm. Where's he at?"

"Chandler's Refitting," I said. "Six-oh-thirteen—"

"Belay it," she snapped. "Just the name, lubber."

I felt a surge of indignation. I know Sensei said never to hit a woman, but didn't that change if she had a security job?

I could almost hear his voice: *No exceptions, Ramou— unless she's trying to kill you, and has a good chance.*

I sighed. I'd known some women apt to slay me, but I didn't think that was what he'd meant.

The old bird was nattering at the phone, but she was rude enough not to keep her mike open. I craned my neck and could just barely make out the captain's face on the comm. She glanced at a smaller screen above his face, triggered two patches, nodded, and disconnected. Then she reached for her mike again. "Okay, lubber, the captain says you're legit, and the computer says it was really his voiceprint. Just to be sure, I asked him a couple of questions that couldn't have had prerecorded answers. Come on in."

Something clunked inside the door, and I stepped in, speculating about the nature of her questions. Okay, so she was in her sixties, but so was McLeod, nearly, and you never knew what she'd looked like forty years ago . . .

"What're you staring at?" she snapped. "Get upstairs!"

"Uh, yes, ma'am." I ducked into the lift. The doors closed, and I was on my way up; presumably she had entered the floor. I wondered if the building really did have stairs. Probably; fires were still possible . . .

The doors opened; I stepped off and followed the numbers on the wall until I came to 1007. I pushed on the door, but it gave about as much as a banker without collateral. I frowned and pressed again. "Open up, damn it!"

"Watch yer language, lubber!" the old lady's voice crackled from a speaker beside the door. "You could be polite to a lady, telling her you've arrived!"

I mentally weighed the evidence for her being a lady, but only said, "I'm at the captain's door. Would you please let me in?"

"Right. I'm timing you."

Nice to be trusted. I pushed; the door opened, and I stepped into the neatest room I'd ever seen that claimed to not belong to an institution. Everything was square corners and precise folds, and there was almost nothing that looked personal. I scanned quickly on my way into the bedroom and did notice a couple of holos in brass frames. The bedroom had wall holos of ships in space and a planet that I didn't recognize. That was it, aside from a lingering aroma of cologne. I began to wonder if I really wanted to live on McLeod's ship, after all.

The door slid back at a touch; the suits and slacks and robe hung in perfect verticals, the shoes and slippers lined up precisely beneath them. I repressed a shudder and picked up the big squarish suitcase, almost a trunk. Somehow, it reminded me of a sea chest. I was tempted to open it to check, but McLeod had said it was always kept packed, so I didn't ask. He had just been waiting his chance to get back into space, hadn't he? For the first time, it occurred to me to doubt his story about being allergic to double-helix control systems, but we weren't exactly in a position to dicker. Still, his record might have made interesting reading.

I thought about all this on my way back to the door, remembering what the old battle-ax had said about timing.

I stepped through the portal; it closed behind me, and I called, "I'm out."

"I know y' are, lubber," her voice said from the wall behind me. "Downstairs now, double-quick. If the captain says he needs that trunk, he needs it *now*!"

"Yes, ma'am," I grumbled, and wondered what Virginia would be like in forty years. I backtracked to the lift, stepped in, and stood watching the closed doors. They opened and I bolted out, heading for the doors and calling, "Thanks, ma'am!"

"Well, it does have some manners, after all," she said. "Smooth lifting, son."

It took me half a block in the cab before I realized she wasn't accusing me of theft.

Fortunately, the cab had waited, even though I'd taken two minutes longer than I'd said I would. It suddenly occurred to me that I didn't have the faintest idea where Barry lived, so I gave it Horace's address. Then I leaned back in the seat, suddenly glad I was going someplace familiar, even if I'd only known it for a few days.

I was just terminating a rather unpleasant chat with Elyena Slavnaya, one of the two ladies young enough to play ingenues but old enough to play mature leads who had indicated an interest in coming. Upon discovering that I expected her to be ready to depart at dawn, she had questioned my sanity, my gentility, and finally my ancestry in terms no lady should know. To do her justice, Ms. Slavnaya had never claimed to be a lady. I had just disconnected with a sigh, trying to sustain my nerve long enough to call Ms. Oleander, the other lady of indeterminate age, when the door said, "Male guest of five nights past desires entry."

"Ramou?" I looked up with a massive surge of relief—not that I'd been worried about the lad, but it gave me an excuse to postpone La Tempesta for a few more minutes. "Do admit him!"

The door opened, and Ramou burst in, all excitement and aglow, with a footlocker on his shoulder. I felt a pang for my lost youth, when everything was hugely important and waking was an adventure. "Horace! Merlo found him! He—" He stopped short, staring at the sheet of paper that scrolled off my desk and down to the floor. "What's that?"

"The hard copy of my checklist." I sighed. "I didn't want to have to keep bringing it up on the screen after every call. I'm almost done with the actors—only one to go. I have also ordered provisions and supplies." I turned away, shaking my head. "I had forgotten how much gear and tack it takes to put a company on the road. Mind you, I've functioned as unit manager before this—it was my first job in the theater, actually—but never on such short notice."

He was instant solicitation. "Can I help?"

"You *are* helping, dear boy. You and Merlo are undertaking the largest task of all." I looked back at my list, shaking my head. "The problems will be magnified when I start attempting orders with no address to which to deliver them."

"There's an address! There's an address!" His face was all grin. "Merlo found a captain, and the captain found a ship!"

"Did he really!" I stared, just then realizing that I had really expected to put in this whole night's work to no purpose—only to be told that we could not lift off, after all, for lack of either a captain or a ship, both of which are rather necessary to voyaging. But here this lad was telling me that Merlo Hertz had done the impossible, finding both in only a few hours' time. It occurred to me to wonder about the caliber of both, but I put it behind me—I was actually becoming eager for this venture, after all. I sat up with renewed vigor, called up the notepad on my screen, and said, "Give me the address, then."

"Chandler's Refitting Yard!"

I paused, waiting.

"That's it," Ramou said.

"I'll need a name," I told him. "Or at least a number. Something to identify the ship."

He looked abashed. "I didn't think of that."

"Neither did Merlo or your captain, apparently. What was Chandler's commcode?"

I punched it in as he rattled it off. As the screen flashed blue, with the WAITING legend, Ramou said, "That's all I was supposed to tell you, actually—to call Merlo."

"Wise." I nodded. "After all, if you hadn't found me, what use would any other information have been?"

The screen cleared, showing me a face that I instinctively did not trust. I made a mental note to use it as an example of poor body language. "Chandler's Refitting Yard."

"Good morning. I'm Horace Burbage, and at the moment, I am functioning as Mr. Barry Tallendar's managerial assistant."

"Uh—yes sir, Mr. Burbage!" Chandler's eyes grew huge. "I, uh, recognize ya from the 3DT—I mean—"

I smiled; it is always pleasing to be saluted by one's admirerers, which includes nearly everyone, when they are meeting you in the flesh and offstage—or off-camera, in most cases. "How kind of you, my good man. But may I speak with my associate, Mr. Hertz? I believe he is at your shop."

"Uh, yeah, sure! I mean, yes, of course. Just a second, Mr. Burbage." He ducked out of sight.

"Merlo said the line might be bugged," Ramou said. "Sorry; I forgot to mention it."

I stiffened, and I'm afraid my smile stretched a little thin. If the line were truly attached, our opposition had a full, up-to-the-minute picture of our progress. I really should have thought of it sooner—though what I could have done, with so many people to contact and so little time, I really didn't know.

In any case, the damage was done. I would merely have to attempt to be as circumspect as possible in future exchanges.

At last Merlo drifted into the picture, a little far away, which was just as well, because his distance enabled me to see the gentleman beside him, looking for all the world like the captain of a New England clipper from the great days of tall ships. He wore a peaked and visored cap, a jacket with brass buttons and stripes around the cuffs, and iron-gray sideburns. With an actor's practiced eye, I knew him instantly for a poseur. I couldn't help wondering if he was a con artist—but surely Merlo would have asked to see his master's papers. Barring that, he had a deep-seated need to identify himself with the sea captains of old—but who am I to look askance at another man's eccentricity? I merely said, "Horace Burbage at your service, sir." And, before he could answer, "My assistant has told me of you; I am pleased to make your acquaintance. If you'll excuse me, I must exchange a word or two with my assistant."

He nodded with a seraphic smile, looking so detached and unworldly that I wondered if I were shipping with an alcoholic. Then I saw the same look on Merlo's face, and realized it was simple euphoria. "Good evening, Merlo. I take it you have found the commodity we both seek."

"Boy, have I ever!" Merlo burbled. "You should see this item, Horace, it's great! Just like the old days! Talk about charm and grace! Hey, this one was really elegant in its day!"

I glimpsed the shabby damask of the walls behind him, the dust on the tabletop, the general air of neglect, and had to swallow very hard before I could say, "Very good, then. Go ahead and complete the transaction."

Merlo nodded with a foolish grin, and Chandler's face came between the euphoric pair and the screen. "Uh, Mr. Burbage, I really appreciate your support in this, but—"

"You need something a bit more firm than a verbal promise to pay." I nodded and fished through the pile of hard copies on my desk. Hooking the proper target for the instance, I fed it through the slot. "I am faxing you a copy of the authorization from our underwriter. You may check that number against the one in the directory and call it; you will find a rather sleepy-looking clerk who has been roused out of bed on double wage to undertake the expediting of our little crisis." I let my smile grow warmer. "It has been a pleasure meeting you, Mr. Chandler."

"Uh, yeah! And you, sir! Uh, good-bye!"

I disconnected, reflecting that the glamour of the profession has its uses.

I swiveled about in my chair with a tired sigh. "Well, if anyone is truly eavesdropping on our communications, Ramou, I'm afraid the cat is well and truly out of the bag. We will just have to hope."

"Uh, yeah." The lad swallowed, his eyes flicking to the communicator's screen. "Sorry to drag you into this, Horace. But we tried Barry, and even his answering machine was tied up . . ."

"That was because I had engaged him in a rather lengthy discussion, while Marnie was no doubt trying to get through to rage at him for such short notice and to demand that he solve her problems in packing, possibly personally." I sighed, shaking my head. "One is tempted to hope . . . but never mind. Are you sure this captain Merlo has found is really dependable?"

Ramou nodded. "Solid. Oh, he's a lush, but he sobers up fast when you give him the medicine."

"An alcoholic?" I stared. "And Merlo is willing to ship out with him?"

"Doesn't seem to worry him." He spread his hands. "Don't ask me why—but I've got this gut feeling about Merlo."

"I know what you mean." I shook my head. "When I worked with the man, I found him infallible, except in matters of actresses, and of set designs . . . Well, we shall have to trust in his judgment."

"Captains aren't easy to come by, on short notice," Ramou supplied.

"Very true; I'm amazed he found anyone. And an antique ship, eh?"

"Fifteen years old."

I nodded. "In technology, that could be an antique. I take it the captain is the same?"

"Yeah. That's why he's available. They don't run his kind of ships anymore."

"But we do. Well, you might as well doss down and see

if you can get a bit of sleep, my boy." I riffled unhappily through my stack of papers.

"I can sleep in space! There's gotta be something else I can do to help!"

"Come to think of it, there is." I looked up with a frown, suddenly remembering a loose end—one that probably couldn't be tied back into the tapestry, but worth a try. "I've managed to contact all the company members except two . . ."

"Did they all say they'd come?"

"The minimum number did, fortunately. One of the more mature actresses has refused to pack up on a moment's notice—I'm about to wake the other—and so has one of the young character actors."

"What'll you do without them?"

"Change costumes—very quickly, and very often."

Ramou nodded. "Who didn't answer?"

"Susanne Souci." I glanced at him keenly and saw the expected widening of the eyes. "The screen politely informed me that her communicator has been disconnected. I might give her points for the ability to make prompt arrangements, except that she could not possibly have heard of our imminent departure. Could you run over to her apartment and knock on her door?"

"Well, I can try." I had my doubts about security doors; they tended to be very tough, and had very smart mouths. "Where's she live?"

"In the Village." I referred to my notes. "Corner of Christopher Street; Sheridan Square. Do take care, my boy."

"Do I have to?" I could swear he sounded disappointed. "Yeah, I know—we can't afford any run-ins with the police right now, even if I'm on their side. Don't worry, Horace, I won't leave any evidence."

Not the most reassuring statement in the world. I turned back to my desk. "Good hunting. It would be pleasant if you could bring the young lady back in the flesh, but a definite refusal is better than no word at all."

"Not for me, it isn't. See you later, Horace."

He was out the door before I could begin to wonder what he'd meant—but then, why wonder? I was fairly sure I knew.

His departure left me no alternative but to get back to work. I referred to my list and punched in the number of the grocer with whom I had already placed an order that would guarantee his year's overhead; now I could give him an address for delivery. I would have to do the same with the orders for the year's supplies of water, soap, paper sludge, and bedding, and the innumerable other minor items that people need for a halfway civilized existence. I had hesitated long over the order for alcoholic beverages, but had decided that Ogden in withdrawal was worse than Ogden drunk. The indulgence would kill him, of course, but that was his own decision, and beyond my ability to influence.

Work might woo him away from the bottle, though. If he could just remember his lines . . .

20

"Entry prohibited," the door said.

There was no old battle-ax to reason with here—just a
steel door with a barred speaker in its center and a computer
in the basement. Other than that, the Village hasn't changed
much in six hundred years—it's not allowed to. Historic site,
retaining all the quaint charm of late nineteenth-century
New York, and twentieth-century coffeehouses. It's a maze
of low apartment buildings of brick and/or stone, with steps
and stoops, artists, poets, and affluent businessmen who
want to feel as if they're creative.

The doors, though, are very up-to-date. I eyed a window
speculatively, but I knew that those quaint old sashes were
hardened alloys that only looked like wood, and held armorglass. "Ramou Lazarian, to see Ms. Susanne Souci," I
said.

The computer paused a second while it checked its data
banks; it was a very minimal model. "Ms. Souci is incom-
municado," it said.

Bad. Not only had she cut off communicator service,
she'd canceled her lease. She might still be in there—I
couldn't really see her going to a hotel for the night—but she
couldn't be reached. "I have an important message for her,"
I said.

"No communications can be accepted."

My mind raced. "The message was that I was interested
in renting her apartment."

"Subleases are not allowed!" the speaker blared.

I reamed out my ear and answered, "Hey, I can't rent

from her if she's already canceled her lease, can I? I'm still interested in renting the apartment."

The door clicked and swung back instantly. "Second floor, number two," the computer said.

I headed upstairs, grinning. It was a trick that wouldn't work a second time, of course, and I was surprised some enterprising burglar hadn't thought of it before. On the other hand, how often did a lease expire in New York City? Practically never, and then only if the tenant went broke, in which case there was nothing left to burgle. For centuries, New Yorkers have preserved the quaint old custom of subletting. That means that when one person wanted to move out of an apartment, he or she would offer it to a friend. The friend would take over paying the rent, and the apartment would not have changed tenants officially, so the rent control laws wouldn't let the landlord raise the rent.

Of course, it really *was* a matter of subleasing—the former tenant might decide to move back in any time, and when the subleaser decided to move out, he had to check with all the previous tenants, or at least all those who were still living. And as time went by, the earlier ones actually did start moving back in—the kids were grown, so they wanted to ditch the suburban life and move back into the Big City. They didn't particularly like the neighborhoods they'd started out in, but what the hey, it was cheap.

Smart? Maybe too smart—the landlords stopped making profits, so they started abandoning the buildings. After all, the rents weren't going up, but the taxes were—so some of the more enterprising landlords turned their rental buildings into cooperative apartments, or condominiums, and the tenants had the option of buying their apartments—if they could get mortgages—or of moving out.

So a really new tenant was rare—and when one did come, so did a hike in the rent. A big hike. In fact, as I climbed the steps (didn't trust the look of the asthmatic and arthritic elevator), I wondered why Susanne hadn't found a subtenant of her own. Of course, it was kind of short notice—but how had she learned about our imminent departure?

Maybe she'd just heard Elector Rudders herself, and drawn her own conclusions.

Number two was only one flight up. As I came up to the door, it said, "Do not attempt to enter. This room has been sealed, and all services suspended, due to nonpayment of rent."

Well. That explained why Susanne hadn't found a subtenant. No doubt she was planning to stay for another four weeks, until the company's original estimated date of departure—but her rent had to wait until she got her first paycheck from Barry.

It also explained why her comm was disconnected.

"You're behind the times," I told the door. "Check with the central computer. I'm here to look at the apartment, maybe rent it."

"We are not interconnected," the door told me.

Oh. I could see some sense in that, as a security measure— or as the result of a landlord trying to shave pennies. Still, what had worked with the one computer might work with the other; neither of them was exactly a genius. "I would like to take a look at the apartment, though. Might want to rent it."

"Tenant is still on premises," the door informed me. "No entry without tenant's permission."

Still here! That was a relief, two ways. I'd been worrying that Susanne might be camping out somewhere until Barry paid her her first installment—after all, we had been planning to rehearse on Terra for a month, while Barry arranged for a spaceship and crew by more orthodox channels than Merlo had used. It also took care of the burglar problem— there are other things to steal besides material goods.

There was also a very simple solution. I knocked. Then waited a few minutes. Then knocked again.

"Just a minute," a sleepy voice called out.

I waited.

Then the door opened, and my heart stopped.

She was beautiful. She was enchanting. She was undressed.

Well, actually, she was wearing a very long pajama jacket that came halfway down her thighs, and I was instantly ragingly jealous—but being too large, it draped nicely to hint at every curve and contour, and she had plenty of both. Her blonde hair was disheveled, and her blue eyes were heavy-lidded with sleep. When she saw me, those eyes opened a little wider, and something connected; suddenly, I was intensely aware of her femininity and knew she was aware of me as a man, not just a face. I don't know what kind of dreams she had been having, but I could guess, because desire seemed to ooze from her every pore. I stared, and my tongue thickened.

"Hello." Husky with sleep, and something else—an invitation implicit in the word. "You're . . . here a little late, aren't you?"

"I am indeed," I said, "and at your service." Right then, I felt that I would be at any service she could think of, and I hoped she was thinking of the same ones I was. "I am a man with a message."

"Come in." She stepped back from the doorway, and I entered a realm of perfume and ruffles, of intense femininity impressed upon a plain and functional room in spite of an extremely pinched budget. It verily embraced me.

She closed the door. I turned to her, and I could almost swear that she wanted what I wanted, and would be a lot less reticent about it. Me, though, I still had my old reserve, which had nothing to do with puritanism but resulted in the same effects, so I said quickly, "We've got to hurry. Elector Rudders is on our trail."

She snapped a hundred percent awake, eyes wide, pheromones fading. "Rudders? Why us?"

I shrugged. "Why not? And why speculate? Only Rudders knows for sure. But he's trying to get a court order to restrain us from leaving Terra."

"Does this mean the company's broken up?" She looked tragic, without the slightest hint of relief. Could she actually have thought the Star Company was her Big Chance? Or maybe just her meal ticket?

Or did she care? I suddenly realized I might be dealing with a more complex mind than I had thought. All at once, I was seeing her not just as a sex object, but also as a person, and very much as both.

"Not yet," I said. "Barry isn't giving up without a fight. Merlo has found a captain, and the captain has found a spaceship, and Horace is going crazy ordering supplies, and we lift at dawn."

"I'll finish packing." She turned away; her voice floated out of the bedroom. "There's coffee powder in the cupboard, if you want to brew."

I was doing that very well already, thanks to her, but I decided I might as well do it to the coffee, too. I turned on the tap, but all it gave out was a trickle and a groan. I stared, then turned it off quickly and looked around, wondering why she bothered keeping powder on hand anyway. Then I saw the coin slot on her food synthesizer, and wondered no more.

Inside the cupboard, right next to the big jar of coffee powder, was a jug of spring water. There wasn't much else in the cupboard, though.

I stirred brown powder into cold water, and it started steaming; the crystals reacted with water to release heat. It's a very interesting reaction, and I don't know how the chemists ever dreamed it up—but there's no residue; the heat-making crystals are totally used up in the reaction, and the coffee tastes better than anything from a cheap food synthesizer like Susanne's, anyway.

The coffee was steaming and fragrant when she came out of the room, hauling a suitcase with both hands, fully dressed, a vision of loveliness even in a female *complet* and without makeup—or was that just my hormones talking? Heaven knows she had given them enough content for a month's conversation. I set down the cup and leapt to take the suitcase from her. Unfortunately, she was just setting it down by the front door. She looked up, saw me hovering, and lit up with a mischievous smile. "Thanks, Muscles. There's another one back there."

I was in her bedroom in two steps—it was a very small apartment. Pinkness and chintz seemed to envelop me in a languorous embrace; I breathed deeply, filing the aroma among my permanent memories, and picked up the other suitcase.

Her eyes widened as I came back out; I wondered why. "Isn't that . . . a little heavy?" she asked.

"What, this?" I glanced down at the suitcase. "Not really. I warm up with fifty-pound dumbells, see, and . . ." My voice trailed off at the look in her eyes. Sensei was right, never brag—or, I might add, never be too honest. "Skip it." I forced a smile. "But let me carry the grips, okay?"

"Glad to." She eyed me nervously as she sidled around me back to the bedroom.

"I'm harmless," I called out.

Her head appeared around the doorway with a merry glint in her eye. "Too bad." Then it was gone, back to the domain of feminine fripperies, and I took a deep breath and strode back to gulp my hot coffee. There was an excellent chance that I was missing an even more excellent opportunity—but I had sworn to do so; better regret than remorse, and better to make my life a little less full than to wreck someone else's. In this situation, the minimum number of wreckages is two, and the chances of enhancing even one are negligible.

Besides, there wasn't time—we were in a crisis, and had a spaceship to catch.

She came back out with a small travel bag, tossed me a smile that held both regret and gratitude, and said, "We'd better go."

I nodded. "You pack very quickly."

She shook her head. "The landlord wouldn't have sent roustabouts to roust me out, but if I ever left the apartment, the door wouldn't have let me back in. I was just about out of food, and they'd shut off my water."

"Well, Merlo Hertz has found you new lodgings." I nodded my understanding. A tenant behind in his rent was in a state of siege. Why pay good money to have a tenant evicted, when natural processes will do it for you? Provided you can keep him from getting back in. "So. You were packed to move out, even if we hadn't called."

She looked up. "Did you call? Sorry you couldn't get through."

I shrugged. "Believe me, I've never been happier to be a courier."

This time the mischievous smile held not only gratitude and invitation, but also hinted at a plan of attack. I froze for a second, then answered it with a slow smile and stepped in.

Her lips were honey and roses. Then her mouth enveloped mine, and for a few minutes, I couldn't have said where hers left off and mine began—I only knew that I had a foretaste of ecstasy, greater than anything I had experienced with Virginia or any other girl, and that I didn't want to stop, but to go on and on in that kiss forever and do anything else to deepen that closeness, to approach nearer to that ecstasy, and my hands began to stroke and caress her back without my realizing it, lower and closer to the front, our bodies were moving together like waveforms coming into phase—

I suddenly realized what I was doing, and gently drew back from the kiss, staring down into her eyes—and for a wonder, she was staring back up at me with just as much surprise and, yes, perhaps a little fear, even as I was.

Then she smiled and winked, and handed me her little bag.

I laughed, far louder than the joke deserved. I handed it back to her, picked up the two suitcases, and said, "Come on. I can make it down to the curb, at least."

"Then I'm slipping." Before I could respond, she opened the door and stepped back. I went out into the hall. She joined me, turning back to say, "Lights off." The room darkened as the apartment's computer obeyed. She was silent a moment before she added, "Good-bye, apartment. Good-bye, New York." Then she turned away, head bowed. The door closed behind her and answered, "Good-bye, Ms. Souci." I must have been imagining things; I could have sworn it sounded gentle and sympathetic, but surely the landlord would not have wasted a few BTU's on such a subprogram.

The lift doors opened, though they probably would not have if she'd been going up. We stepped in, and she was busy with a frilly handkerchief, so I studied the molding, noting carefully that there wasn't any, and we observed silence. Then the doors opened, we stepped out into the lobby, and the street door clunked and opened for us as we approached. "Good-bye, Ms. Souci," the door said as it closed. It clunked, and she whispered "Good-bye," dabbed at her face, then tucked the hanky away and managed a roguish smile. "Where to now, handsome?"

She lied, but it felt good. "To the nearest mart; I have to call Horace and relieve his worried mind." I looked about me; the air was chill and smelled remarkably fresh. The sky was beginning to lighten. For me, at least, it had been a short night. "Could you show me where?"

"It's half a block," she said dubiously.

I nodded. "Convenient. Nice neighborhood you have here."

She gave me a funny look, but turned away. I caught up, and we chatted a few inanities about Horace and Barry before we came to the mart. This one was a little bigger than average, having two walls, each with two dispensary doors and a comm. I set down her bags, fed in a bill, punched a number, and wondered if I should hit up Horace for a little more cash, or if the bills I had would last for a few more errands.

The screen cleared, showing Horace's lined and worried face, which also cleared to a smile of relief. "Ramou!"

"Safe and triumphant," I agreed. "I have the honor to be escorting Ms. Souci, with suitcases."

"Oh, what a relief!" he sighed. "Ms. Souci?"

"Yes, Mr. Burbage?" She poked her head around between me and the screen. I stepped back.

"I trust Ramou has acquainted you with our current condition of crisis?"

"Oh, yes, Mr. Burbage. He's been very honest."

"He does have a problem that way. Are you still willing to ship out with us?"

She nodded. "I wouldn't miss a chance like this for the world, Mr. Burbage."

"That is exactly what you will be missing," he said with a smile. "I'm delighted you've chosen as you have, Ms. Souci. The car is already making its rounds, to pick up you and your fellow actors. I shall tell it to stop by your building."

She glanced up at me. "The mart in the middle of the block would be better, Mr. Burbage. I've already, uh, checked out of my apartment."

"If you say so." He looked doubtful. "Ramou, please remain with the young lady. We cannot risk any misadventure."

"Gotcha, Horace!"

"Very good." He cracked his warmest smile. "Then I will see you aboard ship."

"Bye," I said.

The screen went to blue again, and I turned to smile at Susanne. "My turn to treat. Coffee?"

"Why, yes, thank you." The roguish smile was back in place. "Cream and sugar, please."

She could afford it—and so could I. I fed in the bills, handed her the cup and took my own, and stood there leaning against the wall, while she sat on her suitcase, apparently oblivious to her low-scooped neckline though I certainly wasn't, and we chatted and watched the sky lighten and the east turn rosy. In spite of the pressure and the rush, in spite of the looming loneliness of the Unknown and the Waste Beyond New York, it was an enchanting half hour, being alone with Susanne Souci and having all her attention, in the hour between night and morning, amid the silence and the predawn breeze. You could actually hear a few birds beginning to chirp, and for New York, that's silence.

Then, out of the paleness, a huge dark car came gliding up, looking as long as a whale and twice as streamlined.

"Mr. Ramou Lazarian and Ms. Susanne Souci?" the res-onant voice asked through the grille.

"The same," I told it.

"Both," she said.

The rearmost door opened. "Please step in." The trunk lid sprang open. "Luggage in the rear."

I hefted the cases into the trunk, just about filling it, and followed Susanne through the door.

There were four people in the rear compartment already, and I could see six more in front, through the smoky glass, but there were still empty seats. I was with the young folk, and they were all laughing and chattering. There was Larry Rash, who immediately started trying to cozy up to Su-sanne, and I was instantly insanely jealous, the more so because I paled into insignificance next to his lush male— well, beauty is the only word for it.

But Susanne sure didn't pale into anything at the sight of Lacey Lark. If anything, she seemed to brighten and become more vivid, so that it was almost a contest between the two of them to see which one could light up the car all by herself. They instantly started swapping girl talk and gossip, for all the world like old bosom buddies—but did I detect an edge to their voices, a dim echo of cats yowling? No, surely it must have been my imagination. I just sat back in silence and simmered; I began to realize that this was probably going to be my role in the company. After all, what was a mere tech assistant, compared to a juvenile?

I know the answer to that, now. I know a lot of answers, but I've still got twice as many questions. Horace says that's life.

21

ure that somehow terminated in a hand outward
I pulled out the crumpling bills—what use was th
how to want his fate of th hotel, and
that you sov?" Paddy's hack at quite trial wo

To my surprise, the limo didn't pull into Chandler's—it went up to the passenger terminals, like any other limo. It stopped in front of the side door of Terminal D, which was for "Charters and Private Vessels." The actors piled out in a happy, chattering throng and swept on into the terminal without a thought for the baggage—except Susanne, who all of a sudden realized I wasn't there and peeled off from the group with apologies and a quick explanation, and ran back to me. "Why aren't you coming?"

"Somebody has to see that the luggage gets loaded," I explained, while my heart overflowed with gratitude to compensate for the chill of having felt so thoroughly left out of the actors' conversation.

"Won't the car take care of it?"

"It can't," I explained. "Its computer has its limits."

A skycap came strolling up. "Help you with your baggage, sir?"

"Yes," I said. "Lots. Can you get this stuff onto the *Cotton Blossom,* fast?" I pointed to the trunkful.

He looked at it, lips pursed thoughtfully; I'm sure he was calculating his tip. Then he took out his dog whistle, put it to his lips, and blew. Two seconds later, a luggage cart came rolling up. With relief, I got busy yanking out bags.

"Hey, now! I'll take care of that, young fellow! You go join your party!"

I looked up at the man. "You sure?"

" 'Course I'm sure! It's not your union. You go ahead, now." He waved toward the terminal in an expansive gesture that somehow terminated in a hand cupped to accept. I pulled out all my remaining bills—what use was I going to have for them? But I saw the total, and conscience took over—that was way too much, even for this kind of work. I peeled off two and pressed them into his palm as I went past. "Thanks a lot!"

Three paces later, I risked a glance back. He was staring at the bills. I hoped that was a good sign.

"That was way too much," Susanne hissed beside me.

"Right now, I'm not about to sweat the small stuff," I assured her. "We need speed, and lots of it."

She stared at me, alarmed. "You mean we're not safe?"

"I'll say we're safe when we're past the orbit of Luna," I said, "but for now, I'll settle for lifting off."

We went through the air curtain and saw the mob. A dozen actors were milling around Horace, who saw us and beckoned us over. "Ah, at last! What kept you, Ramou?"

"Baggage," I said simply.

He looked up, startled, then grimaced with chagrin. "Yes, I should have realized no one else would think of it. Thank you, lad. Well, we can go, now."

"I hope." I fell in beside him as he called, "This way, my friends!" He beckoned with an overhand swing that wound up pointing toward the right-hand end of the concourse. We set off walking fast over the terrazzo, and it was a delight to see the old man flushed with excitement, eyes bright with enthusiasm. "So the great adventure begins, my lad!"

"So it does." I found myself grinning in response, and deciding the man was amazing. To go kiting off into the unknown was one thing at my age—but at his, it was an entirely different matter. Had he always been that way, I wondered? Or did it go with being an actor?

I had been massively relieved to see Ramou's face on the screen, especially since he had had Susanne Souci beside him, and I was more relieved than I cared to show when I saw the two of them coming in the door together—relieved, to know the whole company was finally together, but also to see that there would be a counterbalance to Lacey Lark in Ramou's emotions. The fact that Souci, alone among them, had turned back to see why Ramou lagged, I found to be a very good sign—but then, I've generally trusted soubrettes more than ingenues anyway, finding that they tend to have a much larger dose of fellow feeling. Biased, I'm sure—no doubt a large proportion of hideously selfish and insecure ones is to be found in both types; certainly it seems to be the same among mature leading ladies, who draw from the ranks of both. But then, leading ladies have more experience, not all of it joyful or triumphant; they have greater reason to be wary. The young ones do, too, of course, but they don't know it yet.

Be that as it may, I was somewhat concerned for my young friend; Ramou's expression was a benumbed sort of combination of exhilaration, disillusionment, and exhaustion. The first I attributed to Ms. Souci's presence; the second is an occupational hazard; and the third came from a very full night of running around bailing out us older folk.

Really, I don't know what I would have done without the lad. Well, no, I know what I would have done—managed to get everyone together somehow, probably without Ms. Souci, which (as things eventuated) would have been a major loss indeed. However, that was just myself; when I learned the full story of Merlo's hunting expedition of the night before, I realized that we very well might not have had a spaceship if it hadn't been for Ramou. Come to that, we might not have had anything left of Merlo.

But I don't think the lad realized any of that, just then. I was to realize that he always underestimated his own worth.

At the moment, though, I wasn't done with my need for his assistance, and gauged that he would profit from knowing how much of a help he was being. "All right, here's the gate. Lag behind with me, Ramou, and help me make sure they all get on."

He snapped back to alertness in surprise, then nodded and said, "Sure, Mr. Burbage," and stepped back against the far side of the gate.

"Horace," I reminded him, and stepped aside as my fellow thespians swept past us in a glorious chattering gaggle. I counted heads, and Ramou scanned the immediate area. "I don't see any laggers, Mr. . . . Horace."

"Good lad. And I've counted all heads." I motioned him in, stepped in behind him, and called, "All personnel loaded."

"Closing," the ramp warned, and the doors slid shut behind us. "Holding for baggage," it informed us.

Horace looked nettled. "Do hurry, please."

"Just putting the last case in now, sir," the skycap's voice assured him. We heard a cavernous slam as he closed the baggage door, and his voice said, "Have a pleasant journey."

"Thank you, my good man!" Horace called out, though the skycap was probably already on his way back to his station. "All present and secured!"

There was a hissing; we didn't feel anything, but the terminal outside the windows moved lower, so we knew we were rising on our air cushion. We did feel the pull of acceleration as the ramp-bus drifted across the tarmac, but it wasn't even enough to make anyone want to sit down.

"Where's Barry?" I asked. "I mean, Mr. Tallendar."

"Already aboard, trying to settle Ms. Lulala into her cabin," Horace answered.

"In that?" Susanne asked, staring out the window.

Horace looked over her shoulder and nodded, smiling. "Yes, young lady, that's the *Cotton Blossom* herself. Not a bad sight for an old ship, eh?"

Well, sure, if you could call fifteen years "old." I mean, I was thrilling to space comics when that ship was built. Of course, the fact that she had logged more light-years than I expected to live was something to consider—but in the morning light, I thought she looked marvelous, a tall, soaring, tapering tower, a porpoise ready to frolic in the seas of space. Sure, I know there was a certain phallusy in her symbolism, not to mention gender confusion—but streamlining is streamlining, and the fish were here long before the human libido.

"Don't we get to see out?" Lacey sounded somewhat petulant, and Larry shuddered. "Cooped up for months in that? I'm feeling claustrophobic already."

"There's a great deal more room than it looks to have from here," Horace hastened to assure them, and I pitched in. "There're plenty of windows, but they're all electronic."

They subsided, satisfied. "Electronic" was the magic word—they knew it worked, but hadn't the faintest idea how, so it solved everything. I allowed myself to feel a bit of complacent superiority and began to understand what Merlo had meant about the tech/actor split.

Then the ramp slowed and stopped. I was alert for the jar, but even so, I scarcely felt it—the operator had a smooth computer, or vice versa. The actors were peering up through the ramp windows at the sheer wall of metal before them, and someone said, "It doesn't look so shiny from here."

"Don't worry," Horace said, "you won't be seeing it from this angle." He pushed himself to his feet and strolled over to the forward door, just as it rolled open. On the other side, the lights glowed, warm and friendly; the Oriental carpet led on between tapestried walls, and the ceiling had crystal fixtures. The ladies exclaimed in delight and headed for the luxury appointments, with the men right behind them.

I just stared. Chandler's repair crew had been very busy, and very good. We had gotten *this* at a bargain price?

Horace saw my gape, and winked. "Not all old things are bad, m' boy. Now, ladies, gentlemen—as you pass, I'll give you your cabin assignments." He glanced down at his computer-pad. "The signs on the wall will direct you, just as in any good hotel. If you're displeased with your accommodations, I'm quite willing to discuss it after lift-off—we have several unused cabins."

I liked his knack for understatement. We had maybe fifteen people total, and the ship had been built for a hundred. I began to wonder if we were going to make a profit, after all.

"I had understood that I was going to be playing young leads," Lacey said firmly, and behind her, Susanne stared in surprise.

"And your cabin shall be commensurate with your rank," Horace assured Lacey. "However, it will also correlate with your experience in the theater, relative to other members of the company."

She flared into indignation. "You mean that the older you are, the better your room! I won't accept that, Mr. Burbage."

Horace looked unutterably sad. "If you really feel you would prefer to remain on Terra, Ms. Lark, we shall certainly understand, and it's not quite too late. Still, I should inform you that one of the smallest cabins will be allocated to a gentleman in his fifties, who has elected to join us though he has no prior experience in theater."

Lacey frowned, not understanding. I did, though, since I knew about Charlie Publican. Then she shrugged in irritation and said, "Oh, well, we have to suffer for our art. What's my cabin, Mr. Burbage?"

"C-three," he said with a warm smile. "Please web in right away, Ms. Lark. Luggage will be available shortly after lift-off. You'll understand that we can't quite take the time for the usual amenities? . . . Yes, thank you. Ms. Souci?"

"Hear, now!" Larry Rash frowned darkly. "Why am I not next?"

"Ladies first, Mr. Rash. We of the theater adhere to a code of gentility quite as old as our profession. Ms. Souci, you are in room C-seven."

Wise, I thought. Not next door to Lacey.

"Ms. Drury?"

"Oh, my! Yes, Horace?"

The warm smiled widened even further. "You're in B-four, Grudy my dear. Now, Mr. Rash . . ."

On he went, and the troupe paced past him one at a time, Winston Carlton looking a bit nettled by the younger actors' temperament, but taking it all with good grace. I watched them filing past, wondering if I was supposed to sleep under the bar.

Finally Wellesley rolled though the door and down the hall—companionway, I was to learn to call it—and I stepped up. "Lazarian, Ramou."

Horace gave me a twinkle of the eye. "C-eight, my boy, and don't take advantage of it, eh? But before you do, would you go through B and C decks, and coax them all to lie down and web in? There's a good chap."

"Uh, yeah, sure, if you'll show me what 'webbing in' means."

"Delighted, especially since I may need your help with Ogden. This way, my friend."

First time he had called me that. I followed, feeling honored. I was beginning to realize that there was more to Horace than ham.

We went up the lift, and I couldn't help wondering what the experience would be like when we didn't have much gravity. I noticed handholds built into the walls—and the ceiling, and, unobtrusively, at the sides of the floor. I wondered.

The door opened, and we stepped out into a corridor of faded elegance. The crystal lighting fixtures had evolved into small chandeliers, the walls had sprouted brocade, and the carpet was rich and plush. We stopped at an open cabin and Horace knocked, then sallied in, crying, "Ah, there, Ogden! And how do you like your home away from home, eh?"

"Nicely—it will do quite nicely, Horace," the tottering tower wheezed. "But I'm afraid you forgot to set out the brandy."

"No time for the last-minute niceties, as I said," Horace said smoothly. "Now, Ogden, we may be lifting off momentarily, so I really would appreciate it if you would either sit down, or lie down, and web yourself in."

"Oh, well, I suppose I must," the old actor grumbled, and more or less toppled into the armchair. Horace stepped up beside him and pressed buttons; the chair smoothly tilted back and lifted its front, occasioning a startled oath from the massive man. He stiffened in panic, reaching out to grab something that wasn't there, but Horace was talking smoothly all the while. "Reclining is the most effective position for taking a thrust of acceleration, you see, old man—I'm sure you've taken the ballistic several times during your career . . ."

"Well, yes, Horace, but they never leaned back as much as this!"

"They didn't have to accelerate this strongly, either. Now, just pull the webbing out from its recess in the right-hand side of the seat, like this—take those clips, would you, Ramou? And just insert them in the buckles on the left, there's a good chap . . ."

I snapped the two buckles in. It left Ogden secured in his seat by a network of white webbing that spread all across his chest, abdomen, and thighs, for all the world like the prey of some giant spider—a spider called "gravity." I hoped the simile wouldn't be too apt.

"There, quite secure," Horace said with a smile. "Do keep your cranium back against the headrest when you feel acceleration begin, old chap—the viewscreen's right there next to the door, you can see quite easily. All comfortable, now?"

"As much as I can be," he wheezed. "Is it really necessary to go through all this so soon, Horace?"

"As I say, old man, we may be lifting off at any second, and certainly with very little warning. Do stay webbed in, now."

"Well, if I must, I must," he sighed. "I say, Horace—I don't suppose you could find your way clear to sending up a bottle of some sort of liquid refreshment, eh?"

"If there's time before take-off, Ogden—but we're rather shorthanded, don't have a kitchen staff or attendants, I'm afraid. We'll pick them up when the budget allows, but for the time being, I fear you'll have to make do with the food dispenser in the wall over there. Ramou, would you dial Mr. Wellesley some sort of potation? Yes, how kind."

I stepped over, looked at the chart, and punched in the

combination for a martini—then, as an afterthought, for "half-strength." I brought it back and set it in the recess on the table beside the chair. "Try to finish it off when you feel the first stirrings of acceleration, Mr. Wellesley—you know how it is, that moment of zero-G when we're out of the gravity well . . ."

"I assure you, young man, I've made the trip to Luna a few times in my dotage," Wellesley said with some asperity, then relented. "But thank you for the courtesy."

"My pleasure." I meant it—anything I could do for Dr. Moebius, I would.

I was careful to close the door behind us, then hurried to catch up with Horace. "Uh . . . I made it half-strength . . ."

"I'm sure he'll detect the difference, but he's in no position to argue."

Behind us, there was a muted roar.

"Yes, he did." Horace didn't slacken his pace. "Thank you for your assistance, Ramou. Now, if you would see to the people on C deck, I'll take care of B deck."

I guessed that Barry was taking care of A deck. "Uh, Horace . . ."

"You're concerned for Ogden's welfare."

"Uh, yeah. I mean, that's an awful lot of bulk for one poor human heart to keep pumping blood through, Horace, and his alcohol content . . ."

". . . won't strengthen him in the slightest." Horace nodded, grim-faced. "But would he rather die in the obscurity of a Government Assistance home for the aged, or in the struggle to begin one more season? He knows the risks, my boy. Let us accord him the honor he deserves."

I swallowed hard and followed him to the lift.

He went on down the companionway; I went into the "down" door. I had it figured out—older actors were on B deck, younger actors on C deck. I hoped they wouldn't mind having a member of the crew in with them. On second thought, they'd better not . . .

With that in mind, I stopped by Larry Rash's cabin first. I knocked; he called, "Who is it?"

"Ra—" I decided on a little more formality. "Mr. Lazarian, Mr. Rash. Mr. Burbage asked me to show you how to work the cabin." Which was sort of true.

The door snapped open. "Thank heaven, a porter! This blasted dispenser won't give me any sort of a drink, you know, and I did want to sip some champagne as I watched old Earth recede."

Porter?

Oh. Now that we were in space, he had decided to try to put me in my place. I weighed him at a glance and found him wanting—in both muscle and skill, at a guess. But I dutifully disregarded the crack about the porter, stepped over to the machine, and frowned at it. What could be wrong?

Then I realized that the power patch was dark. I pressed it; it lit; I stepped back and said, "Try it now."

"Oh, do it for me, my good man." He was in his chair now, with a languid wave.

I froze, even to the face. He saw the look and gave me a mocking grin—but he was where I wanted him to be, officially, anyway. If I didn't get the drink, he'd have to get up, and might not get back—so I punched for champagne, then brought him the glass. "Sure. Glad to do you the favor."

He frowned; "favor" implied equality.

I set it down beside him. "Know how to work your webbing?"

"Well, yes, but not just—".

"Like this." I pulled the webbing out and snapped it into place.

"Here, now! I was going to invite Ms. Lark in . . ."

"Confined to cabins until after lift-off. Captain's orders." I looked directly into his eyes, and thought how much fun a good fight would be right now—or even a bad one. And I let it show. He stared, appalled. Then he rallied with anger. "Why, you imbecilic tradesman, how dare you . . ."

"Buddy." I clapped him on the shoulder—and probed with a thumb. I hit the pressure point, and if he hadn't been webbed in, he would have hit the ceiling. As it was, he let out a yowl that must have gone right through the soundproofing. I let up and said, "Glad I didn't push hard."

He stared at me, the whites showing all around the irises. I let the grin slacken into the old friendly smile and said, "Let's get it straight right now. I'm not a tradesman, and I'm not a servant. If you know anything about the martial arts, you can call me 'Sensei'—if I decide you've got any potential. As to brains, as far as I'm concerned, if you can't do calculus, you're illiterate. I'll be glad to do you a favor, if you need one—and I'll expect you to help me out if *I* need it. Because we're both in the same company together. Right?"

He'd mustered some poise again. "Why, how crude."

"The crude man is the one devoid of compassion," I said, quoting Sensei. "The crude man, by his manner, makes others be direct."

Anger flashed in his eyes, but behind it there was self-doubt, and I had his measure. Not that I hadn't pegged him for a case of low self-worth, anyway—but it was nice to be sure.

I stepped back with my friendliest smile. "Just call me if you need a hand. But till we're out of the gravity well, I'd appreciate it if you'd stay in your seat." I went out and closed the door behind me, but not quite enough to keep from hearing him start cursing. I heaved a sigh and gave my head a shake, but it didn't clear the bad feeling.

I hate to throw my weight around, especially when the other guy hasn't—but he had tried to, really, and hadn't left me much option. I could have faced that scene then, or later, but it was really only a question of time.

Three doors for empty rooms; then I knocked on Lacey Lark's. "Who's there?" said the speaker beside the jamb, and I answered, "Ramou Lazarian, on ship's business."

The door clicked, and she said, "Come in."

She was pacing about, and turned on me as I came in the door. "Of all the inconsiderate, insensitive arrogance! Do they really expect me to put up with *this*?"

I looked around at pale damask walls and a plush carpet, with chair and sofa, and beyond, a bedroom. "Looks pretty nice to me."

"Well, yes, I suppose it is, but it's so small!"

I shrugged, "It's a ship, Ms. Lark." Somehow, I didn't feel like calling her "Lacey" at the moment. "Even the captain's probably going to have to make do with rooms the size of a Government Assistance special. And I know the upholstery's a little worn, but it's not *that* bad."

She glared at me, but I could see the calculations ticking off behind her eyes, and she suddenly relaxed into a warm smile. "Well, it's not your fault, anyway. But do you think you could get the food dispenser working?"

"Why, sure." I stepped up and pressed the power patch. It lit, and I punched for Chablis. I turned halfway, so I could enjoy her stare out of the corner of my eye as the glass filled, then turned to hand it to her. "There you are. Now, Mr. Burbage says we're due to take off any minute, Ms. Lark—"

"Lacey." She batted her eyelashes at me. "I thought we'd been through that last week, Ramou."

So I'd been promoted again. I gave her the warm smile and said, "So he wants us all to web in, Lacey. Know how to work it?"

"Why, I think so." She sat down, set the glass on the table, and tugged at the webbing. A flicker of annoyance crossed her perfect complexion. "It's so stiff! Could you help me, Ramou?"

"Be glad to." I stepped up beside her, just incidentally moving her glass into the recess on the table, and pulled the webbing out. It came easily, so it wasn't the machinery that was resisting. "Just stretch it over and clip it in . . ."

She turned as I pulled, bringing a breast into contact with my moving hand. My knuckles seemed to glow where her curve had been, and her smile was all warmth. I smiled quickly, hoping it would hide my real reaction, then forced myself to look down as I pressed the clips into the buckles. Didn't help much; she was just managing to squirm so that the buckle was right next to the other curve, and I brushed it again. At least, I suppose you'd have to say it was me who did the brushing. Now it wasn't just my knuckle that was on fire. I'm afraid my smile was a little shaky, but I said, "All firm then, Lacey."

I could have bitten my tongue, but she smiled, amused, and said, "It's so boring, waiting like this. Why don't you stay and chat with me, Ramou?"

"I'd like to." It didn't take much faking to sound as though I meant it. "But Horace has nine more jobs for me before we lift. Now, you need to recline your chair, Lacey."

"Like this?" She pressed the button and the chair began to lean.

"That's it," I said. "Remember to keep your head back when you feel acceleration starting."

"Like this?" She laid her head way back against the headrest, and since her body was almost exactly horizontal, the profile was breathtaking. I managed to take the breath back, though, and gulped out, "Yes, that's fine, very fine. See you in space, Lacey." And I got out of there fast.

I stopped next door. The portal was open, so I could see Marty leaning back in his recliner, webbing in place, drink in hand. He looked up, saw me, and grinned. "Hi, Ramou. Let me know when we're in space, will you? I'd prefer to wait until after lift-off"—he grimaced—"to dial up something with alcohol in it."

I stared. "You sure you're not a techie?"

He glanced furtively to either side, then whispered, "I ran lights on three shows."

I nodded. "That explains why you knew how to get the dispenser working."

He stared. "You mean somebody didn't?"

"It mixes better if you turn it on," I said. "Sure you don't need anything?"

"How about an audience?"

I grinned. "We'll have you one in four light-years."

"Well, I'll have to rough it," he sighed. "Think you could cobble up a laugh track?"

"I'll try," I promised, "as soon as they give me some spare time. See you in space, Marty."

I went on, feeling considerably better. Only one more to go, now. I went down three doors and knocked.

"Who's there?" Susanne said.

Let's see, now—who could have been there? Only a dozen of us, and only one she hadn't met. Were all New Yorkers so automatically cautious? "Ramou Lazarian, Ms. Souci."

"Oh, Ramou, come on in!" The door clicked. "And what's this 'Ms. Souci' stuff? Forgotten my name?"

I grinned as I walked through the door. "How could I, Susanne?" Then I stopped short, staring.

She had already done everything just fine by herself—she was webbed in and reclined, head back, but turned toward me at the moment with a smile, and I sucked in a deep breath. Seen in profile, she had a definite advantage over Lacey. But she winked, and my paralysis loosened. I stepped over. "Just came to see—"

"If I had sense enough to web myself in?"

"You could put it that way," I admitted. "I don't suppose you could think up something I could help you with?"

The roguish smile again. "Well, I could use a drink, and I can't figure out how to get the dispenser working . . ."

"Say no more." For the fourth time, I stepped over to a "malfunctioning" food dispenser and pressed the power patch. *It won't work, Mr. Stagehand. Plug it in, Mr. Actor.* "What's your choice?"

"Champagne! It's a festive occasion, isn't it?"

It was, but the reminder of who else had taken champagne made me bristle. I drew the glass and forced the smile as I turned, feeling a strong impulse to jam Larry Rash's smile off his face, just in case he should get ideas about inviting Susanne anywhere—but I stifled it; she was her own woman, and I wasn't in love.

Was I?

No, of course I wasn't. As long as I was asking the question, I couldn't be in love.

But her smile was so warm and friendly that mine thawed

out, too, and I grinned as I handed her the glass. "It goes in the little recess on the table, you know."

"Oh, yes, I know all about recesses." She sipped at her champagne just long enough for me to wonder about the line, then said, "We used to have them in grade school, all the time."

I wasn't sure that explanation was all that much of an improvement, but I grinned and sat down on my heels beside her. "Cabin okay?"

"Okay? I haven't lived in this kind of luxury since I played Niagara-on-the-Lake, and they put us up in a Victorian hotel! Two rooms, Ramou! On a ship, I was expecting a fold-down bed!"

"We lucked out," I agreed, very much aware of how close I was to her. "I'm just across the hall from you and two doors down, if you need anything."

"I'll think of something. Your room nice?"

I grinned. "Haven't seen it yet—but I think they're all pretty much alike."

"Mr. Lazarian," a metallic voice interrupted. "Mr. Ramou Lazarian to the bridge, please."

She stared at the strange voice, a little frightened, I think.

"Captain," I explained, and stepped over to the grille in the wall. "May I?"

"Uh . . . yeah, sure!"

I keyed the pickup and said, "Right away, Captain." I turned back to her. " 'Scuse me. Gotta go."

"Duty calls." She smiled. "Duty has a rather raspy voice."

"Too much yelling," I agreed. "See you after lift-off, Susanne." I could hope, couldn't I?

"See you then, Ramou." Probably just wishful thinking, but it sounded like a promise to me.

Then I was out with the door closed behind me and on my way to the lift.

I stepped into the "up" car and said, "Bridge."

"Access restricted," the lift informed me.

I frowned. "Ramou Lazarian here. Captain has called me to the bridge."

We didn't go anywhere.

Then the lift started moving, and said, "Confirmed."

I relaxed—in more ways than one. All things considered, I decided it wasn't a bad idea to be able to keep the actors out of the control room.

I stepped out and felt the tension so thick I wished I'd brought my bolt-cutters. "Lazarian reporting, Captain."

"Acknowledged." McLeod swiveled his chair to face me, and his hand twitched; then he frowned. "I can't return your salute if you don't make one, spacehand."

I stared.

Merlo started to talk, but I got there first. "Begging the captain's pardon, but I don't have the right. I'm not crew."

Horace and Barry, just behind the captain, looked very uncomfortable.

"Ah," McLeod said. "Yes."

"That's what we wanted to talk to you about, Ramou," Merlo said.

I frowned from one of them to another. "What is this?"

"Technicalities," McLeod explained, "but ones with good reasons behind them. We can't even ask Earth Control for clearance to lift if we don't have a minimum crew."

I began to get that old, familiar sinking feeling in my stomach. "How many is that?"

"Three," said McLeod. "The absolute, bare-bones minimum crew for any space vessel is three."

I stared. Then I found my voice. "Who's *number two*?"

"Right there." McLeod nodded at Merlo.

I pivoted to him, staring.

22

Merlo cleared his throat, not meeting my gaze, and said uncomfortably, "Well, yeah, I guess so."

"Guess so?" McLeod snapped. "I just saw your first officer's papers! It better damn *well* be so!"

"You?" I couldn't help staring.

Merlo fidgeted. "You know how it is. When I was a young idiot, I enlisted in the Merchant Marine, and I wanted higher pay, so I studied for my papers on the side."

"Well." So that was why Merlo hadn't been worried about McLeod's drinking. I shook my head, enthralled. "You got any other surprises for me, boss? Gonna turn out you know how to design a planet from scratch, maybe? Have a paper in your back pocket that just happens to be a passport out of a black hole? A revolutionary theory for hyper-radio?"

"Don't be foolish." Merlo frowned. "You know faster-than-light radio's impossible."

McLeod scowled. "What I can't figure out is how come he seems ashamed of it."

"It means he lost faith in the theater," Horace explained.

Merlo shrugged impatiently. "What can I tell you? I was twenty-seven, and I hadn't even made technical director, much less any kind of a track toward designer. I decided I didn't have what it took, so I looked around for something that would pay the most with what I knew."

"You should be damn proud of it, man!" McLeod snapped.

"Yeah," I said, "you should."

Somehow that seemed to help Merlo.

"Yes, proud." Horace, ever quick to save the other guy's face. "Especially since you gave up all that money to come back to the theater, Merlo."

Merlo shrugged. "I could afford it by then—and I'd missed being backstage, right from the first. After five years, I was downright homesick—couldn't even bear to go watch a live show anymore. That's when I knew I had to come back, and the hell with the money."

But McLeod was nodding in approval. "Bravely done—it required no small amount of courage. But didn't you ever miss the sea of stars, Hertz?"

"Well, yeah," Merlo mumbled, "but I couldn't have 'em both."

"Well, you do now, Number One! But we still need a second."

All four of them turned to look at me.

"Me?" I croaked. "What do I know about spaceships?"

"You know electronics," Merlo explained, "and you don't have to have any papers, just the captain's official appointment. And a willingness to learn everything he wants to teach you about being a spacehand. And you'll have to obey his orders, of course."

"Uh . . ." I was numb.

"You'll be paid for both positions," Barry assured me. "Technical assistant, and spacehand."

I swallowed. "I don't mind doing two jobs, Mr. Tallendar—but I am worried about who I take orders from. We all have to obey the captain's orders, don't we?"

"In space, yes," Merlo said. "If you sign on as crew, though, you'll have to obey the captain's orders even dirtside—and even if he disagrees with Barry. You don't, and you go to prison as soon as we make the next planetfall."

I turned to Barry. "You've got my first loyalty, Mr. Tallendar."

"Yes," he whispered. "Thank you, Ramou. But I need to lift off, very badly. Odd as it may seem, your first duty to me is to become responsible to somebody else."

I turned, feeling the thrill build. "Okay, Captain McLeod. I'll be honored."

"Well said, second mate!" he snapped. "Sit down on that couch over there, and mind the sensors!"

Merlo was right behind me, pointing and explaining. "That's the radar screen. The center is us; all the other little dots are metal objects around us. Next to it is the heat sensor. Dull red is for life-forms; yellow is for artificial heat sources, like fires and engines; white is a spaceship's exhaust, or the sun. You'll need that mostly on the ground. The linear scale next to it is a spectrometer—don't worry about what it's for, I'll tell you in space."

"Thanks," I said. "Anything else here I really need to know right now?"

That brought him up short, and I could see he was thinking about getting angry. I shorted that by asking a question as I pointed to a grid. "Audio sensor, right?"

"No, that's radio right now—the one beside it is audio. You can put on a headset and split those two into right ear and left ear. The screen in front of you is your standard comm, right now, but you can change it to RF comm, or laser comm, with that selector there."

The screen lit up, showing a harried-looking man in a gray *complet* with an insignia over the breast. His collar was open, and he had a double headset on. "Earth Control. *Cotton Blossom,* get clearance or get off the apron."

"Cotton Blossom applying for clearance," McLeod said.

The controller looked startled, then fell back on routine. "We only have captain logged, *Cotton Blossom.* Gantry McLeod?"

"Speaking," Gantry said. "First officer is Merlo Hertz."

The controller frowned, entering the data and looking down at his readout. "Acknowledged. Hertz hasn't shipped out in twelve years."

"His papers are still valid."

"Yes, they are." The controller looked up, frowning. "You sure you know what you're doing, Captain? Neither of you has shipped out in anything I'd call recent history."

"We're not in the books yet," McLeod snapped. "Second officer is Ramou Lazarian."

I started, then felt the slow grin growing. That's right, I was an officer, wasn't I? Never mind that there weren't any rankers.

"Entered," the controller sighed. "No prior record . . ."

"He's new, but he's qualified."

"Captain McLeod, you've got two men so rusty that you're flaking, and a greenhorn! Are you sure—"

"Yes, I'm sure," McLeod cut him off, eyes snapping. "We're one hundred percent safe, Earth Control. So is our ship—you should have Chandler's test results right there."

"Yes, I've seen them," the controller sighed, "and you didn't blow up on the test hop from his yard to the apron. I have to certify you for lift-off, if you're still determined."

"Determined and ready, and thank you for the unsolicited advice," Gantry retorted. "Applying for clearance to lift off."

"Acknowledged." The controller looked very grumpy, but he punched on his keyboard.

I looked up at Merlo and mouthed, "Has he had anything to drink?"

Merlo shook his head and dropped down to mutter in my ear. "Says he never drinks while he's on duty, and when he's on a ship, he's on duty. I pushed hard, but all he'd admit to was the occasional nightcap, and that only when there's no reason to expect a snafu."

"Unbelievable!"

Merlo nodded. "That's what I think—but I hope I'm wrong."

"What's he made out of, steel?"

"Molybedenum alloy is my guess. Besides, he's had a taste of Gran'ma's Hangover Remedy."

Well now, *that* made sense.

"We can give you clearance in two hours and twenty-five minutes."

"Too long," McLeod snapped. "I've got passengers webbed in, and I don't want to have to run around to check on them again. This is earliest morning, Earth Control, and your traffic's at a minimum. You can clear us within the hour."

"Look, you don't know what I've got stacked up."

"No, but I've been listening to the traffic talk, and I can guess. You've got nothing stacked up, only three in orbit, and only one landing within the next half hour. I've only heard two request lift-off clearance. Why're you dragging your feet, Earth Control?"

The controller flushed. "Your craft and crew aren't exactly in the greatest shape to inspire confidence, McLeod."

"Then you should want us out of your hair as soon as possible. If you really thought there was any chance we'd blow up on the way, you wouldn't let us lift at all."

"Call it a gut instinct."

"His instinct is to curry favor with the authorities," Barry murmured. "He's heard about us, and about Elector Rudders."

I stared. "You mean he could be in the LORDS party?"

They all stared back at me, startled. Then Horace nodded. "Not in the party itself—it's only open to plutocrats and politicians—but an aspirant, a young man on the make. Yes, Ramou. Excellent insight."

"We're within the rules," McLeod snapped.

"Only just barely," the controller griped. "This whole thing is kind of last-minute, isn't it?"

"We've been informed of a lucrative engagement on New Venus, if we can be there within the month," Barry ad-libbed smoothly. "We had to move our schedule up rather suddenly."

"I'll just bet you did." The controller glowered at his readout, punched buttons, and said, "You're scheduled for 0655. That suit you?"

It was 0610.

"It'll have to," McLeod sighed. "Number Two, inform passengers they can release webbing."

Merlo leaned over—his console was between Gantry's

and mine—and pointed to a set of patches. "There's the intercom."

I punched for "all stations" and said, "Captain's compliments. All personnel may release webbing and move about their cabins. Please be ready to resume seats and webbing on a moment's notice."

I released the switch and looked up into Gantry's approving nod. "Nicely done, young fella. Taken a lot of ballistic flights?"

"Only a few." I flushed with entirely irrational pleasure.

The grid spoke back to me. "Ogden here."

I glanced down and saw a triple row of tally lights, each with a cabin number. Ogden's was lit. "It's rather difficult for me to arise from this position. I don't suppose anyone would be free to fetch me a bottle?"

I looked up at Horace; he shook his head, mouthing "no." I pressed the patch next to Ogden's room. "I'll be down if I can get the time, Mr. Wellesley, but they're keeping me pretty busy here. Try to nurse that one I gave you."

"If I must, I must," Ogden sighed.

Lacey Lark's tally lit up. "I'll come and get it for you, Mr. Wellesley. What cabin are you in?"

"Two-B," he told her. "Bless you, child."

Both their tallies went out, and Ramou looked to me for guidance. I frowned and shrugged—nothing we could do about it now, without being too obvious, not to say rude. Didn't the Lark chit realize what lift-off could do to a man in Ogden's condition, and that intoxication would make it worse?

Or was it possible that she was actually trying to be helpful? I found that rather hard to credit; she was more likely to be currying favor with the older actors. I would have thought she would already have relegated Ogden to the list of people who couldn't do her any good. No, all things considered, I found it most probable that she merely wanted to see how the older actors lived. I braced myself for shrill complaints as soon as we had lifted off.

"Ramou," Barry said, "enter a commcode for me, please."

I looked up, surprised, but he was reciting numbers and letters, and Ramou was entering them. I recognized them, of course—Valdor's private line.

The screen cleared to show Valdor's face. He looked harried and worn, but managed a smile. "Ah, big brother! How is progress?"

"We're scheduled to lift off in forty minutes, Valdor—but I believe our Earth controller is being obstructive. Is this at all hazardous?"

Valdor's face had turned grim as he listened. Now he nodded. "It could be indeed. Someone seems to have told Rudders that we're trying to rush lift-off. Ever since you agreed to buy the ship, the elector's office has been in a flurry of activity, waking lawyers and judges. He has no legal authority within New York or New Jersey, of course, but he has enormous influence. The mayor of New York City has applied for a court order to prevent your lifting off."

"Of course; it takes pressure off his theater district." Barry nodded, face grim. "I had thought better of the man. But didn't the law require a resident of New Jersey to petition a New Jersey judge?"

"Yes, but the chairman of the Newark Conservative Party was happy to oblige, and woke up his favorite golf partner, who also happens to be a judge."

Barry blanched. "Then the papers are signed and on their way."

"Not yet." Valdor smiled. "I have a few friends, too, and *they* have friends. My New Jersey lawyer is currently explaining to the good judge how this action might affect his chances for reelection. Even when he does sign the restraining order, my lawyer will find it has three loopholes and five misplaced commas, which will take a fair amount of time to argue over. And, of course, there is the problem of actually serving the papers on you; the bailiff can't refuse, mind you, but he doesn't have to rush, either."

Barry exhaled a sigh of relief. "*Thank* you, Valdor."

"It's my investment, too, brother, though I must admit I'm tempted to keep you home for Christmas. Still, the crisis is far from past—Rudders's resources are barely scratched, and I must mobilize the rest of mine. I have a few more friends to call, and a favor or two to call in. If you'll excuse me, Barry . . ."

"Of course, Valdor. We'll call you from orbit." He gestured to Ramou to disconnect. Privately, I thought him amazingly optimistic.

Rightly. The controller appeared on our screen again, and he looked much tougher. "*Cotton Blossom,* I've been advised to demand that you show cause for such abrupt conduct."

"Who advised you?" Merlo snapped instantly.

The controller shrugged, irritated. "My boss." Nice general term, that. "Any particular reason why you have to leave so suddenly?"

McLeod opened his mouth, but nothing came out. On the instant, I said, "Why, yes, there is. If I may, Captain?"

He looked up, startled, then gave me a slow grin. "Why, of course, Mr. Burbage!" He turned back to the screen. "Here's the owner's representative. You understand, I just do what the owners want."

"Of course." But the controller looked wary. "Who am I talking to?"

"Mr. Horace Burbage, assistant to Mr. Barry Tallendar, the owner of the spacecraft." I stepped forward, McLeod swiveled out of my way, and Ramou leapt to slide a chair in behind me—I don't know where he'd found it. I sat down easily—the whole thing went so smoothly you would have sworn we'd rehearsed it—and glanced up at Barry. He nodded, a tight smile of amusement in place, and I turned back to the screen. "Mr. Tallendar is occupied with other duties at the moment . . ." Indeed, he was watching the outside visual screen—our electronic 'window,' if you like—for signs of activity. Fortunately, there weren't any. "You do understand that we are a company engaged in an entertainment enterprise, young man?"

He was forty if he was a day, but the term made him look just a tad nervous. "Yeah, sure, I've been watching the news."

"Then you must realize that we are embarked on a bold and unanticipated enterprise, the actual embodiment of an idea as old as Thespis, yet as new as the colonies."

He began to see what was coming. "Yes, but, Mr. Burbage, what—"

"An enterprise of valiant striving and priceless derring-do," I went on, overriding his attempt to interrupt. "We seek to carry the benefits of Terran culture to our benighted brethren in the galactic hinterland, to bring the rain and reign of mercy upon these parched souls in the desert of material groping, to uplift these poor fellow creatures sunken beneath the burdens of daily strife—"

"Okay, okay, but what does this have to do with—"

"We have, of course, ascertained that our repertoire is of the most elevating, designed to uplift and educate." Well, after all, Feydau's bedroom farces did educate one about late-nineteenth-century French culture, didn't they? "We have striven to be certain of the moral validity of each of our plays." Surely the New Orleans bordello-turned-hotel in Backer's *Didn't He Ramble* exemplifed the degenerating effects of moral bankruptcy. "Our mission is to enrich the souls of all humanity, wheresoever they may be, no matter how many parsecs we must wearily traverse, never asking relief, never asking more than a modicum of applause . . ."

The controller knew he was lost, but he made one more feeble attempt. "All very laudable, Mr. Burbage, but we really must—"

"Must extend ourselves to the utmost in our determination to rescue our fellow human beings from the night of Infinite Space!" I was only beginning to hit my stride. "To bring them once again into contact with all that they hold most dear, with the fullness of their cultural heritage, with the wellsprings of the human soul, streaming forever from Terra out to all her orphaned children light-years removed from the ground that gave them birth . . ."

I saw the controller's eyes click into resignation. He knew he was not going to be able to terminate this discussion by anything short of outright rudeness, which could only be justified by a genuine emergency, or a real change in our status. I confined my smile within myself and continued to extoll the merits of our noble and selfless, but ultimately commercial, enterprise.

Finally, the controller capitulated. "All right! All right!" He pecked at his keyboard, then looked up. "You're cleared for lift-off in five minutes! I surrender!"

"Why, how noble of you," I purred.

"Warming engines!" McLeod snapped, and far below us, something whined, then fell silent, but the whole ship seemed to thrum with power.

"Ramou," Merlo snapped, "call 'em back to bed."

Ramou triggered the intercom. "Captain's compliments! We lift off any minute! Back in your chairs and web in! Fast!"

As he clicked off, Barry said, "Check on them. Quickly. Please."

Ramou nodded and raced for the lift. I found out later that he had found Susanne strapped in and patient, but with Larry at her door. Lacey was insisting that she didn't need webbing, Ogden had a full bottle of gin at his elbow, and Marnie was pacing her cabin like a caged lioness. He reinstated her by a combination of flattery and pleading; swept Lacey off her feet quite literally, but with a stream of polite chatter, and webbed her in; poured Ogden one last martini-in-a-bulb and took the bottle with him. He never did tell me how he got Larry back into place, but was at pains to point out to me that Mr. Rash hadn't a single mark on him. Somehow, in spite of all of that, he was back out of the lift and dashing into place with a minute and a half to spare. "Everybody's tucked in nice and tight," he panted as he slid in behind his console.

"No problems?" I asked.

"I did have to do a little persuading," Ramou admitted.

"For example?"

"Well, Mr. Wellesley kind of resented having to be fastened down beyond arm's reach of a bottle. I had to tell him it would only be for a few minutes."

"He would," I sighed.

"All passengers secure?" Captain McLeod snapped.

"They were when I left 'em." Ramou looked up at the exterior vision screen and stiffened. "Hey! There's a guy in a gray *complet,* shooting toward us on an air-scooter!"

I looked up at the screen, startled. Sure enough, here he came, arrowing straight toward us on a sort of flying sled with a seat and handlebars, looking for all the world like a banker on his way to work—but he had no business being there. We all had the same thought—*process server.*

But Ramou had a haunted look about him. I thought he recognized the man. "Where have you seen him before, Ramou?"

"In the background," Ramou said, "when the reporters caught Marnie walking her dog. And hovering around, when that mob jumped us on our way out of rehearsal."

"How long before we can lift, Captain McLeod?" Barry asked, his voice tense.

"Not before we're supposed to, Mr. Tallendar," McLeod ground out. "The engines won't be able to generate full thrust for another minute and a half—but that's right on schedule."

"I estimate that scooter will reach us in a minute and fifteen," Merlo said.

"Good estimate," McLeod snapped. "I make it a minute twenty-five, myself."

The controller appeared on our screen again, smiling with triumph. "*Cotton Blossom,* hold! Idle your engines and wait for an official communication!"

"Official communication?" McLeod barked, genuinely angry now. "What the hell kind of an official communication can be on its way a minute and a half before lift-off, Earth Control?"

"I don't know about that." The controller grinned. "All I know is, that your clearance is—"

McLeod pressed a patch, frowning. "Earth Control, I've lost your image! Also your voice! Earth Control, what's wrong?"

The controller turned purple. "Nothing's wrong, you blasted liar! Your clearance to lift off is—"

"Can't hear you, Earth Control! Could be our receiver—wait a minute. Maybe it's our transmitter, too . . . Commence countdown, Number One. Are you receiving me, Earth Control?"

"You know damn well I'm receiving you!" the controller bellowed. "And you're receiving me!"

"Ten seconds," Merlo said, reading the clock. "Nine . . . eight . . ."

"I know you can hear me, *Cotton Blossom*!" the controller raved. "You can hear me perfectly well, hear me tell you that your clearance is . . ."

"Zero!" Merlo yelled.

McLeod hit the patch, and a giant roared beneath us. For a moment, our ship hung poised, the view of the spaceport trembling in our viewscreen, with that idiot in gray trying frantically to sheer off at the last second . . .

Then the spaceport began to sink in the frame, and the scooter and the man in gray went tumbling about in our wake. I saw him manage to straighten out, streaking away from us, just before the picture turned into a blur, and the Midgard serpent crushed us in its coils, trying to hold us down to its bosom. We rode through the roaring and trembling, myself struggling for breath, and thinking, oddly perhaps, that I hoped Ogden was well, then surrendering to the singing elation within me as the Star Repertory Company left town in the finest tradition of the old American touring companies—one step ahead of the sheriff.

About the Author

CHRISTOPHER STASHEFF spent his early childhood in Mount Vernon, New York, but spent the rest of his formative years in Ann Arbor, Michigan. He has always had difficulty distinguishing fantasy from reality and has tried to compromise by teaching college. When teaching proved too real, he gave it up in favor of writing full-time. He tends to pre-script his life but can't understand why other people never get their lines right. This causes a fair amount of misunderstanding with his wife and four children. He writes novels because it's the only way he can be the director, the designer, and all the actors, too.